Harry's R

Evil Came to Portland in a Fast Car

A novel by Anthony Holt

Copyright © 2017 Anthony Holt

ISBN: 978-0-244-35547-0

All rights reserved, including the right to reproduce this book, or portions thereof in any form. No part of this text may be reproduced, transmitted, downloaded, decompiled, reverse engineered, or stored, in any form or introduced into any information storage and retrieval system, in any form or by any means, whether electronic or mechanical without the express written permission of the author.

Harry's Revenge is a work of fiction. Names and characters are the product of the author's imagination and any resemblance to actual persons, living or dead, is entirely coincidental. None of the events described actually took place and although some real place names are used, this is merely to establish the setting of the story in South Dorset

PublishNation
www.publishnation.co.uk

Acknowledgement

Without the companionship, unstinting support, guidance and lasting patience of my Wife, Irene, this novel would never have been able to emerge.

Dedication

This book is dedicated to my four grandchildren, Tom, Amelia, Jenna and Caitlin.

Author

Anthony Holt MBE served as a pilot and seaman officer in the Royal Navy for over thirty years. In 1992, he left the Navy with the rank of Commander and was appointed as Chief Executive of the Naval and Military Club, better known as the 'In and Out' in Piccadilly. After six exciting years, 'putting the club back on its feet', he moved on to spend the next eleven years as Chief Executive of the Army and Navy Club in St James's Square.

His naval service took him all over the world, including a two-year secondment to the Royal Australian Navy, and a further three years in the unique appointment of Flag Lieutenant to the Admiralty Board, as well as sea service in every type of ship, and flying with the Navy and RAF.

He has lived in Dorset for over forty years where his roots go back to 1610. He is married to Irene and now spends his time writing, sailing, working as a Volunteer Coast Watcher and as a school governor, in addition to entertaining his four grandchildren.

This is his seventh book and second novel

www.anthonyholt.org.uk

Also by the Same Author

Spoofy
Vanguard press (2012)
ISBN 978 1 84386 886 6

At least we didn't sink
Vanguard press (2013)
ISBN 978 1 84386 793 7

Privateer
Vanguard press (2013)
ISBN 978 1 84386 774 6

Four of clubs (2014)
ISBN 978 1 291 83500 7

Nine stories of the sea (2014)
ISBN 978 1 291 95778 5

Twelve of a kind (2015)
ISBN 978 1 326 24213

Chapter 1

The westering sun left a vivid but hazy red glow along the horizon as it disappeared below the distant edge of Lyme Bay. An elderly man was strolling up the sloping rough grass field from the pub car park towards the National Coastwatch Lookout. His thatch of silver-grey hair contrasted markedly with a ruddy, weather-beaten face and sharp blue eyes. He used a sturdy wooden walking-stick to help him negotiate the big grass tussocks as his dog trotted fifteen yards ahead, tail wagging, and nose frequently investigating the bases of the small stunted bushes that dotted the hillside. Overhead, a single short-eared owl swooped silently, low over the field, clearly identifiable despite the advancing twilight by the golden bars under its wings. The man stopped for a few minutes, leaning on his stick as he tried to follow the rapid but graceful movements of the big bird.

The owl dropped swiftly into a patch of thicker grass, and immediately launched back into the air again, clutching the first victim of the night's hunting. The bird flew away towards the east, as silently as it had arrived. The man watched it out of sight before starting uphill after his dog once more.

As he trudged along, he called to his dog. The dog didn't take much notice and he opened his mouth to call again, but he was interrupted by the noise of powerful car engines approaching fast from the direction of Southwell.

A convoy of about half a dozen big smart-looking cars came powering down the road, turned sharply onto the single track road winding up towards the Lookout and roared out onto the grass in front of the compound around the building.

The man, sensing danger, shouted again to his dog as loudly as he could. 'Cassie!' he yelled. 'Cassie, come here!'

But he was too late. With a sickening crunch, accompanied by a gut-wrenching scream from the animal, a big black Range Rover smashed into the dog and pulverised it. The man started to run forward but before he could reach the cars he saw a tall man hop down from the black car, grab the dead – or dying – dog, and drag it towards the cliff edge before tumbling the body into space.

The remaining cars began to circle around the stationary Range Rover, engines revving loud in low gear while full beam headlights probed the darkening sky, turning as the cars circled.

As the man stood, transfixed, horrified, tears running down his face, shocked by the horrific death of his dog, he was struck from behind on the back of his neck. He fell, stunned, face down into the long grass. Seconds later, more figures had leapt from the cars, and in the gathering gloom, they surrounded the figure lying prone and trying to roll onto his side. Led by two young and attractive women, like a pack of hyenas savaging a carcass they darted in towards their victim, kicking and stamping on him, screaming and laughing as they did so. As the attack continued some of the assailants could be heard chanting a word that sounded like 'Frug.'

At length the assault ended. The assailants, their shoes and trousers liberally spattered with the blood of their victim, stood around the inert and bloodied body for a while, giggling, while some stood back and snorted cocaine. Others passed around a bottle of expensive malt whisky. One man stood behind the group filming the others, finally focusing in on the body lying in the trampled grass. Eventually, a small wiry man and a blonde athletically-framed woman stepped away from the group, opened the boot of a big sports car, dragged the bleeding body towards it and heaved it inside.

The victim, still alive but seriously injured, bounced around in the back of the car as it sped off, heading north towards Fortuneswell. One by one the other cars followed, lurching down the hill and keeping close together. Within thirty minutes all the cars were parked haphazardly around the square in Fortuneswell and the dozen or so occupants were celebrating their evening's fun with whisky, champagne and beer.

The elderly victim still lay in the boot of a car, slipping in and out of consciousness, while images of what had befallen him passed through his head. In his moments of consciousness he was reliving what had happened to him. In the darkness of the car boot he still heard the wild, raucous screams of men and women and felt the pain of feet thudding into his unprotected body as if the frenzied attack was continuing even now.

When the pub closed, the car with its victim drove off towards Weymouth. The other cars raced each other to Portland Bill and back. Most of them continued on across the causeway still generally heading north; but one, a big powerful sports car, left the road north of Easton and smashed into the dry stone wall that lined the western edge of the road.

A police patrol car arrived quite quickly; and as they were breathalysing the driver, the other car, carrying the body of that evening's victim, was backing carefully into an alleyway near the centre of Weymouth. A man and woman emerged from the car, opened the boot and tumbled the body, which they presumed to be dead, out onto the pavement. They got back into the car and drove out of Weymouth.

Chapter 2

'You're lucky ter' be alive, mate.' The disembodied voice was neither near nor far, but somewhere within the endless grey film that seemingly encompassed everything. The man in the bed could see nothing – other than marginal changes in the density of the greyness. Nor could he remember anything, nor feel anything. But now his hearing had begun to return, although he was unaware of when this had happened. It was just that suddenly he had become aware of noises around him and then, just as suddenly, he realised that he could distinguish speech. He began to think, to interpret the sounds, and later, to link various sounds together. It was some time after this that he realised that at least one of the voices was addressing him. He was surprised. He wanted to respond but his body and mind could not yet combine sufficiently to move the muscles which might enable speech.

There was one voice in particular that seemed to spend a lot of time near him and which seemed to be talking to him rather than about him. The voice was that of a woman: soft, gentle, encouraging, and repeating the same things over again.

This brought about increasing realisation within the man; and with the realisation came hordes of questions, tumbling one upon another. Who was he? Who was she? Why was he here? Where was 'here'? What was happening to him? What had happened to him? What was going to happen to him? There were no answers so the questions changed form and came to him repeatedly.

There was one single word that recurred again and again. It came from near the man and from further away. The word was 'Harry'. It took some hours before the man registered that this word was a name. Whose name? Was it his name? Then, slowly through the eternal mist, came another sensation. Feeling was returning to his body; and with feeling came pain. He began to move in the bed and the pain moved around and intensified. He heard the woman's voice very near to him and then he heard her cry out. Within moments there were other voices in the room, talking to each other at first, and then to him.

'Harry.' It was a man's voice, speaking very close. With the single word came awareness. He was Harry. And this discovery was followed immediately by a new sensation. He could smell the man. He knew what it was to be able to smell.

'Harry,' the voice said again, very close to his ear. 'Harry, can you hear me? If you can, try to move your head.'

Harry moved his head, not quite realising how he was able to do this. Instantly several voices started to speak at once, and Harry – he was strangely delighted to have a name, to be something positive, something identifiable – could not pick out the words. He moved his head again.

'Harry, my name is George, George Grainger. I'm a doctor and you have been very ill for a long time. You are in a hospital and we've been looking after you. You will recover but you must be patient because you need time to heal and regain your strength. But we will help you to get better. Do you understand?'

Harry moved his head again.

'That's good, very good, Harry, but now you must rest.'

Harry tried to move his head in response, but he wasn't fully aware of what he had been told. He could still hear the voices, although they were becoming fainter, but he could also hear other, different sounds surrounding him; and he worried, with primeval instinct, that these might be a threat – lurking in the greyness that was swirling within and without his being.

The pain that had arrived with the first notion of feeling was now creeping insidiously all over his body. It was like something alive, determined to devour him, and he knew fear.

More voices, mostly talking, it seemed, about somebody – or perhaps something – else. At first he had no notion of time, but as the pain increased, he recognised the agonised minutes and hours passing. The pain seemed to encapsulate his body; but then there was a new pain in his thigh, and all the pain drained away. He rested and fell into a deep drugged sleep.

Still unaware of time or of his surroundings, the days and weeks passed, the pain gradually dividing itself into separate pains, of differing types and from different places. The greyness became lighter, the voices clearer, awareness and understanding improved.

And the flashbacks began.

Paving stones, scuffed boots with knotted laces, white shoes, a woman's voice – excited, brash, harsh and shrill, raucous, snarling; the smell of blood, crunching, snapping sounds like breaking twigs or a crackling fire. More blood, a word – 'Frug'. What was 'frug'? Did it matter? Where did it fit? He didn't care; it was too difficult, too painful.

The real voices began to talk to him again, and they drew him gently from the drug-induced sleep and the horrors of the dream. At first he was unable to remember his circumstances; but recent memory began to return and he was once again able to think, although he didn't know how to speak. The woman was back and he could hear her soft soothing voice talking to him as she moved around the room. It comforted him and enabled his body to relax, giving him more opportunity to think.

They called him 'Harry' so that must be his name. Harry what? He didn't know. He didn't care. There were more people in the room and as they began to move him about he could hear and feel the rustle and movement of linen or clothing material. He found he had a sense of smell. The odours were familiar and eventually they began to relate to an earlier time for him. When? Childhood? But how old was he? He wasn't a child. He must be an adult – but what kind, how old? How big? What colour?

He began to identify the voices but still he didn't speak. His first voice – London, he thought – had remained for a time but had now gone. Most of the others seemed posh. How had he identified that? Was he posh? Some were men, some were women; sometimes they came together and talked among themselves, occasionally remembering his existence, awkwardly it seemed. He knew what 'awkwardly' was. Wonderful! He had knowledge and could use it, little though it was, to make deductions, assessments, to think.

****

He could hear, he could smell, he had feeling in most of his body and he knew that the greyness was at least partly brought about by the bandages he could now feel over his eyes.

The new voice was deep, authoritative and powerful. 'I think we can take the risk, Sister; all the signs are that he should have full sight recovery in at least one eye – can you hear me, Harry? How are you today? Can you feel my hand on your foot there?'

Harry heard a voice say 'yes' and realised it was his own.

A new smell – a light and delicate perfume – filled Harry with pleasure; and gentle fingers began to remove the bandages section by section from around his eyes and the upper half of his face. The greyness became lighter until he could see shapes: blurred and indistinct, but nevertheless discernible. In minutes only, or so it seemed, he could see people – two men, and two women dressed identically in crisp white. He could see a window with rain running down the panes, a shiny floor, polished metal stands supporting some sort of machinery, a cupboard and bright cream walls.

'Can you see me, Harry?' The older and larger of the two men leant towards him and Harry smelt tobacco. The other, younger and smaller, said nothing and stood a little distance from the bed on which Harry was lying.

'I can see you.' Each word came slowly and hesitantly.

'My name is George Grainger – I have been running the team that has been looking after you. Do you know your name, Harry?'

'Harry,' said Harry. 'You call me Harry.'

'Do you remember your other name – your surname?'

'No.'

'You are called Harry Chaplin and we think you are sixty-four years of age.'

'You have been through a very difficult time.' The younger man spoke for the first time in a clipped, precise voice with a slight lilt.

Harry moved his head slightly towards the younger man, realised there was no pain to accompany the movement, and took in the fact that the speaker had a light brown skin, a fixed but engaging smile, sleek, short black hair and a pristine white coat, open over a well-tailored and immaculate mid-grey suit. Harry turned his head to the other side where the two women stood; the nearer one, still holding a confusion of crepe bandages, was the one with the elegant perfume. She was looking enquiringly towards him with a gentle hint of a smile playing about her lips. She seemed to exude an air of calm authority and Harry perceived kindness and intelligence bundled into a pleasing open face framed with short brown hair. The other nurse, who was much younger and very pretty, seemed to be absorbed in reorganising the various pieces of tubed and chromed machinery which occupied so much space in the room.

George Grainger began to speak. 'You've been with us for over three months now; but before that you were asleep for a very long time. You are a credit to the miracles of modern medicine.' The voice was pleasant and completely matter-of-fact, and it seemed to match its owner. Grainger was a big, fit-looking man framed in a white coat, with a ready smile beneath twinkling grey eyes. He seemed sincere and friendly. 'You were found in the street,' he continued, 'broken lower leg, broken forearm and depressed fractured skull; damage to both eyes. You had been stabbed several times and you had lost a lot of blood, but no major organs have been irreparably damaged. Your kidneys have taken a bit of a beating but they are recovering. Shall I go on?' He had now moved closer, still smiling engagingly.

'Where do I live?'

'You were found on the pavement near the town centre.'

'Which town?'

'Weymouth.'

'But where do I live?'

'We're not sure, really; but we think you were a sailor and we think you might live on Portland.'

Memories began to stir. Harry thought he had something to do with the sea. But was he a sailor? And if so, what kind of sailor? Suddenly he knew of Portland. It was clear in his mind

– a picture, almost. A tiny cottage, neat with sturdy stone walls and a long garden. The rough uncultivated garden was leading down to the edge of a cliff overlooking a narrow shingle beach with turbulent sea beyond. Was it real, or had he imagined it? He decided it was real. But what was it? Who owned it? Did he own it? Did he own anything?

'Yes, I know Portland. I think I lived there, but not for long, I believe.'

'That's good,' murmured Grainger. Harry noticed that they were now alone, although he had not been aware of the others leaving the room. 'I think you should rest now and we can talk again later.' As he spoke, Grainger moved quietly away from the bed, and Harry felt sleep creeping forward steadily to cover him like an incoming tide. Darkness came, his body relaxed and his mind emptied.

****

It was bright, clear, and the sun was shining from a pale watery sky. A Portland morning, thought Harry. But where did that thought come from? He was still contemplating this and the pain in his legs when the door opened and Grainger entered. Harry wondered what the time was – he had no watch.

'Good morning, Harry,' said Grainger, smiling dutifully as he walked towards the bed.

'What time is it?'

'It's early.'

'Yes, but what time is it?'

Grainger examined the instrument screens beside the bed before reaching down for the clipboard hanging on the end of the bed. He spoke without turning round. 'You have had a great deal of trauma, Harry, and your brain decided to shut down for quite a long time before we were able to coax it to start up again. You have come a long way; but you have far to go before I can say that you are completely recovered. We don't want to worry you with any concerns or thoughts other than those that will help your body to heal.'

'Am I in one piece? Are there any bits missing?' Harry looked anxious.

Grainger smiled gently. 'I can assure you, Harry, that there are no bits missing, as you so interestingly put it.' Then he turned away from the screens and stood looking fixedly at his patient. 'Harry, there is a real chance of relapse in your case so it is important that you try to be patient and wait until your body completes the healing process. This will take all the time your body and your mind need. It's a process that can't be rushed, but as you heal I hope that you will begin to recover your memory. This will help you to come to terms with what has happened and help you to rebuild your life.'

'Can I have a watch?'

The doctor paused for a long time before answering.

'Can I have a watch?'

Grainger seemed to come to a decision. 'Yes,' he said, 'you can have a watch, but not today. Today you will sleep and when you sleep you will become stronger.'

Grainger left and was replaced almost immediately by the younger nurse carrying a tray. Harry didn't feel very hungry but he drank most of the hot sweet tea and ate the slice of bread and butter that she offered. He was asleep before the nurse left the room.

When next Harry woke the room was in semi-darkness and he could hear heavy rain drumming on the window. He took time to remember where he was and what he had been told. He had no idea how long he had been asleep but he felt that it must have been quite some time. He remembered a cottage and a beach far below it before he dozed off once more. When he awoke this time, the rain had stopped and the room was brightened by weak sunshine creeping around the edge of the vertical blinds. The door opened.

'Good morning, Harry,' said Grainger. Harry's reply was cut off as he saw two other men following Grainger into the room. He was alarmed. This was a disturbance to his routine and not what he expected. As he shrank back into the bed, Grainger sought to reassure him. 'You wanted a watch, Harry. Here it is,' he said. 'I think you are getting better and because of that I want to talk to you with my two friends here. This is William, and this is Robert.' He waved an arm at each of the two men in turn. They smiled in unison and nodded. Harry stared silently back at them, troubled, not knowing how to react at first. Then the one introduced as Robert offered a hand in greeting and Harry tentatively shook hands. The grip was firm and dry, and Harry saw a genial, lived-in face surmounting a bulky frame in a suit that was just a little too tight. William, who merely raised a hand in greeting, was quite different: sharp-featured, with pale blue eyes partly hidden by thick lensed spectacles, thin and tall, wearing a fashionable tweed jacket.

'Old friends being re-introduced.' Harry was not sure whether he had spoken aloud or whether it was just a thought. Nobody acknowledged it so he decided it was a thought. He reached out tentatively and took the watch, while the three men pulled chairs forward and settled themselves comfortably around the right side of the bed.

'We want to help you to remember, which will help you to recover,' said Grainger. 'The best way is for us just to chat. How do you feel about that, Harry?'

Harry nodded.

The man introduced as William fiddled inside a folder he was carrying and produced a large coloured photograph which he handed to Harry. It showed a small terraced cottage viewed from the back. 'Do you recognise it?' he asked.

Harry reached for the photograph and nodded.

'Do you live there?' said the other man. Harry nodded, staring at the photograph. Another photograph was produced and Harry nodded again. This one was of a dog – a handsome-looking light-coloured golden retriever. Harry stared at the picture as images flashed through his mind. He knew the dog. It was his dog. He saw fields, children, a young woman and another dog – an Alsatian. The images kept coming.

Robert spoke for the first time. 'What's his name, Harry?'

'He's a she,' said Harry. 'Her name is Cassie.'

The photographs kept coming and gradually the conversation became more fluent although still occasionally punctuated by long periods of silence. After an hour, Harry was confident of his name and he had some idea of his mode of living, and where he had lived in his life before the hospital. He also knew the time, the day and the date. He had discovered with a shock how long he had been in hospital and in the clinic, recovering. But he didn't yet know exactly what he was recovering from. Later, as the drug-induced curtain of sleep crept over him once more, he experienced a new feeling. He felt contentment.

Chapter 3

The talk with George Grainger, William and Robert was the first of many. Every two or three days the three men would appear, unannounced, and gather around Harry's bed; and as the days turned into weeks, Harry began to come back into the life he had once known. Two weeks after the first meeting, Harry welcomed the three men into his room from a wheelchair. Another week after that he was passed into the hands of the physiotherapists and he began the long and frequently painful process of learning to use his body again.

With the information drawn hesitantly from Harry, William, who was a senior Social Services officer, was able to provide Harry with a surname. Harry became Harry Chaplin, or even sometimes Mr Chaplin. His life was being carefully and slowly rebuilt; but although he thought he knew who and what he was, or perhaps had been, he still didn't know what had happened to him and who or what was responsible. His new knowledge seemed to cover only a segment of his life, leaving him feeling as if he had walked into the middle of a film. He knew about the here and now but he had little idea of what had gone before. He felt more unsettled with this partial picture than he had been when he knew nothing at all.

Eventually, and with patience, he prized out more of the information that he needed to know, but enormous gaps remained in the recent history of Harry Chaplin, and in part, this was because the men talking with him were also probing in ignorance, hoping to prompt a returned memory by some word or phrase haphazardly thrown into the conversation. The process was likened by Grainger to fishing by dipping a line in and out of uncertain water.

Gradually, ever so gradually, pieces of information started to emerge and the three men around the bed – or occasionally around a wheelchair – found themselves mentally fitting together a virtual jigsaw puzzle.

After the first month they had established that Harry had been the victim of an unprovoked attack late one night while he was out walking his dog, after spending a couple of hours in a pub on a warm, balmy summer evening. That was as much as they felt able to share with him; but after each session of mild interrogation, they would meet in Grainger's office and go over what had just taken place around Harry's bed or sometimes, his wheelchair.

'I wonder if he's consciously hiding things from us.' William leaned forward and stubbed his cigarette into his coffee saucer. The three men were seated in Grainger's office, reviewing their latest session with Harry. Grainger glanced up at the prominent sign on the wall which forbade smoking. William Russell had many good points, but his smoking habit wasn't one of them. Grainger swallowed his irritation and continued with the discussion.

'I don't think so,' he said. 'He's always been keen to find himself ever since we took him off sedatives. I think the blanks in his knowledge really do worry him and, if you watch him carefully, you'll see small signs of – not relaxation – but what I would describe as the easing of tension.'

'Yes, I've seen that as well.' Detective Chief Inspector Robert Majury continued to make notes on his ring-binder pad as he spoke. 'He's certainly more comfortable with us now.'

Robert, or Bob to his closer friends, had entered the Dorset Constabulary after twenty years with the Hampshire force. He had intended to take early retirement from the police but had been unable to settle. 'Policing,' he was often heard to say, 'is in my blood.' After six months as a civilian he had applied to the Dorset Constabulary and had been taken on as a detective inspector. That was five years previously and he was now a detective chief inspector and head of the local CID, as well as running the Victim Support Group.

This was why he had been invited to take an interest in the mysterious case of the man he now knew as Harry Chaplin. Robert's second title as Officer in Charge of the Victim Support Group sounded impressive but in fact he had only three assistants, minimal funds and not much professional support with which to follow up the steady stream of crime victims emerging from rural Dorset. What he did have, however, were the ability and authority to delve into local and national police records. He was also pretty good at using his easy-going persuasive personality to gain access to records and information belonging elsewhere.

The three men continued through a further round of coffee without advancing much into their quest. Grainger decided that it would be appropriate to defer the next meeting for a week and allow Harry to concentrate on improving his physical wellbeing. William was already thinking of other cases that he could turn his attention to; but Robert had become more intrigued and was anxious to get back to his office in the new Weymouth Police headquarters to see if he could place a few more pieces in the puzzle.

When Robert arrived back in his stark, airless office high up in the building, he slung his raincoat over the easy chair in the corner of the room and placed the plastic beaker of coffee he had collected from the machine in the canteen carefully on the old table that served as his desk. He flopped into the comfortable chair behind the 'desk', placing his notebook on the table in front of him where he could read it while using both hands to fiddle with the lid of the hot coffee container. Despite his care, a small blob of coffee stained the table-top as the lid eventually came off. He reached behind to a pack of tissues on the window sill, pulled one out and mechanically wiped away the spilled liquid. While he was performing this little chore his eyes remained fixed on the notebook in front of him. He reviewed over and over again what he had heard during the latest interview with Harry. After a while he leaned forward, flicked back some pages and examined what had been written previously. For the next half-hour he just sat behind his table, clasping his rapidly cooling plastic coffee beaker while allowing his mind to rove around possibilities and theories.

An hour and a half later, Robert climbed back into his raincoat, threw the remains of the now cold coffee out of the tiny window onto the flowerbed below and trudged off down the stairs towards the ground floor entrance.

While he drove towards the centre of town he reassessed and worried back and forth the information that he had discovered about the attack on Harry Chaplin. It had been vicious and unprovoked but had seemingly generated only passing interest at the time. The problem, Robert mused as he parked his car in the expensive waterside car park, was that to be noticed, you have to have your dramatic event on a quiet news day. The attack on Harry Chaplin had taken place at the height of summer when Weymouth was seething with visitors and when the news was all about anticipation for the forthcoming sailing Olympics, soon due to take place in the bay.

Robert pushed open the glass door of the town library, strolled across to the administration desk, waited while three borrowers had their piles of books stamped, and then asked to speak to the librarian.

'What about?' was the somewhat peremptory response. Robert fished his Dorset Police badge from his pocket and held it at arm's length and eye level so the attendant could see it.

'I see. Just a moment, please.'

Robert waited. Five minutes later a grey-suited youngish man emerged and peered at Robert through black-framed spectacles while running his hand over thinning brown hair. 'How can I help?' he said, clasping both hands together in front of him.

'Can we speak somewhere more privately?' said Robert, smiling with what he hoped was an engaging expression.

'Would you like to come to my office?' The young man gestured towards the door from which he had just emerged.

'Thank you,' said Robert, following the librarian, who was already walking briskly towards the sanctuary of his office.

They entered a light and airy office, packed with books and documents, many stacked around the edges of an elderly wooden 'knee-hole' desk, others on chairs and on the floor. The librarian moved twenty or so books from a small armchair to join others on the carpet. 'Please,' he said, indicating the chair. 'Can I offer you a coffee?'

'Thank you, but no.' Robert hovered over the chair. 'My name is Robert Majury and I head up the Dorset Police Victim Support Group, Mr er…'

'Booker, Paul Booker.'

Robert suppressed a smile, as Booker continued, 'Apt name for a librarian, don't you think?'

Robert smiled again and inclined his head in response as he sank into the comfortably padded elderly chair. He leaned toward the desk and said, 'I'm investigating an incident that took place a few years ago and I wanted to see if you have any press records covering the period.'

'How far back?' said Booker.

'Well, at least five years, maybe seven or more.'

Booker smiled. 'No problem there, then. We have copies of all the local and regional papers going back at least forty years. They used to be on microfiche, but we're up to the minute now. They're all stored on databases. What would you like to see?'

'I'll start local and work out, but it would help me a lot if I could work discreetly, perhaps in a small office space?'

'We have students' reading rooms, more a set of cubicles really, but you won't have anyone looking over your shoulder. Would that do?'

'Thanks,' said Robert, 'I'm sure that would be very good. Could I start with the Dorset Echo, and then the Bournemouth Echo?'

Booker stood up and moved around the desk. 'Follow me,' he said.

Robert followed, and he was led along a brightly-lit, narrow corridor running behind the main Library rooms, up a staircase and into a large, dusty room where the far end had been divided into five small cubicles. Each cubicle consisted of two wooden partitions surrounding a fixed work surface behind which, set in the back wall, was a series of sockets and wires providing power and communication. Two adjustable black vinyl office chairs and a multi-directional desk lamp completed the furnishings. Only one of the five cubicles was occupied, by a frizzy-haired girl hammering feverishly on the keyboard of a laptop.

'I hope this will do. Settle down and I'll bring you a terminal and the information you need.' Booker said this over his shoulder as he retreated back down the corridor. Robert pulled out the chair, sat in it, placed his notebook on the work surface, and waited.

A young freckle-faced girl popped her head around the side of the cubicle and said smilingly, 'Can I get you a cup of coffee, sir?'

Robert thought it would be churlish to refuse twice although he was becoming uncomfortably aware of a full bladder. 'Thanks, yes please,' he said. 'A little milk and no sugar, please. By the way, is there a loo I can use?'

'Just along the corridor, on the right.' With that imparted, she was gone.

Robert put his notebook back in the pocket of his raincoat, stood up and set off down the corridor.

A few minutes later he returned to the cubicle, where there was now a steaming, slightly chipped mug of coffee adorning the work-surface. He sat down again to wait but almost immediately, Booker returned, carrying a fairly battered laptop under one arm and a small box, rather like a cash-box, in his other hand. He placed the laptop carefully on the desk, leaned across to connect it to a power supply and then placed the small box beside it. 'Everything you need will be in there,' he said, pointing to the box, 'dated and catalogued. But if you need help, I'll be just along the corridor. We shut at six today,' he finished, meaningfully.

Robert shrugged off his jacket, took another sip of the surprisingly good coffee, put his notebook down beside the laptop and peered into the box. There seemed to be about twenty USB memory sticks, and a similar number of SD cards, each wedged into a cloth-lined slot with a catalogue of the two-digit code name and subject matter of each unit pasted into the lid of the box.

He studied his notes. Harry had been in a coma for nearly four years. He had been 'in recovery' for about six months so it would be safe to start the search five years previously. He picked out a memory stick allegedly representing the output of the Dorset Echo for the first six months of 2010 and slipped it into the appropriate USB port on the side of the laptop.

Chapter 4

Harry was walking on the treadmill, very slowly. The routine they had prescribed for him was to walk at a gentle, steady pace, with the machine set on a level plane, for ten minutes; then a note would sound, the machine would decelerate to a smooth stop and the attendants would help him out to a chair. There he would sit for twenty minutes after which he would be helped back to the treadmill. It was a long, slow process; but his emaciated legs were beginning to work and the doctor had said that this treatment would need to continue for some time in order to rebuild the damaged muscles wasted by years of lying in bed. Harry wanted to walk again so he worked at the treatment as hard as his physiotherapists would allow.

During the twenty minute rest breaks he had nothing to do other than perhaps sip at a glucose drink, so usually he sat back in the chair, closed his eyes and allowed his thoughts to wander. Again and again he found himself addressing the big questions of his life. Why was he here? Who was the cause of his state? Why? What had he done to contribute to this? What had he done at all during all those years of his previous life which still remained frustratingly blank?

Behind his closed eyes, Harry kept coming back to three things. An image of white shoes: tennis shoes, he thought. But then again they were not tennis shoes – at least not like the tennis shoes of his youth 'plimsolls', he called them. These shoes were smarter, bigger, and with colourful decoration. But what were the colours? He didn't know. But he did know that these shoes were associated with the damage done to his body. His thoughts moved to why he should have such a clear image of these shoes as well as another image of dull brown leather ankle-boots with knotted laces. There was an obvious reason, but Harry's processes of logical deduction were weak and it took many rest periods before he reached the conclusion that the shoe images were so clear because he must have been lying on the ground when he first saw them.

Somehow he knew that at one time, not so long ago, these images had been associated with fear; but he felt no fear now. Indeed, he felt nothing but curiosity. But gradually, it seemed that as he returned again and again in his mind to the images, he began to see more. Or, he wondered, could he be inventing something else to develop the shoe images?

Then there was the word. 'Frug.' Who had said it? No, that wasn't right, he thought; it wasn't said, it was shouted; and whenever it had been shouted he had felt sickening pain and he had seen the shoes and boots in stark detail. He realised he was being kicked. He knew there had been many such kicks but he also knew that, after a while, they had ceased to hurt him, even though the vicious attack had continued.

After completing the session on the treadmill, Harry was helped back to his room, subjected to the regular routine physical examination, and then given another pep talk by Doctor Grainger. He was 'doing well' and his leg muscles were improving, he was told.

'When will I be able to walk normally?' he asked, not for the first time.

'We must be patient, Harry; these things take time,' was the usual non-answer. Harry asked again about his home and was told not to worry. Then he asked about his dog and was again told not to worry – although, he noted, with less certainty.

It was late afternoon as Harry finished his modest supper; he had been sitting in a wheelchair looking out of the window for a while but then he set the plate back on the tray and eased himself from the chair onto his bed. Before sleep overtook him he found the images were once more creeping out of his subconscious into his eyes. But now they were clearer and there seemed to be more to see. Curiously, although Harry knew there was more to each image, he was unable at first to identify what that additional element was.

Later that night, when the room was in darkness and the building offered only the usual tiny night sounds, Harry woke and recognised what it was that had now been added to his realisation. The boots were more than just knotted laces. The boots were brown and of soft dull leather. He knew what type of leather it was but he couldn't remember the word for it. Then there was clothing. Trousers! Dark trousers of rough material. The dark of the material became blue. He knew what this was! They were jeans. He knew about jeans. He remembered jeans. He felt triumphant. But not all the legs had jeans. There were also bare legs. These were women's legs. He didn't know why or how he knew they were definitely a woman's legs but he also realised that they were the ones with the white shoes. Harry slept peacefully for the remainder of the night, and when his breakfast arrived together with watery sunshine lighting up his room, he was actually smiling.

****

It was near the end of the third consecutive afternoon spent in Weymouth Library before Robert's search produced any sort of result. It was a small article found in the Western Morning News in July 2010 which he then found repeated in a copy of the Bournemouth Echo dated a week later. Each report was short and shallow and described a group of young men and women who had hired a private room for a sumptuous dinner party in one of Bournemouth's smarter restaurants. The party consisted of twenty men and women celebrating their graduation from Oxford University. The second article claimed that there were twelve in the party and that they were undergraduates from several Cambridge colleges. Both articles agreed on the fact that huge amounts of champagne had been purchased, some of which must have been drunk, but much more had been used to spray the celebrating students and anyone else who got in the way.

A follow-up article claimed that twenty thousand pounds worth of damage had been caused to the restaurant but, on interview, the restaurant manager had been surprisingly sanguine and had said there was no question of anyone pressing charges; even the waiter who had ended up in Accident and Emergency after having been struck by a thrown champagne bottle was strangely reticent.

Robert found the whole thing a bit puzzling. If damage to the tune of twenty thousand pounds had been caused surely more people must have noticed – and why was the manager apparently so content? He answered his own second question. The manager had been paid off, and handsomely, it seemed.

Before continuing his search, Robert sat back over his fourth mug of coffee of the afternoon and thought about what he had read. Students, by definition generally, were poor and not given to outlandish displays of extravagance such as champagne dinners in expensive restaurants unless, of course, one or more of their number happened to be very wealthy – and, he reflected, stupidly arrogant. He had heard of Oxford-based dining societies busting up premises; but these were all male affairs, and according to both of the reports there were women included in this group. There was confusion in the reports over which university they came from; or perhaps, he thought, they had come from more than one university.

In short, he thought, all of the reports were of misbehaviour in Bournemouth. He was looking for more local misbehaviour. He returned to the memory stick for the Dorset Echo and began once more to pore over each page and each article as it came up on the screen.

Two hours later Robert picked up the next piece of information. The Dorset Echo was in the habit of lining the outer edge of each page with small articles of fifteen words or so announcing forthcoming events, fairs, markets, jumble sales and so on, as well as other tiny newsworthy snippets. Halfway down the edge of page four was a slightly longer report. It was headed 'Drunk Driver Arrested.' A young man had been arrested late at night and charged with driving his Aston Martin through the village of Easton, Portland at excessive speed before colliding with a stone wall. He had been breathalysed and found to have nearly three times the permitted level of alcohol in his bloodstream. His name was given as Sam Steen and the time and date of the incident was given as 2 a.m. on Monday 19th July 2010. The broken body of Harry Chaplin had been discovered late on the evening of Sunday 18th July 2010.

He scanned the subsequent pages and later copies but there was no further reference to Mr Steen or to his expensive vehicle.

One more report in a paper a few days later also caught his eye. A group of revellers, it said, had caused a disturbance during the third day of the Weymouth Harbourside Seafood Fair, a three day event which began on the afternoon of Friday 16th July 2010.

Robert noted down all the salient details and returned the laptop, saying he would be back again, probably the next day.

****

At the clinic Harry was having another chat with William Russell. Despite the fact that Russell was a senior caseworker for Social Services, he tried to present himself to Harry as simply a passing acquaintance who enjoyed Harry's company over a cup of tea.

What William was actually doing was trying to follow the delicate and winding track into the depths of Harry's mind to see if he could help to locate the missing pieces of fractured memory without inadvertently implanting information or causing anxiety with his questions.

Harry was still an enigma. William knew where he had lived and some of the circumstances he had lived in but he didn't know where Harry came from, what he had done beforehand, nor whether he had any of the circle of friends, acquaintances or relatives that most people relied on to ease them through life. Of course, he also wanted to know why Harry had been beaten up so badly and by whom. He had an open case file with a lot of blank pages which needed to be filled before Harry could rejoin the world.

'So, Harry, have you ever been to sea?' said William, seeking a new route to probe. Harry looked blank.

'You do know what I mean by the sea?' said William.

Harry didn't answer at once, then his expression softened and he nodded. 'Yes, I do. I know a lot about the sea.'

'So you've spent time on the sea?' William continued.

'At sea,' said Harry. 'We say "at sea" not "on the sea".'

'I see,' said William, and then he laughed at his own remark. Harry smiled and then laughed a little. William was surprised because this was a 'first'. The laughter marked a new waypoint in Harry's progress.

Neither spoke for a few moments; then William tried again. 'Where did you go to sea, Harry?'

There was a long silence. Harry was trying to conjure up a memory of a time at sea, time which he knew had taken place but which he could not recall or identify. 'All over, I suppose,' he said eventually.

'Did you fish?' asked William.

There was no answer.

'Were you a sailor?'

Again, no answer.

'Were you in the Navy?'

This time there was a faint light of recognition in the eyes looking back at him. William waited.

'Yes, I think I was,' said Harry, 'but it was a long time ago.'

William decided that the 'patient' had had enough for today so he finished his tea, looked at his watch and said, cheerily, 'Well, Harry, I should be off now. See you again in a day or so.' With that he picked up his coat, headed towards the door, turned with a wave of his arm, and disappeared out into the corridor.

William Russell didn't leave the building immediately. He turned right instead of left towards the outer door, and knocked on the partially open door to George Grainger's consulting room. Grainger looked up from his seat behind his desk and motioned Russell to come inside.

'I think I'm making progress,' said the social worker. 'He reacted and showed interest about the sea. He even corrected me when I said "on the sea". It should have been "at sea", he said.'

Grainger put down his pen. 'Really, that is progress indeed.' He spoke slowly and thoughtfully. 'Well done!'

They talked for another ten minutes before Russell stood up to move towards the door. At the doorway he paused and turned. 'By the way, we never get any care or subsistence bills. Your treatment must be pretty expensive. Who is paying?'

'To be perfectly honest, old boy, I don't really know.' George Grainger leaned back in his swivel chair and seemed to seek inspiration from the ceiling. 'The cheques just come rolling in – and I am delighted to say they cover our costs quite handsomely.' He rocked the chair back to an even keel and gazed towards Russell over folded arms.

Chapter 5

Bob Majury eased his five-year-old Mondeo into one of several vacant spaces at the end of a row of haphazardly parked police vehicles. All the way back from the library he had been puzzling over the facts, such as they were, that he had been able to uncover. There wasn't very much to start with other than that a local man going about his business late at night had been set upon by persons unknown and beaten to a state of near death. The big question was not only who had done it, but why? Bob was uncomfortably aware that a four-year-old crime that had already been investigated but which remained unsolved was well outside his present responsibility and he was running the risk of being accused of interference or of wasting his time. Nevertheless, he mused, it was a matter that had been properly drawn to his attention because there was a victim who still existed as such; and as well as heading CID, Bob was responsible for Victim Support.

As he pushed through the glass swing doors and walked towards the pair of lifts he started to evaluate what else he knew about the incident, but by the time the lift doors had opened at the third floor the only conclusion Bob had reached was that even with the new information he had gathered from the library archives, the list of unanswered questions far outranked the list of facts he had now gathered. He shrugged off his raincoat, tossed it over an empty chair and flopped into the worn pseudo-leather swivel armchair that was the third item of furniture in his sparse office after the green four-drawer filing cabinet and the long wooden table which did duty as his desk.

'Hiya, Boss. Coffee?' The tousled ginger head of Acting Detective Constable Gerry Treloar appeared in the doorway.

'Yeah, thanks,' said Bob absently as he delved into his briefcase to drag out his notebook. He raised his voice and called after Gerry. 'Any luck with the background on the "No-name" case?'

Ever since Bob had first become involved with the recovery of Harry Chaplin the 'case' had been dubbed the 'No-name' case, largely due to the simple fact that when first Bob had become involved, the man lying in a coma among the tubes and dials of the hospital bed had been just a body, clinging precariously to life, with no name or background, no worried relatives, no cards or driving licence or wallet that would give any clue to who or what he was. George Grainger and his medical team had not been unduly worried by this. Their job had been concentrated on the delicate business of coaxing the mess of torn, bloodied flesh and broken bones back into something resembling a human being. Who or what that human being was or had been would be of no interest to them until the silent body was able to communicate with them and respond to their repair work.

In the beginning the presumption was that their patient would be unlikely to survive, and if he did he would very probably not be able to become much more than a vegetable. But the man in the bed seemed possessed of an extraordinary will to cling to life. With the comatose patient, the team had been able to isolate individual injuries and infections and deal with them separately, adopting a process similar to that of repairing a damaged building. After the first five months the attitude of the doctors and nurses had begun to change and there had been much more emphasis on the recovery of the man rather than just the repair of his body.

It was about this time that DCI Robert Majury had been asked to look into the 'case' and it became the case of 'No-name' because that was what Gerry had written on the cover of the thin red folder that formed the case file. It should have been relatively simple to look at the list of missing persons, crew lists of visiting ships and the records of hotels and guest houses. But it was not simple at all. Hospital records had been investigated, looking for patients who matched evidence of the unknown man's previous injuries; but also to no avail. In the end it was a third check of dental records which produced a name and the information that Harry Chaplin might once have been a merchant seaman. By this time Harry was showing distinct signs of emerging from his coma, aided by the medical and non-medical staff spending hours talking to the unresponsive patient.

Gerry, who had only recently moved into the CID world, had been given the task of putting together a pattern of what had been happening in Weymouth and on the Isle of Portland during the afternoon and evening of the day when Harry's broken body had been found. He hadn't got very far.

The problem that Gerry had been trying to overcome was that although the investigators knew the date of Harry's attack – or to be more precise, they knew the date on which his body had been found and of course they knew where it had been found – that was really the sum of their information concerning the attempted murder of Harry Chaplin. Harry had been found late at night in an alleyway in the centre of Weymouth, but he had been seen earlier in the day walking along a path through the unkempt fields which looked down on the lighthouse car park at Portland Bill. Grass and dirt found on his clothes suggested that he might actually have been attacked in the open fields near the Bill. The area was well used by dog walkers, ramblers and bird watchers as well as casual tourists wandering down to see the turbulent waters of the Portland Race. It had been estimated that Harry's injuries had occurred several hours before he had been found and, despite the public location, nobody, absolutely nobody, had seen anything at all. It was as though he had been dropped from the sky to lie unheeded in amongst the buildings of Weymouth.

Somebody had attacked Harry, given him a comprehensive kicking and left him to die. His injuries could not have been incurred without there being noise and movement which must have been evident to anyone in the general vicinity. Marks on Harry's body and clothes also suggested that several people must have been involved, as many as eight or ten, Bob thought. Yet apart from the earlier possible sighting of Harry, nobody had seen anything significant either at the Bill or in Weymouth.

Gerry had been sent to pore over the desk logs in every police station in Portland, Weymouth and the surrounding towns to see if there had been any reports of fighting, drunkenness or other disturbances. Then he had been sent around the hospitals with the not very hopeful task of seeing whether there were records of people turning up at A&E with minor injuries consistent with fighting or drunkenness, or people who were hopped up on drugs. There had been plenty of such instances but nothing to link with Harry Chaplin.

The other active foot soldier in Bob's team was Jim Creasy. An easy-going, fit-looking man with an athletic build and an open, friendly face, Jim had once had a promising career as a detective sergeant in the Met until a hit and run driver outside Harrods in Knightsbridge had ended any chance of him being able to complete the running section of the Metropolitan Police Annual Fitness Test. Jim felt himself to be fortunate in that the multiple fractures to his left leg had not resulted in amputation, but the injury still slowed him down and caused him to limp slightly.

As soon as he had recovered and was able to walk and drive again after the 'accident', he had resigned from the Met, gathered up his young family and moved to the south coast. His victim compensation was not going to keep him for the rest of his days and so, leaning on favours from old friends, he had initially secured a clerical job with the Dorset Constabulary, based at the headquarters in Winfrith, near Wareham. For an active, outdoor man, the job was incredibly boring; so when the formation of the County Victim Support Team was announced Jim was in like a whippet. He was accepted into the Dorset Force with the rank of detective sergeant, which rank he had previously held in the Met and which took into account his former very successful career as a 'thief taker'.

Bob settled himself in his chair, placed his notebook on the table, pulled the 'No-name' file out of the left-hand drawer, and bawled 'Coffee!' in the general direction of Gerry in the communal office. Gerry was already coming through the open doorway into Bob's office with two mugs of hot coffee in his hands. One white china mug was decorated with the inscription 'Property of HM Prison Parkhurst. Not to be removed.' This was Bob's mug and Bob's private joke.

The DCI picked up the notebook and flipped through the pages of scribble as Gerry placed the mug of coffee on a Carlsberg beer mat which did duty as a coaster.

'Whadda we know, Boss?' asked Gerry as he sat and faced his boss across the table.

Bob sipped his coffee, holding the mug carefully, feeling its warmth through both hands. 'I went to look through the newspaper records in the library,' he said.

'Yes, I know,' said Gerry. 'What did you find?'

'Not much, but enough to be interesting, I think.'

'Shoot,' said Gerry.

'Well, in the local press – not the immediate local press, that is – there are a couple of reports of antisocial behaviour at around the time that Harry was found,' said Bob.

'What sort of reports?'

'A restaurant hired for a very expensive evening out in Bournemouth, and then trashed, big time. But the interesting thing is that the owner of the place seemed happy and content not to get excited about his loss of business or even to want to press charges.'

'He's been paid off!' Gerry looked disgusted as he spoke.

'I think that's right, but not just paid off with a whip-round; he's been given a proper "bung". A hell of a lot of money must have changed hands.'

Gerry nodded.

Bob continued. 'Then there's a stupid rich tearaway getting boozed up and crashing his Aston Martin outside Easton.'

Gerry nodded again. 'You don't see many cars like that on Portland!'

'Finally,' said Bob as he flipped a page in his notebook, 'there was some sort of dust-up among the stalls during the Seafood Festival. And before you ask, yes, there is a pattern, albeit a weak one. Each of these reports hints at a group of people arriving from out of town – with, obviously, a great deal of money to throw about. One final thing.' Bob raised a hand to forestall the interruption that he could see coming. 'All the reports I saw were minimal fill-ins and I could not find one single follow-up in any of the papers I looked at.'

'Court reports?' asked Gerry.

'Nothing. Not even a blot on the paper!'

'Really?' Gerry sought inspiration in the depths of his own coffee mug.

'There is something else,' said Bob, carefully laying a page torn from his notebook on the table in front of Gerry. 'All these unusual events happened on these dates, very close together. See if you can find out what else happened then.'

Gerry picked up the paper, looked at it, raised one eyebrow and folded it before tucking it into the breast pocket of his shirt.

'I want you to go down to records and see if there is anything on file about any of these.' Bob was bringing the discussion to a close.

'Will tomorrow do? It's getting late and the lazy bastards running records have probably locked up by now.'

'Okay, tomorrow. But I want you to take the stuff I've got here and set out a time line with anything else you can pick up – as soon as you can

Chapter 6

Harry was having a bad night. He had been dreaming intermittently and within his dream his brain was rehearsing the experiences of the day. Inside his head it was rather like a slideshow where the slides vary in quality and are never left on the screen long enough to assimilate the whole picture.

Eventually Harry twisted and tumbled in his bed until the discomfort of the tortured bed linen brought him awake. He lay there in the darkness, sweating profusely in a tangle of sheets and pillows, and tried to remove the images from his head.

The window blinds had not been drawn shut and as his eyes became accustomed to the dim light from the three quarters moon he was able to take in the familiar surroundings of the room. He could also recognise the fresh, slightly antiseptic conditioned air that surrounded him. He could hear in the distance the faint routine sounds of the clinic at night. All this began to settle him. His breathing slowed, the perspiration eased and he felt calmer – and, curiously, perhaps for the first time, he felt more aware and in control of himself. The bed was in a mess and briefly, he considered calling for the night attendant but he quickly dismissed the idea. If he was found awake and sweating with his bed awry they would probably give him a sedative and he'd sleep quietly until morning.

Harry didn't want that. He wanted to think. He was sure that in his turbulent dreams he had uncovered things he needed to know. He tried to marshal his thoughts but it was difficult because inconsequential things intruded and his mind would drift off.

Harry breathed slowly, lay still and tried again to concentrate, but already the substance of his interrupted dream was drifting away. At first all he could concentrate on was a belief that he now knew more than he had once known – but he couldn't remember what that new knowledge was. He was as yet unable to identify the additional knowledge that he believed he had now gained, but he was certain there was something. He reached out a tentative hand for the water container on the bedside cupboard, put the drinking tube in his mouth and enjoyed the cool water trickling into his throat. He felt refreshed and more comfortable. He settled down to think, without realising that this very act marked a new advance in his healing.

His life was like a jigsaw puzzle with gaps in all the important places. He lay in the bed and tried, one by one, to recall the images that had appeared in the night, and then to see if there was a space into which they might fit. He didn't sleep again that night.

The moon had set but dawn had not yet arrived and so the room seemed darker. Harry was able to close his eyes, relax and recall – and it was working. He knew, almost exactly, where he had been attacked. He knew he had owned a car, a blue Ford Focus estate, nearly eight years old but serviceable. He knew where his home had been but then he had already been told that. Now, however, he was able to visualise the rooms, the furniture and the small south-east facing back garden. He knew he had been a seaman, not in the Navy but working as a boatswain in a variety of tankers and container ships. He had a clear picture of an austere but adequate cabin he had once occupied, situated high up in the after superstructure of a huge ship. He knew about chain cable and cordage, anchors and safety harnesses. He knew also that all this had been a long time ago and it had been many years since he had left the sea.

Although he tried to push it away from him, Harry recalled more about his attack and his attackers. He had been walking on the windswept field which rises gently behind the lighthouse when his attention had been attracted by rowdy noise coming from the pub behind the lighthouse car park. Ten or a dozen young men and women were spilling out of the pub, throwing open and slamming car doors, shouting obscenities at each other and to the air surrounding them. One or two people had stopped in the car park to watch the performance as car engines revved, gravel sprayed and five or six expensive cars drove fast and erratically from the front of the pub, accelerating up the road towards the village of Southwell.

Then, without apparent rhyme or reason, it had happened. Instead of continuing north along the road towards Weymouth, after half an hour the cars had reappeared, driving fast towards the lighthouse. But they turned off onto the narrow road leading up towards the Coastwatch Lookout. Harry watched. Something dreadful, something appalling, had occurred. But he couldn't remember what had happened. He lay on his back, desperately trying to remember what had happened next – but his stubborn mind seemed to have closed itself off. And then, on the verge of sleep, it came to him. It came like a hammer blow into his head. It was his dog. They had killed his dog; but he still couldn't recall how it had happened. His mind seemed to have shut the knowledge away behind a gate – however, he was acutely aware that Cassie, his seven-year-old retriever, was dead. He forgot everything else and lay in his bed weeping, until nature took over and he fell asleep.

With the early morning light came more recollection, but the pictures in his head were disjointed. He remembered two cars stopping and reversing rapidly with gears screaming. In the gathering dusk he had been surrounded by men and women, all of them young and all of them shouting and angry. He had no idea why. He was knocked to the ground and as he tried to roll into a foetal ball, kicks and punches rained down on him from all sides. He had lost consciousness. The rest remained blank until that first voice had told him he was lucky to be alive. He knew that a long time had passed, but he did not know how long.

But there were other things Harry now recalled about his attackers. There had been at least one woman, possibly two. They had shouted to each other the word 'Frug' which seemed to increase their frenzy. Although he couldn't remember any other shouted words, he knew that the accents were all alien to him. He had spoken with a typical Dorset burr but now he had learned to speak once more his words were more 'proper' – what others might have called 'home counties'. That was what his attackers had sounded like.

Also their cars: he remembered, as they had roared towards him up the hill. They had been big, new, powerful, expensive; and some had been sports cars. Finally, and most important, he had the images of two faces, spitting and snarling before the merciful darkness had overtaken him. Now, however, he remembered them; and in the early light of pre-dawn, he knew he would never forget them.

All this Harry remembered, piece by disjointed piece, in the deep hours between midnight and dawn.

Chapter 7

Gerry started with the drunken Aston Martin driver. That should have been a very easy case to locate, given the fancy make of car involved. Aston Martins were not exactly common around South Dorset and a brand new one written off in a crash should have been headline news. It should also have resulted in a great fat file full of all the juicy aspects of the case: the car, the driver, drawings and measurements of skid marks, the weather, the condition of the road and, of course, the sentence eventually handed down.

At first he couldn't find any file at all. He searched through motoring cases for 2010, then 2011, then, as a long shot, through 2009. After that he started on the computer files for cases of drunkenness. Again, nothing!

He decided to take a different approach and went back upstairs to the office to contact the DVLA in Cardiff. As usual, he got the standard runaround until he started making threats about official complaints. Eventually he found himself speaking to a man who called himself Anwar. Anwar duly searched the records for driving licences issued to one Samuel Steen. There turned out to be seventeen of these in all. Six of them were over the age of seventy, four lived in Scotland, and one in Northern Ireland. Four would have been below the age of seventeen in 2010 and none of the rest fitted the age bracket.

Gerry then cajoled his helper onto a different tack. The vast vehicle registration records were tapped but none of the three hundred or so registered Aston Martins had ever belonged to anyone called Steen.

Unfazed, Gerry phoned the Aston Martin Company. They were at first reluctant to provide information, pleading client confidentiality. Gerry scoffed openly at this, and with a little more persuasion, his questions were being answered, though not usefully.

Did the company have a register of all Aston Martin owners?

Well, yes, they did have a register of all first owners and some second owners, but no, nobody with the name of Steen appeared on any of their records.

Did they keep records of what happened to the cars they have built? Specifically, did they record cars written off, in accidents, for example?

Yes, they did.

Was a car written off in an accident in Dorset in or around 2010?

Yes, there had been an insurance write-off in a collision with a deer on the Isle of Portland in mid-2010.

Gerry punched the air in delight. At last, he thought, some progress.

He was still smiling from the progress he had made when he picked up the next piece of good luck. Mary Flint was the youngest and prettiest member of the team, although she tried hard to hide her good looks, tying her golden blonde hair back into a severe ponytail and affecting black-framed spectacles. She suddenly breezed into the office clutching three battered and stained brown cardboard files. 'Is this what you're looking for?' she announced triumphantly as she dumped them firmly on the desk, producing a cloud of dust.

'Where did you get these?' said Gerry, looking up at the tall girl standing on the other side of the desk.

Mary smiled. 'In the trash,' she said.

Gerry frowned in surprise, 'What do you mean?'

Mary smiled again, obviously delighted with her discovery. 'All the old files or files for disposal have to be checked before they are shredded or burnt. Everybody sends their obsolete or de-activated files to the trash storage but nobody seems to have the time or inclination to get into the trash store to do any checking. Files stay there for ages; so I just went down to do some checking, had a root around, and here's what I found.'

'You are just brilliant!' said Gerry, as he reached across to pick up the files. He opened the first one, which had a title scribbled on the outside: 'DUTI', it said, which meant Driving Under The Influence. Inside was a charge sheet alleging that a Mr S J Steen had been arrested at the scene of an accident on the A354, otherwise known as Southwell Road, travelling north from the village of Easton. That was almost the only information the file contained. There were five or six additional sheets of paper, including two which were headed 'Witness statement'. Every other piece of information except one statement on the final sheet had been heavily blacked out – 'redacted', it was called now.

The final remaining statement said, 'All charges withdrawn – lack of evidence.' Below this there was an indecipherable scribble of three initials.

The second file was not much more forthcoming than the first. This had no title on the outside but enclosed several sheets of paper, again heavily redacted, offering up references to disturbances during the Weymouth Seafood Festival and complaints by three or four pub landlords of antisocial behaviour aimed towards unnamed groups of people. Once again, witness statements had been obtained, blanked out, and then the whole thing had been wound up, the final remark being "No Further Action".

The third file referred to questions which had evidently been raised by the Bournemouth and Poole police forces, but it didn't provide any answers.

Gerry spread the files open across the desk and started to compare the sparse information offered. He pulled a piece of scrap paper towards him and began to jot down dates and times. Then he pulled out the 'No-name' file and started to add more dates to the piece of paper.

While he was doing this, Jim Creasy limped into the office, dropped his jacket over a chair and came to stand behind Gerry.

'What gives?' he asked.

'It's the No-name case. Boss has got the bit between his teeth.'

'I thought that was a dead end,' said Jim.

'No, not now it isn't – and I could use some help actually.'

'What do you want me to do?'

'I'm chasing the people, but I need to try to run down the crashed car. Can you have a go at that?'

'I'll give it a go,' said Jim as he gathered up the notes headed 'car' and walked across the room to a vacant desk by the window.

Gerry began to construct a timeline, listing all the information he had lifted from the four files. He worked at it for the next hour, referring back and forth between the files and ignoring the cup of tea that Mary had placed on the desk.

At five o'clock that afternoon he was perched on an old upright farmhouse chair in the corner of Bob's office. He heard the familiar measured tread of his boss coming down the corridor and he eased himself up from his chair as the detective chief inspector breezed through the door, wet raincoat skirts flapping to either side of him.

'What's that bloody thing doing in here?' Bob said by way of greeting, pointing at the heavy old chair Gerry had been sitting in.

'It's my thinking chair, Guv'nor. I dragged it in from the office. Helps me think,' he finished lamely.

'Well, you can bloody well drag it back out again.'

Gerry put his papers on the table and started to move the chair.

'No, wait,' said Bob. 'You've got something for me. You've got that look.'

Gerry brightened. 'I have, Guv'nor, and I think you're going to like it.' Bob shrugged off his wet raincoat, hanging it carefully on the clothes hanger on the back of the door, and eased himself into the chair behind his long table.

Gerry stood on the other side of the table, placed a sheet of paper on the blotter, turned it so that it could be read by his boss, and then referred to a similar sheet in his hand.

'There is a very neat little pattern of dates,' he said. 'In 2010, most of the universities ended the academic term on or around Friday 9th July. Just over a week later on Saturday 17th July a major disturbance takes place in and around a private room booked for an expensive dinner party in a smart Bournemouth hotel. For some reason, unspecified, the hotel closed for about two weeks afterwards. On the face of it, at the start of the holiday season, this seems unlikely to have been a planned closure. The next day, Sunday 18th July, there is a fight in and around the Seafood Festival along the Weymouth Harbourside. Some stalls are damaged and a few cuts and bruises handed out. It seems to have been alcohol-fuelled but...' he paused: 'and this bit is important. The group in the hotel numbered between eight and twelve, depending on who you believe, and the troublemakers at the Seafood Festival were about eight or nine youngish men and women.' Gerry paused again, waiting while Bob peered at the sheet of paper in front of him.

'Go on, then,' said Bob, leaning back.

'In the early hours of the morning of Monday 19th July, an Aston Martin car travelling north out of Easton left the road and collided with the left hand dry-stone wall. The car seems to have been a write-off and it also seems likely that the driver gave a false name. The insurers were told it had hit a deer, but there's no indication of any deer, or any other animal for that matter. By Tuesday 20th July, investigations had been started and crime files were raised. At about midnight on Sunday 18th July, a body, badly beaten, was discovered by a patrolling team of a PC and a PSO lying in an alleyway just off St Mary's Street. The body was at first presumed to be deceased, but an ambulance and paramedic were called. The body was rushed to Dorset County Hospital more dead than alive and then, in a coma, transferred to the Chesil Clinic just outside Chickerell. On or about Monday 26th July, all investigations were closed, charges dismissed – note, they were not to lie on the file, but dismissed. Here ends the story!'

'Well, well.' Bob peered over his steepled fingers and Gerry dropped back into his chair, waiting.

Chapter 8

Harry had suffered another disturbed night. The dreams had returned after a gap of four peaceful nights. This time the images in his dreams seemed even brighter; more stark, as though someone had sharply increased the contrast on a camera. But as well as this, the images were sharper and there seemed to be many more, different, faces. There were other things left by the dreams in his mind. The faces were clearer, he saw clothing that seemed sometimes familiar, and he recognised a strong smell of wet grass. He heard car engines. He had been in a car, there had been a short fall onto hard ground, banging his head before fading into oblivion. Then the dream ended, with the last remaining sense being the smell of urine and vomit.

Harry decided once more to keep the dreams to himself. He wasn't sure why, but he didn't want to volunteer information on what was entering his mind in the quiet hours of the night. As the days of physiotherapy and psychiatric confidence-building continued, one after another, he found that he was thinking more logically and rationally. He became more aware of the here and now, of the taste, likes and dislikes he was developing for the food he was being given. He stared through his window towards the trees, bushes and grass outside. He watched the birds, the squabbling sparrows, the bullying starlings, the occasional rook, but most of all, he became fascinated by the diligent foraging of the blackbirds. There were at least two pairs of blackbirds who seemed to be patrolling the lawn whenever he awoke. They became important to him. If at least one of the birds was not easily evident when he first looked through the window he would begin to feel discomforted and saddened.

Harry was also dwelling silently on what the future might hold for him. He was now certain that he had done nothing to provoke the vicious attack that he had suffered five years previously and his thoughts dwelt more on the sheer random unfairness of what he had suffered. As he lay awake at night thinking, a slow burning anger began to assert itself within him; but he never spoke aloud of this feeling. Instead, it became the force to push him to try even harder each day to recover his faculties. He became the most perfect and willing patient.

William Russell came regularly once or twice a week to talk to Harry. He sometimes brought with him a selection of newspapers, always a week or so old, and he used the articles to bring Harry forward through the nearly five years lost to him. Harry learned about political changes, locally and nationally, new laws which had been enacted and the generally rising irritation with all things European. They talked of who had entered and who had left the national scene, the mass misbehaviour of politicians and of the wars in Iraq, Sierra Leone, Afghanistan and elsewhere. They talked of the music scene, but Harry showed little interest in that. He was more interested in what had happened locally – to his environment – and in particular he seemed fascinated by the Olympic Games which had taken place three years previously. At night, alone in the dark, he rehearsed everything he had learned during the day and slowly but steadily he filled in the blanks and built the picture that was Harry Chaplin.

But when he slept the dreams would often come again. They had become repetitive and so, like short video clips repeated over and over, the dreams began to lose impact. Harry no longer woke in a sweat among tangled sheets. Instead, he felt almost as though each night it was necessary to memorise certain images. Each night they came and then they went. He slept peacefully and calmly until it was time to look out for the birds already at work on the damp lawn.

Harry's growing mental strength began to reflect itself in an improvement in his physical state. Within two weeks he was able to walk unaided except for a walking-stick; and his ability on the treadmill was improving at an impressive rate. So much so that George Grainger felt it necessary to have an avuncular chat with him.

'Your mind is racing ahead of your physical state, Harry,' he said.

'What do you mean?' said Harry.

'You're much straighter in your head, and once that process has begun it can continue at a rapidly increasing rate. You've overcome the fog you were left in and now you have what I might call the mainframe of your mind back again. Think of it like a series of shelves in a store cupboard. You have rebuilt the store cupboard but only a few of the shelves are occupied. As each shelf becomes occupied you will quickly begin to learn to use the contents to help fill the adjacent shelves, each side, and above and below. The more shelves you are able to fill, the more opportunities there will be to expand into the remaining empty shelves. Then when they are all filled you will have a library of information which you can use to bring in more information. Do you follow what I am saying?'

Harry sat and thought for a few moments. 'Yes,' he said slowly, 'I think I do.'

'My point is,' continued the doctor, 'that building muscle and teaching muscle to operate properly does not work like that at all. Each muscle needs to develop little by little and when that is complete, the whole collection of muscles need to integrate with your nervous system in order to produce a functioning arm, or a leg. You can't rush that. You can't do it with drugs or by spending ever more hours on training machines set at ever more demanding rates. If you overdo it you will break or pull something and find yourself right back at the beginning.'

'I can work harder,' said Harry, staring back at his mentor.

'No,' said George Grainger, emphatically. 'You can only work at the rate your body will allow. You are not a young man, and on top of that your key muscle groups have been idle for years. Trust me. I know. We will take you forward as fast as we can but the rate of progress will always be governed by what your body can accept and withstand.'

Harry nodded in agreement but he didn't really mean it.

Chapter 9

Giles de Courtney Wellton was enjoying life. As he powered the Jaguar F-Type north along the M11 he turned up the heavy rock music belting out of the eight speakers and thought about the sweetness of life. A Member of Parliament for only two years, he was now the youngest Minister of State and Privy Councillor since Pitt the Younger and he knew that he had the coveted place at Rural Affairs entirely on his own merit. It had absolutely nothing to do with being the son of a former Cabinet Minister – although, Giles thought with a wry smile, the old man had been the most successful Minister for a century; and now he, Giles, was going to achieve even greater fame and fortune.

As the powerful car ate up the miles at twenty-five miles per hour above the motorway speed limit, Giles allowed his thoughts to wander onto even more pleasurable events. The sex with Sandra had been superb, even though it meant that he had not slept at all last night. Not to worry, he thought, a couple of uppers followed by a can of Red Bull had him firing on all six cylinders. As he thought about the heavy scarlet satin sheets and the wild contortions that she could achieve, he drifted back to another occasion.

The first time they had made love was immediately after they had snuffed the old man. Kicking and beating him to death had aroused both of them to a level they had never experienced before; and the frantic coupling, rolling around on the wet grass, still covered in the man's blood while they ignored the rest of the Frugs who stood around drinking whisky from a bottle and smoking joints, was an experience impossible ever to repeat.

Of course, the little shit Simmonds had chickened out at the last minute and spoiled it all when he crashed his car while trying to run away. Somebody had a brainwave and moved the body so none of the guys on Portland could be connected. And now with a few strings pulled here and there, the fun of untrammelled youth was over and forgotten. 'Well, over but maybe not forgotten. Perhaps we should put the old team together and do it all again,' mused Giles, as he slowed marginally for a set of roadworks reducing the motorway to two narrow lanes and the hard shoulder. Giles eased the Jaguar smoothly onto the hard shoulder and began to stream past the speed-restricted traffic in the two remaining lanes. He made a conscious effort to transfer his thoughts to the inevitable dullness and boredom of constituency matters.

'The little shit Simmonds' was in fact only a few miles to the west of the speeding car. He was sitting in his opulent drawing room looking out over a hundred acres of manicured parkland, part of an estate of over two thousand acres, and contemplating his new life as Sir Arthur Simmonds, now Seventh Baronet. He looked older than his twenty-seven years, and since inheriting the estate and title, his dress and appearance had been changing gradually into that of a typical country squire. He wondered, sometimes, whether he was turning into his father. The thought depressed him.

At length he turned back to the spread of papers littering the huge oak bureau beyond the window, 'waiting to smother him,' he thought. Reluctantly he turned away from the window and settled himself in the Regency chair. He flicked the pages of a leather-bound desk diary lying open on the fine green and gold leather of the bureau; he studied the entries on the page and reached for a Coutts cheque book.

He made out a cheque for £2,000 to the Chesil Clinic and stuffed it with nervous fingers into a plain envelope, already conveniently stamped by his Estate Secretary. He scribbled the address and flicked the envelope into the 'out' tray before turning back to gaze through the window once more at his new domain.

He was a worried man. Since the sudden, early and harrowing death of his father he had been thrust into a world where he was expected to assume the role of the responsible and trustworthy leader of his extended family and of the people who ran his estate and business interests, who relied on him and gave him their trust.

As well as the cares of his position and his estate which now burdened his once carefree persona during the daytime, his nights were deeply disturbed and frequently sleepless. Almost immediately after he returned to live at the family seat he had become subject to dreams and nightmares which seemed to emphasise his dissolute and irresponsible youth. His deceit, his drinking and drug taking came nightly to accuse him and to destroy him. He was suffering an acute attack of conscience brought on by the final words addressed to him by his dying father.

In a matter of days Arthur's father seemed to have aged twenty years and shrunk in every respect. Nevertheless, his final remark to his son came like a hammer blow, destroying utterly the young man's self- respect. The dying sixth Baronet had curled a white bony finger, drawing his son nearer to the great bed. Arthur had to lean close and strain to hear his father's words.

'Arthur,' the old man said. 'I know what you've been and what you've done and I've covered your vile behaviour. You are a bloody disappointment to me and to my family. You don't deserve the inheritance. You are a fucking disgrace.'

And then he died. For the first time in years, Arthur wept, not only for his father but for himself.

****

Giles gunned the motor just to feel the acceleration. He slipped into the outer lane to pass an articulated Tesco lorry, cutting in front of another car before sliding right back across to the inside lane. The 'one mile' sign slipped by, warning of his departure point. He allowed the car to coast down to seventy, then sixty as the slip road signs appeared, and he started to think about his constituency surgery. In fact, he began to estimate the minimum time he would need to spend with the boring agent and his carping drones, which was how he thought of his constituents.

As it turned out, the session was none too onerous. He spent an hour and a half listening to a selection of the usual moans and bleats, half listening until each story was spilled out, before offering the response already prepared for him by the agent. He then had to endure cloying tea and cake with the ladies of the fund-raising committee, smiling on cue and accepting their adulation with as much grace as he was able to muster. He gave the little speech written by his political secretary, shook a couple of hands and left as quickly as he reasonably could.

He was pleased by the scraps of conversation he heard as he stood outside the community hall putting his papers back into his briefcase.

'Such a nice man!'

'Very busy with government business…'

'We're so lucky to have him…'

He was already weighing up the possibility of a casual reunion with the nimble Sandra as he drove out of the car park, ignoring the farewell wave of the agent.

As he drove back towards London he tried to call Sandra, using the two numbers in his phone memory, but without success. By the time he reached the Chelsea flat he was in a foul mood.

Chapter 10

Jim Creasy had two follow-up visits to complete before the afternoon was over so he tucked the file and papers into his rucksack and chucked it on to the back seat of his rather smart Toyota Prius. As the car cruised silently out of the car park, he was thinking of the route he would take in his attempt to pick up the trail that would inevitably have been left by the crashed car.

After several cups of tea and the distribution of leaflets giving a range of advice on home security to some recent burglary victims, he climbed back into the Prius and headed for home. He was greeted by his wife and an intriguing smell of cooking coming from the kitchen. Sarah looked knowingly at the collection of papers now clutched in Jim's hand, sighed, and busied herself once more at the stove. Jim went straight to the dining room and spread the papers over the far end of the eight-place dining table.

Half an hour later they were both working their way through generous portions of spaghetti Bolognese.

'Busy day?' said Sarah.

'So so.'

'What does that mean?' Sarah twirled an inch thick rope of spaghetti around her fork, then thinking better of it, she started again and came up with a smaller forkful.

'Well,' said Jim, 'it means quite a lot of dogsbody work doing follow-up visits on unsolved housebreaking, followed by the opportunity to do some interesting research about a crashed car.'

When dinner was finished, Sarah cleared away the wreckage, loaded the dishwasher, noted that all the main television channels were predictably offering only puerile rubbish – 'as usual,' she thought – and then wandered into the dining room carrying a bottle of Cabernet Shiraz, just under half full, with two glasses.

'Can I help?'

'You're helping by bringing that.' Jim angled his head towards the bottle. 'But two brains might be better than one.'

'Fill me in, then,' said Sarah, pleased at being able to work with her husband as part of an investigating team once again. For a moment she allowed her thoughts to drift back to her days as a young detective, sitting by a paper-strewn desk with a clutter of empty coffee mugs, debating the quality of evidence with Jim, as she had done so often before they were married.

'In summary...' Jim began, before pausing to move his chair back and reaching for the wine bottle. He examined the label, then poured the remaining wine equally into their two glasses. Sarah waited patiently for him to continue; they both picked up a glass, and raised them in silent toast. Sarah had been here before and she experienced another startlingly clear bout of déjà vu. Jim put his glass back on the table and examined the contents critically, squinting through the dark red liquid towards the light. He picked up the empty bottle and studied the label once more before continuing. 'In summary, we have a tearaway, almost certainly a wealthy and possibly well-connected tearaway. He drove an Aston Martin until he crashed it. Oh, and he was apparently as drunk as a skunk!'

'Did he repair it or replace it?' interrupted Sarah.

'I presume you mean the car?' Jim sipped his wine.

'Yes, the car.'

'Good question – and I don't have an answer yet – but as it happens, there's nothing to indicate either repair or replacement. The car just disappeared.'

'But surely we can find out?'

'We can try,' said Jim. 'But there are other questions – was there an insurance payout? If the car was scrapped, where is the wreckage? Did anyone see and remember the crash? Who was it registered to, why did the driver give a false name, and who covered it all up? That, my dear, is the most important part. All the records seem to have disappeared.'

'If there has really been a cover-up, that suggests some pretty high level input from the police.' Sarah doodled on a piece of scrap paper as she spoke.

Jim's head jerked up sharply. 'Explain,' he said.

'Easy,' Sarah pushed back a lock of auburn hair that had fallen forward, hiding her face. 'Our tearaway gives a false name and no-one checks on it; or if someone did, they took no action. How many times do you come across a crashed Aston Martin – and on Portland of all places! A Sunday night patrol coming across anything at all on Portland would work it until they had squeezed it dry. And can you imagine anyone with an Aston Martin crash to write up not talking about it back in the canteen?'

'No, I can't.'

'Neither can I. Coppers talk about anything and everything to anyone who will listen when they have a break or finish the shift.'

'Yeah, but not this time,' said her husband pensively, as he searched his pockets for cigarettes, before remembering that he no longer smoked.

'Another thing,' continued Sarah, staring intently across the table at her husband. 'Did anyone see a driving licence? Was a licence produced? Was the driver's identity checked, or the car registration? It's a simple procedure and easy, any time of the day or night. The first thing any traffic cop would do was to check whether the car had been nicked. Any check of the driver's name would have come up with all lights flashing. Yet you say there is nothing. Nothing anywhere! To my mind there is only one explanation. Someone, probably several someones, were lent on.'

'That's an assumption, Sarah,' said Jim, absently shifting the table mats about.

'You don't believe that and neither do I. I bet the Boss doesn't either.' She stood and began to pace up and down the room.

'Sit down. I can't do with you marching about like that. Can't think.'

'Look!' said Sarah. She returned to stand behind her chair but didn't sit. 'An Aston Martin is a bloody expensive car. The driver crashes it with no other vehicle involved. He gives a false name. Nobody thinks to check that. Why did he crash? No explanation. No breathalyser either, or if there was then those results have been binned as well. Now nobody can trace the car and apparently nobody has ever attempted to trace the car. Even for a Morris Minor, the RTA investigation boys are normally all over the site within minutes, buggering up the traffic flow for hours if they can manage it. It stinks!'

'You've got one thing wrong. He must have been breathalysed because there is an initial report saying he was drunk – just before the 'no further action' bit. Yes, it certainly does seem to have a bit of a smell lingering about it.'

'Another thing.' Sarah was back in her stride once more. 'Think of it like this. Who drives around in outrageously expensive cars like Aston Martins?'

Jim shrugged.

'People who are bloody rich, that's who. People who have got money to burn, and – particularly – people who give false names so that whatever naughtiness they have been up to can be shovelled under the carpet...'

'With a golden shovel,' Jim finished the statement for her. Sarah started to say something else but Jim held up his hand in a familiar gesture. She closed her mouth and waited, still standing behind the chair.

'The Boss wants Gerry to give him a timeline linking the trouble in the Bournemouth restaurant with the hassle in Weymouth and the attempted murder in Weymouth, or maybe on Portland. But I think I might be able to give him a bit more than that.'

'Don't make up a story. If he susses you out doing that he'll throw a serious tantrum. You know what he can be like.' As she spoke Sarah remembered very well what Bob Majury could be like. She had once worked with him as his detective sergeant – his 'skipper' – and she knew that he would poke holes through any story not backed by facts, and false conjecture would have been likely to produce problems for the person presenting the case.

Chapter 11

Harry had begun to read again. The books he had been given were undemanding but lightly entertaining. He knew, though no-one had told him, that each book had been carefully vetted; nevertheless, he was enjoying the books and his brain had something positive to concentrate on, so he was quietly pleased with himself. He believed the books marked another waypoint in his progress back towards the man he had once been.

Another improvement appeared in the form of a small flat screen colour television set. This seemed to have been given to him as a reward for the improvement he had made in his physical condition, but nothing had been said to that effect. He was also able to spend more time out of the wheelchair and could even walk quite fast for short distances, aided by nothing more than two walking-sticks.

The dreams still came regularly but now there seemed to be no fear in them. It was almost as though he was a spectator – a spectator to a frenzied attack by a gang of men and women, kicking at a shapeless form moving listlessly on the ground. It was only when an unbidden rogue thought interrupted the dream, telling him that the lump moving on the wet grass was him, that the dream ended. Usually, this was the trigger to spring him back to sweating, shaking wakefulness.

When he woke in this fashion he would lie in his bed in the darkness, no longer sweating but feeling his heart pounding. As he did so, faces began to form behind his closed eyelids. There was one in particular which appeared again and again until Harry was sure he would always recognise this man. The man was slim, young, with the build of an athlete. He wore a white jacket over a black satin shirt open at the neck and the first two buttons. Black hair curled out from under the shirt and curled and twined around a medallion on a gold chain. The white jacket was stained red, and green with grass stains. The red was Harry's blood.

The face was small, fine-boned, aristocratic and sun-tanned. Thick locks of unnaturally black hair hung down on either side of the head and sometimes flicked forward to cover the face. It was a cruel face, an arrogant face, a powerful face. Above all, it was a face to be afraid of.

There were others but the faces in his subconscious did not appear as clearly as that of the leader. That the man was the leader Harry had no doubt. Among the other faces there was one with close-cropped ginger hair, striking blue eyes and thick snarling lips which poured out a stream of obscenities accompanied by drool and spittle. Harry hated this face more than the leader, and like a slow computer hard drive, his subconscious began to record and catalogue this face. He would also recognise this face if he saw it again, although he didn't yet know this.

There was a woman. Later he realised that there were two women. He began to identify the kicks from the women. The kicks were aimed powerfully but they were inept and failed to carry the force of the others. In his dream Harry began to anticipate these attacks, to welcome them almost. Then, to his sadness, the women withdrew. He heard complaints about the blood – his blood.

One woman began to stand out from the crowd. She was always close to the leader and she snarled incoherently as she kicked. Sometimes her kick missed completely and she fell, swearing, onto the grass. Her face also became memorable. She was like a female version of the leader. Fit, slim, long athletic legs, long black hair and sun-tanned with red lips.

Each night when the dreams came, Harry, when he woke, found himself in a mild state of shock. His chest would be heaving and his heart pounding, almost, he felt, as though the beating had only just occurred. But then as he came fully awake he began to realise that he had retained a picture embedded in his mind of the dream faces of his tormentors. He knew them, or so he believed. He also knew that no-one else knew of his discovery. This fact, or perhaps it was just an assumption, Harry thought, gave him power. He remained confused; but curiously, he felt more content than he had since first waking in the clinic.

Then one evening about ten days later, while seated in his armchair watching his television, he saw the leader of his tormentors. Unusually, the television had been left on to show the evening news. The picture showed the Houses of Parliament with an earnest young man standing on a lawn with a microphone in his hand. He turned to the camera and said, 'and now I can ask the Minister of State.' The camera flicked away from the interviewer to show another young man, smiling slightly, immaculately dressed in a double-breasted blue pinstripe suit.

Harry sat bolt upright, dropping the paper he had been holding. It was HIM. It was the man who had led the attack on him, for no reason other than that Harry happened to be there. He stared at the screen, listening but hearing nothing of what was being said. The one thing he did hear – and remember – was the man's name.

He was the Right Honourable Giles de Courtney Wellton, Minister of State for Rural Affairs.

Chapter 12

The Victim Support Group assembled in Bob Majury's office at nine o'clock the following morning. They sat in a variety of straight-backed chairs spread around the big table, an assortment of mugs set before them, filling the room with the sharp aroma of coffee.

'You wanted a timeline,' said Jim.

'Right.' Majury nodded. 'I've got a timeline of the events from Gerry, so give me yours and let's see what comes out of it.'

Jim shifted in his chair. He was uncomfortably aware that he didn't have much more to offer than Gerry had already uncovered. 'Okay,' he began. 'Day 1 – that's Friday 9th July. I put that in as an afterthought but it might be relevant because it's the day that university terms end, at least most of the big ones, that is. Day 8 comes next – that's Saturday the 17th of July and it's when the local story really starts. Ten or possibly twelve men and women, all white, all apparently well-spoken and aged in their early twenties, assemble at the Gardenia, a fashionable Bournemouth restaurant. They sit down to a pre-booked dinner at about seven-thirty in a private room and eventually drive away some time after midnight in six or seven different cars. They had ordered champagne and, by all accounts, they paid for a lot of very expensive wine.' He paused, then finished with, 'They also wrecked the joint,' before waiting for questions or comments. There were none.

'Day 9, Sunday the 18th of July, is the third day of the Weymouth Sea Festival. A group of about ten young men and women, some allegedly drunk, disrupt the Seafood Festival, damaging stalls and insulting bystanders. There is some sporadic brawling near the Queen's Arms and police are called. Beat officers arrive quite quickly but the aggressors have dispersed and there is no consistent or sensible evidence except that words like 'posh', 'flashy' and 'la-di-dah' have been used in descriptions.' He paused again, looking expectantly around the group.

No-one spoke. Bob started doodling on a dog-eared blotting pad. Jim scanned his notes, breathed in, exhaled and continued, 'Day 9 again, or possibly early in the morning of day 10…'

'That would be Monday morning.' Mary glanced sheepishly across the table towards Jim, her cheeks reddening as she realised that she had blurted the obvious.

Jim cleared his throat and continued. 'At some time during the night we know that an Aston Martin, travelling north from Easton town centre, left the road and crashed into the dry stone wall on the left – west side of the road. There was a report from a traffic officer and a file was raised but all we have now is the empty file cover. There is no record of anyone being admitted to any of the local hospitals with injuries consistent with an RTA and no record of recovery vehicles being called out or local garages being involved.'

'It would be Anderson's at the top of the hill.' Bob was doodling on a blotter as he spoke his thought aloud.

Jim continued. 'I've questioned the Aston Martin makers. They seem proud of the fact that they can trace the history and ownership of all their cars – but they can't find this one!'

'Maybe it wasn't an Aston. Maybe that's a blind. Maybe it was another make altogether.' Mary looked pleased.

'Good lass,' said Bob. 'We'll make a detective out of you yet.'

Jim made a note in the margin of the pages he was reading from. 'I'll go back to that,' he said, then continued, 'that same day, or rather, night, an elderly man was found unconscious behind the old town hall, off St Mary's Street. An ambulance was called and a paramedic attended as well. He was taken by the ambulance straight to the Dorset County Hospital in Dorchester. His injuries consisted of...'

'Spare us that.' Bob's voice cut sharply through the room. He paused, sighed, then continued, with a milder tone. 'We know he was beaten and kicked near to death but we also know that he has no knowledge of what happened to him that evening. However, he seems to be making a steady recovery and will probably be well enough to leave the clinic in a matter of weeks. He can't help us yet so we need to concentrate on whatever information we've got – sparse though it is.' He eased himself back in his chair, steepled his hands and looked pointedly towards Jim.

Jim started again. 'There isn't much else,' he said. 'About a week after our victim was found...'

'Give him his name,' growled Bob.

Gerry got in quickly before Jim could continue. He was trying to swallow his irritation because a lot of Jim's report had actually been recovered by the junior man of the team. 'About a week after Harry Chaplin was found, there was a small unattributed report in the Bournemouth Echo alleging that a private room had been wrecked and other parts of a large restaurant had been damaged to the extent that the restaurant had to be closed, without notice, for two or three days.'

'Damage that hasn't been acknowledged or even admitted by the owner, the manager or by any member of staff of the restaurant.' Bob Majury was doodling again as he spoke.

Jim looked around the table, then said, 'There is one last thing. We know that normal police procedures were followed after Harry was found and after the car crash was reported.

Reports were made, files were opened and investigations started. Then, suddenly, everything stops and every piece of relevant paper disappears. We wouldn't even have known that if Mary hadn't discovered some of the empty file covers in the archive waiting for disposal.' He slapped his sheaf of notes, none too gently, onto the table, signifying the end of his report.

'Right,' said Bob. 'Nothing – nothing and nobody simply disappears into thin air. We're all like slugs. We leave a trail and we can't help doing it. Start with what we know. We know the date when the attack on Harry Chaplin happened. It had to be the evening of July 17th. So we need to find out who was who in the station at that time, who was on traffic, who found Harry, and most important, who, in this nick, has got some beefy outside connections.'

'What about the gang who wrecked the restaurant?' Gerry Treloar had reverted to silence after his previous input. He continued, speaking thoughtfully and slowly, 'They look as though they were all one and the same. They must have been involved in the Weymouth fracas.'

'No assumptions, just hard facts.' Bob looked pensive as he continued, 'I don't want to jump any fences before we have to, but I'm bound to say that my copper's nose tells me there must be a connection, albeit with only circumstantial evidence. Let me sum up. We seem to have a gang of up to a dozen young toffs out on the razzle, getting pissed, or high, or whatever, and causing mayhem in a posh restaurant followed by a wrecking spree among the innocent harbourside traders of Weymouth, then they disappear just before the cavalry arrives.'

'Look, Guv'nor.' Jim leaned forward, staring earnestly across the table at his boss. 'This mob. We're calling them toffs. The Bournemouth restaurant is an upmarket place – not for the common man if you take my meaning. It was wrecked –

we know that, and we know that the damage was sorted, and quick. We know that the mob who caused the bust-up at the Weymouth Seafood Festival were described as lah-di-dah and posh. We also know that the Aston Martin is a bloody expensive car. What does that tell us?'

'It tells us to tread warily, be watchful and keep shtum,' said Bob. 'And that is because the one factor that is screaming at me out of this case is that we are dealing with power, wealth and influence – and a very great deal of each. Also, remember we're looking into this as Victim Support, which is not necessarily thief catching.'

'Do you mean we should back off?' Jim looked worried.

'Shit, no. Not on my bloody watch.' Bob pushed his chair back and began to pace the room. As he walked he raised his arms, stretched and began to run his hands through his thinning hair. After three or four turns back and forth across the room he reached his side of the table, turned, and leaned forward, placing both hands flat on the table top. 'This is what we do,' he said. The others waited.

'As I see it, we need to pursue two lines of enquiry. The primary one is: who attacked and attempted to kill Harry Chaplin – and what was their motive? The second line of enquiry is much more delicate. Harry Chaplin could have been beaten up by anybody, and if he didn't die, routine investigations would follow. But the second line of enquiry starts with a car crash with, so far as we know, only one vehicle involved. These road traffic accidents happen all the time but what makes this one different is that firstly, the car involved was very expensive indeed, and secondly – and this is the important bit – somebody was so excited by the crash that they hauled in some very high-powered help to hush up the whole thing. Now why would you do that? Not for a car crash,

I'm sure. So it suggests that there might be something else, more embarrassing, connected to the crash.' Bob stopped his pacing and returned to his chair.

'We concentrate on the second line of enquiry. We go back four or five years and find out who operated from this nick at that time, from the 'brass' downward. We need to know where they lived, what they drove, who they were married to, where they took their holidays and what they did off duty.'

'That's about sixty or seventy people!' Jim sounded shocked. 'And how do we go about gathering that sort of stuff without somebody wanting to know why?'

Gerry chipped in again. 'Yes, but the probability is that whoever was involved in a big cover-up would probably have moved on.'

'I haven't finished,' said Bob. 'These bloody Aston Martin chumps reckon they can trace every car from the cradle to the grave, so we push them hard. Make them do exactly bloody that. Then you, Mary, get back down to the archives and see what else you can find. Tell the mastermind down there that I've lost some important files on a series of robberies a few years ago and we are being embarrassed by insurers – or anything else plausible.'

'Right, Boss,' said Mary, looking pleased.

Bob continued, 'We must find the patrol car drivers who dealt with the Aston crash. Then I'm going to go over to Bournemouth and do a little bit of specialist leaning on the overpaid twerp that runs that restaurant. Any questions?'

'That's a bit hard, ain't it? Calling a bloke you've never met a twerp?' Jim smiled as he spoke, but his boss was no longer listening. He had his telephone in one hand and was flicking through the pages of his notebook with the other.

Jim left the room then, but Gerry waited patiently until his boss ended the call and replaced the receiver.

'Boss,' said Gerry, 'there's a way we can chase down the real owner of the Aston Martin. We can get a list of the cars built and sold in Britain in, say, the last ten or twelve years. Then we can do a trawl through the motor insurance companies and build a list of all the insured cars and see if we can identify any cars that suddenly disappeared from the insurance world.'

'That's a helluva big call, Gerry.'

'It's a lot of phoning, but I think it can be done.'

The DCI sat in thought for a minute, then leaned forward and said, 'It might be easier just to get onto the DVLA and get a list of Aston Martins where payment of the road tax stopped. They should have all the information you will need.'

Gerry looked sheepish for a moment, then he brightened and said, 'Either way, Guv, I'll get Mary to help and we'll give it a go.'

Chapter 13

Harry had changed. He was a different man. Gone was the unsmiling 'zombie-like' countenance. He was taking an interest in everything around him and he was eating better.

George Grainger was delighted. He tried to hide his pleasure at the sudden and sustained improvement in Harry, but the mood of the patient seemed to infect George and his staff. Nobody suspected any ulterior motive when Harry started to devour the Daily Telegraph each day, and when he asked if he could see The Times and the Daily Mail, it was just thought to be his way of mentally climbing back into the world.

In fact, Harry was concentrating his attention on the social columns and political reports. He was hitting paydirt and was amassing a considerable store of knowledge of the lifestyle, friends, duties, hobbies and social world of Mr Giles de Courtney Wellton, newly appointed Minister of State for Rural Affairs in the Second Coalition Government.

The improvement in Harry's mental outlook also seemed to be having a marked beneficial impact on his physical state. He was now able to move around almost unaided and had advanced through the range of exercises prepared for him.

'The Doc' – as Harry now thought of George Grainger – decided that, with the weather improving, it was safe to allow Harry out into the grounds, always accompanied, of course. Harry was able to walk about, staying on the paved paths that wandered through the lawns and shrubs. He was usually followed by a taciturn man dressed in a white uniform and pushing a wheelchair. Sometimes the unspeaking attendant was replaced by a pretty young girl who beamed and chattered about everything they saw as they passed through the grounds.

With the male attendant, Harry was left in untrammelled silence to gather and arrange his thoughts; and on these occasions he found he could review and mentally catalogue each day's snippets of news. When he was with the girl he was able to interrupt her chattering with comments of his own. In this way he could inject questions, which were always kept carefully vague but enabled him to add to his store of knowledge centred on The Right Honourable Giles de Courtney Wellton.

He was unable to commit any of this information to paper so at night after his tours through the grounds, he often lay awake, reviewing what he had learnt from the papers and his other unwitting sources so that he was able to build a better picture of the man who was now always uppermost in his thoughts.

Within a few weeks, Harry was walking through the grounds, at last without being accompanied by an attendant pushing an empty wheelchair. Shortly after this he was sometimes allowed to wander around outside without a companion – another mark of progress, although on these occasions he retained an uncomfortable feeling that he was being watched. He tried to dismiss the thought, putting it down to paranoia. But it wasn't really paranoia, because he was indeed being watched. George Grainger was immensely proud of the progress his patient had made and he was assessing whether the time had come for Harry to leave the clinic and try to resume life in his old home on Portland.

George was anxious to proceed but worried that Harry might meet obstacles in coping with normal life which would test him both physically and mentally. In fact, by now Harry's mental capacity and mental strength were both far greater than his doctor realised. George really had no need to worry.

He might have worried if he had known what Harry had already begun to plan.

Chapter 14

The first break came at the Aston Martin car plant. Gerry had spent nearly a week going through records trying to identify every car they had built, who had bought each one and where it had been registered. It seemed that in a good year the factory turned out about six hundred cars but this could drop as low as two hundred and fifty. Over the last four years the output had been steady at just over five hundred. Of these, about three hundred and fifty had gone to overseas buyers, leaving a core of about six or seven hundred cars for him to trace. A lot of those cars had changed hands, some several times. A helpful man from the accounts office unexpectedly provided Jim with a list of cars which were currently for sale with various dealers around the country. This further reduced Gerry's task but he still had to research about four hundred and sixty cars. None of these seemed to have been written off in accidents. Aston Martins seemed to be the survivors of the car world. However, Gerry did have a list of eleven cars which had been de-registered, mostly – according to the Driver and Vehicle Licensing Authority – because they had been exported.

While Gerry was chasing his theory, Jim was walking through the yards and parking bays at the back of the Aston Martin factory smoking an illicit cigarette and considering what to do next. He had arrived at the factory about an hour previously but despite telephoning ahead to warn of his visit he had been left cooling his heels in a smart and glitzy reception area until his patience snapped. Jim forcefully repeated his demand to see the manager, which then produced an immediate result. A deeply polished mahogany door labelled "Manager" opened and the occupant emerged.

Jim took the outstretched hand of the suave and smiling individual who introduced himself as Wilfred Warren, explaining simultaneously that he was in fact the Deputy Manager. As he spoke, his other hand produced a slightly over-sized, ornate, gold-edged business card.

'Wilf,' he said, 'call me wilf'. How can I help?'

In response, Jim held out his warrant card and explained that he was investigating a serious crime and he wanted to look at the remains of cars written off in accidents. As he spoke he assessed the man in front of him. Warren, he thought looked very glossy and rather expensively important. He was probably in his mid-forties but used the sharply tailored lightweight fawn suit, pink shirt, regimental tie and tinted gold rimmed spectacles to appear younger. Both men were still standing and Warren was having to look up to the detective despite his gleaming built- up shoes.

Jim explained in more detail what he was looking for, and Warren, flashing expertly whitened teeth, with his wide smile still in place, responded by waving at a wall-mounted plan of the factory site.

'You're welcome to go anywhere. Would you like anyone to show you round?' Warren looked so eager to please that Jim thought he might be wagging a tail.

'No thank you,' said Jim. 'I would rather just wander around on my own.'

Warren nodded assent, still with his smile in place, as he accompanied Jim to the office doorway.

****

Apart from a parking area and a space earmarked for delivery lorries, the tarmacked paving behind the factory seemed to be a dumping ground for empty crates, pallets and various bits of discarded machinery. Jim strolled along behind the building, stopping here and there to look inside empty crates or to poke about among small stacks of misshapen metal. Rising boredom encouraged him to walk across to the boundary hedge to see what lay outside; he climbed precariously onto a couple of concrete posts lying near the base of the hedge, parted the top of it and leaned forward to look through. What he saw caused him to lean further into the hedge until he was on the verge of collapsing into the greenery. Just below him and a few feet to his right was a skip, which appeared to be filled with builders' rubble, broken wood and pieces of metal. Peering beyond the skip he could see that the hedge divided the smart factory premises from a small patch of distinctly unloved land. It might once have been a paddock, perhaps home to a child's pony. Now it consisted of patches of bare land dotted with flint stones, clumps of coarse grass and thick flourishing areas of tall weeds, mostly nettles. Then his gaze settled once more on the skip.

It was a large metal skip of the type used by builders to remove rubble. It was quite long, covered with a mixture of faded orange paint, rust, curling strands of ivy and some blackberry brambles. Jim stood on tiptoe, attempted to part the top of the hedge further with his hands and leaned forward to peer into the skip.

It was indeed – or rather, had been – a builders' skip and it seemed to be about two thirds full of rubble and bits of broken furnishings. Jim had placed his cigarette between his lips while he tried to see into the skip. He squinted as the smoke curled up into his eyes but then the cigarette fell to the ground at his feet, as what he saw caused him to stare open-mouthed.

He was looking at pieces of metal and fibreglass which were mixed with the builders' rubble. They were damaged car body panels and some of them were painted green. Somewhere, he couldn't remember exactly where, but possibly from the document that named the driver as Sam Steen, he had been told that the crashed Aston Martin on Portland had been painted green.

Jim stepped back from his temporary perch, ground out the still smouldering cigarette stub with his toe, turned and walked briskly in the direction of the Deputy Works Manager's office. Moments later he was in the office of the suave but generally unforthcoming deputy manager demanding access to the land on the other side of the hedge. Did Warren look furtive? Jim wondered, as he stared hard at the man.

'That land is nothing to do with us,' smiled Warren.

'Well, whose is it?'

'Um, I'm not sure.'

'Well, who has been dumping parts from your cars in a skip on the other side of the hedge?'

'Oh.' Warren appeared to capitulate. He rose from his seat and stepped across to a glass-fronted key cabinet. 'We might find a key to the gate in here,' he muttered; then, more forcefully, he said, 'It's not our land though. The builders seem to have been using it during the extension.'

Jim wondered what extension the man was talking about but put the thought quickly aside. 'I want to see what is in that skip and I'd be very grateful if you would lend me a man to help me look.'

The deputy manager picked up his phone, pressed one button and said into it, 'Reg, can you send a couple of your lads to the office? I've got a little job for them.'

Jim held out his hand, looking pointedly at the large old-fashioned key held by Warren. The deputy manager handed it over and they stood looking at each other. Warren shifted his feet and seemed nervous.

Two men in loose-fitting brown overalls arrived at the office door. 'You gotta job for us, Boss?' the older one asked.

'Yes, this man is a policeman and I want you to go around to Martin's Field and help him look into the skip.'

With an inward feeling of satisfaction Jim noted that despite earlier claiming ignorance, Warren knew of the skip, probably knew what was in it, and knew the name of the field.

The key was handed over and Jim followed the two men out of the office, across the top end of the factory floor, passing three already gleaming cars undergoing detailed polishing and cleaning, and then out through a side door marked Emergency Exit into the yard, which was doubling as a car park, on the other side of the main building. Nobody spoke as the three men continued out into the lane and turned right, walking alongside a high hedge before passing a traditional farm gate which was secured shut with bailer twine and barbed wire. A few yards further on they came to a smaller gate set in a gap in the roadside hedge, locked with a heavy-looking padlock. The key worked easily and the group wound their way through and around the nettles to reach the skip.

Jim explained that his damaged leg meant that he wasn't much good at climbing and asked the two men to begin to empty the skip. They climbed in and began enthusiastically dragging objects out, dumping them haphazardly around the skip. Piles of old breeze blocks, pieces of masonry and timber began to grow until Jim called out that he wanted to concentrate on car parts, particularly body panels. The heaps began to change. Wheels, tyres, chunks of gearbox and engine began to appear as well as battered body panels.

Jim gazed down at the heap of wreckage. It wasn't a car, just bits of several cars; but as the men delved further, body panels and sections of suspension emerged, which sparked his interest. Doors were piled beside body panels, window frames, damaged seats, bumper sections and other parts which were unrecognisable. He stood and looked at the sad-looking heaps of junk and as he did so an idea began to form in his mind. He started to drag bits of metal and plastic away from the rest, and forty minutes later he had separated the original collection of car parts into five or six separate groups. Each group looked to Jim's untutored eye as though it contained parts from a single vehicle.

Jim sat himself down on a section of breeze-block wall and called to the men still working in the skip. 'Go and get yourselves a brew, lads, and then ask the deputy manager to come here, will you? I'll wait here.'

It was at that point that he found it. It was a battered piece of metal that had once formed part of the left front wing of one of the famous cars. What had attracted his attention was that the original curve of the body panel had been ground flat and scored with deep scars running from front to back. It had once been painted a colour well-known on car racing circuits: British Racing Green.

He took out another cigarette, remembered again that he was supposed to be giving up or at least cutting down and then put it back in the pack. He was looking at the dark cloud formations developing to the west and wondering whether he was about to be soaked when he heard the small gate on the far side of the field clang shut.

Mr Warren was working his way across the overgrown field towards the skip. 'I am a busy man, you know,' he called, not bothering to hide a frown directed towards Jim.

'And I'm a policeman investigating a serious crime.'

The deputy manager responded, using a more conciliatory tone and matching it with a change in his facial expression. 'But you haven't told me what crime it is that you are investigating,' he said.

'No, I haven't.'

Warren waited, listening for something more while he stood looking at the piles of motoring junk and the spread of rubble around the skip.

'Each of these piles seems to me to contain the remains of one individual car,' ventured Jim as he waved an arm in the direction of the half dozen piles of metal and plastic.

'Maybe; I'd have to look in detail to be sure.'

'How would you know? What would you look for?' Jim stood up.

'Well, the Aston is a pretty expensive car and so most of the parts are marked with a serial or reference number.'

'So you could check those numbers and confirm whether each heap comes from the same vehicle?'

'Yes.' This came hesitantly and quietly.

'So, if you can find these corresponding serial numbers, presumably you can go back into your records and identify the original car?'

'Yes.' Again the reply was quiet and uncertain.

'So if you can identify the original car, I imagine you can tell me when and where it was sold and to whom?'

'Yes.'

Jim resisted the urge to punch the air in triumph. 'Start with this lot,' he said, indicating the pile with the once green-painted damaged wing panel on it.

'I'll need to take it back inside the factory to do this identification,' said Warren.

'That's okay, but I need to make a phone call first.' A drop of rain fell as Jim pulled out his mobile and punched in the 'quick-call' buttons for Bob Majury. It took a few moments for the phone to be answered.

He wasted no time. 'Guv'nor,' he said, 'I'm at the car plant and I'm on to something. Can you get here, and can you get a loan of a couple of constables for an hour or so? I'll need somebody to keep an eye on things.'

There was a prolonged pause before Bob replied. 'Okay,' he said. 'I'm on my way and I'll sort out some support once I'm moving.' The line went dead. Wilfred Warren who had overheard the call, began to look concerned.

Chapter 15

Harry was now back in his cottage. The move from the clinic had taken place without giving him much warning. His recovery had been proceeding well and he was much more mobile. He had been invited into George Grainger's office 'for a chat', and when he walked into the office, still using his two walking sticks but feeling increasingly less reliant on them, he was surprised to find that the man from Social Services was also present. Harry hadn't encountered him for several weeks and during that time his thoughts had been concentrated elsewhere. He thought the man was called William but he couldn't remember the surname. This was resolved when the doctor stood to help Harry, unnecessarily, to a chair.

'You remember William Russell,' said George.

'Yes, of course,' Harry replied, beginning to wonder what might lie behind this little gathering.

Russell beamed at Harry. 'Tea?' he asked.

Harry noticed the tray of teacups and biscuits for the first time. He nodded.

Russell, who was nearest to the tray, poured a cup of tea for Harry, moved it across the desk and hovered a milk jug above the cup.

'Thanks,' said Harry. He eased himself in the chair and looked expectantly across towards George Grainger.

'Well, how are you?' began George, rather inconsequentially, Harry thought.

'Fine, thank you,' Harry replied automatically.

They carried on discussing a series of banalities until the teacups were empty and half an hour had passed. By this time,

Harry had reached the conclusion that the two experts were assessing him, although he was not quite sure to what end.

Eventually it was Russell who moved the discussion to Harry's future. He talked about how impressive Harry's physical improvement had been in recent weeks, at the same time feeding in little remarks which were not quite questions but which would elicit responsive comments from Harry.

Then Grainger came out with the sixty-four thousand dollar question. 'How would you feel about going home, Harry?' he asked.

To his own surprise, at the moment the question was posed, Harry didn't really know how to answer. There was a long pause before he said, somewhat neutrally, 'I'd like that.'

George Grainger had been expecting a more enthusiastic answer, but he continued in what he hoped was an encouraging tone. 'We wouldn't just dump you, Harry. We would introduce you back to your old home quite gently, perhaps just a day at a time, at first.'

'And of course we'll provide you with help in your cottage until you are settled and feel able to cope,' Russell interrupted, leaning forward towards Harry.

'All right,' Harry heard himself say. 'I need to get back to normal as quickly as I can, and going home is the right way to achieve that. But what is my cottage like now?'

'Shining like a new pin!' said Russell, beaming again at Harry.

****

That had been three weeks ago, thought Harry to himself, as he looked around the sitting room. His sitting room, he pondered.

It was certainly true that a great deal of effort had gone into making his old cottage clean, warm and comfortable. A rather smart and well-spoken home-help lady came in every day at first. She still came each day except Sundays but now she spent only a couple of hours keeping the place clean, ensuring that everything worked as it should and that Harry had a ready supply of food available. Once each week, a smart black car, adapted to carry a wheelchair, would arrive and he would be invited to climb into the wheelchair to be taken for more exercises, more tests and a probing discussion with George Grainger. Although he always arrived at the clinic in a wheelchair, he always walked to the car, using his sticks, for the return ride.

This routine left Harry a lot of time to think – and to plot, plan and expand his knowledge of his former tormentor.

At home in his cottage, Harry spent most of his time reading newspapers, watching television and listening to the radio. In this way he was slowly able to build a comprehensive mental dossier on the Right Honourable Giles de Courtney Wellton. He had already decided that Wellton was a shit – a prize shit, in fact. But more usefully, Harry had been recording in a small notebook every fact and snippet that he could find regarding Mr Wellton, who he believed would provide the key he needed to help him discover who had attempted to kill him, and why.

Harry knew what Wellton did for a living, broadly where and how he travelled, the general location of his home and, probably, the identity of his current steady girlfriend.

Sandra Somerville was the darling of the tennis circuit. She had climbed steadily up the tennis rankings and was now considered to be a strong contender for the Wimbledon Championships. No less than three national newspaper gossip columns – one Sunday and two weekdays – had linked Ms

Somerville with Giles de Courtney Wellton; and so Harry started a new file on Ms Somerville.

About this time, as Harry was settling back into what he thought of as 'an ordinary life', several things happened, each of which served to brighten his outlook.

A fat, official-looking tan-coloured envelope arrived containing numerous forms and standardised letters making various 'what-if' recommendations. However, it was a single typed sheet of headed paper which really concentrated Harry's attention. It appeared to be from something which called itself the Public Protection Office and it informed Harry that arrears of a State Pension owed to him, together with interest now accrued, was about to be paid into his bank account. The sum mentioned was a staggering £88,463. When he read the amount, Harry was shocked into silence. The letter ended by wishing him well and inviting him to fill in three forms, one of which was something from Her Majesty's Revenue and Customs, and the others seemed to be complicated declarations of having received the money.

The second letter among the small pile of mail was the only other item which would not fit under the heading 'Junk' and when he opened it he extracted two sheets of paper. The first was a statement confirming receipt of £88,463. The second was a letter on a single sheet of paper under the grand heading of Drummonds Bank, informing Harry that two accounts had been opened in his name. One was a current account into which £5,000 had been placed and the other, an investment account, contained the remainder of Harry's new fortune. The letter went on to recommend that Harry should contact the writer, one Andrew Symonds-Barr, as soon as possible so that his new wealth could be made more productive. It wasn't put that way. The language was rather more flowery, but it meant the same.

He put down both letters and wandered off in the direction of his kitchen. He needed a strong cup of tea.

Harry took a biscuit from a tin on the kitchen worktop to accompany his tea and carried both into his small sitting room. He placed the tea on a wooden side table and eased himself carefully into the heavy old brown leather-covered armchair which dominated the room. He sipped his tea, put it back on the table and picked up the brand new TV remote control.

He pointed the remote at the TV, switched back and forth until he found channel three for ITV, and settled down to wait, allowing the waterfall of inane advertising to wash over him while he waited for the six o'clock news. He sipped his tea again, reached for the biscuit and realised that he had already eaten it.

Harry had slipped into a near doze while he waited for the news. As a result he missed the opening remarks of the newsreader. Because of this it was the picture filling the screen that shocked him into sudden wakefulness, spilling his tea in the process.

Ignoring the spilt tea, he leaned forward, peering earnestly at the haughty face now filling the screen. It was the man who had disrupted his dreams. His enemy. The man he hated.

Harry listened to the reporter describing his enemy. Apparently Mr de Courtney Wellton had made some sort of announcement. Harry was not interested in this, but he was interested in the attractive woman who stood just to one side of Wellton. She was strikingly and elegantly beautiful, tall and slim, with the build and poise of an athlete. But it was not her attractiveness that had drawn Harry to stare at her. She was also familiar to him. She was one of the women who had screamed and shrieked as she had tried ineffectually to kick the life out of him. Harry stopped, rubbed his eyes and then looked back at the screen. The announcer had moved on to a new report. Harry waved the remote at the television, switching it off. He stared at the blank screen, wondering at the meaning of what he had just seen. He considered whether he might be allowing his imagination to mislead him; but no, he thought. And speaking aloud, he said, 'I know these people. I wonder if they will remember me?'

Chapter 16

They needed a long-wheel-base transit van to collect all the car parts from the skip and transfer them back to Weymouth Police Station. There they were unloaded onto a tarpaulin spread across the concrete on the far side of the car park.

While Jim started to poke about among the motoring wreckage, Bob disappeared towards the back door of the station. He had been summoned by the trill of his mobile phone. The call had been brief and terse.

'What kind of a half-arsed operation are you running, Bob?' The superintendent sounded angry and panicky.

Bob started to answer, but was saved from having to construct a plausible response by the next outburst. 'You may not have enough to do,' spluttered his boss, 'but I'm not going to have you wasting the time of people like forensics who are busy.' He paused for breath, snapped a pencil in half and added, 'And bloody expensive.'

'So that's it,' thought Bob. 'He's wound up again over the monthly budgets and he's worked himself up into a panic.' The superintendent was at least twenty years younger than Bob and had been parachuted into his present role three months previously by the process of Special Accelerated Advancement.

'Can I come and see you, sir? I've got something brewing that might become very hot indeed.'

At first there was no answer. Then as Bob was beginning to think he had been cut off, the familiar petulant voice returned. 'Oh, all right. But I am bloody busy. I'll give you two minutes. Two minutes. Got that?'

'I'm on my way, sir.' Bob headed quickly for the stairs.

Less than forty seconds later, and slightly out of breath, Bob tapped on the elegant glass-panelled door.

'Come!' The superintendent was seated in a comfortable, tall, black leather swivel chair, and dressed, as usual, in his immaculate dark blue uniform with a polished silver crown marking his rank on each shoulder. He was a small, rather intense man who worked hard at being seen to be 'in charge', but the DCI could not avoid the unbidden thought that his boss should really have been an accountant.

Bob could not help noticing that the desk and single in-tray were remarkably devoid of files and paper for a man who was so busy. He put the thought to one side and carefully closed the door behind him. He was not invited to sit but he did anyway.

Before the 'Super' had a chance to speak, Bob leaned forward conspiratorially and spoke. 'This thing I am working on is becoming red-hot. I think we may be looking at corruption at a very high level. I need to tread carefully and I need to keep it discreet. Can I have your support, sir?'

'Tell me more.' The superintendent spun his impressive chair to face Bob and leaned forward. 'But please be concise.'

Bob took a deep breath and started. 'I'm looking into an attempted murder which took place over four years ago and from which the victim, an elderly man, is only just recovering. Circumstantial evidence suggests the involvement of a group of young and well-connected men and women. But the really fascinating point is that the three lines of enquiry which were started, including an enquiry into a single vehicle road traffic accident caused by a seriously drunk driver, were all abandoned almost immediately. All of the records and reports have been destroyed and no one seems to know anything. The car involved in the accident was an Aston Martin, worth about a hundred and fifty grand.'

The superintendent sat in silence while he considered what he had just heard; then he said, 'But these things happen. The victim has recovered and it was all a long time ago.'

'With respect, sir' – Bob spoke quietly and slowly – 'you're missing the point. When these investigations into several serious crimes were stopped, they were stopped in this nick.' The last six words were spaced out carefully, emphasised with an accompanying slap on the corner of the desk. He added, 'It means we have or have had one or more very corrupt and very senior coppers in this nick, who were able to make these investigations go away.'

The superintendent stared at Bob, his expression alternating between shock and worry. The DCI waited, determined not to be the first to break the sudden silence between the two men. The superintendent eased himself from his chair, stood and paced to the far side of his desk. He turned and looked squarely at Bob. 'I see what you mean,' he said. He stood, without speaking, for several minutes; then he said, 'You have my agreement to continue with this. But I don't want you charging in and saying anything that you can't properly substantiate. There may well be alternative explanations to what you've found; but if records really have been destroyed and investigations abandoned, then I want to get to the bottom of it. However, what little you've told me seems a bit sensitive, not to mention laden with assumptions; so we need to keep it absolutely under wraps. Only you, your team and I will be involved, but I want you to keep me in the picture. Go to it.'

Bob took this as an end to the interview. 'Thank you, sir,' he said, rather formally, as he got up and walked to the door. As he shut the door gently behind him he wore a satisfied smile on his face.

Behind the door, his boss was also smiling. He said to himself, barely audibly, 'That should keep him busy and quiet.'

Most of the Weymouth Station was populated by individuals who Bob thought of as 'old-fashioned coppers' and some of them didn't try very hard to hide their contempt for the young man with a first class degree in Classics who was now their boss.

Bob did not belong to this group and he took the phlegmatic view that the county hierarchy must have been sufficiently impressed with the young man to award him such a key appointment, and anyway, he believed that a friendly and helpful approach, applying diplomacy, lubricated with a touch of respectful deference was more likely to produce the results he needed.

In this assessment, Bob was right. Buttering-up the 'old man' – the 'young old man,' he thought – was always going to be the best way. It had certainly helped in the present situation, and as he strolled back across the yard to join Jim, he was whistling an out-of-tune pop song to himself.

Jim looked worried. 'How'd it go, Guv'nor?' he asked as Bob stopped at the edge of the tarpaulin. 'Are we bollocked and blown out?'

'I don't think so,' said Bob thoughtfully. Jim looked brighter and waited for more.

'I convinced the Super that we stumbled across this as a case that has remained unsolved for years. I told him that this has just fallen on top of the Victim Support Group and convinced him that we could follow it up without costing him anything except a tiny bit of forensic and that we would not disturb any of the regular "coppering".'

'I imagine he liked that.'

'Particularly when I hinted that there may be more than a smell of corruption surrounding it. I mentioned some of the missing files, but kept it vague.'

Jim raised an eyebrow.

'He's my new best friend,' said Bob.

They spent the next couple of hours trying to identify individual car parts from the heap of expensive motoring junk in the yard; but by the late afternoon, light was fading and they had made little progress. However, Jim had managed to separate into a sizeable heap a great many twisted and shattered body parts, all of which had the same shade of dark green paint.

He looked up. 'Guv'nor, we need to go to Portland.'

'No, we need to go home,' Bob responded wearily.

'Humour me, Guv.'

'Why?'

'Because I think I've seen this green paint before, on bits of a dry stone wall, just to the north of Easton.' Jim had assumed the look of a pleading dog, and Bob gave in.

'Okay,' he said. 'I'll give you an hour, max. You drive.'

They walked around the building to where Jim's car was parked. Bob took his hat off and eased his bulk into the front passenger seat. Jim took off his jacket, folded it and threw it into the back seat before settling himself into the car.

It took forty minutes to thread through the ridiculously congested Weymouth traffic, then crawl at walking pace along Wyke Road before coming up behind a heavily laden builders' lorry with Crook and Son painted across the tailboard. The steep uphill climb through the narrow streets of Fortuneswell and then the even steeper road to the top of the rock that formed the Isle of Portland did little to improve the Detective Chief Inspector's mood, so that by the time they pulled up opposite the former drill hall, Bob had become quiet and taciturn. His 'bubbling volcano mood,' Jim called it.

Sensing that he wasn't going to be allowed much time, Jim left the parked car and without waiting for his boss, he began to walk along by the dry stone wall playing his flashlight on the stones as he passed. He was conscious of Bob following about twenty yards behind, still remaining silent.

After he had covered perhaps a hundred yards, walking towards the outskirts of the village of Easton Jim thought he had found what he was looking for. A section of the stone wall was new. The stones had not weathered in the same manner as the rest of the wall. The difference was not great and he thought that the section of new wall only stood out from the rest because of the peculiar effect of the orange light from the tall sodium street lights.

Clutching his torch in one hand, Jim climbed up and over the waist-high wall. On the far side he found himself standing in a soggy stretch of rough couch-grass, decorated at intervals with sorry-looking patches of nettles. He shone his torch in front of him and picked out an elderly, sagging fence made of wooden posts standing haphazardly at various angles with three strings of barbed wire. Some of the wire strands were broken and there was just enough light to make out the white shapes of sheep, mostly standing motionless, in the field beyond.

He moved the beam of his torch slowly along the strip of rough grassland between the wall and the wire fence. He heard his boss arrive on the other side of the wall but he continued to concentrate on the beam of light illuminating the rough grass a few yards ahead. As he did so, he walked slowly forward. With surprising suddenness he pitched forward into the muddy wet grass, dropping his flashlight in the process. He had tripped, hitting his foot on a big stone block hidden by the grass. In an attempt to regain his balance he had stepped on a second smaller stone which rocked under his foot, tipping him off balance, to fall forward onto his hands and knees.

'Jim, where are you?'

The call was answered quietly as Jim struggled to his feet. The torch beam was shining through the grass a foot or so to his right. He bent down to retrieve it, before realizing that it had rolled into an isolated clump of healthy nettles. 'Bugger,' said Jim. Then as he rubbed the nettle stings in his smarting hand: 'Bugger, bugger, bugger.' He shone the torch beam down in front of him, confirming that his jacket and trousers were each liberally covered in mud – and some other substance that was generating an obnoxious smell.

Bob Majury stood impassively on the other side of the wall. 'Was that worth it, lad?' he asked.

Jim was still rubbing his stinging hand, the torch tucked under his arm. 'I think so, yes,' he said hesitantly. 'I think this is where that fancy car left the road and ran into the wall. The wall has been patched with new stone…'

'Not so new now, lad,' interrupted Bob.

'No, but it's different to the original wall. This patch of wall stands out from the rest. And as I've just discovered, the idle sods who did the patching simply chucked the damaged stone into where I'm standing. We need to collect all of that stone and see if there's anything that matches up with the bits of car we've got in the yard.'

To Jim's surprise, Bob did not demur. 'You may be right there,' he said, 'but we can't do much tonight. Let's get you home and cleaned up a bit and organise some bright young coppers to do the shifting first thing tomorrow.'

Jim started to climb back over the wall. 'For Christ's sake, what's that bloody awful stink?' Bob reeled back away from the dilapidated figure emerging above the wall and clapped a hand over his mouth and nose.

'I think it's vintage dog shit.' Jim looked down at his filthy trousers, made a move to brush away the filth and then thought better of it. He stood still, uncertain of what to do.

Bob bent down and pulled a small stick from the grass at the base of the wall. 'Here,' he said, 'scrape off what you can and we'll drive back with the windows open.' They walked towards the parked car. 'I should be a bit reticent when you get home,' he continued. 'I dunno what your missus is going to say.' Jim stayed silent and looked unhappy.

As they pulled away from the kerb, Jim brought the car around across the wide, and temporarily empty, road in a single curving one hundred and eighty degree turn. 'That's interesting,' said Bob, 'it's a wide, straight road, with brilliant lights, so how do you manage to run a flash motor off the road, across the pavement and through that wall?'

'Pissed,' said Jim.

They drove back to the station in silence with all the windows open while the DCI held a handkerchief over his mouth and nose.

Chapter 17

Harry spent most of the next week sitting in his armchair, reading the Daily Telegraph in the morning and the Dorset Echo in the evening, both of which were now being delivered daily. He didn't know who had arranged the deliveries, but since the people at the clinic knew that he preferred to read the Telegraph he assumed it must have been someone from there.

As the early spring weather began to improve he ventured out into his back garden. He had expected it to be wild and overgrown but the lawns had been mowed and the shrubs and flowerbeds looked reasonably well presented. Using a single walking stick, he made his way down the long sloping garden until he could see the cliff edge and the sea beyond. With a steady wind blowing from the west, his garden was sheltered by the cottage and those on either side. He looked to his right and could see some people making their way carefully down the steep winding path to Church Ope Cove. There were children as well as adults and they all looked carefree and happy. He envied them, but then he thought that perhaps he should just be grateful for his survival. He tried to be grateful but he really couldn't. Harry turned around and made his way back up the garden.

As he entered the kitchen, the phone was ringing in the hall. He reached out to pick up the receiver but the ringing stopped. He retraced his steps back to the kitchen and busied himself making a single mug of instant coffee. He was carrying the coffee back towards his living room when he noticed a small red light flashing on the telephone base unit. Placing the hot mug carefully on the cloth-covered table he picked up the receiver again. There was a recorded message. Harry listened to the usual telephonic preamble which was then replaced by a pleasant female voice informing him that a follow-up visit had been arranged for him at the clinic next morning. A car would collect him, it said in conclusion.

Harry was pretty pleased with himself as the white station wagon drew up outside the cottage next morning. The driver was a younger man than usual whom he had not met before. He was pleasant enough but didn't take up any of the conversational openings offered from the comfortable rear seat.

When the car cruised to a stop outside the main entrance to the clinic, Sam, one of the attendants, opened the car door, smiling a welcome before manoeuvring a wheelchair alongside the car.

'No thanks,' Harry said as he set his walking-stick firmly into the gravel, leaning on it and easing himself carefully out of the car. He walked slowly and steadily towards the door of the clinic followed by the procession of Sam and the empty wheelchair. The front door opened silently. One of the familiar nursing sisters stood just inside, looking uncertainly at Harry and at the empty wheelchair.

As she turned to lead Harry towards a consulting room, the voice of George Grainger boomed out from the consulting room doorway. 'Well, well,' he said, 'showing off our independence now, are we?' Harry started to speak but then he just took the outstretched hand. 'Something like that,' he eventually managed, as he sat down facing Grainger across the wide desk.

'Well, tell me how you are.' Grainger leaned far back and the black leather chair creaked.

'I'm coming on well,' said Harry. 'As you can see, I'm walking better, and I'm feeling better…'

'Good, good.' Grainger cut off the sentence as he climbed out of his chair. He came around the desk, put a hand under Harry's elbow and eased him to his feet. Neither of them spoke until they had entered the adjacent Examination Room, when Harry was invited to undress and begin the process of being weighed, measured and checked in every faculty.

It was mid-afternoon before the process was complete. The doctor had retired to examine and analyse the results of the day's tests, leaving Harry in one of the sitting rooms with tea and biscuits, a copy of the Daily Telegraph and a television set. He was munching a digestive biscuit and starting to reach for his teacup on the side table when his attention was riveted onto the picture which had just formed on the screen. It was HIM.

This time he was dressed casually in a cream linen jacket and a dark blue satin open-necked shirt. He was striding away from a reporter, looking terse, and with the same incredibly attractive woman on his left arm. Inconsequentially, Harry dwelt for a moment on the thought that the stunning raven-haired tennis star in the figure-hugging white silk dress was slightly taller than her evil consort.

Harry stared at the screen.

The reporter, almost running to keep up, was firing breathless questions at the backs of the retreating couple.

'Can you confirm that you do not own the house, sir?' shouted the reporter. He received no answer other than the slamming of a car door and the noise of wheels spinning on the gravel.

The reporter gave up the short chase, turned to face the camera and took a deep breath. 'As you can see,' he said, drawing breath more easily now, 'the Minister has declined to comment; but I have it on good authority that IPSA is starting an investigation into the expenses claims submitted by Mr de

Courtney Wellton. I have also been made aware, from several sources, that the house which is the subject of the claims has been permanently occupied by Sandra Somerville, Britain's number one lady tennis player. Apparently Mr de Courtney Wellton has stated that Miss Somerville has only been using the house as his guest while she is in training for Wimbledon. He has also denied that the two are romantically involved.'

'That's a bloody lie for a start!' Harry muttered to himself quietly. He sat wondering what use he could make of this unexpected televisual tit-bit. There were questions. Where had the encounter been filmed? Where was the house that had been mentioned? Who was the woman? He stopped at that point. He knew who the woman was, or rather, he knew that she had been connected with the man Wellton because he was convinced she had been one of the figures that had appeared in his dreams.

He was interrupted by the door opening. He turned to see the large frame of George Grainger filling the doorway. Grainger looked concerned. 'Are you all right, Harry?' he asked. 'You look as white as a sheet.' He advanced towards the chair, offering a hand to help Harry to his feet, but Harry beat him to it. Leaning heavily on his stick he used the springs of the chair cushion to bounce himself into the vertical. Grainger adjusted his approach to clutch Harry under the elbow and turn him towards the door.

'Time for the results, old chap.' Grainger spoke with a bluff heartiness that made Harry wonder whether it was genuine. They passed into the doctor's consulting room and Grainger continued to fuss until Harry was settled in the upright chair, then he walked around the desk, flopped into the capacious swivel chair and leaned back in a manner Harry had come to recognise and respect before smiling and speaking again.

'Well, old chap, you're in pretty good shape I think. Blood pressure, heart rate and lung function are all pretty well as they should be. Muscle tone seems okay so far, but you need to keep up the exercise regime.' Harry reckoned that there was an air of censure in this remark and, he thought, it was probably deserved. He had become a bit of a couch-potato as he had been easing himself back into the comfort of his cottage.

Harry realised that Grainger was still talking – still addressing him. 'What was that?' he asked, trying to remove the recent television images from the forefront of his mind and concentrate on what was being said. He need not have bothered because Grainger was already off into small-talk.

'So what do you intend to do with your time now, Harry?' he asked.

'I don't know,' Harry replied weakly. 'I'd like to get out more and I walk to the shops in Easton but to go anywhere else I have to wait for a bus.'

'Ah, that reminds me,' said Grainger. He opened a drawer in the desk, slid out a folder, extracted an official-looking form and pushed it across the desk. 'Sign that,' he said.

Harry drew the form towards him and started to study it. As he did so there was a polite knock at the door and a woman he had not seen before came in carrying a tray.

'Tea!' said Grainger. 'Thank you, Mrs Waring,' then, to Harry, 'I'll pour; help yourself to a bun.' As well as the teapot and mugs, the tray contained two plates, one with slices of rich fruit cake, the other filled with fancy biscuits. Harry selected a biscuit.

Harry lifted the form with his free hand. 'What is it?' he said as he crunched biscuit.

'Application for the return of your driving licence,' said Grainger. 'All filled in. You just have to sign it.'

'I don't really remember driving, but I suppose I did,' said Harry uncertainly. 'I wonder if I'm safe to drive,' he continued.

'As I said, all taken care of,' said Grainger. 'We know you did drive because you had a licence. The form has to be endorsed by two authorities. I have to certify that there is no reason of physical health, infirmity or mental reservation that will limit your ability to drive a car – and I have done that.' He beamed triumphantly across the polished desk surface before continuing, 'And a qualified driving instructor – instructor mind, not examiner – must certify that you have completed a driving refresher course and that you are familiar with the Highway Code and the usual driving technique applied on British roads.'

'Oh,' said Harry. He couldn't think of anything else so he concentrated on his tea.

'First driving lesson – no, session, that should be – starts tomorrow,' said Grainger, adding, 'assuming you're not doing anything else, that is.' He lifted his tea mug and his lower face disappeared behind it for a moment.

'Thanks,' said Harry. 'No, I'm not doing anything else.'

They sat in silence for a few more moments, crunching biscuits and drinking. Then, seeking to continue the conversation as well as keeping it light, Grainger said, 'I saw you watching the television. What do you think of that lying hypocritical bastard Wellton?'

The form of the remark suggested what opinion Grainger held on Mr Wellton but Harry decided to play dumb. Another part of his mind was already congratulating himself on even being able to make such a decision. 'Who?' he said.

'You know. It's been in all the papers. Britain's youngest government minister, one of Britain's richest MPs as well. On the take. Fiddles his expenses. Big time as well, apparently. As I said, a lying, thieving, hypocritical bastard.'

'Yeah, I see; yeah, I watched it but I wasn't sure what it was all about.' Harry put down his near empty mug and reached for another biscuit.

'What it's all about...' Grainger spoke through a mouthful of cake: 'is that the Right Honourable Giles de Courtney Wellton, lately Minister of State for Rural Affairs, has decided to resurrect the parliamentary expenses scandal by using taxpayers' money to buy himself a rather nice, comfortable house, conveniently situated between Westminster and Wimbledon, for the occupation of his tennis-playing girlfriend who he is screwing to the point of distraction. Well, maybe that last bit is conjecture, but there seems to be a deal of circumstantial evidence.'

Harry could see that Grainger was exercised by the subject but he could not quite understand why he was being told. Then he wondered whether it was just topical and Grainger needed something to talk about. Either way, Harry was seriously interested, but he tried to remain outwardly indifferent.

'So where is this house?' said Harry, still trying to hide his rising excitement and remain outwardly calm and only mildly interested.

'Apparently it's a rather large and luxurious pad in a gated complex just off Wimbledon Common and handy for the tennis club.'

That was the moment when Harry decided to go to Wimbledon.

Chapter 18

Bob sat uncomfortably in the young 'Super's' office waiting for his boss to finish his phone call. He had decided that he couldn't continue the expanding investigation without getting some proper top cover, and his previous interview with his boss had been somewhat vague on this point, or so he thought. The young man in the smart new uniform tunic brought his telephone conversation to an end and spun the expensive 'executive' chair around to face Bob and the immaculate but empty desk.

'What can I do for you, Robert? Have you made any progress?' Superintendent Julian Holmes smiled at Bob, who wondered, not for the first time, if he was doing the right thing. He took a deep breath and plunged in.

'Do you mind if I close the door, sir?' he said. 'This could be sensitive.'

The young man facing him allowed a worried frown to appear briefly. 'Not personal, is it?'

'No, sir, nothing like that. But it could become quite sensitive and it could ruffle a lot of feathers – highly placed feathers.'

Julian Holmes decided to take charge of the interview – as he perceived it to be. 'All right, man,' he said. 'I presume that this is the same delicate but aged enquiry we discussed a few days ago?' Without waiting for an answer the 'Super' started to speak again, but he was interrupted.

Bob had already prepared himself. Taking a deep breath, and spotting the approach of another homily from his superior officer, he started speaking quickly, cutting off the other man as he was opening his mouth to speak. 'As you know, I think I have accidentally uncovered an attempt to hide a serious crime and I think that attempt may have involved officers from this station.' He paused but the Super, who was now leaning forward with his chin resting on locked knuckles, his elbows resting on the desk, was waiting for the rest.

'Go on.' The Superintendent continued to peer at Bob above his locked hands.

'What it amounts to is this. About four years ago an attempt was made to beat an elderly man to death somewhere either on Portland or on the outskirts of Weymouth. The victim was shifted and left in a narrow cul-de-sac off St Mary's Street in the town centre. The body was discovered by a beat officer and the man was found to be still alive, but only just. He was rushed to A&E at Dorchester but he remained in a coma. He seemed to have suffered a lot of head injuries and was thought to have a very slight chance of survival. But then he was transferred to the Chesil Clinic at Chickerell. The Chesil Clinic is a small medical research establishment which specialises in the study of severe trauma to the brain.

'Harry – that's the name of the victim – was very severely injured. He had damage to his internal organs as well as multiple broken bones – several ribs, both lower legs and one forearm among other injuries. The clinic didn't expect him to survive but the injuries to the brain exactly matched their area of research. Harry showed no sign of coming out of the coma so they took the opportunity to treat the other injuries, using some pretty smart state-of-the-art techniques, and at the same time continued to treat and monitor the victim's brain. Until recently, nobody expected the victim ever to come out of the coma.'

'Call him Harry, like you did at first.' The elbows had come off the table and Superintendent Holmes was making notes on a lined pad of paper.

Bob nodded acquiescence. 'The thing is, against expectations, Harry did come out of the coma.'

'When?' An expensive silver Cross biro was poised over the pad.

'About four months ago.'

'I see. Please continue.' He was all abrupt efficiency now.

'Well, Harry has made a remarkable recovery, particularly given his age.'

'Which is?'

'He was sixty-six when the attack took place and he is now just over seventy.'

'Uh huh.' The biro flashed as it flitted across the page.

'Harry came out of the coma with complete amnesia but he has made a steady improvement since then. He knows who he is, where he lived – and lives now – and has some incomplete memory of his life before the attack.'

'How did you become involved?'

'I was called in as the boss of the Victim Support Group,' said Bob, shifting in his chair. 'Harry had no idea why he might have been attacked, nor where the attack took place or who did it, although interestingly, he now seems to be aware that the attack involved several people.' He paused again while marshalling his thoughts; then he continued.

'I thought I would have a look at the Crime Report for the incident but there's nothing there.'

'Explain.' The biro paused, hovering above the pad.

'Well, sir, what it amounts to is that every piece of information relating to this case has been destroyed or removed. There are no records. There are, however, one or two snippets of information that have been uncovered by my team, but to be honest…'

'Please do,' the station commander interrupted humourlessly. The biro was still.

'Well,' said Bob, measuring his words carefully and speaking slowly, 'about three or four days before the victim was discovered, a group of wealthy young men and women held a party in the Gardenia, a very fancy restaurant…'

'I know it,' interrupted the superintendent.

Bob ignored the interruption and continued without pause '…which offers smart private banqueting rooms. There was one small report in the Echo stating that the restaurant had been comprehensively wrecked.'

'How old were they?'

'Early twenties, we believe.'

Bob waited to see if there was a further question coming. There wasn't so he continued. 'The next day, a group of well-heeled young men and women were involved in a fracas in the middle of the Weymouth Seafood Festival. From witnesses quoted in the paper, they seemed intent on trouble, but they didn't get off scot-free. At least a couple of them apparently got a fair hammering. It was in the early hours of the next morning that the victim was found. At about the same time that night a very expensive motor car came off the road near Easton and crashed into a dry stone wall. There was no other traffic about.'

'If there are no records, where did you get all this?' asked the Super, looking unconvinced.

'Local paper mostly, but we have picked up some bits of evidence, cross references in other files, that sort of thing.' Bob let his boss absorb this, then said 'Oh, and we think we've found the car, or at least what is left of it. It was an Aston

Martin, and funnily enough no one seems to remember who owned it or who was driving it, or who collected the wreck, or who was driving the patrol car that found it, nor where the wreck was taken and where it was dumped. The forensic boys are even now collecting bits of Portland stone that once comprised part of the wall alongside the A354 just to the north of Easton. If we can match stone residue to any of the wreckage we have recovered, or if the stone has traces of oil or paint, we will have moved a long way ahead.'

'Tell me what you think happened,' said Holmes. 'Use your "copper's nose".'

Bob wondered if his boss was being sarcastic. He glanced across the desk and decided this was not the case. 'I think,' he said, speaking carefully and slowly, 'that a bunch of rich young men and women, possibly university graduates, came to Dorset to get some kicks. I think they started by wrecking a restaurant, then wandered down to Weymouth to get some more kicks and possibly get boozed and or high before going off to find a victim on which they could do a snuff job.'

'Snuff job? What's that?' The superintendent looked genuinely puzzled.

'It's where a certain type of criminal gets their kicks by killing a victim, selected at random and for no reason.'

'And you think that's what happened here?'

'There's more,' said Bob. 'After all of this took place, someone demonstrated that they had the wealth and power to subvert a lot of coppers, as well as probably a restaurant owner and one or two others so that they would forget the whole thing and destroy any existing evidence – but they were not as efficient as they thought.'

'Who could do that?' The Super was beginning to look worried.

'I don't know,' said Bob. 'Money had to be applied but power and influence as well. Government, security services, senior coppers, who knows?'

There was a discreet knock on the door. They waited in silence as the door opened. The head of Jim Creasy appeared in the gap with a triumphant look on his face. 'We've got a match, Guv'nor,' he said.

'Come in.' The superintendent gestured to a chair on the far side of the office. 'Have a seat, Sergeant,' he said, 'and tell me that again, adding, if you would, what it is that you have matched and what might be the import of that discovery, please.'

Jim looked as though he was bursting to tell more, as indeed he was. 'Sir, early this morning we sent a team over to Portland to locate and recover the stones that the Guv'nor and me discovered yesterday evening. They were told to bring back as many as they could find. They brought about twenty sizeable chunks and at first sight at least eight of them have scraping marks along them which could be consistent with being hit by a car at a shallow angle. Further to that there are some which have small patches of discoloration which could be paint. Forensics are looking at them now and they say they have a preliminary match with the paint from some of the car parts we recovered. They're also looking at the damaged car parts to see if they can find traces of stone.'

He paused for breath and was about to speak again when the 'Super' said, 'Well done! What do we do now?'

Bob opened his mouth to speak but Jim beat him to it. 'There's more!' he said, somewhat louder than he had intended. The other two men both turned to look at him. 'Two things,' he said. 'First, if we do have a match between the car parts and the paint found on the stones from the wall, we will be able to identify the actual car, because all of the parts are serial numbered from which you can find the car. So, if we identify the car we can also identify the owner. Oh, and the serial number we have on the parts we've recovered identifies a car manufactured in 2006 which, according to DC Treloar's research, ties in with one of the cars that stopped being taxed and insured in 2010. Second, I think we might have a witness.'

'A witness to what?' said Bob, with a trace of disbelief in his tone.

Jim plunged on. 'A man came into the station at Dorchester this morning. He said he wanted to talk about something that had been bothering him for some time. It was some kind of fight late at night down on the common land near the lighthouse car park at Portland Bill.'

There was silence in the room for at least thirty seconds as the other two absorbed what they had just heard. Bob spoke first. 'Who is this man and where is he?'

Jim could hardly contain his air of triumph. 'He's down in the interview room and his name is Peter Wright.'

The superintendent stood up and began to move out from behind his desk. 'Right. Let's go down and see what he has to say.'

Bob stood as well, not quite obstructing his superior's route to the door. 'With respect, sir,' he began, 'I think it would be better if I just go down with Jim. If a very senior officer turns up to question him it might spook him. We might need to take him gently and of course we don't know anything about him yet.'

The senior officer hesitated, then returned to his chair. 'Yes, you're right. But this is a tricky situation all round so I want your report as soon as the preliminary interview is finished.'

'He knows all the right words,' said Jim as they walked towards the stairway. Bob ignored the remark and they walked on in silence.

The interview room was only marginally different from a large cell. The unadorned walls were painted a uniform light grey. Dull afternoon light from the cloud-covered sky filtered weakly in through two fixed windows of wired glass which were set high up near the ceiling on one wall. The only furniture in the room was a plastic topped table bolted through thin carpet tiles to the concrete floor, and six chairs. Two were set against one wall and the other four surrounded the table – two on each side. The table contained a digital recording machine simultaneously running two audio tapes from a multi-directional microphone mounted in the centre of the table. An unsmiling uniformed constable stood beside the wood veneer-covered steel door One of the upright chairs at the table was occupied by a tall, sparely-built man with a leathery nut-brown face and thick silver-grey hair swept back far enough to hide his collar. He was wearing a thick blue woollen seaman's jersey, brown corduroy trousers and aged, scuffed brown sailing shoes.

Bob fixed a big smile on his face as he walked into the room, at the same time gesturing to the young constable to wait outside. He thrust out his right hand and in a friendly, jolly voice said, 'It's Peter, isn't it?' Jim had followed him into the room and was headed for one of the chairs opposite the seated man.

Bob waved his hand expansively, taking in Jim as well as their witness. 'Has anyone given you a cup of tea, Peter?' Peter Wright shook his head.

'Jim, can you fix tea for three, please? How do you take it, Peter?'

'Milk and one sugar, please.'

Jim stood and went to the door, relaying the order to the constable outside. As he returned to take his place at the table Bob was still transfixing Peter Wright with his beaming smile.

Wright looked distinctly nervous. His lined and deeply suntanned face wore a worried frown and his hands were twisting together while his deep blue eyes flicked left and right, then down to the table. Jim had at first decided that the man was shifty with something to hide but then, taking in the salt-stained and worn seaman's clothing, the story he had to tell, and the fact that he was here voluntarily, he concluded that the nervous reaction came simply from the unfamiliar situation of a police station and the pressure of the interview.

Jim growled an attempt to clear his throat and leant forward across the table. 'We're investigating a crime that we think took place five years ago where an elderly man was seriously assaulted and I understand you may be able to tell us something about it.'

Bob interrupted, still smiling. 'Thing is, Peter, why have you turned up now to talk to us? Most people couldn't even remember what happened five years ago.'

'I've been round the world.' The statement was simple but the shock effect on the two officers was considerable. Bob recovered first.

'Can you put that in a bit more detail, Peter?' he asked. The smile was slipping.

'It was a Sunday,' said Peter, shifting in his chair, partly to find a more comfortable position but also to try to avoid the unblinking gimlet stare from across the table. 'It was my last watch before I went on my cruise. I should have reported it to somebody but I was scared to get involved and I didn't want to delay my sailing. I thought if I got involved I would have to spend weeks waiting around answering questions. My mate Eddie was already in the boat and he's an impatient bugger – sorry, but that he is, or was. Like as not, he would have sailed without me.'

Bob interrupted gently, hoping not to disrupt the flow of information. 'Where is Eddie?' he asked. 'How can we get hold of him?'

'You can't. Eddie's dead. He's buried in Fiji.'

'Oh, I see.' The smile had disappeared and been replaced by a worried frown.

'Heart attack,' said Peter.

'You were telling us about your last watch,' said Bob, trying to bring his witness back to the crux of the story. 'Where were you keeping watch, Peter?'

'I am – was – a Senior Watchkeeper in the NCI.'

'What's that?' said Jim.

Bob answered before Peter could speak. 'National Coastwatch Institute,' he said. 'They keep a lookout at various difficult places around the coastline and try to stop people getting into trouble on the sea.'

Jim nodded.

Peter continued. 'I remember the date clearly. The 17th of July 2010. It's haunted me, that day, and what's happened, ever since. I made a stupid decision and I couldn't go back on it. It's haunted me!' He looked close to tears.

The door opened and the constable came in carrying a tray with three mugs and a plate of digestive biscuits.

'Take a break; have some tea.' Bob watched Peter sip the hot tea and waited for him to continue.

'Yes, it was the 17th July, and we sailed at six o'clock on the 19th. I tried to put what I'd seen out of my mind but I couldn't. It just got bigger, and the bigger it got, the more I was feared of tellin' anyone.'

'Come back to the day itself,' said Bob, as gently as he could.

Peter began again. 'It was my last watch before my circumnavigation. I was on the last watch – three till seven that is. Well, I gathered up my kit, locked up the lookout with my colleague Joe Sherwood, and then I drove down to the Marina. It was nearly nine when I realised I had left my small sailing bag with my passport and cameras in the lookout. My old car was going to be collected by Fancy's Garage next day so I hopped back into it and drove back to the lookout. It was a fairly bright night with a good half-moon so I didn't bother to put any lights on when I got inside. I unlocked the lookout and I had just picked up the bag when I saw something through the front window. I looked but I didn't want to…' He stopped speaking.

'What did you see?' said Jim, speaking very quietly.

The room was very still. 'There was a man, elderly I think, and I think he was walking a dog. They were both going slowly so the dog was probably quite old as well. Five or six cars roared up, nose to tail, in a convoy. The man with the dog had reached the flatter grass a hundred yards to the south of the lookout. The cars – all expensive jobs and at least two convertibles – roared out onto the grass and started driving around the man and his dog, like Indians around a wagon train. Then one of the cars drove right into him. He was hit a glancing blow and fell to one side of the car. The car continued and drove right over the dog. A load of men and women came leaping out of the cars, whooping and screaming, and they started hitting and kicking the body on the ground.'

'How could you see all this?' Jim interrupted.

Bob frowned, 'Go on, Peter,' he said.

Peter answered the question. 'Headlights,' he said. 'Clear as day.'

'I see,' said Jim, unnecessarily.

'I thought they were mad, or maybe mad drunk. They were waving bottles and shouting and screaming. I thought they'd killed the man and then they would come after me. They'd certainly killed his dog.'

'How do you know?' Bob bit his lip but couldn't help interrupting.

'It was a bloody mess,' said Peter. 'Anyway one of them dragged the dog past the lookout and tumbled it over the cliff. I was petrified and I stayed absolutely still in the lookout. Suddenly, though, they all piled back into their cars and roared off, bumping and bouncing over the grass, then off down the little narrow road, nose to tail, and they disappeared.' Peter stopped. He had turned pale under the tan and was trembling.

Bob didn't want to waste the moment. 'You said they were shouting. Could you hear what they were saying?'

'Not much,' said Peter, 'You can't hear much through those windows but the inner door was open and I could pick up one or two words.'

Bob cocked a quizzical eyebrow. Peter continued. 'Frug, I think, and what sounded like "snuff".'

'Are you sure? "Frug" – are you sure?' Jim looked sceptical. He scribbled a note on a pad in his hand.

'I told you. I couldn't hear much. I was shit scared. How can I say I'm sure? I'm just telling you what I believed I could hear.'

'But it was a very long time ago. Four years or more. How sure can you be of any memory over that time?' This time it was Bob who spoke.

'I told you, that horrible shameful night was burned into my brain. I lived with it, dreamed it and couldn't get it out of my head no matter what happened during those five years, in storms, in near disaster, even when my buddy died and I was left to run that boat single handed. I will never forget. That's why I'm here. It's my shame and I need to confess and hope I can learn to live normally again.'

'Okay, I understand,' said Bob, 'and I want you to know that I appreciate what you are doing. We'll take a break now, and then I want to ask you if you can recall any detail. Anything at all, faces, colour, gender, sizes of the people and anything about the cars; the makes or ages or colours for example.'

'Okay.' The reply was weak and quiet as though Peter Wright had drained himself of all emotion and all feeling.

'Just one more thing.' Jim stared fixedly at the witness. 'You said the details of the incident were burned into your memory. How sure are you that you would be able to recognise those people after all this time? Could you pick them out of an identity parade? Do you think you would be able to stand up in court, with no doubt, and identify those people with absolutely no doubt whatsoever? That's what a cross examining barrister would be testing you on.'

'I might not be able to recognise every one of them, but I would be absolutely clear on three of them, possibly four, maybe five if you include the second woman.'

Bob made a show of standing up. 'We need to move to a more comfortable room and you could do with a break, and some food, I think. Come with me, Peter.' They trailed out of the room, Bob leading.

Chapter 19

When Harry was deposited back outside his cottage, in the same comfortable car, driven by the same driver, his mind was still occupied by what he had seen on the clinic television and by George Grainger's remarks concerning Mr de Courtney Wellton. He was only brought back to the present by the feel of the driver's hand attempting to assist his progress towards his front door, clutching Harry's left forearm in a firm grip. Harry stopped walking, turned to his 'assistant', smiled and said, 'Thank you very much. I appreciate that you are trying to help me but it's really much better for me if I try to walk on my own.'

The driver let go of Harry's arm. 'I understand, sir,' he said. He took a step back and stood on the pavement, watching intently as Harry walked fairly steadily to his front door, hardly leaning on his stick at all. Harry fished in his pocket, transferred the stick to his other hand and fumbled with the door key for a few moments while the driver continued to watch. Eventually the door opened, shifting back a pile of papers and envelopes as it did so; Harry turned, gave a friendly wave and shut the door. The driver looked relieved as he strode back towards his car.

Harry stepped over the litter on the doormat, walked back through the short hall, placed his stick where he could reach it and busied himself in the kitchen. Five minutes later, he walked carefully into his sitting room carrying a biscuit barrel in one hand and a mug of strong brown tea in the other. His stick remained in the hall, temporarily ignored and forgotten.

He placed the biscuits on a polished coffee-table, fished about for a coaster and set the mug carefully on top of it. He stood silently for a few seconds, still thinking of the new information the day had brought, before turning back to the hall. He picked up his stick as he passed, reversed it and used the curled handle to scrape the letters away from the doormat. Leaning on the stick, he bent down and picked up the letters and papers one by one. As he straightened up, two envelopes slid from his grasp and fell back on to the carpet. 'Sod it!' said Harry. He put his bundle on the stairs and bent once more to collect the rest.

Harry glanced at the more prominent envelopes, strolled back into the sitting room where he settled himself back in his armchair, took a few sips of his powerful tea and selected a biscuit. He sorted through his communications and set them beside his tea mug in three separate piles: sealed letters, daily papers including two 'free' papers, and the rest – the biggest pile – which looked like junk mail.

Harry allowed himself to continue to think for a while about the information he had gleaned earlier that day and was excited by the prospect of getting a little closer to what, for the first time, he thought of as his quarry.

He finished the tea, resisted the temptation to turn on the television, bit into his third biscuit and started on the pile of junk mail. Most of the papers were flyers inviting him to patronise local businesses for groceries, pizzas, shoe repairs and so forth, all of which went straight into the waste-paper basket by the fireplace. Near the end of the pile, however, he found a plain sealed envelope with his name handwritten on the outside.

Inside the envelope was a handwritten note on a sheet of headed paper which, among other information, listed the various qualifications of the writer. The note was dated that day and explained that the writer had been invited to help

Harry to recover his driving skills. It suggested 'sessions' – not 'lessons', Harry noted – which should start the following morning. Harry was asked to telephone to confirm that he was able to comply.

Harry started on the second, much smaller, pile and forgot about the television. The first letter contained a bill for groceries which had been delivered from the Metro supermarket in Easton; the second was a telephone bill together with a small sheaf of paper giving instructions concerning the installation of internet broadband, which made Harry wonder who had made the arrangement on his behalf.

He opened the next letter which, together with several others, appeared to have been forwarded from the clinic. There were three sheets of paper. A short covering letter explained briefly that Harry had been awarded compensation from the National Injuries Compensation Board relating to his injuries. The next document was an official receipt form which Harry was invited to sign to declare his acceptance that the sum of money was full and final compensation for his injuries and associated losses. The third document had a cheque printed over the lower third of the page. It was for the eye-watering sum of £245,000. Harry sat and stared at it.

Harry sat motionless for three or four minutes. He peered again at the cheque, examining it to see if there was some catch or flaw to it. There was none. He turned to the last few envelopes, and started to rip them open, still mesmerised by the huge sum of money he had just been given. Five minutes later he was in shock. He had four more cheques spread out on the table beside him. The biggest was £100,000 from the Mariners' Mutual Insurance Company; a further £12,000 was from the Seaman's and Waterman's Benevolent Fund; £50,000 came from the Providential Accident and Life Assurance Society;

and the last was from the Department of Work and Welfare covering four years of sickness and unemployment benefit and amounting to £76,546 – including interest, it said.

He was shocked and numbed. Only a few weeks ago he had been not much more than a cabbage; now, with this sudden and unexpected windfall of cheques together with the previous money from the Public Protection Office, he had instantly become a rich man. He jotted the figures on a scrap of paper, added them up, checked his arithmetic twice and then sat staring at the total sum scrawled on the paper. He couldn't really take it in at first. He eased himself out of the chair and walked in a daze to the kitchen, where, without thinking what he was doing, he made himself another cup of tea. As he made his way back to his sitting room and flopped into his chair, he was wondering if what he had just seen was real – or was it all just a cruel joke? He picked up the letters one after the other and examined them again. Yes, he thought, they are real. He seemed to be suddenly worth the extraordinary sum of £572,009. He spoke aloud as he picked up the piece of paper. 'That's over half a million pounds,' he said.

His swirling thoughts were interrupted by the shrill clamour of the telephone. Mechanically, he reached across the papers and envelopes, picked up the receiver and spoke, weakly and hesitantly. 'Hello, yes?' he said.

At first, he had no idea what the caller was talking about. Then the man introduced himself once more and explained that he was seeking to arrange the first of several 'driving refresher sessions'. Harry agreed to be ready for collection the following morning at 10 a.m. – but he was not really concentrating. He was still thinking of the various sums of money that had just fallen into his lap.

The driving instructor, as Harry thought of him, rang off with a cheerful assertion that he was looking forward to meeting Harry in the morning. For the first time since emerging from his coma, Harry felt he needed a drink, an alcoholic drink. His second tea mug was empty and he searched through the cupboards in the kitchen but he couldn't find anything alcoholic so he settled for a chilled can of lemonade from the fridge. Harry sat down again in his sitting room, sipping his lemonade and staring at the blank television screen. Several times he said to himself, 'I'm rich; I'm seriously rich.'

Harry spent the rest of the evening skimming through the Daily Telegraph and then the Dorset Echo. After a while he got up and prowled round the kitchen. He found a ready-to-eat meal in the small freezer, glanced at the instructions, then stuck it in the microwave oven for the requisite four and a half minutes. He slid the meal out of the packet onto a warmed plate and ate the contents while sitting at the kitchen table.

At five to ten he rinsed his plate and put it back in the cupboard before walking through to the sitting-room, easing into his armchair and pointing the remote control at the television.

After a few seconds the screen began to light up. Harry stared at it blankly as a series of inane and meaningless adverts floated across the screen. Then the noisy musical introduction heralded the ten o'clock news. The newsreader, looking serious but engaging, leaned forward and gave a short preview of the items to follow.

The second item caused Harry to jerk forward in his seat. It was HIM again.

Chapter 20

Jim led Peter Wright down the long corridor to the canteen at the back of the Station while Bob slowly climbed the stairs to the superintendent's office on the second floor. He knocked on the partially opened door, waited a few moments, then stepped quietly forward and peered around the door.

The young man looked up from behind his desk. He closed the buff-coloured file he had been working on and gestured to a chair. 'What have you got for me, Bob?'

Bob noted the use of the familiar version of his Christian name. Bob, it was now; not Robert, nor even Chief Inspector. He was moving rapidly towards the status of 'close associate' to this awkward and unpredictable young man.

'I think we've got the beginning of a break-through, sir.'

The superintendent leaned forward, peering over steepled hands, elbows propped on the desk. 'Tell me more,' he said.

'Well, unless he's spinning us a complex yarn, and I don't think he is, I think we've got a witness to an attempted murder, an attempted gang murder, I think.'

'What about the crashed car? You were working on the crashed car,' said the Super, somewhat inconsequentially.

Bob refocused his thoughts while trying to maintain control of what he had been planning to tell his superior. 'DS Creasy is working on that, sir,' he said.

'Oh.'

Bob pressed on, intent on overcoming any further distracting interruptions. 'It's about the witness, sir. We have a man who has come forward. He says he witnessed a group of young men and women brutally attacking a man. He says that although it was dark and difficult to identify the cars or the people, he seems to think he could identify at least four, and possibly five of them. Actually, he said their faces were burned into his memory, not because of who they were, but because of what they were doing. I think he was traumatised by what he saw, and because of that he might make a good witness – but of course he'd be challenged over how accurate his memory would be after five years. He also confirmed that there were two women among the attackers, and that ties in with what we've learnt so far.'

'You mean he stood there and watched a gang trying to kill a man and he did nothing?' The Super sounded shocked and incredulous. 'Why didn't he try to intervene?'

'Oldest reason in the world I think, sir. He was frightened. Scared shitless would be more accurate.'

The superintendent looked uncomfortable at the coarse description. He began to flick offending specks of dust from his tunic. Then he said, 'It's been five years, Robert. That's a bloody long time to stay scared. And why pop up now? What caused your man to have a rush of conscience five years after the event?'

It's back to Robert, noted Bob to himself. Aloud, he said, 'He was scared. He hid, then ran away from the scene in a state of shock. He went to a sailing yacht in the Dean and Reddihoff Marina at Portland. He shared ownership of the yacht with another man and they were both due to set to sail on the early tide next day, to go around the world.'

'Where's the other man, the joint yacht owner?'

'Dead!'

'Convenient.'

'Maybe so, but we'll check his story thoroughly.'

'Where is your witness right now?'

A shiver of alarm ran through Bob's body from top to bottom. He hoped his boss was not about to think he could become an interrogating detective. 'Jim Creasy has taken him to the canteen to get some food into him. Relax him a bit. We need to give him a break,' he said.

'All right,' replied the superintendent hesitantly. Bob exhaled the breath he had been holding and opened his mouth to speak but he was interrupted again.

'What I can't accept is why a man would wait five years and then spill the beans?'

'I don't know.' Bob spoke slowly, rubbing the stubble on his chin as he did so. 'Could be all sorts of reasons, I suppose.' He paused. 'But he did tell us, quite a few times in fact, that when his friend died at sea and he was left alone he began to worry about what he'd done, or rather what he had not done. He might know more but it's been a long time and I don't think he's consciously hiding anything. He's our only real lead...'

'Except the car.'

'Yes, except the car. But the car can't talk and this man can. I want to continue to pump him but I need to take it very slowly.' Bob glanced at his watch and the Station Commander took the hint.

'You'd better get back to him then, while he's still warm.' A brief smile lifted the corner of the Super's mouth for a moment. He was pleased with himself for remembering and deploying a piece of current police jargon.

Bob stood up. 'Right then, Guv'nor.' He took the cue to revert to 'copper-talk' and shuffled out of the room towards the stairs.

Back in the interview room, Jim and Peter Wright were already seated, facing each other across the table. A different uniformed constable was standing just inside the door. No-one was speaking.

Bob fixed what he hoped was an engaging smile on his face, took a deep breath and strode briskly and purposefully into the room. He slipped easily into the vacant chair alongside his detective sergeant.

'Had a good lunch, I hope?' He addressed the remark towards Peter in the hope of breaking the icy silence. Peter was looking decidedly wary and nervous. Inwardly, Bob was anxious because, in the mood that he could see developing in front of him, witnesses – particularly nervous witnesses – were likely to shut down, taking a huge amount of time and effort to be coaxed back into providing information. Peter Wright was looking very nervous.

'Can we have some tea, Constable?' Bob called over his shoulder. Turning to smile across the table at his witness, he said, 'Let's run this through just once more, shall we, Peter? Take it from where you arrived at the lookout. Just describe the lookout for me, will you?'

Peter shifted in his seat and looked from one to the other. He was about to speak when the tea arrived. Bob hid his irritation, sipped his tea and waited. Presently he repeated the question.

Eventually, Peter placed his mug on the table. He cupped both hands around the warm white china. 'It's a Coastwatch Lookout Station,' he said. 'We are all volunteers and we keep a lookout for people getting into trouble in the sea or on the cliffs. I had the last watch that day. It was actually going to be my last watch before I sailed away…'

'To sunshine and adventure.' Bob smiled warmly, trying to put his witness at ease.

'Yes.' Peter sat quietly, staring into the steam rising from his mug. At length he looked up and began again, speaking so quietly that the two policemen had to lean forward to catch what he was saying.

'I went back to the lookout when I realised I had forgotten my sailing bag. I had just arrived at the boat when I saw that I'd forgotten my bag with my binoculars, laptop, phone and so on. I couldn't leave without that so…'

'What time was that?' Jim interrupted, his voice sharper than he intended.

'I left the boat about half nine and I got back to the lookout at around ten, opened it up and collected the bag. And that's when I saw them come roaring in with their cars…'

Jim interrupted him again. 'Stop there, Peter,' he said, trying hard, but not quite succeeding, to keep his voice steady and even. 'I want you to think carefully. Try to go back to that night; can you do that?' Bob glowered at the sergeant, annoyed by the unnecessary interruption.

'It's ingrained on my brain. I've thought about it every day, for five years. I can never forget what I saw…' Peter Wright's voice tailed away, and then he continued, almost inaudibly, '…and I ran away.'

As he continued speaking, he seemed very emotional and near to tears. Both of his hands had begun to shake so much that the tea was spilling out of his mug. Bob reached across and pressed the shaking hands. Peter looked up, eyes glistening through tears.

'I want to ask you some very specific questions.' Bob spoke almost as quietly as the other man. 'Just give me the best answer you can to exactly what I ask. Don't try to elaborate and don't worry about getting it wrong. You're not going to be cross-examined on what you tell me now. It's just that we need help to solve a very nasty crime and I think you can give us at least some of that help. Do you understand, Peter?'

Peter nodded. Bob waited a few moments and then continued in the same quiet voice. 'How many cars, Peter?'

'Six; no, seven.'

'Six? Or is that seven?'

'Six.'

'Now the first car – what colour was it?'

'It was in the dark.'

'Okay, was the car dark coloured or light?'

'Dark.'

'What type of car was it: sports, saloon, estate, big, small?' Bob stopped, realising he might have gone too far with this question, but Peter answered quite quickly.

'It was big. It was a big dark coupé. It could have been a sporty Bentley, something like that.' He stopped, his breath coming in audible gasps, hyperventilating; hands drawn away from Bob's restraining hand; the half full mug shoved aside, abandoned and forgotten.

Bob pressed on. 'Who stepped out of it, Peter, man or woman?'

'Both.'

'Can you describe either of them? The woman – what was she like?'

'I only saw her for a fleeting glance, when she stepped through the headlights of the next car. She was tall – and she was beautiful.'

'You mentioned the next car. Did you recognise it?'

'Yes, I did. At least, I think I did…'

'Go on.'

'It was a big sports car, an Aston Martin I think.'

'Was it dark or light?'

'It was lit up by the headlights from the other cars. I think it was green. Dark green.'

'The driver – man or woman?' Bob rattled out the next question, not giving time for the witness to think. He wanted an instinctive reply.

'Man, a big man; looked too big for the car.'

'Go back to the first car. You saw the man. He was the driver? What did he look like?'

It was like a fox mesmerising a chicken. The questions were being fired out and the answers were coming back rapidly, spontaneously, unthinkingly; and that was exactly what Bob wanted.

'He was slim, thin, a bit shorter than the girl.'

They continued in this vein for the next three hours, by which time Peter had been reduced to a sweating, shaking automaton. But Bob had the answers he was looking for and he was confident that the man in front of him was incapable, at that point, of lying. He was bound into the horror of that night, which had burned itself into his subconscious for five years. He was unburdening himself, almost as if he was in a confessional, facing the darting sword of questions from an insatiable priest.

As the afternoon sunshine was fading, Bob drew the proceedings to a close. He got up, walked around the table and placed a fatherly hand on the shoulder of the drained man hunched over the table.

'I want you to stay with us, Peter, but you need to get some rest so we're going to put you up in a small hotel. You happy with that?'

Peter nodded.

Jim was puzzled but tried not to show it. This approach was new to him.

Bob walked across the room, gesturing for Jim to follow him. When they had both reached the door he turned to his assistant and said quietly, 'We'll put him in the Glenside, but I want you to stay with him. No more questions for the moment. Just stay with him, make sure he doesn't leave and keep him well fed and comfortable – oh, and just in case he likes a drink, let him have one or two, but no more. Got that? Any questions?'

'I'll need to tell Sarah that I won't be home.'

Chapter 21

The driving sessions began well. Harry seemed to retain an instinctive familiarity with the basic handling of a car although he remained hesitant and nervous at first. Tony Harrison, the driving instructor, was an easy-going man in his early fifties. A former Royal Marine, he had been active and fit in his younger days but more recently, several years of riding around with a variety of aspiring drivers had taken the edge off his physique. He had now established a shape that he described as 'comfortable'. The car was a Volkswagen Golf fitted with dual pedal controls and it was responsive and straightforward to drive.

Tony had an engaging, easy manner and only a few minutes after he pressed the bell on the front door of the cottage they were both settled happily in the car, chatting like old friends. The lesson started with Tony driving up the wide street back to and through the centre of Easton before turning into a quiet residential street where he climbed out of the car and swapped seats with Harry. When they had both strapped in again, Tony spent the next twenty minutes explaining the car and reminding Harry of the basic principles of driving. The engine was then started up and they set off at not much more than walking pace, motoring back and forth through the empty streets, all the while chatting away about anything and everything, only occasionally returning to the subject of car driving. The experience was rewarding and enjoyable for Harry, who, as they entered the second hour, realised that without having given it much thought, they were bowling along the busier roads surrounding Weymouth.

After just under two hours behind the wheel, the car was stopped and parked by the kerb in front of the cottage. Harry suggested a cup of tea and they both ambled across to the cottage. Harry was by now carrying his walking stick without any attempt to use it for support.

When they were settled in the fireside armchairs, Tony peered over the rim of his mug and asked, 'How did you think that went, Harry?' The emphasis was on the word 'you'.

Harry took his time before answering. 'All right,' he said eventually.

'Good. I thought you did well,' said Tony. 'But the main thing is, how do you feel about it? Do you feel confident to go out on the road by yourself?'

'Not yet.' The answer was firm and came quickly. Tony didn't respond but waited for Harry to continue. Harry sipped his tea and said nothing. They both sat in silence for a long ten minutes before Tony spoke again.

'Two more sessions,' he said, 'and you'll be competent for local stuff, but if you want to go further afield we'll need maybe another couple of goes, then perhaps a stint of motorway driving. We could do it all in a week; say, ten days at the outside – if you've got the time, that is.'

'I haven't got much else to do.' As he spoke the words, Harry felt embarrassed. He was lying to this nice man who was only trying to help him. He had plenty to do. He had to plot his revenge. He wondered if his deceit showed in his face.

Tony finished his tea and placed his mug carefully on a side table. 'When do you want the next session?' he asked.

'How about tomorrow morning?'

'I can't do the morning but I can do the afternoon.'

'That's fine by me. What time?'

They agreed on another two hour session starting at two o'clock.

The next session went at least as well as the first one but this time Harry could feel his confidence returning in waves. His progress continued in much the same manner for the next two weeks. Although Tony judged his pupil to be fully competent to drive a car under all conditions, Harry had asked to continue the 'course' driving by night and in rain on motorways and trunk roads; and the whole thing had been finished off with an extended afternoon session on a skid pan in Southampton.

When they returned to Portland they sat once more by Harry's fireside and Tony produced the form which would reinstate his client's licence. As he was signing it, Harry leaned forward in his chair and spoke earnestly.

'There is one more thing you can do for me,' he said.

Tony looked up, raising an eyebrow. 'What's that?'

'I need a car. Can you help me find one?'

Tony smiled and raised a hand in a kind of half-salute. A gesture he had used before when dismissing something as insignificant. 'Of course,' he said.

They talked for another hour, discussing the pros and cons of various makes of car before agreeing to meet to go 'car hunting' two days hence, on Friday morning.

It was nearly eight o'clock before Tony saw himself out through the front door, leaving Harry staring into the flames of his gas-powered imitation coal fire. He sat quietly, plotting first what he needed to do to discover the identity of his attackers, and then how he planned to deal with them. By now, the appearance of the outwardly tired, elderly victim was hiding a dangerous man bent on vengeance.

It was after midnight when Harry climbed out of his chair, locked up and went to bed. By this time he had formulated a way ahead. He needed a reliable but nondescript car and he would also need a small van, but he would not buy the van locally. He wanted something like a medium-sized Citroen, big enough to accommodate a wheelchair in the back. He would also need to acquire a lock-up garage, paid for in cash with no questions asked. By the time he fell asleep he had jotted down a list of other essential requirements together with some idea of where he might be able to find these things, again with no questions asked.

Next morning, Harry telephoned the local branch of his bank and was delighted to learn that his account now held something in excess of half a million pounds. The young-sounding woman who provided this information asked Harry to hold on for a moment and almost immediately he found himself talking to a man who explained, quickly and enthusiastically, that his name was Mark Barrington and he was now Harry's personal bank manager. Harry wondered what had happened to Mr Symonds-Barr but nevertheless he listened attentively to what Mark Barrington had to say. Mr Barrington wanted to come and see Harry to discuss investments and banking arrangements; but Harry was in no mood to be tied down to a meeting in the next week, so he explained that he would like a credit card and a current account with fifty thousand pounds in it to be set up, but he did not feel well enough for a meeting within the next week or so. Mr Barrington seemed disappointed but said he would follow Harry's instructions and would telephone again to arrange a meeting in ten days.

As soon as Harry ended the discussion with Barrington he picked up the phone and called for a taxi. Fifteen minutes later a toot on a car horn from outside signalled the arrival of the cab. Harry locked his door and, leaning on his stick more than was necessary, he walked across the wide pavement before climbing awkwardly into the back of the Wey-Line taxi. He quickly explained to the driver what he wanted, and sat back to enjoy the ride.

The taxi cruised through thinning traffic across the causeway, up through Wyke Regis and around the inner harbour to the centre of Weymouth, before stopping in the parking area by the parade of shops just to the north of the railway station. They pulled up outside the electrical goods store, Currys, and thirty minutes later Harry strolled back out to the waiting taxi followed by a young man in a Currys uniform carrying two largish cardboard boxes and two plastic carrier bags. Harry was now the proud possessor of a laptop, a printer with copying and scanning features and a selection of necessary accoutrements such as paper, ink, additional software and the means to access the internet. The boxes and bags were loaded into the boot; Harry thanked his assistant – who ten minutes before had been his instructor in basic computer techniques – and the taxi drove him back to Portland.

On arrival back at the cottage the taxi driver carried Harry's purchases into the cottage and was rewarded with a tip which brought a smile to his face. Once the cab had gone Harry set to, opening the packages, reading the instructions – including the additional instructions jotted down by the assistant from Currys – and connecting up wires and plugs. It took an hour, but by then Harry was staring at the bright colourful screen of his new laptop computer while attempting to achieve connection with the internet. In fact internet connection took another five days, some telephone calls and form-filling, in addition to a visit from a pleasant young man wearing a thin beard, spectacles and an old jacket almost as threadbare as the beard, who came from an organisation calling itself The Tech Guys.

At last, after a few guiding nudges from his visitor, Harry was able to start a tentative communication with a whole new world which waited behind the screen.

The Tech Guy left with a cheery 'See ya!' just before one o'clock. It was nearly seven before Harry moved himself away from his new toy. He stood and stretched his arms high above his head and then made his way to the kitchen where he filled the electric kettle and switched it on. As the kettle began to hiss and burble, he made himself a cheese sandwich and then, ignoring the kettle, he fished a small bottle of beer from the shelf in the refrigerator door. He took both back into the sitting room and settled once more in front of the computer, where he stayed until past midnight.

It was Friday morning and Harry had barely finished breakfast when the front doorbell announced the arrival of Tony, ready to go car hunting. Harry realised with a shock that he had forgotten all about his arrangement to search for a suitable car, guided by the amassed experience of his new friend.

It was quickly agreed that Harry should do the driving. 'Build up the experience and familiarity with the road,' Tony had said. They spent the rest of the morning driving around the various car agencies, examining different makes and sizes of vehicle and discussing the pros and cons of each type before stopping at the Riverside Inn in Upwey village for a comfortable lunch. By the time they had finished a home-made steak, ale and Stilton pie, Harry realised he was recovering his appetite. It was at this point that they had finally settled on a vehicle.

'The Astra, then?' said Tony.

'That's the one I think suits me best.' Harry wondered whether he should try a pudding.

'Nice little motor.' Tony lapsed for a moment into the jargon of the trade.

'Yes,' said Harry after a pause. He had made up his mind. He would have a slice of lemon meringue pie.

Tony thought the lemon meringue pie would not help his failed attempts to control his weight so he sat and chattered about cars – specifically Vauxhalls – while sipping black coffee.

They finished their lunch, complimented their hostess, and set off for the big Vauxhall agency on the Granby industrial estate. After further examination of two high specification hatchback Astras and a hesitant test drive by Harry, a deal was agreed. The car seemed in excellent condition, was about one year old, had only 7,000 miles on the clock and offered an equipment fit that even included a satellite navigator. It also came with a two-year warranty.

'I like the colour,' said Tony; 'a nice dignified blue.'

They drove in convoy, relatively slowly, to the irritation of several following drivers, back to Harry's cottage and parked both cars outside while the two men went inside for more coffee and some fancy biscuits. After another hour of discussing the merits of Vauxhall Astras, Tony took his leave. He drove off, leaving a tentative arrangement to go out with Harry to help familiarise him with his new car.

Chapter 22

Bob Majury settled himself behind his table, leaned back and stretched his arms upward and behind his chair. He felt comfortable and content in the familiar surroundings of his office. He leaned forward again, bringing his elbows to rest on the table surface while he waited for Jim to arrive with the tea. The afternoon had collapsed once more into a gloomy evening. The first heavy raindrops were pattering noisily against the single-glazed window pane as Jim appeared on the other side of the table. He carefully placed two thick china mugs onto cardboard bar mats, and hooked a chair towards the table before flopping down into it. Bob pulled open a drawer in the table and extracted a two-thirds full bottle of Famous Grouse. Neither man spoke as Bob poured a generous tot into each of the mugs.

For a while neither man spoke, each apparently wrapped in thought as they peered vacantly across the steaming mugs. They could smell the whisky. It was as though they were each sitting in a bubble of their own thoughts, isolated, oblivious to everything outside the bubble.

At length Bob broke the silence. 'Well, what have we got?' He spoke over the rim of his mug before taking a generous sip of the tea-whisky.

'Well, thanks to Peter Wright we know what happened and where.' Jim unthinkingly copied his boss as he took a sip of the now cooling but powerful liquid.

'And when.'

'But not why.'

'I think we're close to "why".' Bob spoke quietly. 'It's simple, I think. Kicks. They were out for kicks – nothing less, nothing more.'

'But Guv, surely not to go so far as to kill a man? A completely innocent old man.'

'Why not? It's happened before. In fact it's probably been going on throughout history. Think of the Nazis…'

'Are you suggesting we're dealing with a bunch of Nazis?' Jim sounded shocked. He put his empty mug back on the table.

'Not the sort of Nazis you're thinking of. I don't reckon there would have been anybody strutting about in black uniforms shouting "Heil Hitler!" But you can find plenty of people with the same outlook on life.'

'Bastards!'

'Yes, Jim, but bastards that we have got to catch and put away, if only to stop them from developing a habit from their nasty games.'

Jim interrupted. 'We've also got enough to identify the car and probably trace it back through its owners.'

'Righto, but let's go back for a moment to Peter Wright. His statement is dynamite, but it's vulnerable. I mean vulnerable to being pulled apart by some smart-arsed lawyer purely on the suggestion that he wouldn't be able to remember the detail or recognise the faces after five years.'

'Well, we both heard him and I, for one, can believe him. His statement is clear and it's very obviously in his own words. Nobody could look at it and accuse us of coaching him. He saw it. He'll never forget what he saw, and there are no holes or inconsistencies in his statement. Once we've nailed these sods, and put him up alongside the car evidence, we'll already have the basis of a strong case.' Jim waited for his boss to challenge his reasoning.

'Yes,' said Bob, 'Peter Wright's evidence will help us a lot. But we shouldn't forget that we also have to chase the cover-up. And, of course, there's the not-so-simple matter of identifying the gang and catching them.'

'…and we already know we're looking for at least eight, possibly nine, individuals – with basic descriptions of at least two of them, as well as the knowledge that the gang included two women.'

'Probably,' said Bob. 'But that is not a certified fact.'

'It's a start, and it's pretty close to being a fact.'

'I want to dig in a different hole,' Bob continued. 'I want to know what was going on in this nick. Who took a bribe to wipe the memories? Who paid – or blackmailed – a senior copper, maybe more than one, and who had the power to make every scrap of record or information disappear? Who were the traffic officers and where are they now?' He paused for breath and reached for his mug. He put it back on the table when he realised that it was empty.

'Mary is chasing that one.'

'Yes, and I've arranged some impressive top cover for her.' Bob smiled as he continued, 'The Super has agreed to her using his name. She has carte blanche to run all over the place, asking questions to get information for the compilation of an Honours Display Board. Writing up the story of Weymouth Nick, you might say.'

'What about the traffic cops?'

'Yeah, that'll take longer. It means going back into County records. But since those cunning little buggers at Human Resources, who spend their time producing bloody silly forms, will know the name, date of birth and address at the time of every copper who has ever worked anywhere in the county, we just need to be patient.' Bob looked at his watch and eased his chair back away from the table.

Jim realised that the briefing was over but he chipped in quickly. 'So we know how many were involved, we have an idea of what they looked like and what their cars looked like. We think we might have a theory about motive and we should soon know the names of some of the key players who helped to cover it all up. We still don't know why so many good cops could be suborned like that. When are we going to talk to the Super with this?'

'Eight o'clock tomorrow morning,' said Bob, 'which is why I am going home now.'

****

It was just after seven thirty when Bob arrived back in the office next morning. Jim was already present and the electric kettle was just starting to hiss and bubble. A single sheet of paper occupied the centre of the otherwise empty table. Bob stared at it as he shook the rainwater off his coat and hung it behind the door.

He nodded towards Jim and took two steps towards his chair, picking up the paper on the way. It was a cryptic note, handwritten, from Mary:

Bob smiled as he started to read:

Station Commander was Chief Superintendent Alex Croft. Left Dorset for the Met at the end of May 2010. Promoted to Commander but retired within one year. Address on retirement was Felixstowe. Pension is paid monthly into NatWest Bank in Felixstowe. Deputy Station Commander was Superintendent Andrew Marsden. He also left Dorset for the Met at the end of

2010. Also promoted to Commander and it looks as if he was given Croft's job when Croft retired. Also retired from the Met but more recently. He lives at Longfellow Court in Ham. It's a small exclusive estate of low-rise flats near Richmond, mostly occupied by retired people. I have spoken to HR and will have the names by this afternoon of the six traffic officers operating from here at the time. Also three possible desk sergeants, two watch inspectors and the records clerk. The sergeant in charge of Records and Admin in 2010 is dead.

Bob read the note again, then stuffed it into his pocket, beamed, and said 'Brilliant! That girl is brilliant! We're getting the stuff we need and we're on our way, Jim.' Jim followed his boss, who was almost bouncing with delight, out of the room and down the stairs to the Super's office.

At precisely eight o'clock Bob tapped on the partially open door and peered tentatively around it. Superintendent Holmes was seated at his desk, scribbling a signature across the bottom of a document. He placed the rather smart fountain pen carefully on his desk and looked up.

'Come in,' he said. The two detectives spent the next hour and a half going through, repeating and explaining the evidence they had gathered, and suggesting their future actions.

Chapter 23

Harry woke early, fixed himself a light breakfast of nutty crunch and Weetabix and set the bowl on the kitchen table beside his new computer. He took a mouthful of breakfast, switched on the computer and while it was going through the start-up process he filled the electric kettle and waited for it to boil.

By the time the computer presented itself as ready to work, Harry had finished his cereal and the kettle was boiling. He dropped a teabag into a mug, applied boiling water and turned back to the computer. He cautiously tried a few keystrokes and then sat back in admiration. He was connected to the internet.

For the next couple of hours Harry familiarised himself with his new toy. He had purchased two instruction books to complement the rudimentary instructions that came with the laptop but as he played with the various facilities on offer, he found that the machine was forgiving of his mistakes and the books gradually became superfluous. Harry ploughed steadily into the layers of information offered up to him. He had found a whole new world which was going to assist him in what he had begun to plan.

He began to amass information on the Right Honourable Giles de Courtney Wellton but most of this seemed to be gossip column tittle-tattle which he had already seen in the newspapers. He stored the information in a file and started to look for sellers of small commercial vehicles. He began to compile a list of businesses, their telephone numbers and addresses as he went along. He had already reached the conclusion that it would be better to make his purchase somewhere outside the borders of Dorset so the list he eventually produced showed addresses scattered around three counties.

The next item he would need was a lock-up garage, again located a fair distance from where he lived. Finally he looked for alternative accommodation. This took a long time until he realised that his requirements could probably best be met by acquiring a boat. He needed a fairly big vessel to use as a 'live-aboard', but big vessels tended to cost a great deal of money and Harry realised that even with his new-found wealth he would need to look for something seaworthy but older to fit in with his budget. However, this boat wouldn't need to go to sea; or at least not very far.

Harry started to make telephone calls to the garages on his list, occasionally crossing out the entry so that he was left eventually with only five names, one in Wiltshire, two in Devon and two in Somerset. While making his telephone calls he had realised that he would need some other pieces of equipment to further the plan he was developing. So he began to use his rudimentary knowledge of the internet, the area telephone directory, the Thomson Directory and the 'Classified' columns of the Dorset Echo. It took about an hour, by which time he had identified a list of nine or ten items, some of which had already been dispatched to him and others which would await his collection for payment in cash.

He realised that it was lunchtime and he was hungry. He gathered the notes he had been making, slid them into the narrow drawer in his small desk and strolled into his kitchen. Harry was anxious to get on with his research so he delved into the fridge, pulled out a sizeable chunk of strong cheddar cheese and made himself a sandwich. He considered opening a can of beer but thought better of it and settled for a glass of water.

Forty minutes later he collected his walking stick from the hall, closed and locked the front door and walked across the pavement to his car. Remembering what Tony had told him he looked quickly around the outside of the vehicle, satisfying himself that the tyres all seemed evenly inflated and there were no signs of leaking fluids or any other indication of defects.

Harry climbed into the car, settled himself comfortably and strapped in. He checked his mirrors and set off, driving carefully in the direction of Weymouth.

He drove across the causeway road connecting Portland to the mainland and up through the congested centre of Wyke Regis. As he drove around the complicated Boot Hill roundabout heading towards the town centre he began to think about other things he would need to purchase and he decided that he should not make all his purchases in one place. In any case, he would need to visit some fairly remote places in order to collect a couple of the more unusual items he had located through the internet. Having decided this, Harry turned the car purposefully towards Dorchester.

He parked in the big Charles Street car park and made his way towards the Carphone Warehouse shop, where he listened for ten minutes to an enthusiastic young salesman trying to sell him the latest in smart mobile phones. Eventually he emerged from the shop with a fairly basic and cheap pay-as-you-go and moved on into the shopping centre. Half an hour later he had three small mobiles, all pay-as-you-go, all connected and each charged with fifty pounds' worth of prepayment.

Before leaving Dorchester Harry went in to the NatWest bank and, using his debit card, withdrew £600 in cash. He believed this would be sufficient to cover the next few purchases he needed to make.

From Dorchester he drove off down the A35 towards Poole and the big PCWorld electronics store. It was nearly seven by the time he arrived but the store was still open. He bought a small compact Lumix digital camera and a Garmin portable GPS navigator. Thoroughly satisfied with his afternoon, he drove back towards Portland, briefly diverting into the countryside to the south of Blandford where he called at a rambling cottage attached to an overgrown smallholding, and here he paid cash for several other items he thought he might need. His transaction complete, he locked the latest purchases in the boot and set off once more for Portland.

He was driving along a variety of roads and lanes, all the time becoming more familiar with his new car and with the skill of driving, which he was still re-learning. It was a quarter to ten when he parked the car outside his cottage. When he had locked the front door behind him, he switched on the gas fire in the sitting room, made himself a cup of strong instant coffee, switched on the television and sat down in front of it.

The third item on the BBC ten o'clock news concerned the latest gossip on the man who he now regarded as his principal enemy. The reporter talked of the growing scandal in relation to parliamentary expenses claims and then cut to a film of the tennis star, Sandra Somerville. The voice-over continued, dropping heavy hints about where the woman was living and probing rumours of a relationship with the former Minister. Harry stared hard at the screen and felt the stirring of memory. He had seen this woman before in his dreams; but also, he was sure, in the flesh.

The final part of the news item showed the reporter attempting to intercept de Courtney Wellton, dressed in running kit, as he returned to his house. The reporter signed off by giving his name, which passed over Harry's head, and saying "from Wimbledon Common", which didn't!

Bingo! Harry now knew where to go for the start of his hunt.

Harry spent the next few hours engrossed in his computer, examining various internet websites.

****

Harry did not get to bed until well after midnight but despite this he was up before seven the next morning. He sipped his cooling tea and followed this with mouthfuls of cereal while he scribbled entries on a scruffy piece of paper. By eight o'clock he was pulling away from the kerb in the car. He drove down through Fortuneswell and joined the stream of slow-moving traffic across the causeway before turning off into the Sailing Centre complex. He parked at the edge of the line of cradled boats and walked across to the Chandlers shop, only to discover that it would not be open until nine. Frustrated and annoyed, he realised he had half an hour to wait, so he returned to the car and sat behind the steering wheel, waiting and thinking.

It was while he was waiting in the car that he began to resolve a problem that had been worrying him since the previous evening. He needed a fast-acting anaesthetic and according to the online Wikipedia encyclopaedia he had consulted, the one that was most commonly used in the medical world was ketamine. Everything else could be easily obtained but not ketamine – not without risking arrest. He had spent some time on the internet and discovered that ketamine was a Class 'C' drug available only through three possible sources: an illegal drug pusher, or legally, through a vet's practice or in a hospital. It was marketed under a variety of names but in Britain the most common name seemed to be Ketalar. Apparently, ketamine was used by vets to tranquilise large animals, especially horses. It was also used in hospitals as a form of anaesthetic, but there would be absolutely no chance of getting the drug from this particular source. He had also learnt that it was sometimes used among addicts and teenagers to induce euphoria and could therefore be bought on the street.

Harry's lifestyle had never taken him anywhere near that source so he hadn't a clue as to even where he might look. Additionally, he didn't want to risk arrest, which would lead not only to notoriety but also to failure of his carefully constructed plan.

Eventually the doors to the Chandlery opened and Harry strolled across to the shop. Half an hour later he struggled back to his car followed by the shopkeeper, each laden with bundles of Harry's purchases. He spent the rest of the morning driving north to Somerset where he visited the first few garages on his list. He moved on to Devon during the afternoon before making his way back towards Portland, stopping at a wayside pub for a Ploughman's bread and cheese supper on the way.

Harry was dog-tired when he arrived back at the cottage so he left his latest purchases in the car to be unloaded next morning.

It was after eleven by the time he set off next day for his second purchasing expedition. This one was unsuccessful, but he continued for the next four days, by the end of which he returned to the cottage, smiling and happy. He was now the owner of a small Peugeot van with double rear doors and sliding side doors, a fitted GPS navigator, air-conditioning and a combined radio and CD player. The van had no windows in the load carrying section and Harry had taken careful note of the door lock system which the enthusiastic salesman had described as 'burglar-proof'. The van was still at the dealers in Exeter where it was being modified with a winch, ramp, rails and securing points so that a wheelchair could be carried in the back. Harry now also held a two-year lease on a remote windowless barn set on the edge of a copse in sheep grazing land to the west of the village of King's Stag in North Dorset.

Harry still had one purchase to complete. He had made and withdrawn a tentative offer for a boat and a mooring on the river Frome, half a mile from where the river entered into the upper reaches of Poole Harbour. The boat was an elderly converted Motor Fishing Vessel built originally for the Admiralty. In the heyday of the Royal Navy, hundreds of these tough little boats, known universally as MFVs, had been built. They seemed almost indestructible and were commonly used to ferry stores and people back and forth from shore to ship, often riding the most appalling weather. The mooring consisted of a small area of flat grass surrounded by tall reeds and reached by a three quarter mile rough and rutted track just wide enough for a single vehicle. The vessel had two working engines which had been used recently only to charge batteries and make the boat habitable. Although it was over forty years old, the boat – christened, incongruously, *Spitfire* – still seemed to be comfortable and seaworthy, although outwardly it appeared scruffy, unloved and unattractive. It would happily blend in with the floating junk that tended to inhabit many similar small working harbours and river estuaries along the south coast.

It was on the way back from Exeter that Harry struck his most useful piece of luck. He was driving along in steady rain with the early afternoon turning into evening gloom when he heard an appeal on the local radio station for volunteers to help move animals from the still heavily flooded farmland on the

Somerset Levels. Harry reckoned that where there were many animals being rounded up and moved there would be vets. And where there were vets he would find drugs.

Early the following morning he set off for Somerset, stopping to buy a pair of fisherman's waders and an oilskin coat in the fishing shop in Wyke Regis before heading purposefully for the Somerset levels.

As he approached the flooded area he was stopped by a soldier in a high visibility jacket and told that his car, being small and only a two-wheel drive, could go no further. He explained his purpose, lied that he was a retired farm hand, and twenty minutes later he was kitted up in his new waterproof clothing riding into action on a long wooden trailer towed by a tall and powerful multi-purpose tractor. Harry was accompanied on the trailer by eight other men, similarly dressed, ready to help move cattle and horses, but all of them looking rather younger and fitter than he did.

Chapter 24

While Harry was arriving at the flooded Somerset Levels, the two detectives were driving towards the North Dorset estate of Sir Arthur Simmonds. Jim was driving while Bob sat poring over a large scale ordnance survey map. They were having trouble navigating through the narrow, leafy lanes and Bob was in danger of losing his temper as the car edged slowly around a bend in the single carriageway road, a tall luxuriant hedge obscuring the route ahead, only to arrive once more at a familiar junction.

'Shit!' said Bob. 'Another bloody signpost pointing the wrong way.'

'I think the local comedians swivel the signs round for sport,' Jim said as he eased the unmarked police car to a stop.

Bob didn't answer at first. He continued to study the crumpled map which was spread across his knees. 'See if you can back up to the junction,' he said, 'then we'll try the right hand turn. We'll see if we can find a village pub – if they have any villages, that is.' He lapsed into silence.

'Or if they have pubs,' said Jim quietly. Bob didn't answer but jerked his thumb in a rearward direction. Jim slipped the car into reverse gear and twisted around in his seat as they started to move backwards.

'Sod it!' He exploded as he jammed his foot on the brake pedal and knocked the car out of gear.

Bob plunged forward against the restraint of his seat belt. He turned angrily towards Jim, opening his mouth to speak, but he was interrupted.

'Look behind,' said Jim, still peering backwards while sitting twisted awkwardly around towards the back of the car. Bob reached across and moved the interior mirror so he could see behind. What he saw did nothing to improve his mood. The view in the mirror showed the entire lane behind the car completely blocked by a herd of fat cattle, shambling slowly but purposefully towards the stationary vehicle.

Neither man spoke as the cows continued, passing the car like an incoming tide flowing inexorably around an obstruction. The car rocked and bounced as the beasts squeezed past, knocking both wing mirrors out of true and filling the air with a distinctive farmyard smell.

They waited. A tail flicked from side to side and deflected a steaming light brown jet of manure along the side of the once pristine BMW. 'Shit!' said Bob, with feeling.

'Quite! I would say that is shit,' said Jim as the last few cows ambled past the car, driven on by a small, impatient, black and white dog. Behind the dog strode an elderly man wearing a wide-brimmed hat who was waving a longish bamboo cane, occasionally tapping the rumps of the stragglers while apparently shouting encouragement to individual animals by name.

As the man came abreast of the car Jim lowered his window and called, 'Excuse me!' The man continued walking at his steady pace. Jim tried again. 'Excuse me, but can you tell me where the Simmonds Estate is?'

The cowman kept walking. He turned his head slightly and called out, 'Yer on it!'

Jim opened the car door and stepped out, walking quickly after the departing herdsman. 'We're looking for Sir Arthur Simmonds,' he called towards the man's back. This time the man didn't look round. Instead he continued encouraging the cows, some of whom had paused to chew the roadside grass.

'Go back a mile, an' ye'll see the big 'ouse up to the left. That's where he'll be.' He carried on, lengthening his stride slightly. Jim turned to walk the few yards back towards the car. His foot slipped in something and he glanced down. Both of his shoes were liberally spotted with glistening cattle dung. He trudged unhappily towards the grass verge where he began a not entirely successful attempt to wipe off the ordure in the lush long grass and weeds. Bob watched the performance from within the car, recovering some of his sense of humour as he did so.

Jim completed his shoe cleaning and trudged back along the centre of the road, trying, not entirely successfully, to avoid more of the liberally scattered dung before climbing back into the car.

'What did he say?' asked Bob.

'There's a house where his lordship may be found, about a mile back that way, somewhere on the left.'

'He's not a lord. He's a knight.' Bob folded the map, not quite as neatly as it had once been.

'Okay. He's a knight,' said Jim without enthusiasm, as he reversed the car towards the road junction.

'That's "Sir Arthur", not "My Lord",' said Bob, clasping his hands comfortably across his stomach and closing his eyes. 'Tell me when we're there.'

They wound their way back along the narrow road for nearly two miles, rarely reaching thirty miles an hour, before a cluster of red tiled roofs poked above the trees on their left. After another quarter of a mile a tall stone gateway surmounted by a sculpture of a stag came into view. They turned left through the gateway and drove onto a single track road which headed in a straight line towards the huge manor house that now dominated the skyline ahead of them.

On one side of the road, green parkland stretched away towards a line of trees marking the edge of a stand of woodland. The other side was also predominantly well-tended parkland, but here it was cut by tracks leading away to cottages and clusters of farm buildings.

The car rumbled over a cattle grid where the scenery changed abruptly to ornamental gardens. The house now stood almost directly in front of them and the road widened out to become an extensive gravel driveway leading to a big circular space, with a moss-covered fountain in the centre. To one side stood the entrance to a rose garden and on the other side was a track which disappeared behind a group of ornamental flowering shrubs. A dirty green Land Rover Discovery was parked beside a neat red Fiat at the edge of the turning circle.

Bob inclined his head towards the track leading past the shrubbery. 'It must go to the stable block,' he said. 'You can see the horseshoe prints in the mud.' Jim nodded as the car crunched to a halt in front of a set of white stone steps leading up towards a pair of ornately carved wooden doors, blackened with age, which must have been at least twelve feet high.

Bob climbed stiffly out of the car and stood looking at the imposing building, while Jim surreptitiously checked his shoes to confirm that they were no longer an embarrassment.

As they started to walk towards the steps, one of the huge doors slowly opened and a man, evidently a butler judging by his dress, stepped forward. He stood on the top step and looked down on the two detectives. Jim thought that the steps in grand buildings such as this were very likely designed to allow butlers to peer down on unwanted guests.

Bob pasted a smile onto his face and advanced, holding up his warrant card in his right hand. 'My name is Detective Chief Inspector Majury,' he said. 'This is Detective Sergeant Creasy, and we would like to speak to Sir Arthur Simmonds, please.'

Jim wondered if the 'please' part was really necessary, but assumed that the Boss knew what he was about.

The butler looked as though a particularly offensive smell was advancing towards him and said, 'Do you have an appointment?'

'No,' said Bob shortly.

'Sir Arthur never sees anyone without an appointment,' persisted the butler.

'Is Sir Arthur in?' Bob allowed his tone to become distinctly tetchy as he responded. He continued to hold the warrant card where the pompous man in the morning suit could see it. The butler looked uncertain. Bob deduced that the lack of a reply indicated that Sir Arthur was indeed at home.

'Wait here, please.' The butler stepped swiftly back and shut the door, rather more firmly than Jim thought was strictly necessary.

They stood waiting on the second step while a few heavy raindrops suggested the arrival of a shower.

Ten minutes passed before the door was opened once more, this time by a slim middle-aged woman in a dark blue jacket and skirt. She peered sternly towards the two policemen, removed a pair of spectacles and said briskly, 'I am Private Secretary to Sir Arthur. How can I help you?'

'You can't. We've come a long way and we'd like to speak to Sir Arthur; now, please,' said Bob. His voice had sunk from 'tetchy' to 'distinctly frosty', thought Jim as he watched the exchange.

'Sir Arthur never sees anyone without an appointment.' She smiled benignly as she spoke.

Bob smiled back. 'Well, could you give him a message, please?'

'I can take a message for him but I don't know when he will receive it.'

Bob smiled again, but the smile was not quite reaching his eyes. 'Can you kindly tell him, please, that Detective Chief Inspector Majury of the Dorset Police and his colleague are investigating a serious crime and we would like to ask him some questions, for which purpose we have travelled a long way. Could you also tell him that if he wishes to decline my request I will issue a warrant for his arrest and have him taken to Weymouth Police Station under caution, and I will ask my questions there.'

'Oh!' Her eyes widened for a very brief moment, then she recovered her haughty composure, turned and disappeared into the gloom of the hallway. The door was once more shut, leaving the two detectives cooling their heels on the granite doorstep. They waited, listening to the raindrops continuing to plop uncertainly onto the concrete steps behind them.

After perhaps five minutes Bob glanced at his watch, and, nodding to his companion, he pushed at the door. It was unlocked and it swung inward noiselessly. The two detectives crossed the threshold and entered a large, rectangular, high-ceilinged hall with dark wood panelling surrounding several closed doors presumably leading into deeper parts of the house.

The walls were decorated with a series of portraits of unsmiling men dressed in various uniforms and period costumes. Bob shrugged off his raincoat and flopped into one of the elderly brown leather armchairs spread around the hall.

They waited in silence; Bob slouched in the chair, while Jim wandered around the room inspecting the portraits. A door opened in one of the walls and a tall, prematurely balding man aged about thirty strode into the room. He was dressed in a tweedy three-piece suit surmounting a checked shirt and a striped club tie. He was followed by his private secretary who was scuttling along behind him, trying to keep up with her master's long strides.

The man stopped precisely in the centre of the room and scowled at the two policemen. 'I believe you want to speak to me,' he said. The private secretary hovered behind him, now clutching a shorthand notebook and cheap plastic biro in one hand.

'Are you Sir Arthur Simmonds?' Bob prised himself out of the deep armchair with some difficulty. The chair seemed to have folded around him.

'I am.' Sir Arthur seemed to be both discomforted and irritated. He stood, legs slightly apart, dominating the centre of the room and staring down at his visitors.

'I am Detective Chief Inspector Robert Majury.' Bob held his warrant card out at arm's length. 'This is my colleague, Detective Sergeant Creasy.'

Sir Arthur nodded slightly, ignored the warrant card and walked across the room to stand with his back to the empty fireplace. 'Well?' he asked.

Bob, realising that seats were not being offered, moved towards the centre of the room and stood facing the tall landowner. 'We are looking into the ownership of a certain car.' Without looking round he held out his right hand, into which Jim deftly placed a slim cardboard file cover. Without taking his eyes from the face of the baronet, he slid an A4 photograph out of the file and held it up in front of him.

'We are looking for the owner of this vehicle,' he said, evenly.

'I'm sorry. I don't think I can help you.'

'You are Sir Arthur Simmonds?' said Bob.

'Of course I am. Do you want to see my passport or something?' Was this genuine anger, or just bluster? wondered Bob.

'Well, the thing is, Sir Arthur, this vehicle is registered to you.'

For the first time, Sir Arthur looked uncomfortable. He started to speak then checked himself, thrusting his hands deep into the pockets of his trousers and staring down at his feet. The room remained silent for a full minute. Then he looked up, glaring angrily towards the detective. 'It was registered to my father,' he said at length, followed by a long exhalation of breath – which could almost have been a sigh.

'I see,' said Bob. 'And I presume that your father is deceased?'

'Yes.'

'Then, since the car is still registered to your deceased father…'

'Well, yes, it was. But it was written off in an accident some years ago.'

Jim, who had said nothing so far, stared intently at the tall, imposing landowner. As he watched the body language he realised that the man was suddenly becoming quite nervous. A thin sheen of sweat had appeared on his brow and he was somehow beginning to look shifty and evasive.

The knightly gent was making an effort to recover his composure and he had now fished a well-worn black pipe out of his coat pocket. He concentrated on fiddling with the pipe as he addressed Bob.

'This car was written off a long time ago. What exactly is your interest in it?' The question was presented as a challenge and Bob rose to it.

'I want to know the circumstances that led to the car being destroyed. Do you know anything about the accident? Do you know who was driving the car? Where and when did the accident take place?'

'I have already told you,' said Sir Arthur. 'It was my father's car and I really don't know what happened.'

Bob took a pace towards the tall man in front of the fireplace and, measuring his words carefully, he said, 'Come off it. You're telling me that your father crashes an expensive high performance car and you don't even ask him what happened?'

'It was a long time ago. It was my father's affair. He wasn't hurt so it didn't involve me.'

'I don't believe you!' and then, after a significant pause, Bob added, 'Sir Arthur.'

Sir Arthur suddenly stuffed the pipe back in his pocket, looked pointedly at his wristwatch and began to stride from the room. 'I'm afraid this interview is over. My secretary will show…'

He didn't get any further. Bob moved surprisingly quickly for such a bulky man. He stepped in front of the Baronet, blocking his progress.

'The interview is very definitely not over, Sir Arthur. Very far from it. I have a great many questions to ask you and if you co-operate I can do that here. If you decide not to co-operate, I will instruct Sergeant Creasy here to arrest you; and I will take you under custody to Weymouth Police Headquarters.'

'You wouldn't dare. In my own house? Preposterous!'

Bob stepped back. 'Sergeant,' he said, 'arrest this man for obstructing police enquiries.'

Jim stood up. Privately he thought the Guv'nor was going over the top but he started the caution: 'Sir Arthur Simmonds, I am arresting you for…'

He didn't get any further. 'All right, all right,' said Simmonds. 'You had better come to my office.' As they followed the tall landowner towards a large office with a huge window opening onto the parkland, he turned partly and called to his secretary, 'See that we are not disturbed.' Without answering, the woman shut the door, rather noisily.

Sir Arthur sat comfortably behind his desk and the two policemen placed themselves on chairs, slightly to the right and slightly to the left of the desk, so that Sir Arthur was unable to look at both of them at the same time.

Bob ostentatiously hauled out a notebook and a silver biro. 'Why don't you just tell us what happened, Sir Arthur?' he said. 'I mean, when your father's car crashed, that is.'

Jim chimed in on cue. 'Were you driving it?' he asked.

'No. No!'

The response was too quick. Jim also noted that the previous bluster had gone. The man now had a rather hunted look about him.

The interview lasted a further two hours, during which time Sir Arthur recounted an increasingly improbable tale. He said that his late father had a penchant for fast and smart cars but his driving ability had deteriorated with age. The older man had often asked his son to accompany him as he had on this occasion. They had taken the Aston Martin out for a Sunday afternoon spin, driven down towards Bridport and then taken the coast road along through Abbotsbury to Weymouth. They had parked by the esplanade in Weymouth and taken a stroll along the beach, enjoying the sea air. By this time the evening was setting in and it was getting chilly. The elder Sir Arthur had been reluctant to go straight back to the estate so his son had suggested that they could have dinner in one of the harbourside restaurants. The son had driven the powerful car (he said he found it a bit of a handful) carefully and slowly around to the harbour and parked outside the white walls of Vaughan's restaurant.

They both dined on lobster thermidor and the present baronet recalled that the meal was particularly good. They each enjoyed a couple of glasses of New Zealand Chardonnay and this had affected the old man to a greater degree than the son; so the present Sir Arthur had driven the car. His father wanted to see Portland Bill with the lighthouse operating at night so they had driven there, parked in the lighthouse car park and walked along the path by the rocks towards the Pulpit Rock, and then back again to the car. At this point the father had insisted that he was capable of driving and said he would drive the car back to North Dorset. A brief argument followed over this but the father's view prevailed. They set off to drive north, 'increasingly erratically,' said the baronet. As the old man accelerated north out of Easton, he lost control of the car and it veered off the road to the left, hitting a dry stone wall and causing extensive damage, so much so that the car was a write-off. Remarkably, neither occupant of the vehicle sustained any significant injuries.

The car had actually been driven away from the lighthouse car park a few minutes before midnight and the accident had happened about ten or twelve minutes later.

'I think we have enough to be going on with, sir, so thank you for giving us your time.' Bob climbed to his feet as he spoke, rather formally. He stuffed his notebook away in an inside pocket and extended a hand, leaning over the desk. Sir Arthur stood, pushing back his chair with his legs as he did so, and automatically shook Bob's hand.

'We'll see ourselves out, sir,' said Bob, before turning and saying, 'Oh, we may well need to speak to you again – tie up some loose ends. By the way, I must also ask you to let me know if you intend to leave here in the next few days. Do you have any plans that will take you away from here?'

Sir Arthur shook his head perfunctorily.

'Goodbye, Sir Arthur.'

With that both policemen walked from the room. Almost outside they found the secretary, who accompanied them across the hall to the front door.

The huge front door had already closed before the two detectives climbed into their car. Jim was driving and as he started to pull away, Bob said, 'When we are clear of the house and the estate, stop in the first lay-by we come to.'

Jim glanced to his left. 'Right-oh, Guv'nor.'

Twenty-five minutes later, they had left the narrow, leaf-strewn lanes behind and were now cruising south towards Charminster.

'Pull over there!' said Bob indicating an almost empty lorry-park by the side of the road. Jim was momentarily surprised because he believed that Bob had been dozing. He flicked on the left-hand indicator and dutifully pulled into the wayside lorry park, stopping about fifty yards behind a big articulated Tesco truck.

As the engine noise died away, Bob turned to his companion and said, 'What did you think of that, then?'

'Well, he admitted being in the area, driving the Aston and being in the car when it crashed.'

'Don't tell me you were taken in by all that clap-trap!' said Bob. 'Didn't you watch him? He was making it up as he went along.'

'Also he was amazingly lacking in curiosity,' said Jim. 'He never asked us what it was all about. Why were we so interested in a crashed car from five years ago? And he still doesn't seem interested in what happened to a two hundred grand car.'

'That's because he already knows the story,' said Bob. 'It's a pity we weren't able to put a phone tap on that boy – because as sure as God made little apples, he'll be on the phone rousting out his mates even now.'

Jim thought for a moment and then said, tentatively, 'We could put out an all ports check on him. He might just do a runner.'

'Good thinking, lad.' Bob was already reaching for his mobile phone. Three minutes later the order was set in place and any attempt by Sir Arthur Simmonds, Baronet, to leave the country would lead to his detention.

Chapter 25

In fact, the floods on the Somerset Levels had already begun to subside by the time Harry arrived on the long farm trailer. The huge inland sea which had dominated television screens for weeks past had now largely disappeared, being replaced by brown ponds dotted around fields of dead, rotting grass and other vegetation. In the distance, a line of yellow painted JCB diggers dumping bucket-loads of mud and silt on a steadily growing embankment marked the position of the river Parrett.

The tractor stopped at the edge of a small devastated village, where Harry's companions hopped off the trailer and set off in various directions, purposefully heading towards pre-briefed tasks. Harry climbed uncertainly and rather laboriously down from the back of the trailer and stood in the road beside it, not knowing what to do next. As he waited, a truck loaded with cattle pulled in noisily behind the tractor and several men appeared from a couple of shattered farm buildings, moving towards the truck. As they passed, one of them paused and said, 'You looking to help, old timer?'

Before Harry could move or respond, the man in an elderly trilby hat and an outsize green Barbour jacket thrust a clipboard with a pad of forms attached towards him. 'Here,' he said. 'Take these and fill in what I tell you as I check these cattle. It's pretty straightforward. I'll call out the entries as I check each beast. Can you do that?'

'Sure,' said Harry, walking as quickly as he could after the voluminous green Barbour jacket which was flapping open on either side of its owner, rather like a large carrion crow trying to take off. He had nearly caught up with his new leader when the green jacket lurched to the right and partially disappeared into the front of a filthy, mud-caked Land Rover. A moment later the green Barbour reappeared, backing out from the Land Rover cab, and its owner hefted a heavy-looking Gladstone bag, which was held out to Harry. He was able to see the man's face properly for the first time. The face was open and friendly, aged about fifty or sixty. Years of outdoor work had burnished it to produce a ruddy, craggy appearance. It smiled and Harry looked down to see a broad work-calloused hand thrust towards him. The hand's owner spoke.

'Jack Walters is my name. Glad to have you aboard. Can you stay all day? All I need is a bit of help to make the notes and perhaps carry the bag. Can you do that?'

'Glad to,' said Harry. 'I'm Harry Chaplin. Yes, I can stay with you as long as you want.'

Jack grinned. 'Great!' he said. 'Let's go to it!' Harry picked up the big black bag, which was remarkably heavy, and set off, trying to keep pace with the long-striding Jack.

'These beasts have been through a hard time and they're coming back in batches. Mind you, they can't be turned out onto pasture here – because there isn't any, not yet anyway.'

'What are you going to do?' asked Harry.

'Well, they've been kept in difficult conditions in many cases and for a long time. I need to do a final check for injuries or other problems and treat any cattle that need it.'

'I see,' said Harry as he switched the heavy bag to his other hand.

The work of checking cattle did indeed go on all day. The big articulated trucks continued to rumble into the lane about once every hour. As soon as each tailboard was dropped, three or four men would cluster around the rear of the truck, guiding the animals in a thin line down the ramp formed by the tailboard and into a makeshift pen where Jack and Harry waited. Jack would give each beast a fairly cursory check-over and then stand back to allow them to be guided out of the pen. Occasionally he would find something of concern which would disrupt the process. In several instances he would take the heavy bag from Harry, rummage about in it, emerge with a loaded syringe and inject the animal, which would then be dispatched to join the others. The bag would then be handed back to Harry's care.

During the checking of the third batch of cattle – young bullocks this time – Harry fumbled the bag as it was returned to him and dropped it, still open, on the ground, spilling some of the contents onto the grass. Harry called a perfunctory, 'Sorry,' and dropped to his knees, laying the clipboard behind him as he gathered up the spilled medicines and instruments.

He had already spotted what he was looking for. Among half a dozen other items, a brown bottle marked Ketalar had fallen from the bag. As he scooped the bottles and tubes back into the bag he glanced up to where Jack was still hanging onto the neck of the small bullock, his attention focused beyond the animal towards the men at the gate to the pen. Harry flicked the brown bottle back towards his clipboard, still lying on the grass. In the same movement he was able to sweep the clipboard forward along the grass to cover the bottle. Twenty seconds later he was standing with the closed bag in his left hand, the clipboard tucked under his right arm and the brown bottle of Ketalar in his left trouser pocket.

The last lorryload of cattle arrived at about half-past five, by which time both men looked and felt weary. This load contained fewer animals than the previous batches and within an hour Jack was wiping his hands on a cloth moistened with an antiseptic solution, smiling towards Harry and thanking him for his help.

'Can I give you a lift? I've got my car just around the corner.' Jack was already starting to walk in the direction of his battered Land Rover as he spoke.

Harry replied without hesitation. 'Thanks,' he said. 'My car is about half a mile from the village. They wouldn't let me bring it any nearer.'

Suddenly Jack stopped. 'Oh,' he said. 'I've forgotten to pick up the used syringes. They should be just inside the gate.' He turned back towards the pen.

'I'll give you a hand,' called Harry, hefting the case and struggling to catch up with Jack. As they passed through the gate, Harry placed the heavy black bag on the ground by the temporary fence and moved as quickly as he could to help gather the used syringes. They found about a dozen syringes of various sizes on the ground and gathered them up carefully before placing them in a compartment inside the bag. Jack then picked up the bag, which now contained ten syringes. The other two were sharing Harry's left trouser pocket with the Ketalar.

Jack dropped Harry beside his car and waited to make sure it would start all right. It did. Harry deliberately waited a few moments, settling himself comfortably before driving off with a wave and heading towards home. He was content with his day's work and he spent most of the journey plotting his next moves.

Harry slept late next morning and he was only halfway through his bowl of cornflakes, his morning tea still untouched, when the phone rang.

It was the owner of the boat that Harry had been looking at. The voice on the telephone explained that he was about to change jobs and move to the Midlands. He would not be taking his boat and he wanted to make a revised offer to Harry. To

Harry's surprise the boat-owner had knocked one third off the price. Harry was delighted, but he thought it better not to appear too eager; so he continued to haggle for a few minutes. His tea was cold by the time the telephone call had ended but he was well pleased as he switched on his electric kettle once more. For the layout of only £35,000 he was about to become the owner of a comfortable but not very seaworthy twin-engine Motor Fishing Vessel, complete with a mooring tucked away among the tall reeds halfway between Wareham and Poole on the north bank of the River Frome.

Harry spent the rest of the morning poring over his recently purchased maps of Dorset and of the Wimbledon area of London. He had just switched on the radio to catch the news and 'The World at One' when the telephone rang again, this time to announce the imminent arrival of his Peugeot van. An hour later, having moved his Astra to a parking space a hundred yards from his door, Harry had signed a few forms and was inspecting his van, inside which was a folding wheelchair. The van, he was pleased to note, was plain, white and without any distinguishing marks – just like ten thousand others, he thought.

Before he went to bed that night, Harry had formulated the next phase of his plan, which he would begin to put into effect next day. As it turned out, this had to be deferred by one further day because later that afternoon he was summoned once more to the clinic for another routine check-up. He decided that the following Saturday would become 'D' Day!

Chapter 26

By the time the detectives arrived at the police station next morning, Bob's request for port surveillance had already borne fruit. An alert emigration officer had detained a man bearing an Irish passport with the name Arthur Simmonds attempting to board the high-speed Condor cross-channel ferry at Poole. He was presently being held at Poole Central police station in the custody of a nervous inspector who was anxious to get the very angry man off his hands.

'Keep him there,' said Bob. 'We'll be with you in an hour.'

The traffic was light for once and within forty-five minutes the two policemen were walking into the bright and airy entrance hall of Poole Central police station. The desk sergeant recognised Bob and they were both conducted directly to the inspector's office.

'He's blazing mad,' said the uniformed inspector. 'Keeps demanding his lawyer, ranting on about human rights and threatening all kinds of legal action against anyone and everyone.'

'What have you said to him?' Bob settled uncomfortably on a small office chair opposite the inspector's desk.

'Not much. The custody sergeant has explained that he has been detained, albeit temporarily, in order to assist the police with an enquiry into a serious crime.'

'What about the lawyer?'

'He didn't give us a number and we're having difficulty locating him.'

'Good,' said Bob, 'but that won't last for long.'

A few minutes later the two Weymouth officers were following a young constable along a brightly lit, green-painted corridor, past a series of dark grey steel doors. The constable had a big, impressive-looking ring of keys attached by a chain to his belt.

'We put him in the "soft" interview room,' said the constable to the two men following him.

'Thanks,' grunted Bob.

The constable selected a key and turned it silently in the lock before pushing open a stout door – wooden this time – and then stood back to allow the others to pass into the room. As soon as they were inside, he stepped back, closed the door, and waited outside in the corridor.

Although the room had been described as a 'soft' interview room, Jim thought it certainly wasn't very comfortable. He looked around, taking in the high level, single-barred window set too high in the wall for anyone to see much of the outside, the scuffed linoleum floor and the sparse, worn, uncomfortable furniture.

'Good afternoon once more, Sir Arthur.' Bob spoke politely as he advanced across the room towards a rectangular wooden table. On the other side of the table sat the slumped figure of Sir Arthur Simmonds, staring silently at the scuffed surface in front of him. Bob eased himself into the opposite chair.

'I'm glad we were able to contact you, because some things have come up and I wanted to ask you a few more questions.' Bob kept his voice even, while ignoring the irony of the situation. Sir Arthur remained silent, staring intently at the table.

'Where were you going, Sir Arthur?' said Bob, keeping his voice neutral and low. Sir Arthur remained silent. Bob repeated the question, leaning forward and pointedly spacing each word.

Sir Arthur continued to ignore the question and sat staring fixedly at the table. The silence between the two men persisted for perhaps another minute, then suddenly it was broken as Sir Arthur Simmonds leapt to his feet, kicking his chair across the room behind him. In the same movement he leaned forward on the table, his arms stretched out on either side supporting his weight on closed knuckles, and shouted down at Bob seated in front and below him.

'You piece of officious shit!' he shouted, spittle raining onto the table. 'I'll teach you who you're dealing with. I'll have your job for this, you fucking nonentity. I know people in the police who will make you jump. Make you sorry you ever had the nerve to disturb me. You're finished, you ignorant bastard.' He remained leaning on the table, red-faced with anger, breathing heavily.

At this point the door opened and the uniformed constable rushed into the room with a drawn baton. Jim had pressed the emergency button on the doorframe as soon as the tirade had begun.

Sir Arthur saw the constable advancing towards him with his baton raised aggressively. He backed away from the table to the far wall. 'I'll have you!' he said, glaring towards Bob, then, more calmly, 'I want a lawyer.'

During the tirade, Bob had not moved at all, remaining seated and waiting for the tantrum to subside. As though nothing untoward had occurred, he spoke quietly. 'We have been trying to contact your lawyer but you won't tell us who he is or where to find him. I'd call that a bit stupid,' then, turning to the constable, he said 'Cuff him!' The younger man moved deftly across the room and the tall aristocrat suddenly found himself staring with a look of shocked amazement at a set of handcuffs linking his wrists together. In his anger he had not even realised the cuffs were being applied to his wrists. His expression ranged between shock, outrage, and what could have been fear. He flopped back down onto his chair.

Jim realised that his boss had his man where he wanted him. The attempt to intimidate the Chief Inspector had backfired spectacularly, leaving, as the only options available to the baronet, co-operation or a cell. Bob remained silent. He simply sat and stared at the handcuffed man, now seated on the edge of his chair on the other side of the room. After a gap of several minutes but seemingly much longer, he heaved a theatrical sigh and turned towards his sergeant.

'Fancy a cup of coffee, skipper?' he said as he climbed laboriously to his feet and, turning towards the door, he spoke once again, but for Sir Arthur's benefit: 'I think we'll go down to the canteen and let this silly bugger work out how to get out of the mess he's in.'

Then he turned pointedly back towards Simmonds, but continued addressing Jim. 'The funny thing is, he obviously doesn't know what I know, and now I know even more than when we came in. He hasn't got a clue. Silly bugger!'

Jim thumped on the door which was opened instantly. As they strolled through into the green-painted corridor, Bob addressed the constable. 'Keep an eye on him 'till we get back, will you?'

The canteen was fairly quiet, with just a couple of coppers sitting over mugs of tea and empty plates. Jim walked across to the serving counter and ordered two coffees. Bob called after him, 'Add a ham sandwich, will you, Jim? That little tantrum made me quite peckish.'

Twenty-five minutes later, the same constable opened the door into the 'soft room' once more. The two detectives strolled in and Bob flopped into the single empty chair. Jim moved to the corner and leaned back against the wall, facing the slumped form occupying the other chair, which was now placed back against the far wall, as though its occupant was trying to get as far away from the interview table as he could.

The uniformed constable followed the other two into the room, closed the door behind him and stood with his back to it. No one spoke.

The silence dragged on and Sir Arthur Simmonds sat on his chair, occasionally shifting about but all the time staring at the floor. His original bluster seemed to have evaporated.

Ten minutes went by and still nobody had spoken. Then suddenly Bob leaned forward, scraping his chair legs noisily on the floor. 'Frug!' he shouted. The sound was like a gunshot going off in the small room. The effect was remarkable. Sir Arthur's head came up and he stared across the room at Bob. The previous expression of haughty anger had gone, to be replaced, for a brief few moments, with one of terror.

'What does it mean?' Bob was now leaning far across the wooden table staring fixedly at the man opposite. 'And before you start lying,' he continued, 'I might already know the answers. So just talk, and I'll see if you get it right.'

From the far side of the room Jim said softly, 'I bet the "ug" bit stands for undergraduate.' The eyes of the man on the other side of the table flicked briefly upward before his head leaned forward over the table. He muttered something inaudible.

'What did you say?' Bob spoke quietly, his eyes still fixed on his prisoner.

Sir Arthur Simmonds' head jerked up. 'I said, show me some respect,' he said. 'I deserve respect.'

'You deserve nothing!' shouted Bob. 'I'm here to see if you are a murderer. Murderers don't get respect.'

'Oh, Christ,' said Simmonds. 'He didn't die, did he?' The bluster had gone, replaced by a dog-like appeal as he stared, appalled, across the table at his tormentor.

'Oh,' said Bob. 'Who was that who didn't die?' Then, after a long pause, 'Sir Arthur?'

Sir Arthur Simmonds bowed his head, leaning towards the table which was now too far away for him to reach. The room remained quiet and the minutes ticked by, creating an air of oppression while the four occupants waited. At length he looked up, briefly catching the eye of his tormentor.

Bob seized his opportunity. He raised himself partially out of his chair and then shouted across the table again. 'Frug, I said! Frug! What does it mean?' The silence continued.

Then, very quietly, Sir Arthur spoke. 'Free running. It just means free running.'

'There you are!' Bob beamed, speaking loudly and triumphantly; 'that wasn't difficult, was it?' He stared directly across the table but spoke to the room in general. 'What about that, Sergeant? Constable? Didn't seem so awfully difficult, did it? Just a name for a few chums, eh?'

Relief showed briefly through the sweat on Sir Arthur's face, but it disappeared quickly when the DCI started again: 'Yeah, but what does it mean, what *does* it mean? What does it mean when you're shouting it as you thump someone? Is it a war cry? Is it a code? Does it start a fire in your belly? What, really, really, does it mean?' As he finished he leaned further over the table, speaking slowly, directly at the sweating, distraught, man opposite.

From the back of the room, Jim spoke. 'Come on,' he said, 'you can tell us, and then all this can be over. Was it just a bit of fun, letting your hair down, that sort of thing, something that went wrong?'

Tears began to well from Simmonds' clenched eyelids. His shoulders began to shake. When he spoke the words were so quiet as to be almost indistinguishable. 'It wasn't me,' he said. 'I tried to stop it. I tried to put it right.' When he looked up he was in time to see the door closing. He was alone with just the two detectives in the room.

'What do you mean by saying you tried to put it right?' Bob spoke very quietly, so his words were barely audible.

There was no answer.

'What did you mean, Sir Arthur?' The words seemed to be even softer, quieter. Bob waited, allowing the silence to be stretched. The door opened and the constable returned. Bob turned his head and glared at the man, annoyed by the interruption.

'Sir Arthur?' Bob leaned further towards the man on the other side of the table.

Eventually he spoke. Still staring at the floor, he said, 'I paid the medical bills.'

Jim spoke from the back of the room. 'You said you had friends in the police, Sir Arthur – highly placed friends. We'd both like to know who they are.'

Simmonds raised his head and faced Jim. 'Why?' he said. 'Why do you want to know?'

Bob rejoined the dialogue. 'You suggested you could get some important police officers to fix things for you, Sir Arthur. You know, do your bidding. Make problems disappear. Tear up charge sheets, that sort of thing. Who are these friends of yours, Sir Arthur? You might as well tell us, because we really will find out, you know.' Bob kept his voice even, carefully avoiding any notion of triumph.

Sir Arthur remained silent.

Jim spoke again, keeping his words casual, while still leaning against the far wall. 'We would also like to know who was with you on that night in Portland, Sir Arthur. Who else is in your little group of Frugs?'

'It's not my group. I'm not the organiser, only a member.'

'All right, so who is the organiser?'

The baronet remained silent for a long time. Neither of the detectives spoke. Eventually, head hanging low once more, Sir Arthur muttered something.

'What was that, Sir Arthur?' Jim moved closer to the table and stood, waiting.

Sir Arthur waited, then said, very quietly, 'Wellton.'

'Wellton? Does he have any other names, Sir Arthur?'

'Giles de Courtney Wellton. Rural Affairs Minister.'

There was a sharp collective intake of breath from the three policemen in the room.

Bob changed tack. 'Who else was there, Sir Arthur?'

Once again the room remained silent. The interrogators waited.

'Who else, Sir Arthur?'

All the bluster, all the pomposity, all the arrogance seemed to have disappeared from Simmonds. He seemed diminished, almost physically. The policemen waited.

Chapter 27

Harry looked around at the empty street and locked his front door. The pubs had shut and the deserted street suited him well. He had slept all afternoon and into the evening, and now felt alert and refreshed. With a small lightweight rucksack slung over his left shoulder and an imitation-leather overnight bag in his right hand he walked unhurriedly along the pavement for about two hundred yards until he came to his van. He glanced around once more but there was nobody on the street and few lights behind the curtained windows.

He opened the rear doors of the van, peered briefly inside, shining his torch around, carefully checking all the contents. Then he closed and locked the doors before opening the driver's door and slipping in behind the wheel. He switched on the ignition, checked the fuel gauge, then twisted the ignition key. The engine rumbled into life but made very little noise. He looked carefully into each rear-view mirror and then pulled slowly out into the empty road. He drove up through Easton and down the hill through Fortuneswell without seeing any people or other vehicles. On the causeway road he passed a couple of taxis returning from Weymouth, but nothing else.

Within half an hour he was driving along the lonely and dark road to the north of the Armoured Brigade camp at Bovington. The road was pressed in on either side with dense woodland and a thought came suddenly to Harry, he knew not from where. Wasn't this the road on which Lawrence of Arabia had crashed and died on his motorcycle? He shivered and pushed the thought from his mind as he cut the engine and cruised to a stop in a small lay-by, almost hidden under the overhanging, whispering trees.

As the noise of the engine died away, Harry reached behind the passenger seat and pulled out a long, rectangular package wrapped in polythene. He opened the door and, moving carefully and soundlessly, he walked around to the back of the van. He quickly stripped away the polythene and pulled out a rear number plate. It was already prepared with adhesive pads so it was only a moment before the new plate was in place and Harry was doing the same at the front of the van.

He climbed back inside the vehicle and stuffed the folded polythene under the passenger seat. He stayed still, sitting in the silent, darkened van, trying to make sure that there were no witnesses to his vehicle's change of identity.

He started the engine, and as he pulled away, out onto the road once more, he allowed himself a little bit of self-congratulation. He had been extremely careful about the number plates. He actually had four sets of different and false number plates. In each case he had first visited scrapyards looking for damaged or worn-out vehicles of the same make and colour as his van. Surprisingly, he had found several suitable vehicles in each of the half dozen scrapyards he had visited. Having discreetly noted the registration numbers he had then set off to get sets of plates made. Here, he began to run into problems, because usually, proof of ownership of the vehicle which would wear the plates would be required. He managed to blag his way through one transaction, using his age and infirmity to advantage, but after this he realised that in doing so he would make himself more memorable to the seller. So he bought three sets of blank plastic plates and several sets of black letter transfers.

He was reasonably happy that he now had a total of five different identities for his van and unless the van was clocked by a number recognition camera or checked against the Vehicle

Identification Number when actually wearing the false plates, he thought his ploy would probably remain undiscovered.

It took another three hours to drive steadily north-east and it was almost 3.30 a.m. on a now chilly morning when he pulled into a short residential crescent half a mile from Wimbledon Common. Here he wedged his blue 'disabled' badge in the corner of the windscreen before climbing out from the front of the van and then awkwardly back in through the side door, where he spent the next ten minutes arranging his equipment.

The first rays of pre-dawn were just beginning to illuminate the cityscape to the east as Harry stopped his van in a small parking space, surrounded by tallish bushes and protected by a sign announcing that the place was restricted to disabled badge holders. He backed the van up fairly close to the bushes, opened the doors and disappeared inside. He dropped a sloping ramp down from the back of the van, pushed the doors shut after rolling out the wheelchair, then sat in it. The Common seemed quiet and empty as Harry propelled himself briskly along the gravelled path towards his destination. At length he arrived at the spot he had selected, where a young oak tree grew on one side of the path, opposite a stained wooden bench on the other side. He parked his wheelchair beside the bench, facing in towards the path. Quickly he pulled a coil of fishing line from a patch pocket on the side of the chair, propelled himself across the path, running the fishing line several times around the tree before leading both ends back across the path. He pulled a pair of leather gardening gloves from the same patch pocket, put them on and wrapped the ends of the fishing line around his left hand.

He backed the chair up until it was once more level with the park bench and settled down to wait, a copy of yesterday's newspaper in his right hand, hiding the end of the fishing line.

He didn't have long to wait. Half an hour later his quarry came in sight. He had intended to strike on the man's second circuit but he could see joggers and cyclists beginning to appear in various corners of the park, but fortunately, he thought to himself, not near the position he had chosen.

The slim, athletic figure came pounding along the path at an impressive pace. The man was staring ahead but occasionally glancing at an instrument strapped to his wrist. He came abreast the wheelchair containing the old man slumped over a newspaper but took no notice of him. He was still staring into the distance when Harry jerked the ends of the fishing line. The double line leapt suddenly off the path and became taut about nine inches above the gravel. Both of the runner's feet were caught instantly and the man crashed forward, slamming his body into the path. Winded, stunned and in sudden pain, he was rolling over when he felt the jab of a needle in his thigh.

Harry held the syringe doggedly until he was sure all the Ketamine had been dispensed. The body sagged as it rolled onto its back and then it dropped inert onto the gravel. Harry moved as quickly as he could. His long sessions at the gym in the clinic had strengthened his upper body, but it needed a lot of heaving and shoving before he managed to get the inert form sitting, and lolling, in the wheelchair. With some difficulty, he pulled a small black lightweight rucksack from the shoulders of his captive. He hooked the rucksack on the handle of the chair, and gave a couple of flicks on the fishing line, freeing it from both tree and bench. Harry balled it up and stuffed it in his pocket, then set off at as brisk a pace as he could manage in the direction of his van, all the while talking sympathetically to the unconscious body in front of him.

He pushed the wheelchair around to the back of the van, opened the doors and then hooked a four-sheave pulley system into the back of the chair. It was hard but the quadruple mechanical advantage produced by the pulley enabled Harry to drag the loaded wheelchair up the ramp and into the van. As soon as it was in, he fixed the wheels of the chair in the location points on the floor of the van. He pulled the two rear doors closed so he could work in private, then lashed his victim firmly into the chair before taping over his eyes with duct tape. He stretched a cloth over the man's mouth, ensuring he could still breathe, and then secured it behind the man's head with more duct tape.

Harry took a careful look around at his remaining equipment, checked that Mr Giles de Courtney Wellton was well secured in the chair, and then climbed out through the rear doors, locking them behind him, before locking the side door and climbing into the driving seat. The whole exercise had taken less than twenty minutes and Harry smiled for the first time that morning, as he drove slowly towards the entrance to the Common.

Chapter 28

The detectives sat on either side of a yellow plastic-topped table in the corner of the police station canteen furthest from the open ears behind the serving counter. Two china mugs of coffee were placed on the table top.

'We'll have to let him go, Guv.'

'I don't know. I wonder if he wants to go,' muttered Bob over the rim of his cooling mug of indifferent coffee.

'What do you mean, Guv?'

'Well, I think he is a man struggling to maintain a principled position under the enormous pressure of having once seriously injured a total stranger. In fact, he might now be thinking he's killed the man.'

'Are you going to go on letting him think that?'

Bob rubbed his chin, then took a sip from his mug, grimaced and pushed the mug away. 'Yes, I think so. Well, for the present time, anyway.'

Jim didn't answer. He knew there would be more.

'The point is,' said Bob, 'we started out by trying to find out who set about an old man, and why. But then we began to uncover other links, specifically in the police service. Who would have the clout to shut up all those coppers, to make evidence and police records disappear? In short, who could put a blanket over the whole sordid episode – and how could they do that?' He continued, not waiting for an answer. 'You're not going to make all those otherwise honest coppers go schtum just by saying they'd get a bad report. It has to be more than that. Part of it might pop up if we can push matey, the landed gent in there, a bit harder, but I don't think he's Mister Big. I don't think he's been pulling the strings. I think he's just a willing worker. He claims that he's the mystery benefactor behind Harry Chaplin's medical bills, but I don't know about that '

'Why do you say that, Guv?'

'Well, we know he tells lies and we know he's in a spot. He might have paid the bills and he did claim that, but I'll wait for the evidence to confirm it. We only have his word for it. I dunno, though. My hunch would be that he's probably telling the truth; of course he's got a position to maintain. He needs to find something to balance all the shit he's dished out – and he might feel the need to protect his family's honour. But I don't think it matters to us at the moment. It'll be more appropriate when his barrister gets to the mitigation stage.'

Jim looked pensive. 'How could a man like that, surrounded by flunkies and admirers, be forced to spend all that money, getting nothing for it, and stay in the system, so to speak?'

Bob leaned forward to pick up his mug, but then he pushed it further away. A small amount of brown liquid slopped onto the shiny table top. 'I think that's easy,' he said. 'His problem is that he knows he was involved in that horrible game, and maybe other horrible games – and he can't undo that. By luck and family connection he's climbed to the top of the slippery pole. He's inherited the family title. Like it or not he is a grandee. The hold over him, if there is one, is that a few words could bring that whole façade crashing down, and he would rot in disgrace. He knows that and he can't risk that. What he hasn't worked out, though, is that if his master blows his cover, the ripples will spread out to destroy everyone connected, including the master.'

'I see,' said Jim.

There was silence for a few moments, both men reviewing their own thoughts. After a while Bob said, 'How long has he been stewing now, Jim?'

'Forty minutes, maybe more.'

'That should be enough. We might play good cop, bad cop. You haven't upset him directly. You go in and see if you can get him to like you.'

Jim looked surprised; but all he said was, 'Okay.'

'Off you go then,' said Bob. He strolled across the room where a table held several newspapers, selected one, and plumped down in the nearest chair.

Jim walked along the corridor to the custody suite and rang the bell; and when the constable on duty – a different one this time – peered through the strengthened glass, he held up his warrant card so it could be clearly seen, and the door was opened. He followed the other policeman along the stark corridor, waited while the bolts were withdrawn and the door was opened and then strode confidently into the room.

Sir Arthur was sitting with his head in his manacled hands, his elbows resting on the table. He didn't move.

Jim took the seat on the other side of the table, waited for a long few minutes and then said, very politely, 'Sir Arthur, I think you have a problem.' He paused. 'And you don't know how to solve it. You don't even know how to start thinking about solving it.'

He was answered by an almost imperceptible nod of the head and what could have been a sigh or a sob. Jim continued, 'Here's what we think happened. I – that is, we – think that many years ago when you and your friends were all young, rich and with the world at your feet, you went out looking for kicks. Alcohol, drugs; they make people do strange things. Things they wouldn't do in normal life and, of course, as they get older, things they might want to forget.

'But say they can't forget, or maybe they aren't allowed to forget. I'll be straight with you, Sir Arthur: somebody with a great deal of influence in all sorts of quarters seems to have been able to hush up, to draw a cloak over some terrible things that happened, and,' he paused for emphasis once more, 'terrible, disgraceful, things that involved you, Sir Arthur.'

As he stopped speaking, the man in front of him collapsed onto the desk and started sobbing. 'Who is the boss, Sir Arthur?' said Jim, as gently as he could. 'Tell me who arranged this massive and dreadful cover-up of an attempt to destroy an innocent man's life. Who is he, Sir Arthur? You know you can't continue with this; you know you have to tell somebody. Tell me, Sir Arthur.'

The sobbing wreck of the man lying face down on the desk did not respond. All of the pomposity, the arrogance, and the haughty pride seemed to have drained away.

Jim waited. The silence in the room was broken only by the pathetic sobbing and sniffling of the man opposite. After perhaps four or five minutes Jim turned his head towards the constable, still standing inside the door, a look of shock now replacing the former blank expression on his face. 'Get him a cup of hot sweet tea, will you, and quickly please.'

Jim turned back towards the table. 'Sir Arthur,' he said. There was no response. He tried again. 'Sir Arthur, look at me please. You know that you need your lawyer here so you will need to tell us his name. Do you understand? Will you at least tell me his name?'

Sir Arthur looked up slowly. His eyes were red and the tear tracks running down each side of his face seemed to dominate his other features. He nodded once. Very quietly, he muttered, 'Grayson. Grayson-Cummings.'

Jim was about to speak when the door was pushed open and the constable returned with a small metal tray holding a white china mug and a blue plastic plate carrying several digestive biscuits. Jim motioned with his head and the tray was placed carefully on the table in front of Sir Arthur.

'Drink the tea; it'll make you feel better.'

When Simmonds spoke it was barely a whisper. 'I'll never feel better,' he said. He reached for the tea, then stopped as the door opened again. Bob stepped into the room and moved over to the wall to stand near the constable. He waited a few minutes, while Simmonds reached once more for the tea; then he said, 'I think you probably want to get all this out in the open,' he paused, 'Sir Arthur.'

Chapter 29

Harry drove steadily and unhurriedly towards the South West. At first he followed the busy M3 motorway through mile after mile of roadworks, and then, just after the road became clear, he turned off onto the A303, heading towards Salisbury.

It was still very early. The morning commuter traffic had not yet built up, and what there was of it was going the other way. After another mile or two Harry turned off the main road and started along the quieter country roads. There was no sign of movement from the back of the van so after another twenty minutes he pulled off into a lengthy lay-by, conveniently surrounded and shielded from the road by trees and thick bushes of rhododendrons. He sat still for a few minutes, checking carefully ahead, to the sides and through the rear-view mirrors. When confident that he was alone he climbed stiffly out of the van, looked around again, then eased the side door open a few inches.

His captive had moved over to one side of the wheelchair and was beginning to twitch and move. Harry pondered for a few seconds, then decided to give his prisoner another small shot of ketamine. Wellton groaned as the needle went into his thigh but then stopped moving and flopped forward. Harry wondered if he had killed him but quickly reached the conclusion that he wasn't really bothered if he had.

He slid the side door shut as quietly as he could, locked it and climbed back into the driving seat. After another methodical check on his surroundings he started the engine and drove back onto the road. He continued heading south-west, keeping to minor roads where he could, and so the sun was well up and warming the day by the time he reached his destination, a barn on the remote edge of a farm about two miles to the west of the small village of King's Stag.

Harry stopped the van in front of the barn and peered around once again from the driving seat before climbing out and taking a bunch of keys from his pocket. He unlocked two padlocks securing the tall double doors of the barn, pulled them open, walked back to the van and drove in. As soon as the vehicle was inside the barn, he switched off the engine and sat still, listening. After several minutes of silence he climbed out of the van and then, working quickly and with only a little noise, he dragged the big doors shut and locked them from the inside.

He opened the back doors of the van, set the ramp in position, removed the securing clamps holding the wheels of the chair and rolled it down the ramp and round to the side of the van. The occupant was breathing with short shallow breaths but was unmoving and, very obviously, deeply drugged.

Harry pulled open the side door of the van, reached inside, fiddled about in a wooden toolbox and took out a roll of black plastic-backed adhesive tape. With this he proceeded to bind the arms and legs of his comatose victim securely to the arms and sides of the wheelchair. Then he climbed back into the driving seat of the van and settled down to wait.

It took a long time for the drug to wear off and every twenty minutes or so Harry climbed out of the van to check that Wellton was still breathing. Several hours passed before Wellton began to show signs of movement. The afternoon had turned to evening and then to night. It was very dark inside the barn although outside, a nearly full moon had risen to dominate an otherwise clear sky. There was just enough light filtering through the few gaps between the planking of the walls and roof to allow Harry, whose eyes had gradually become accustomed to the failing light, to see the shadows of the van, his captive and the few boxes and bales lying about. He continued to wait in silence, now sitting on a wooden box only a foot from the wretched creature tied into the chair. He was searching through the contents of the small rucksack that Wellton had been carrying on his back. Harry had opened the rear doors of the van, shielding the dim light set in the roof of the vehicle from the man in the wheelchair. He had spread out the contents of the rucksack in a line across the floor of the van. There was a wallet, an iPod, a miniature packet of tissues, a silver Parker ballpoint pen, two unused handkerchiefs, a combined diary and address book and, curiously, two expensive looking mobile phones. One of these seemed to be the latest type of digital phone; however, the other was an older design but nevertheless a rather 'up-market' type.

Harry held the older phone in his hand and started to fiddle with it, pressing buttons at random. Suddenly, the screen lit up accompanied by a little jingle of musical notes. He recalled the advice he had been recently given when he was buying his own phone at PC World. He had been advised that he should devise his own four-digit access code and shown how to apply it. There was no such code applied to this phone and Harry was soon able to look through the lists of recent calls made and received on this instrument. Helpfully, as he highlighted each incoming call, a small coloured photograph of the sender appeared on the screen, with the sender's name printed beneath it. Over the past five days there were eleven outgoing calls listed to two women. Eight had been made to Sandra Somerville, who Harry presumed to be the Wimbledon tennis star and Wellton's latest girlfriend. The other three were to a woman, unknown to Harry, called Jane Lockyer. The accompanying head and shoulders photograph showed a face with attractively high cheekbones, pouting red lips and wide blue eyes framed with a waterfall of luxuriant blonde hair. The list of received calls included only four from the two women – three from Sandra Somerville and one from Jane Lockyer. The duration of the outgoing calls seemed to be somewhat longer than the incoming ones.

Harry left the phone switched on and placed it carefully to one side, picking up the wallet as he did so. He examined the outside of the wallet, peering closely at it in the dim light. It was made of very fine light- brown leather, embossed in the bottom right hand corner with the initials GDCW. Designed to hold unfolded currency notes in one side and provided with a range of compartments filled with various cards on the other side, it looked every bit the property of a wealthy man.

Harry glanced furtively around the door of the van towards his prisoner, satisfying himself that there was still no sign of recovery, before turning back to the wallet. Working separately on each side, he extracted the money, laying it on the floor of the van; then he removed everything else, setting down each item in a row next to the money. In addition to over six hundred pounds in mostly high denomination notes, he was looking at two photographs, a parliamentary identity and access card, an Oyster card – interestingly in the name of William James – and seven rather impressive-looking credit cards, two of which were also in the name of William James. Each card seemed to have been issued by a different bank.

Harry found the last item tucked behind one of the credit cards, the most interesting of all the paraphernalia in front of him. It was a single sheet of pink paper, folded in four. He opened it out and stared at it. It had a series of letters and numbers written in black ink – nothing else. He peered at the first four letters for some time, his hand trembling as he held the scrap of paper. The letters were FRUG. This was followed by B.Hd N.For. 2891830 JS.

As he stared at the word FRUG, the dreams came rushing back through Harry's brain. This was the final proof he needed and he knew that now he had his chief tormentor completely under his control, only a few feet from him. He puzzled for a while over the remainder of the letters and numbers on the paper but then he heard a groan from the other side of the van. Harry scooped up the money and shoved it into his pocket, put the credit and identity cards untidily back into the compartments of the wallet and then turned to study the photographs.

The first photo was in colour and showed an attractive dark-haired, long-legged, slim and sensuous-looking girl facing the camera and staring boldly towards the photographer. She had a lean, fit, tanned and highly toned body. She was indeed a striking beauty. All of this was easy to see because the full frontal photograph showed her stark naked. The name 'Sandy' was scrawled in red ink across the bottom of the picture. The second picture was of a different woman – a blonde this time. The photograph was in black and white and seemed more faded and frayed on the edges. The subject of this picture was wearing more – but not much more – than the other one. She was wearing only a tiny pair of briefs and seemed to be in the act of removing a matching bra. One and a half ample breasts could be seen leaning forward and once again she was facing the camera, but this time pouting with lips opened provocatively towards the photographer. This photograph was unsigned but Harry could just discern the initials JL written very faintly on the back. He slipped both photographs into his pocket.

Eventually, Wellton began to stir. He started to moan, then to move his head slowly from side to side and a little later to attempt to move his hands and feet. The thick rolls of tape held firm. Harry closed the doors of the van and moved around to stare at the figure secured in the chair in front of him. What he saw pleased and revolted him at the same time. Wellton's face was caked in a mask of dried blood from a wound on his forehead caused when he had struck the gravel path in the park. His running vest and tracksuit trousers were torn and dirty and he was far from the cocky, debonair government minister and playboy of only a few hours previously.

This suited Harry very well. He craned forward towards the wheelchair and confirmed that the eyes were now open and trying to look through the dried blood. Wellton moaned, 'Is anybody there?' There was no answer. The next words came out almost as a sob: 'Help! Help me, please! I know somebody's there.'

Harry allowed his feet to scrape on the concrete floor. There was an immediate response. 'Oh, please, oh, please help me!' It was now a long drawn-out wail and was followed by a pause, then, 'I'll pay you if you help me.'

Harry got up from his box, not bothering to hide the noise he made. He walked around behind the wheelchair and picked his way across the cluttered floor to the back wall of the barn. He lifted a small flashlight from the top of an old galvanised water tank and pointed it at the wall, illuminating a plastic bucket filled with water. He picked up the bucket and, playing the beam of light on the floor, he returned towards the bound figure in the wheelchair. The bloodied head craned around to try to see him. As it did so Harry threw half the contents of the bucket into Wellton's face. The head jerked backwards as

Harry placed the bucket on the ground, while shining his flashlight into the eyes of his captive.

Then Harry spoke. 'I am going to ask you some simple questions and I want answers from you right now! Do you understand me?' There was no answer so Harry repeated his demand. Again there was no answer so Harry pushed a foot forward, hooking it under the front bar of the wheelchair and shoving it hard. The wheelchair tipped over backwards crashing down onto the concrete. The high back of the chair saved its occupant from a fractured skull, but the shock of the sudden backward fall produced a high-pitched scream from the man.

Harry moved to the side of the van and rummaged about inside the toolbox once more. He brought out a big pair of pliers and moved towards Wellton's feet, now conveniently fluttering three feet above the concrete floor. 'Oh God, oh shit, what are you doing?' This cry was laced through with fear, although Harry wasn't yet doing anything. Harry said nothing as he moved forward and swiftly removed the running shoe and sock from the foot in front of him. He rested the cold steel pliers on top of the naked foot and then, carefully enunciating his words, he spoke.

'You came to Weymouth, in the summer,' he said. 'You came with your friends and you wanted some fun, some thrills, so you decided to kill an old man. I just want to know the names of your friends.'

'Fuck off!' At last, noted Harry, Wellton was showing some spirit, but it wouldn't last, he thought.

Harry grasped the naked, cold, clammy, left foot in his hand and deftly fitted the jaws of the pliers around the big toe. The foot wriggled and the pliers slipped. Harry hefted the pliers in his hand and brought them down hard across the row of toes.

With his other hand he dropped a burlap sack across Wellton's face, muffling but not quite drowning the long scream of pain from the man. Harry shone the torch on him, noting an expanding dark patch spreading over the man's tracksuit trousers. Harry picked up the roll of adhesive tape and ripped off a longish strip which he used to loosely fix the sacking to the back of the man's head and to the chair headrest.

He stepped away from the chair for a moment and directed the beam of the torch towards his victim, checking that the tapes around the hands and feet were still secure. Then he shone the torch on the naked left foot; it was bleeding and some of the toes looked broken. 'You may be wondering why I am so interested in your foot,' he said, very quietly and gently. 'You see, that is the weapon I think you used most effectively to attack your victim. By the way, do you know what happened to him? No, I suppose you don't.' He finished by answering his own question. Wellton was whimpering under his mask of sacking.

Harry placed his torch on the ground so that it pointed towards the toppled wheelchair, picked up the pliers in one hand and took the foot in the other. He allowed the pliers to rest across the broken toes which attempted to jerk away from his touch. Then he started his questions.

'I think you had ten friends with you,' he said. 'Two of them were women. Let's start with them. What are their names?'

There was no answer, only more whimpering. Hardly seeming to move, Harry swiftly grabbed the big toe in the jaws of the pliers and began to squeeze. The whimper turned to a scream, slightly muffled this time, as the head under the sacking tried to twist left and right. 'I'm not a very patient man,' said Harry. 'If I don't get two answers in the next minute, I will remove these toes one by one – all of them –

with the pliers. I imagine that will hurt you, but of course you will never walk again, either.' For emphasis, he caught the smallest toe with the pliers but without closing the jaws. It worked.

The demented voice from under the sacking started talking. 'Sandra,' it said, then 'Jane, yes, Jane, Jane.' The voice subsided into sobbing and whimpering once more.

'Well, that's okay as far as it goes, but I need to know their full names, don't I?' Harry continued to hold the toe with the pliers.

'Sandra Somerville. Jane Lockyer.' The words faded away into whimpering and moaning once more.

'Gosh, do you mean Jane Lockyer the actress?' said Harry, with feigned surprise. 'So where will I find these two ladies?'

'I, I, oh, I don't...' The attempt to speak ended in another scream as the pliers tightened on the toe. Blood spurted from it.

'I'm getting annoyed now,' said Harry. 'Two addresses, please; and then, I think, another name; or maybe,' he paused again, 'you might like to give me all the rest of the names, at least another seven, I think. It will save you a lot of pain.'

The noises from the floor were indecipherable. Harry leaned down until his head was only just above the sack-covered lump on the floor. 'You see,' he said, pleasantly and gently, 'I know I am asking a lot from you but I can take it a bit at a time and work my way through all the toes on both feet; then there's your teeth.' He emphasised this by tapping the pliers on the sack above where he thought the teeth were. At this point, Wellton gave a great compulsive shiver and passed out. Harry stepped back, gave the body a couple of pokes with his foot and then reached across to where the half-filled bucket stood. He picked it up and threw the contents with as much force as he could muster at the sacking covering the face on the floor. It did the trick. The whole body started to move and wriggle and Wellton started moaning again.

Harry sat on his box once more and waited in silence for another ten minutes. Then he leaned forward and said, 'Can you hear me, Wellton?' There was no reply other than the continued whimpering and moaning. He tried again. 'Can you hear me, Wellton?'

This time there was a grunt in reply, followed, after another space, by a very faint 'yes.'

'Good,' said Harry, speaking briskly now. 'You will want to get this over as quickly as you can, I think. Is that right?' There was a barely perceptible nod from the sack-covered face.

Harry continued speaking, now adopting a very matter-of-fact tone. 'The thing is,' he said, 'pain is always worse when you can't touch the injured area, and the shock is greater when you can't see it. Would you agree, Mr Wellton? Of course, I would have to respect your opinions in these matters, because you are becoming something of an expert. Let's see, maybe I should have another go, start on the other foot, perhaps.' As he was speaking he started to untie and remove the running shoe from the right foot.

This produced a reaction. 'No, no, no, no, no! Oh, please! No, no! I beg you, I'll tell you everything. Everything you want to know. Oh, God, oh, God, please don't hurt me anymore.'

'What, like this, you mean?' The pliers began to close on the big toe of the right foot.

'Oh, God help me!' screamed Wellton.

'Well, he might not,' responded Harry gently, at the same time allowing the jaws of the pliers to move around the captive toe. 'He knows what you've done, you see. You might be beyond help now.'

'Oh, please, please,' wailed the sweaty blood-stained form in the upturned wheelchair. 'I'll do anything, say anything, anything you want. But please don't hurt me again.'

Harry knew he had won. He leaned towards his victim and said, quietly and gently again, 'All right, Wellton. I'm soft, you see. So I'll give you one last chance. I want everything, mind. Everything you know. If you hold back or you don't answer truthfully I will start again; but it will be on the other foot this time. Do we understand each other?' The sacking nodded fervently, twice.

'Right,' said Harry. 'Let's start with an easy one. Frug. What does Frug mean?' At first he thought he wasn't going to get an answer, but then the sacking moved.

'Who are you?' it said. In response, Harry brought the pliers down hard on the damaged left foot. 'I told you,' he said, this time slamming out every word separately, like spaced gunshots. He moved the pliers so the jaws were wrapped around the second toe of the right foot and began slowly to squeeze. It opened the floodgates. Words came pouring out.

'It means Free Running Undergraduates. Don't, please don't!'

'Shut up!' snarled Harry. 'When I say so, you tell me again what Frug means, who is in it and the name and address of every member who came to Weymouth with you. Got it?' As he spoke he stood up quietly and moved across to the open door of the van, where he reached in with one hand, shining his torch with the other, while he switched on a small battery-powered digital recorder. 'Start talking,' he said, 'and don't stop till I tell you.' The sacking nodded once more.

'Frug means Free Running Undergraduates. It's just a name. We got together in a crammer before we went to university. We started meeting and just free running – running and jumping at obstacles and things. Then we became a dining club. We would get dressed up and go out to dinner, spending a lot of money and getting drunk. Most of the places we went to didn't care so long as we paid for the damages and spent a lot. To be a member you have to have a lot of money and spend it. We look for kicks, maybe do a bit of H or a bit of C and get high.' All this was gasped out through sobs of pain.

The flow of words stopped abruptly, to be replaced by the noise of breath rasping through a contorted throat.

Harry swung the bucket so that it hit the side of the sack-covered head. 'Go on!' he said. 'I didn't tell you to stop, did I? What happened in Weymouth?'

'Nothing! Nothing at all! Nothing.' The voice was pleading now.

Harry didn't answer. He just stood, staring through the gloom towards the hooded face, while anger began to boil inside him.

Eventually he spoke. 'If you tell me lies I will really hurt you. I won't stop and when I have finished I will throw what is left of your shitty carcass into the sea. No-one will ever know where you have gone.' As he finished speaking, Harry tapped the exposed left ankle with the pliers.

There was another muffled scream, then, 'Oh God, why are you doing this to me?'

'I think you can work it out, Mr Wellton. You see, I know what you did. Now you have to wonder why or how I know what you did. Come on, tell me what you did when you and your friends visited Weymouth – and Portland, of course.'

'Oh no. It can't be. You can't be the man we...' The quavering voice tailed off. Harry remained silent, waiting. He seated himself once more on the wooden box and looked through the torchlight at the bedraggled, stained, bloodied figure in front of him.

At last, Harry responded. 'The man you what?' he said.

Wellton started snorting and sobbing under his hood. Harry walked away to the far side of the barn and leaned against the wall. Then after a while he called out, 'Do you mean the man you killed?'

Harry could see little across the width of the barn. 'You set out to kill a man. I know that. You wanted the ultimate in thrills. Isn't that so, you disgusting piece of shit?' He took a deep breath, switched on his torch and followed the beam across the barn, stopping in front of his broken, cringing, sodden, slobbering victim. 'Now,' he said, 'we start again. Now you know that I know, but I want to hear it from you. If you get it right, you might live. If you don't, you won't. So talk.'

Wellton started talking, slowly and hesitantly, but he seemed to realise that the stakes were now as high as they could be. He spilled out the whole story while Harry sat on his box patiently listening, occasionally leaning back to check that the recorder was still running.

'When we came to Weymouth we decided to do a snuff job – for kicks. It wasn't meant to go all the way but it got a bit out of control. There were ten of us that time. As well as me, there was Arthur Simmonds and Henry Hayward, Ray Marsden and Cornel Grovey, Jeremy Wilberforce and Don Randell.' At that point he dried up.

'That's not all. Give me the rest. All of them!' Harry shouted at the sweaty, smelly, wet sacking and placed the pliers against the top of the left foot.

'No, no! There was Roger FitzHarris.'

'There were women. Who were they?'

'You know that. I told you, Sandra Somerville and Jane Lockyer.'

'How often and where do you meet?'

'Not often now. Maybe once or twice a year...' The voice tailed off, overtaken by moaning and sobbing as the pain from his broken foot surged up again.

'Where?' This was accompanied by another prod to the foot.

'We choose a hotel or a restaurant in a small town or in the countryside.'

'How do you call a meeting?'

There was a long pause, then: 'An ad in the personal column of the Telegraph. It just says 'Frug' and gives the date and postcode.'

'Thank you,' said Harry. He got up and stood by the recorder. Then he said, 'One more thing. Who is the leader?' There was an even longer delay before the answer came, this time in a trembling whisper: 'Sandra.' Harry waited, deep in thought for a few moments, then he switched off the recorder. Harry walked around to the other side of the van, opened the left door and leaned in. As he did so the internal lights came on, casting a weak glow around the cab of the vehicle and causing an even fainter light to spill out onto the concrete floor of the barn. He pulled the keys from the ignition and fitted one into the lock on the glove compartment. Another small light came on, conveniently illuminating a black plastic washing bag. Harry unzipped the bag, fiddled inside and produced a bottle containing the solution of ketamine together with another syringe with the needle already in place. Without speaking, he stepped back, propped himself against the passenger seat and carefully pushed the needle through the seal on the bottle. When the syringe was full, he held it up so he could see it against the light, and squirted some liquid into the air, just as he had seen on TV hospital programmes. Firmly holding the syringe pointing upward he strolled back to the upturned wheelchair and jammed the syringe through the thin tracksuit trousers and into Wellton's thigh. There was a short gasp from under the sacking hood and almost immediately the body became limp.

Harry stood looking down at the limp form with arms and legs dangling outward from the chair. He leaned down, and with some difficulty tipped the chair back onto its wheels. The body flopped to one side and Harry wondered if he had killed his tormentor. Then he realised once more that he didn't really care.

He walked across to the entrance of the barn, opened a small wicket-door and stepped outside. He stood still, peering into the darkness and listening. At length, when he was satisfied that there was no-one near the isolated building, he stepped back inside, lowered the ramp from the back of the van, and using the winch he had installed, dragged the wheelchair back into the vehicle and secured it with the floor clamps. Then he opened the main door of the barn and backed the van out while keeping the lights off. He stepped out, closed and locked the barn door, and drove off, heading roughly south towards Wareham.

Chapter 30

The two detectives watched Sir Arthur Simmonds drinking his tea. All the bluster had gone from the man. There were drying tear lines on his cheeks and his hands were shaking as he cupped them around the thick china mug. He stared at the floor; and to Bob, he even seemed diminished in size. The detective had seen this happen in previous cases, but he also knew that sometimes the collapse of all resistance, such as had now occurred, could very easily be reversed, and so he decided to frame his questions with great care and move cautiously in continuing to garner the information he needed. Meanwhile, Bob decided to back off for a while, allowing his prisoner to compose himself.

They waited for another hour, completing the paperwork generated by the arrest and by the need to transfer their prisoner to Weymouth. Sir Arthur Simmonds drank strong tea and awaited the arrival of his solicitor.

When the turgid form-filling was finally complete and signatures of approval inserted, Bob walked back into the interview room. Sir Arthur continued to sip his tea as Bob sat down and moved his chair closer to the other side of the table. Then leaning forward until his head was only inches from Sir Arthur's he started to speak, very gently and so quietly as to be almost inaudible to the others in the room.

'I'm not going to ask you to say anything more until your solicitor arrives,' he said, 'but I need to tell you now that the evidence against you and others is mounting. We also know that there was an attempt to cover up at least two crimes…' Sir Arthur's head jerked up and his mouth opened as though to speak, as this registered. Bob ploughed on: '…and we believe that you may have funded the extensive medical care that was necessary to help your victim to recover. That might help you when this comes to trial but it might also serve to tie you in to the crime…'

At the mention of the word 'crime' Simmonds made to speak again but decided quickly against doing so. He sat, unmoving, head bowed, his mouth clamped shut.

At length, he raised his head again and started to speak, but Bob stopped him with a raised hand. 'Not now, Sir Arthur,' he said. 'In fairness to you I want your own lawyer present when we continue the interview. Do you understand that?'

This was answered with a single nod of the head. Bob moved his chair back, stood up and told the constable to fetch more tea. 'And make it hot,' he said, 'so it will last.'

They continued to wait, sitting around the uncomfortable room, until the door was opened and a woman officer came in, went straight to Bob and spoke very quietly close to his ear. He listened, nodded and then she left.

Speaking to no-one in particular, Bob announced, 'The solicitor has arrived.' Sir Arthur looked up sharply as the detective scraped his chair back, stood, and went to the door, shutting it quietly behind him.

The lawyer was waiting, looking aggrieved and impatient, in the reception area at the front of the station. He was a tall man, just over six feet, Bob thought. He was wearing a dark grey pinstripe three piece suit which appeared to be the product of a very expensive tailor; and both of his hands were occupied, one carrying a small brown attaché case and the other leaning on a tightly furled black umbrella. His height and upright bearing as well as his well-coiffured, thick silvery hair and small grey military moustache gave him, as it was carefully designed to do, an air of authority and of a man who would suffer no fools, gladly or otherwise.

Bob marched straight up to the lawyer, thrust out his hand and asked, 'Mr Camborne?'

The lawyer placed his attaché case on the bench lining the wall behind him and they shook hands perfunctorily. 'Charles Grayson-Cummings,' he said. Magically, a silver-edged business card appeared in his hand which he flourished towards Bob.

As Bob glanced at the card, Grayson-Cummings started to speak. 'Now, what is all this nonsense about? Do you realise who you have in there? You've made a blunder which will cost you dearly. One of the most important men in the county! Now, I want this cleared up immediately. I wish to speak to a senior officer – now!' All this came out in one long angry blast directed at Bob and accompanied by a penetrating scowl that, according to Jim, 'could peel paint'.

Bob ignored the outburst and replied in an even voice. 'If you will follow me, Mr Cummings, I will explain why you are here and why your client is here.' He turned on his heel and strode back towards the internal door, pressed a code into the keypad and strode through, holding the door open for the lawyer to follow. Jim, who had followed his boss into reception, fell in behind and followed the lawyer down the corridor.

Bob stopped by another interview room he was using as a temporary office, held the door open and they all trooped in. Bob indicated a chair on one side of the table and dropped easily into a chair on the opposite side. Jim closed the door and sat beside him.

Adopting a rather formal tone while peering directly across the table, Bob said, 'Mr Cummings, are you the legal representative for Sir Arthur Simmonds?'

The lawyer gave a single curt nod and said, with lips hardly moving, 'I am, yes. My name is Grayson-Cummings.'

'Thank you. Then I am obliged to inform you that your client, Sir Arthur Simmonds, is likely to be charged in relation to a serious offence which I am investigating. Additionally, you asked to speak to a senior officer. I am a senior officer. I am Detective Chief Inspector Robert Majury of the Dorset Police.' As he finished speaking, he leaned across and placed his police 'business card' carefully on the table in front of the lawyer.

'What charge?' snapped Grayson-Cummings.

'He hasn't been charged yet; we are still interviewing him under caution. But the charges he may be facing include grievous bodily harm, conspiracy, attempted manslaughter, perverting the course of justice, conspiracy to commit murder, perjury, bribing a public official, affray, wilful damage, dangerous driving, animal cruelty – oh, and failing to report a serious accident. There may be others.'

Both men sat in silence for a few moments, before Grayson-Cummings, now somewhat deflated, asked, 'Can you tell me a little more? The circumstances leading to this, I mean?'

'I think it would be appropriate for you now to come with us and listen while we continue to question your client, who, incidentally, seems willing to co-operate with us.' As he spoke, Bob rose from his chair and moved towards the door. Grayson-Cummings opened his mouth to speak, then stood up, noisily shoving his chair back, and mutely following the detective out into the corridor. Jim brought up the rear once more, closing the interview room door behind him.

Moments later, as they entered the other interview room, Bob noticed that additional chairs had appeared from somewhere. Grayson-Cummings moved around to the other side of the table, placed a chair close beside his client and sat in it. The two detectives seated themselves at the opposite side of the table. Jim leaned forward and pressed buttons on a small recording machine which had now been placed on the table.

'Sir Arthur,' said Bob, 'we are now going to start a formal interview with you. You have not yet been charged with any offence but I must tell you that it is likely you will be charged. Do you understand that?'

Sir Arthur nodded but didn't speak.

'You have already been cautioned, but for the record I am going to ask Detective Sergeant Creasy to read the caution again.' Jim stood up, moved to the middle of the room facing Sir Arthur, and slowly read the standard police caution from a clipboard, while Bob started the recorder.

Bob watched Sir Arthur's face intently as the caution was read. 'Do you understand that, Sir Arthur?' he said.

Again, Sir Arthur nodded. Grayson-Cummings cleared his throat. 'I demand to know what charges my client is facing,' he snapped, speaking towards the senior detective.

Bob leaned forward and pressed a button on the recorder, pausing the recording. 'I have already explained to you that our investigation is continuing and that your client may face a number of charges but no charges will be proffered until this interview is concluded.'

Grayson-Cummings looked uncomfortable, shifted on his chair and then had a bright idea. 'Has my client been given any refreshments?' he demanded. 'Has he been allowed a comfort break?'

In answer, Bob turned towards Simmonds and asked, 'Do you need anything to eat, Sir Arthur?'

'No.' The answer was barely audible.

'Do you want another glass of water, cup of tea, coffee?'

'No.' Again, the response was very quiet.

'Do you need to go to the loo, have a comfort break?'

This time Simmonds merely shook his head.

Bob switched on the recorder and said, rather formally 'Can you confirm that you are Sir Arthur Simmonds?'

'My name is Arthur George Simmonds.'

'Of Clayford House, Dorset?'

'That is my home.'

'Very well, Sir Arthur,' said Bob, adopting a quiet, almost friendly tone. 'We are investigating certain events which took place in and around Weymouth and Portland in July 2010. Can you tell me where you were between the fifteenth of July and the twenty-first of July of that year?'

'That is preposterous. How can you expect anyone to know exactly where they were six years ago?' The interruption came from the lawyer. Grayson-Cummings looked pleased with himself and allowed a brief smirk to pass over his face as he settled himself back in his chair. Everyone ignored him, while Bob peered towards Sir Arthur, waiting for his answer.

'I think I went to Weymouth.'

'What did you do there?'

'We were celebrating.'

'What were you celebrating?'

As his boss was speaking, Jim noticed a brief look of uncertainty flit across the face of the lawyer.

'Nothing much, really. End of term, I suppose.'

'Who is "we", Sir Arthur? Who were you celebrating with?'

'Friends. Just friends.'

Bob paused before putting his next question. 'Were they just friends, Sir Arthur? Or were you all a sort of club? A dining club, maybe?'

Sir Arthur didn't answer.

Pompously, Grayson-Cummings leapt into the vacant space. 'My client refuses to answer such a question. It is impertinent to question a baronet in this insolent manner.'

Bob ignored the outburst and, leaning further across the table towards Sir Arthur, he continued, 'What does the word 'Frug' mean, Sir Arthur?'

Again there was no answer.

'My client declines to answer!'

Bob turned towards the lawyer, fixing him with a withering stare. 'I know,' he said. 'I noticed.'

He turned once more to face the baronet, who now seemed a small shadow of his former self, his presence, dignity and self-regard all much reduced. Bob took a deep breath and slowly exhaled, while never taking his eyes from his quarry, and spoke again, quietly but spacing out his words this time. 'What does 'Frug' mean, Sir Arthur? Why did you and your friends shout that word? Was it a sort of war cry? Did it psych you up?'

Sir Arthur immediately began to look agitated. He turned his head rapidly from one side to the other. His forearms pumped against his thighs, then he lifted closed fists and pressed them forcefully on the table. He moved his hands together, weaving them and pressing them one against the other. All the while, his breathing was accelerating, his mouth was moving and his face was twisting into an agony of anguished expressions. Jim believed the man was at breaking point. Bob continued to stare impassively across the desk, allowing the silence to stretch, waiting for an answer. He darted a glance towards the lawyer, who was also staring at his client, expressions of shock, outrage, surprise and horror chasing each other across his face in quick succession.

Eventually Sir Arthur spoke, his voice hoarse with emotion. 'It means...' He swallowed several times. 'It means Free Running Undergraduates.' He flopped back against his chair, exhausted and trembling slightly.

The lawyer looked as if he wanted to say something, but couldn't think what.

Bob continued to speak, again adopting the quiet and soothing tone he had used previously. 'Sir Arthur,' he said, 'I can understand that this is very upsetting for you. You are implicated in a serious crime but I know that you have taken various actions that seem to be intended to undo the damage you have done. That damage might have been caused by foolish youthfulness. We know that you were not alone and I think that you were not the ringleader. There are others, probably nine or ten – but none of them seem to have shown remorse, as you have, for what they have done. I even wonder whether you really knew what you were getting into when you came all the way down to Weymouth, to let off steam, you thought, I imagine. But it wasn't like that, was it? Somebody in your little group intended to turn high-spirited adventure into something really evil. And you got caught up in it. Am I right?'

The room remained silent again, disturbed only by the laboured breathing of the damaged aristocrat and the occasional scrape of a chair. Jim glanced, surreptitiously, across at his boss. A master, he thought. A real master.

The silence ran on. In a distant part of the police station a phone jangled, then another; then the silence took charge once more. It seemed to become a force locking the occupants of the room into immobility.

Then Sir Arthur looked up, for the first time facing the unblinking stare of the detective in front of him. 'Yes.' He spoke quietly, his body sagging in his chair, looking even smaller to the other men in the room, but with a difference now. He seemed suddenly calm, and, thought Jim, resigned.

'Yes,' he said again, 'yes, that's right. You are right!' The last three words were barked out, almost as though the speaker was trying to spit them away from him.

'Arthur, don't say any more.' Grayson-Cummings spoke earnestly to his client, but he was stopped by a raised hand.

'Just shut up, Charles,' Sir Arthur said, hand still raised. 'Shut up while I expunge my conscience. I need the relief.'

The lawyer looked aggrieved, but he didn't persist.

Bob spoke again. 'Who was with you, Sir Arthur?' he said. 'How many were there? Can you remember?'

Sir Arthur Simmonds was slowly regaining his composure. 'I'll tell you everything,' he said. 'There were ten of us altogether. Wellton was the leader. He's a shit, an absolute irredeemable shit. He was the one with the ideas. The others were impressed by him; they were swayed by him, particularly the women. He was screwing both of them I think…'

Chapter 31

Harry drove slowly into the silent riverside town of Wareham, concentrating on making sure his careful driving was not going to excite interest from anyone who happened to be about in the early morning hours. He drove on dipped headlights until the start of the riverside track that led out from the eastern side of the town. After the first hundred yards of bumping along the gravel-covered track, Harry had to stop to open a gate that led away from the cultivated fields onto a narrower and rougher track between tall reeds with occasional glimpses of the river to his right.

Once he had driven the van through, he closed the gate silently behind him, switched off his headlights and set off, driving very slowly, along the puddled and muddy track. The moon was now low in the sky to the west, behind the van, and although the nearly full moon was still producing a lot of light, it was casting the moon-shadow of the van in front of him, making it even more difficult to see where he was going. He began to worry about losing his direction where the track followed one of the numerous bends of the river and he feared plunging helplessly into the stream.

After half an hour he gave up, stopped the van, got out and rummaged about in the back, emerging some minutes later with his roll of black adhesive tape. He applied the tape in strips to each headlight, leaving a thin slit for some light to emerge. Then he climbed back into the van, switched off all the lights and waited, willing his night vision to improve. He waited fifteen minutes before switching on the dipped headlights once more and moving off at a walking pace along the track.

The ploy worked. Within a further ten minutes he was alongside the wooden planking which formed a rustic jetty for his boat. He got out once more, checked behind the van, and backed it into his parking space among the reeds, leaving sufficient space to be able to open the rear doors. Harry then walked across to the boat, up the two planks that formed a gangway and onto the deck of the elderly vessel. He checked that nothing seemed to have been disturbed, then started the process of transferring his captive to the boat. It took nearly an hour and Harry was exhausted by the time he had finished. He had to pull the flopping body out of the wheelchair, drag it from the reeds to the boat, up the planks to the side deck, then aft to the entrance of a storage space near the stern. He opened the door and tumbled the inert form down the short ladder into the darkened space below. After that he went back to the van, folded the wheelchair, brought it on board and set it up in the store. Once there he struggled and heaved the heavy body back into the chair, tying it securely in position again with the black plastic adhesive tape. He noticed that there was more blood around the body, probably from its unrestrained progress down the ladder into its waterborne cell. He smiled and went forward, where he flopped down on the long saloon berth and fell asleep almost immediately.

In the lightless compartment at the stern of the boat, Wellton remained unconscious for most of the rest of that night, stirring only occasionally as the fresh pain from his smashed nose and broken ribs burst through his subconscious ketamine-induced coma.

Harry woke late, rolled off his makeshift bunk and peered through the crazed polycarbonate window. He could just make out a grey overcast sky with sheets of rain hammering into the surface of the river.

He switched the cabin light on, noted that it was fairly dim, switched it off and started one of the engines. After turning over noisily for about fifteen seconds the engine burst into life, celebrating with an impressive column of black smoke from the transom-mounted exhausts.

Harry stepped across towards the galley, filled a kettle and put it on the gas stove. Then he switched on the diesel cabin heater, shivering as he did so.

When he had poured his tea, he started to go through the wallet and other items that had once been the property of Giles Wellton. Most of it was not very interesting, although since Mr Wellton had been thoughtful enough to write the relevant pin code on the back of each credit card, Harry realised he had a useful source of petty cash, without bothering his own bank, so long as he was careful.

He counted the cash he had taken from Wellton, six hundred and forty pounds in all, and stuffed it in a large envelope which he folded and placed in the cutlery drawer. Then he settled down to study the coded statement on the pink slip of paper. He looked at it for quite a long time before he realised what it was. It was a 'calling notice', calling a meeting of the Frug gang. He first managed to unravel the group of numbers, after which the rest came fairly easily. The numbers represented a date and a time. The first three digits – two, eight and nine – meant the twenty-eighth of September. The next four, he thought, referred to a time, 1830 in the twenty-four hour clock, or 6.30 p.m. He wasn't sure what the letters 'J' and 'S' meant but he surmised that it might be a joint signature – Jane and Sandra.

The remainder of the message was more difficult. 'Frug' was easy; from his interrogation of Wellton he knew it was the name of the group, but it was also their battle-cry. The rest took him a lot longer to work out but when he did he was shocked by how straightforward it was. After several more hours of staring at the letters, he stumbled onto the solution. It came like a ray of sunshine, suddenly striking in and illuminating his mind. The second and third letters 'Hd' gave the game away. 'Hd' was almost certainly shorthand for Head. The date and the time suggested a rendezvous or meeting place, so where would this gang meet? The answer was either a geographical location such as Bolt Head, or more likely a pub or restaurant. Very few restaurants had 'Head' in their names so it was more likely to be a pub. It could be a headland somewhere, but this crowd, he thought, would prefer to get tanked up in comfort rather than venturing out to some cold and windy headland in September. At this point, he realised that, the present date being the twenty-sixth of September, the meeting was scheduled to take place in two days. But where?

Back in the storage compartment in the stern of the boat, Giles de Courtney Wellton never regained consciousness. While Harry was trying to work out the location of the planned meeting place, Britain's one-time youngest Government Minister died quietly from his injuries and from a second overdose of ketamine. It was not until after midday that Harry opened the door into the compartment and realised that the man in the wheelchair, hanging from the black adhesive tapes, was now dead.

Harry decided that he would take his boat to sea next day. But first he needed to do something about the mortal remains of the late Mr Giles Wellton. All he could do at that point was to cover the body; so, using a couple of disposable black plastic bin bags, he pulled one bag over the head and another over the feet, before taping them inexpertly together in the middle.

In the meantime, he set off in the van back to his cottage in Easton. He arrived an hour after dark, parked the van in a communal parking space near the little square in the village centre, bought some groceries in Tesco just before it closed, and strolled back to his cottage.

Harry put the kettle on, lit the coal-effect gas fire in his sitting room, put a frozen Tesco ready-meal in the microwave and settled himself down in his armchair with his new laptop computer on his knees. Half an hour later, with the aid of Google, he believed he knew where the meeting was going to take place. In the heart of the New Forest was an old coaching inn called the Boar's Head. He looked at the set of letters again. B.Hd N For. That could only be the Boar's Head in the New Forest.

He had no sympathy for the man who had destroyed his life all those years ago but he was slightly concerned at the possibility of being implicated in his murder. He entertained no doubt that it was indeed murder but to Harry, this was justified in having removed an evil person from the surface of the planet. The world, he muttered to himself, would indeed be a better place. He finished his supermarket supper, decided to treat himself to a modest whisky, then switched on the television, hoping to catch the BBC news.

The headlines caught his attention immediately. The newsreader gazed earnestly into the camera while he followed the autocue.

'Police are investigating the sudden disappearance of Mr Giles de Courtney Wellton, until recently the Minister of State for Rural Affairs. Mr Wellton was last seen leaving his Wimbledon home early yesterday morning in his car, apparently heading for Wimbledon Common where it was his regular routine to take an early morning run around the

Common. Mr Wellton recently resigned his Government post as Rural Affairs Minister following allegations concerning his parliamentary allowances. Police have found a car abandoned in one of the nearby public car parks and have removed it for forensic examination.'

At this point the camera cut to film of several police officers surrounding a car, followed by another image of the car being lifted onto the back of a flatbed lorry. A short clip followed, showing Wellton embracing a rather pretty-looking dark-haired woman, aged about twenty-five or thirty.

The announcer continued. 'Mr Wellton has been romantically linked with Sandra Somerville, who thrilled the crowds at Wimbledon this year by reaching the women's quarter finals with a powerful and impressive series of wins...'

Harry switched the television off. He cleared away the detritus of his supper and went to bed.

The following morning Harry stayed in bed for an hour after his alarm went off. He was enjoying the luxury of a lie-in, but also planning his next move, which would involve interception of the group about to assemble in the New Forest.

Chapter 32

While Harry was luxuriating in bed, a small convoy of three unmarked police cars was speeding along the dual carriageway section of the A35, a few miles east of Dorchester. The first car was an escort vehicle, fitted with discreet blue lights and sirens. The purpose of this vehicle was to ensure that nothing – traffic jams, accidents, roadworks or anything else – could disrupt the journey from Poole to Weymouth. The second car was driven by a uniformed traffic officer. Bob Majury was seated next to the driver in the front seat and Jim accompanied Sir Arthur in the back seat, now rather more composed. The third car, also driven by a uniformed traffic officer, contained the lawyer, Charles Grayson-Cummings, in the back. A police press officer was seated in the front.

The convoy slowed as the first vehicle joined the queue of traffic at the end of the dual carriageway. Blue lights came on and the three vehicles moved out into the centre of the road to pass the crawling traffic, before threading their way around the roundabout marking the beginning of the Dorchester bypass.

Bob turned around in his seat, addressing Sir Arthur. 'We'll be arriving in Weymouth in about fifteen minutes, Sir Arthur,' he said. 'When we get there, either Detective Sergeant Creasy or myself will accompany you into the station; and in your own interests, I must ask you to speak to absolutely no-one else, no matter who they are or what they say. Just us. Do you understand that, Sir Arthur?'

'What about my lawyer?'

'Yes, you may speak to your lawyer, but one of us will also be present when you do.'

Sir Arthur didn't answer.

Bob continued. 'There will be one other exception. We will have a police doctor available and if you feel unwell at any time please tell us and he will be brought in to see you.'

Bob had given a good deal of thought to what would happen on arrival at Weymouth. He remained acutely conscious of the evidence he had uncovered that pointed to police corruption reaching up to a high level. It was readily apparent that someone had already wiped out most of the evidence relating to the original crime. That 'someone' had also collected and destroyed most of the documentation and managed to silence and disperse the police officers directly connected. The only fact that he could be reasonably certain about was that the individual who could deploy such influence was probably highly placed at the time and likely even higher in the system now. At least one senior copper was bent, he thought, and if there was one, there might be more; but where were they?

The convoy swept around the roundabout marking the centre of Granby Road and slowed as it passed the entrance to the football ground on the left and the large euphemistically worded sign on the right, Weymouth Police Headquarters and Custody Suite. As usual, the words 'Custody Suite' brought a wry smile to Bob's face.

Fifteen minutes later, they were all seated in comfortable imitation-leather padded swivel chairs around a conference table. The group had been joined by two women, a stenographer called Kate Travis, a darkly attractive and diminutive young woman in her early twenties, and Elizabeth Curry from the Crown Prosecution Service. A uniformed police constable, picked by Bob, sat on an upright wooden chair just inside the door. As soon as they arrived, Sir Arthur had been taken to a small room where he was briefly questioned by the police surgeon on duty. Then, accompanied by Jim, he was taken to the otherwise empty lavatory and shower room, while Bob waited outside the door. The two detectives then led Sir Arthur to the interview room.

Once they were all seated and the door was shut, Bob moved across to a panel of switches on the wall and switched off the video cameras monitoring the room. He was ensuring that no-one else would be able to witness what was about to take place in the room until he was ready to release information. For Bob, the corrupt but unidentified police manipulator seemed to hover like an evil presence just behind his chair.

Bob started speaking as he walked back towards his chair. 'Sir Arthur, I believe you know most of the people around this table, though possibly not Miss Travis, who is a stenographer, and Mrs Curry who represents the Crown Prosecution Service.'

Sir Arthur glanced across the table, apparently taking in the presence of both women for the first time. Kate Travis, the young stenographer, kept her head down and her eyes fixed firmly on the small machine on the table in front of her. Elizabeth Curry was a tall, trim forty-something woman dressed entirely in black, with brown hair pulled severely back behind her head and tied with a black velvet ribbon. She glanced briefly across the table, allowing a ghost of a smile to flutter around her lips.

Bob forged on. 'Sir Arthur,' he said, leaning forward in his chair towards the Baronet, 'it is normal procedure in circumstances such as this to record what is said at this meeting, by having the discussion taken down by a stenographer and by recording the proceedings electronically. Two simultaneous copies of the recording are made. One of these will be made available to your legal advisor. Do you understand this?'

'Yes. Why is she here?' Sir Arthur inclined his head towards Elizabeth Curry, who seemed about to reply, but Bob cut her off.

'As I said, Sir Arthur, Mrs Curry represents the Crown Prosecution Service and she will be deeply involved with this case as it develops. You may object to her presence at this stage if you wish but I think that might be unwise. There are certain facts that will come to light which will weigh in your favour. Although no charge has yet been proffered we will be charging you...'

'What with? My client is...' Grayson-Cummings got no further. Bob held up a hand, and ignoring the interruption, he continued, raising his voice slightly as he did so.

'...as I was saying, we will be charging you in due course but how we then proceed will be subject to discussion and consideration which will take in all the evidence, some of which, I have reason to believe, may be in your favour. I must say to you that the presence of Mrs Curry will be more likely to benefit you in the long run, than otherwise. Do you object to the presence of Mrs Curry?'

Sir Arthur stared at the table for a full minute, then perfunctorily shook his head.

'Can you say yes or no, Sir Arthur, for the tape, please?'

There was another long pause at the end of which Sir Arthur, still staring at the table said, 'No.'

'Good. Now I am going to ask you some more questions, then we will ask you to make a statement. Do you understand that, Sir Arthur?'

Again, Sir Arthur nodded.

'Yes or no, for the tape, Sir Arthur.'

Almost inaudibly, the answer came: 'Yes,' then again, louder, 'yes.'

Bob turned towards the lawyer. 'Anything to add, Mr Grayson-Cummings?' Grayson-Cummings shook his head and Bob let it pass. Grayson-Cummings couldn't add anything useful and in any case, Bob thought, his personal views were not relevant and, judging from recent experience, his advice was likely to be rejected by his client. The process had reached a stage which Bob had encountered often in the past. The key facts of evidence, which the suspect knew he could not overturn, had driven away the original sense of bluster and grievance, leading to passive acquiescence. Sir Arthur Simmonds knew that he was going to be implicated in a crime which now appalled his conscience and which, even in the unlikely event of his being found innocent, would lead to public disgrace for himself, his family and his name; in fact, for everything he stood for. He just wanted to get it all over with as quickly as possible.

Bob started his questioning: 'I want to take you back to your visit to Weymouth in July 2010.' He paused. 'In particular to the weekend of Friday the 16th, Saturday the 17th and Sunday the 18th of July.' He paused again, allowing the question to sink in. 'But before that, about a week before, you and your friends visited Bournemouth. What was the reason for your visit?'

'We had a dinner to celebrate the end of term. There were about fifteen of us and we were all from the Free Runners. We let our hair down a bit and some damage was caused but we paid for it so nobody was put out.' The voice emerged as a droning monotone, almost as though he was reading from a particularly boring book.

'When was this?' Bob moved his chair an inch closer to the table. To his right the stenographer's fingers were dancing over her machine and Elizabeth Curry was scribbling in a notepad.

'Term ended on the 10th and we met in Bournemouth about four days later.'

'Would that be Tuesday the 13th of July?'

Sir Arthur frowned and his lips moved as if he was counting. He looked across at his inquisitor and frowned again, 'Yes, I suppose. I thought it was the 14th, but it might have been the 13th.'

'When the dinner was over, who paid for the damages in the restaurant?'

'I did, I shared the cost. I paid half and the others were to pay me back later,' there was a long pause, 'but they never did.'

'What did you do after the dinner? Did you stay in Bournemouth?'

'Yes, it was sunny and most of us spent the days on the beach.'

'What about the evenings?'

Sir Arthur was surprised at this question. He knew where the questioning was heading but he didn't understand why Bob was dragging things out. After a few moments he said, 'We travelled around a bit and visited some country pubs. I went home on a couple of evenings. Some of the others went home as well, and they didn't all come back.'

'How did you get home, Sir Arthur?'

'I drove.'

'What kind of car were you driving?' Bob's eyes were now fixed, drilling into those of his victim, across the table.

The shoulders sagged. 'The Aston.' This was muttered quietly and the baronet's head was down once more. He was unable to make eye contact with anyone seated around the table. His shame became almost a physical thing.

'The Aston,' repeated Bob. 'Was that your own car?'

'It was registered to my father.' He was still mumbling.

'Did your father drive the car at all?'

'Not much.' It was an even quieter mumble this time. Jim began to worry that his boss was wandering off the track. He leaned forward, elbows on the table, ready to intervene. Then he realised where this was going. A pit was being dug, ready for Bob's victim to fall into, and destroy once and for all any credibility he might retain as an honest man.

'Sir Arthur, you told me, in considerable detail, that your father drove you round parts of South Dorset at about this time. Was that true?'

'Is this really relevant?' This came from Grayson-Cummings. The voice was loud, harsh and braying. It broke the atmosphere that Bob was trying to build up.

The DCI spun round rapidly in his chair to face the lawyer. He was just as loud. 'I'll decide what is relevant. And yes, it is.'

The lawyer jerked backward in his chair, as though he had been struck. The powerful counter-attack had not been expected. Bob turned back to face his subject and repeated his question. 'Was that true, Sir Arthur?'

'No.'

'He was too ill to drive – wasn't he?' There was no answer. Grayson-Cummings looked uncomfortable but stayed silent. The CPS pencil could be heard scratching on the pad.

'Sir Arthur, your father, I believe, was too ill to drive at this time. Isn't that correct, Sir Arthur?'

'Yes, it is.' The voice was barely a croak. Sir Arthur had only then realised where the line of questioning was going.

'So what you told me previously about your father driving the Aston Martin was a lie.' The word 'lie' hung in the room like an unexploded bomb.

'Yes,' said Sir Arthur. 'It was. I'm sorry.'

Bob waited for that to register while Jim scribbled a list of driving offences in his notebook.

After a few minutes of silence broken only by shuffling feet and chairs, Bob took an ostentatiously deep breath, fixed a neutral expression on his face and turned once more to face the baronet. The unexpected questions about the car had not been wasted. He had now established that the former upright pillar of the community was easily and readily capable of lying. Another rung of respectability had been knocked away.

'Let's move on.' Bob spoke briskly now. 'After your few days on the beach and in the pubs around Bournemouth, what did you do? Did you move on from Bournemouth?' Leading the witness, thought Jim, but he didn't say anything out loud. He had no wish to upset his boss by a second unhelpful interruption.

'Yes, we did.' Sir Arthur now seemed more composed.

'Who is we? Do you mean everyone who had attended the dinner in Bournemouth?' The word 'dinner' was said with a slightly sneering emphasis, as though the detective was describing something rather nasty, as in fact he believed he was.

In responding, Simmonds spoke ponderously, as though he was ticking off the names as he listed them. 'There were ten of us,' he said. 'About six or seven cars. I don't know who decided but suddenly we all zoomed off to Weymouth. We were enjoying ourselves and we thought it would be fun.'

'Fun!' Bob allowed the word to hang in the air. Nobody else spoke. Then he said, 'I want you to tell me the names of all these people who went with you to Weymouth. Take your time.'

'Well, there was Giles Wellton.'

'Do you mean the MP?'

'Yes, and he had Jane Lockyer and Sandra Somerville with him.'

'Who is Jane Lockyer?'

Sir Arthur seemed surprised by the interruption. 'She's an actress now, not very well known I think, and Sandra is the tennis player.'

This piece of information seemed to shock the other occupants of the room. How could the nation's darling, the young queen of the court, be mixed up in something as sordid as this?

Sir Arthur continued, unaware of the effect his previous pronouncement had had on the rest of the room. 'There was Henry Hayward, and Ray Marsden. He's a barrister now, a QC,' he added helpfully.

Like the others, Jim was fascinated by the names which were emerging, but particularly by this last one. Ray Marsden was a spectacularly successful young QC who had made his career and polished his reputation by defending the indefensible – and regularly winning his cases, much to the continued embarrassment of several police forces and a whole legion of Crown Prosecutors. Among the more acceptable epithets applied to him was 'villain's friend'. It was even rumoured in some quarters that this man would soon be destined to become a judge.

Then, like a firework exploding in his head, Jim realised that this was the connection they had been looking for. 'Bingo!' he thought, wondering immediately whether he had spoken aloud. He had not. But he was desperate to tell his boss what he now knew. Marsden was the son of a former Deputy Commissioner of the Metropolitan Police. Jim missed the next few exchanges as he concentrated on trying to work out whether Marsden's father had still been serving in 2010. He thought he had. If so, they had identified the 'copper bender', the man who could make evidence disappear.

The litany of names was still being trotted out and Sir Arthur seemed to be warming to his task, explaining the key points and attributes of people he had begun to think of as his successful friends rather than as psychopathic killers. 'There was Cornel Grovey, always in the papers; then Jeremy Wilberforce, or should I say the Reverend Jeremy Wilberforce. His father is Lord Bodmin, you know, and he's already a canon and chaplain to a bishop. I'm not sure which one though.' He stopped speaking, placing a forefinger against his temple, trying to remember this important piece of information about his friend.

'Let me see,' he continued, 'who else was there? Oh yes! There was Don Randell and Captain Roger FitzHarris.' He stopped speaking and peered round the table looking, Jim thought, as though he was expecting a round of applause – for having answered all the exam questions correctly.

There was no round of applause.

'Who is Captain FitzHarris? What does he do?' Bob was taking charge of the interrogation once more. The short period of focus on the baronet was over and Bob was rather surprised at how easily all the names had come out.

'Captain FitzHarris: I suppose he might be a major, or even a colonel by now; he was, at the time, an officer in one of the Guards Regiments. I haven't actually seen him for some time,' Sir Arthur finished rather lamely.

'And Don Randell?'

'I'm not sure. I think he might be something in the city.' After his few moments as the focus of attention, Bob realised his man was running out of steam.

'I think we should take a break,' he said. 'Sir Arthur, would you like something to eat? Some tea perhaps, or a cup of coffee?'

Sir Arthur said he would like some food so, accompanied by his lawyer, he was escorted by the uniformed constable towards a room off the canteen where strong tea and indifferent sandwiches were being made available.

Bob headed purposefully towards the staircase leading to his office, followed by Jim, bursting to impart his recent deduction. They walked at a brisk pace into the big office and Bob called across to Gerry Treloar, the only other occupant.

'Coffee for two, Gerry. Make it three if you like. But make it hot and strong – very strong.' He eased into his chair behind the table. Jim dragged a chair forward and perched himself opposite. 'Guv'nor,' he said. 'Do you realise what we've just been told? We've got the connection. We know the fixer!'

'Thanks, Gerry, you must have known we were coming.' Gerry had arrived with a metal tray carrying three mismatched china mugs, which he arranged on the table, placing each one carefully in front of each chair. 'Right, Jim, what is this you're bursting to tell me? Pull up a chair, Gerry; three heads might be better than two on this.' He looked expectantly towards Jim.

'The big thing with this case, right from the beginning, was where had all the evidence gone? We knew there had to be someone with sufficient clout to pull some pretty big strings. This man shut down the case and covered up the evidence within twenty-four hours. You've gotta be higher up the pecking order than sergeant, or even chief inspector, with respect, Guv, to do that.'

'Let's just establish who we're talking about. I have an idea, but tell me,' said Bob, while Gerry just glanced from one to the other, cupping his hands around his mug of coffee.

Jim spoke patiently. 'It was when he mentioned Ray Marsden, the QC. His old man is former Deputy Commissioner Andrew Marsden of the Metropolitan Police.'

'I think he might be Sir Andrew Marsden now,' said Bob. 'I think he might have been knighted when he retired. However, the fact that he is the father of one of these scumbags doesn't prove he was destroying evidence and corrupting the occupants of this nick. In fact, I don't ever recall him visiting here, or even telephoning here for that matter. I don't think he was ever in a county force. He was always in the Met. He was in fact the blue-eyed boy of the Met.'

Jim listened, then replied thoughtfully, 'You say he was always in the Met but I think I heard that he was seconded, doing something else for a while, and if my memory serves me right it came as a bit of a surprise when he got his knighthood. They don't usually dish these out to deputy commissioners, not unless they've been a chief constable somewhere, or done a big job in ACPO or with the "complaints" or something like that. The word at the time, I think, was that he got his gong for doing some very special coppering, somewhere else.'

Bob made a steeple of his hands, thought for a moment and then said, 'You may be closer than you think, Jim. The thing is, where do these smart-arse rising stars go when they do their special coppering?'

Jim waited, holding back his answer.

'Well, they don't go to Marks and Sparks to check on the security, do they?' said Bob. He seemed to be working out his conundrum as he continued speaking. 'They go abroad to advise some brown-skinned gentleman how to spend the dosh that our grateful government gives him for his policemen and not to put too much of it in a Swiss bank. Or they go to do some government work…'

Jim interrupted. 'Some go off to do staff courses with the Army or the Navy.'

'Yes, that's true; but usually they are not quite deputies in the Met when they do the courses and they most certainly do not have the Queen hanging a nice pretty bauble around their necks for passing the course.'

Gerry interrupted the flow. 'Actually,' he said, 'they get a star, not a neck decoration.'

'Can it, Gerry!' said Bob. 'You'll disturb my concentration. No, I'm thinking: important special senior coppers with sons who are QCs (and a pain in the arse, to boot) will only be deployed to do something special, something that doesn't get into the papers, even for publicity-hungry self-serving buggers like Sir Andrew. I'm thinking security – and that would provide him with all the power he would need to do pretty well whatever he liked. We need to pursue this, but very, very carefully. The first thing is to find out whether Deputy Commissioner Sir Andrew Marsden was still serving when Harry Chaplin was found more dead than alive. I want you to do this, Jim, but on tiptoe, understand. It's just possible that this man still has sufficient arm-length to get both of us retired without a pension.'

'Got it, Boss,' said Jim. 'I'm on the case, and nobody will even know I'm there.'

Bob looked at his watch. 'I think we'll charge him now. Then we can keep him overnight.'

'What will we charge him with?' Jim said.

'We'll just use a holding charge, good enough to keep him till morning. I'd also like to keep him away from that brief of his. While we're also looking for bent coppers we need to be careful about who knows what, who knows who, and what we say to anyone. For now, I think we'll charge him with conspiracy to commit murder.'

'Yeah, I think that should be enough to prevent him walking out of here tonight, 'specially considering that we picked him up on his way to France.' As he spoke, Jim stood up and started to gather together some loose notes he had made during the prolonged interview with Simmonds.

Gerry picked up the empty mugs while the other two stood and started to make their way to the door. On the way down the stairs, Jim turned to his boss and said, 'Don't forget you've got to brief the Super, Guv'nor.'

'Yes, I've been thinking about that.'

Chapter 33

Harry had not been idle while the police were conducting their enquiries. There had been a brief announcement in the Dorset Echo about a local landowner assisting a six-year-old police investigation, but nothing more. The disappearance of the former Government Minister, however, was occupying a lot of headline space, and this made Harry feel rather uncomfortable, considering that the corpse was still occupying part of his storeroom.

He realised that he had to act, and act quickly. Already the smell of decomposition was evident around the storeroom and even lingering outside the after part of the boat. Harry had already decided that it would be necessary to go on a little fishing trip and get some sea air. He went to the shed at the end of his wooden jetty, then climbed into the back of the van, emerging with two heavy-duty black refuse sacks, each filled with various bits and pieces.

He had only driven this boat twice and then only for short distances but he felt fairly confident that he could find his way out to sea provided the sea remained benign and the weather didn't play up. He was conscious that his damaged memory suggested he might at some time have worked as a merchant seaman, but as he faced the prospect of taking his boat to sea unaided, he became convinced that his seagoing work must have been limited to painting, cleaning and other deck duties. He could not conjure up any recollection of ever having worked as part of the crew of a small boat.

He had to learn as he went along; so first of all he sat himself behind the small chart table and did some research. He found a chart of Poole Harbour, including part of the River

Frome where he was now berthed. He opened the chart and folded it so that the centre section, showing the main part of the huge harbour, fitted on his navigation desk. He spent an hour poring over the chart which at first looked formidably complicated; there seemed to be buoys, islands, moorings and channel-ways scattered haphazardly all over the surface of the paper.

After a while Harry began to discern a pattern. From the bookshelf above the chart table he took a paperback guide to Poole Harbour, and then he found another small book, issued by the Royal Yachting Association. The title was International Regulations for Preventing Collisions at Sea. Tucked inside this was a four page pamphlet headed The Cardinal System of Buoyage.

It was nearly midday when Harry considered that he had taken in enough information to get his boat down the channels of the harbour and out to sea without running aground or hitting something. His biggest remaining worry was how he would be able to cope with the chain-ferry at the narrow entrance to the harbour. He reckoned he could probably deal with this by simply following what other small boats did. He had also worked out that when heading out of the harbour he should leave the green buoys on his left and the red ones on his right. If he could keep clear of other vessels, avoid any big ships, follow the buoys and watch the depth-sounder, he might just get away with it – provided the weather remained kind, he didn't encounter fog and didn't stay out after dark.

In fact he need not have worried. The little bit of study had provided him with the bare minimum of information but enough to wander down the river and then follow the buoyage system across the inner harbour. Once past the Royal Marine Amphibious Base which he would need to pass on his left, he would encounter the more complex cross-channel ferry terminal which would lead him out into the big deep water channel, running down the centre of the wide expanse of generally shallow water, which formed the outer harbour.

The weather did stay kind throughout the morning, and a short while after casting off from his reed-bound berth, Harry's boat emerged from the river and joined a haphazard line of yachts and small motor boats as they plodded slowly along the winding main channel. It took nearly an hour before the boat cruised around a bend, passed across the stern of a crowded tourist boat heading in to Brownsea Island, and joined a group of yachts and motor-cruisers waiting before the chain ferry at Sandbanks. He had a short bout of nervousness when he saw that the chain ferry was halfway across the entrance, but he held his nerve, knocked the throttle lever into neutral and stopped his boat with a short burst of astern power; then he lay drifting, surrounded by the other boats, until the ferry ramp was sitting firmly on the concrete slipway, the chain behind the vessel had dropped below the surface of the water, and the other half dozen boats were surging forward past the cumbersome-looking ferry and out to sea.

Once past the ferry, Harry counted the numbers on the green buoys to his left until at last he realised he was clear of the dredged fairway. Then he opened the throttle slightly until the electronic log of his boat was registering ten knots. As he passed Old Harry Rocks, he glanced across at the tall, white pillars of rock and said aloud to himself, 'They're named after me. That must be an omen.' At the same time he turned his boat about fifteen degrees to the left – to port, he unaccountably realised – so that he was heading south east, towards the open and apparently empty expanse of Poole Bay.

Harry kept going like this for nearly another hour before he closed the throttle, peered diligently all around the horizon and allowed the boat to drift, moving slowly on the ebbing tide. As soon as the boat seemed stationary it lay across the wave pattern and started to rock rhythmically from side to side. Harry hadn't allowed for this and the movement made his work much more difficult as he tackled the next part of his task.

He wrapped a scarf around his face before unlocking the storeroom door and descending the few steps. He dragged several of the big heavy-duty refuse disposal bags down the ladder behind him and dropped them on the deck. The stink in the confined space was almost unbearable and he started gagging as he approached the corpse. He turned back to the steps and the open door, breathing deeply of the salt-laden air. After three or four minutes he clamped his teeth together, tightened the ineffective scarf around his face, and turned back into the compartment. The mortal remains of Giles de Courtney Wellton were already covered by two black plastic refuse disposal bags and Harry started to drag two of the big heavy duty bags, one over the feet, and one over the head. He taped the bags loosely in place and dragged the black bundle across the deck and up the steps. Although Wellton had been a slightly built man, the task was much more difficult than Harry had estimated. It took him another hour of heaving and struggling before he had the ungainly bundle on deck.

The process took a heavy toll on his energy and his rebuilt body, and when he had finally dragged the shiny black stinking bundle over the hatch coaming and onto the deck he ran out of energy. He flopped down on the wooden deck, panting and gasping for breath. By this time the early afternoon breeze had died away and the foul stench from the bundle lying on the wooden planks beside him seemed to reach out and envelop him and the whole boat. Eventually he crawled to his knees, braced himself against the movement of the boat, and clutching at the handrail along the coach-roof staggered to his feet. Nausea overcame him and he started retching. He tried to clamp his teeth together but it didn't work. He vomited comprehensively over the deck and the wrapped corpse of Giles Wellton. Again he found himself gasping for breath as he leaned back against the cabin side. It took a great deal of effort and willpower to do what was needed next, and his work continued to be punctuated by recurrent bouts of vomiting culminating in painful retching from an empty stomach.

The horrible bundle was now slippery with vomit as Harry eased open the temporary join between the two sacks and started to fill them with the objects he had gathered before leaving the river. Eventually the bundle was filled with a bulky assortment of rocks, bits of iron and other metals. He wiped the vomit away as best he could and then he taped the two outer bags together again and dragged two more heavy duty sacks over the others for good measure, winding yard after yard of black self-amalgamating duct tape over the whole lot. Finally, pale and exhausted, he peered once more all around the horizon. He could see no other vessel so he unclipped the wire guardrails on the side facing out to sea, and on his knees once more, heaving, sweating and shoving, he moved the black bundle to the edge of the deck where at last a helpful roll of the boat tipped the whole horrible thing over the side.

Harry stood, traumatised at what he had had to do. He watched the shiny black lump bobbing happily on the surface alongside the boat. It sat stoically in the water, bumping gently on the side of the boat, and a feeling of panic began to creep over Harry. His chief tormentor, he thought, was never going to let him go.

But then bubbles began to appear around the plastic bundle, and slowly, ever so slowly, it started to sink lower in the water. It took half an hour before it was completely below the surface, though still visible and lying only a few feet from the boat. Then, almost as though it was giving up the struggle to stay with the boat, it began to sink more quickly. For a few minutes more, bubbles appeared among the small waves, and then it was gone.

Harry needed more time to recover some strength and push the horror of the last hour to the back of his mind, but then he forced himself to do what was necessary to finish the task. He held his breath as he disappeared into the after store, and working slowly with frequent stoppages to breathe some fresh air, he opened all the windows and ventilators he could find, before heaving himself back up the short ladder to the deck with a leather bucket attached to a short length of rope. He threw the bucket over the side, hauled it up and started the task of washing and scrubbing down the soiled deck.

The sun was low on the western horizon and the breeze had picked up again as Harry turned his boat back towards the fairway leading to Poole Harbour. He could see a few other vessels, mostly fishing boats, closing on the entrance, so it was relatively straightforward to follow them. For the first time in several hours Harry felt able to relax, although he felt desperately tired and washed out. Nevertheless, he followed the line of channel-marking buoys like a master mariner and eventually, in the last of the fading daylight, he bumped the side of his boat alongside his wooden jetty and looped a line around a mooring post.

He tied a couple more lines, checked the boat wasn't moving, switched off the engine and collapsed, exhausted, into a bunk in the forepeak.

Chapter 34

At five o'clock, with the exception of Elizabeth Curry, they all assembled in the interview room.

`'Sir Arthur,' said Bob, 'in a few moments I am going to charge you, but first, Detective Sergeant Creasy will formally caution you once again. Please stand, Sir Arthur. Sergeant Creasy…'

Jim walked across the room until he was standing in front of the tall baronet. He read the formal caution slowly and carefully from a clipboard. Then he glanced up and asked if the caution had been understood. In answer to the question, Sir Arthur nodded and said he understood. Jim then read the charges. 'You are charged with perverting the course of justice…with conspiracy to commit murder…with cruelty to an animal…with driving while under the influence of alcohol and or drugs… with intent to commit murder… with intent to commit grievous bodily harm…with affray in combination with others… with failing to report a serious accident… with attempted bribery…with conspiracy to bribe a public official…'

The litany of offences went on and on, until, when it was over, the baronet collapsed into his chair, leaned forward and held his head in his hands. They all waited in silence until at last the baronet looked up once more, tears streaking his face and his hands trembling. He muttered something quietly as he raised his head.

'What was that, Sir Arthur?' said Bob.

The answer came out more as a sob. 'I'm so ashamed…so ashamed…'

Bob decided he had to press on. 'Friday the sixteenth of July 2010,' he said. 'Tell me what you did then, Sir Arthur.'

'We went to Weymouth.'

'Why did you do that?'

'I don't know. It just came up as an idea, I suppose.'

'Whose idea, Sir Arthur?'

'Well, I suppose it might have been one of the girls; they seemed keen to move on from Bournemouth... or it could even have been Giles, I suppose.'

'Or maybe all of them?'

'Yes, maybe.'

'Did all ten of the people you named to me this afternoon go to Weymouth?'

Simmonds didn't answer at first. He seemed to be ticking off items on his fingers; then he said, 'Yes, all of those people.'

'What did you do when you got to Weymouth?'

'There was some sort of festival going on around the harbour, so we had a few drinks and went along.'

'Where did you have the drinks?'

'I'm not sure. We did a sort of pub crawl through the pubs around the harbour.'

'Were you and your friends drinking heavily?'

'Well, yes, I suppose we were. We were in the pubs for a couple of hours before we went to the fair alongside the harbour.'

'That was the Seafood Festival, I think?'

'Yes.'

'What happened then?'

Sir Arthur waited, staring down at his hands for a long time. Eventually, raising his head slowly, he said, 'There was a bit of a fight, I think.'

'You think?' Bob sounded exasperated as he asked the question. 'Don't you know? You were there, weren't you? Come on now, I'm sure you can do better than that.'

At that point Grayson-Cummings decided to intervene. 'You are badgering my client,' he said.

'I'm trying to get your client to answer my question. It's a simple question and...'

'I'm sorry.' Sir Arthur started to speak once more. 'You're right. It would be foolish of me now to attempt to hide anything and I won't try. I think it was Giles Wellton... and Grovey... and, I think... FitzHarris. I can't be absolutely sure who did what. I had been drinking champagne and I was fairly drunk...'

Jim made a careful note of the admission of drunkenness in his notebook. It was going to be a useful referral when the car crash and drunken driving were considered.

Sir Arthur paused, apparently in thought, then continued. 'Yes,' he said, 'we were all there; but I'm sure those three were the ones most directly involved.'

Bob broke in again. 'Tell me what happened, what you actually saw happening, Sir Arthur,' he said. 'I mean, who did what?'

Grayson-Cummings was on the edge of his seat, about to intervene once more; but the baronet waved him back with a raised hand. He looked down at his hands, a frown of concentration furrowing his brow.

'It started with an argument over a girl serving at a stall. It was a crab and seafood stall. I think Wellton, or it might have been Grovey, was propositioning the girl. Words were exchanged and the man working in the stall with her came round the front and told them to shove off. I think Wellton swung a punch at him and they brawled on the ground. Then the whole stall collapsed. I think the other two pushed it over. There was fish everywhere. Crab, lobsters, prawns, all sorts of things. Somebody must have called the police because suddenly everyone was running away…'

'Who do you mean by everyone?'

'Well, all of us, all of the Frugs.'

Jim noted that this was the first time during the questioning that the baronet had used the word Frug. He was going to cough the lot, he thought.

'Where did you run to, Sir Arthur?'

'Nobody chased us. We went back through the narrow streets to the car park.'

'What then? What time was this?'

'We drove out of town in a sort of convoy. We just kept going until we reached a pub that was open. I can't remember the name but it was a small place near the edge of the town. In Upwey, I think. We had the place to ourselves so we stayed there quite a while. We arrived there about five o'clock. Everybody was pretty pissed off, particularly Giles and Roger FitzHarris. The girls kept egging them on, asking what they were going to do about it. Were they going to let a bunch of plebs push them around? Giles was bloody furious and he came up with the plan.'

Sir Arthur stopped speaking and the room remained silent, expectant.

'What was the plan, Sir Arthur?' Bob spoke the question in an even voice, spacing out the words slowly, his eyes fixed, unblinking, on the Baronet.

'We were going to do a snuff job.' The silence continued, like a brittle presence in the small room.

'Tell us, Sir Arthur, what exactly do you mean by "a snuff job"?' As Bob finished speaking, all eyes turned towards the baronet, many already showing shock and horror at what they had just heard and what they expected to hear.

Sir Arthur Simmonds fiddled with his hands, then pulled a handkerchief from his pocket and blew his nose. He was visibly trembling as he continued, his voice so quiet that those furthest from him had to strain to hear what he was saying.

'Grover said the locals needed to be taught a lesson and either Wellton or FitzHarris said we should grab somebody – somebody who wouldn't be missed at first, and give them a good kicking, maybe do them in.'

The atmosphere in the room was a truly awful mix of horror, tension and shock. Kate Travis was weeping silently as she continued to attempt to record what was being said.

'Do you mean to say, Sir Arthur… Are you telling me that you and all your friends decided to kidnap an innocent victim off the street and to carry out a serious assault on that victim?'

'Not everybody thought that. Some of us, I think, thought that it was just bravado. Or maybe we thought that we might find somebody and just rough them up a bit.' He stopped, then wailed, 'Oh, I'm so ashamed,' before dropping his head into his hands, his shoulders shaking.

Bob spoke very quietly, dropping each word slowly, like pebbles falling into a pond. Nobody moved; there was almost no sound, no scrape of chair, no rattle of crockery, just the sound of breathing. 'Where did you go to do this, Sir Arthur?'

There was no answer.

'Sir Arthur, did you go to Portland Bill?'

'Yes. It was quiet at night and we didn't think we would be disturbed. I hoped there would be no one there and it would all collapse.'

'But it didn't, did it, Sir Arthur?'

'No, it didn't.'

Before he could put his next question, Jim intervened.

'Has this happened before, Sir Arthur?'

There was an even longer silence. Slowly Sir Arthur lifted his head, shook it as though he was trying to throw something off, and then stared directly at the new interrogator.

'Yes,' he said. 'Yes.'

Bob looked grim as he spoke. 'I'm going to have to remand you in custody overnight, Sir Arthur...'

'That is outrageous!' The shouted interruption came from Grayson- Cummings. Jim silently mouthed an obscenity. The man makes a habit of being outraged, he thought.

As the group broke up and Sir Arthur was being escorted to a cell, Jim said quietly to his boss, 'We really do need to brief the Super, Guv'nor.'

'Yes. But I want a special watch kept on our prisoner. Can you fix that first?'

'You mean a suicide watch?' Jim sounded shocked.

'Yes; then we'll brief the big boss.'

Chapter 35

One by one, over the next forty minutes or so, the cars pulled into the extensive tree-lined parking space in front of the Boar's Head Hotel. There were six vehicles in all, not one of them more than a year old and every one worth over fifty thousand pounds. The early evening was darkened by a heavy cloud base, now showing one or two stars through ragged holes in the overcast sky. There was only the thinnest crescent of new moon, which was mostly obscured by clouds. Apart from the new arrivals, the car park was almost empty.

In the dim interior of the rather cosy wood-panelled snug bar, three middle-aged men were sitting on tall stools, sipping occasionally from pint glasses. They were all working foresters, who met regularly in the pub-cum-hotel for a single pint, but when they did meet they had little to say to each other, although they seemed to enjoy the frequently silent companionship of old friends. Eventually, one after the other, they climbed off their stools, bid each other a gruff good evening and went on their way. Two of the men climbed aboard a battered, mud-spattered utility truck and drove off, turning right to head towards Lyndhurst leaving a trail of oily smoke to mark their passage. The third man collected an ancient but sturdy-looking bicycle and began to walk it along the grass verge, eventually turning off to the left along a forest track.

In the hotel saloon bar, several pairs of eyes, bright from the effect of champagne and other stimulants, were watching the man as he walked slowly away with his bicycle. Altogether, there were eight people present, six men and two women. Both women moved away from the windows at the same time and began an earnest discussion. Some of the men joined in as more champagne was slopped into glasses and onto a tray of rapidly disappearing smoked salmon sandwiches. Suddenly, a decision seemed to have been reached and the group, moving almost as a single entity, turned from the bar, strode out past the toilets to the car park and climbed into various cars. They spread themselves between four vehicles, leaving two soft top cars behind. In the pub, their visit was marked only by a small pile of twenty-pound notes on the sandwich tray.

Led by a big steel-grey, four-wheel drive Porsche, the small convoy drove along the road and then noisily into the trees, following the route taken by the man with the bicycle. If they had been less excited and more observant they might have noticed that they were following the tracks of another vehicle, occasionally evident in the mud on the damp track.

The trail ran through a corridor of dark, tall trees in a nearly straight line for about half a mile into the deep forest, where it opened onto a wide flat grass area in front of a pair of well-maintained thatched cottages. The track wound around the edge of the grass before narrowing slightly and disappearing further into the trees, at which point a smaller path forked off to the left of the main track, passing around the back of the buildings. One of the cottages was unoccupied, the other was the home of the forester with the bicycle. Lights were appearing in the ground floor windows as the forester, who lived alone apart from a big dog of mixed parentage, set about preparing his evening meal.

About a hundred yards behind the cottages, Harry Chaplin waited patiently in his van. He had arrived there just over two hours previously when the last of the afternoon light had enabled him to reverse the van deep into the undergrowth where even in daylight it was invisible from only a few feet away.

Harry was feeling pleased with himself, but as the time dragged on, doubt crept into his head. Had he interpreted the coded message correctly? Had they changed their arrangements? Was he in the right place? He pulled the pink paper from an inner pocket and studied it again. He was pretty sure he was at the right place and he had heard the noise of powerful car engines as they arrived at the hotel. Confidence returned. 'B.Hd' meant Boar's Head, 'N.For' meant the New Forest and the numbers formed a date-time group – six-thirty p.m. on the 28th of September; it couldn't be anything else. He didn't know the significance of the last two digits JS, nor did he worry about this. Harry had made his plans accordingly, recognising that he might be entirely wrong or that the meeting might be cancelled; but the possibility of locating the rest of his tormentors was just too good to pass up.

Harry had sorted out the equipment he thought he might need but he still wasn't sure exactly what he intended to do. He thought that his actions would be decided by the circumstances he encountered.

Sitting quietly in his van, he waited, occasionally peering through the open side-window with a pair of binoculars. He heard someone whistling as the forester returned to his cottage and then he was guided by other noises as a door was opened, the bicycle was put away, a dog barked and, through the green curtain of the forest, he was just able to discern a loom of light.

After about forty minutes had dragged by, Harry began to think that he was probably wasting his time, but then he heard the sound of car engines accompanied by waves of loud rock music coming closer. He opened the door of the van, making sure the internal light didn't come on, and eased out onto the wet grass. Holding the door open, he reached in and pulled a canvas haversack from the left hand seat, slinging it over his shoulder. Finally he reached in and pulled out a sturdy walking stick. Leaning heavily on the stick, he shut the door quietly and made his way slowly through the undergrowth pressing in around the van. Placing his feet carefully, so as to create the least noise, he moved along the edge of the path, keeping in the shadow of the trees.

In five minutes as he neared the back of the cottage, the noise of vehicle engines had become much louder and, moving forward, Harry saw that there were four sturdy-looking vehicles circling around the grass area in front of the buildings, churning the surface into mud.

The front door of the nearest cottage opened and the forester appeared. He was holding something in his hand, which he placed by the side of the door as he ran out waving his arms. The lead vehicle, a big grey four wheel drive car, immediately turned towards the forester and charged at him. Belying his apparent age, the man threw himself to one side but he was caught a glancing blow by the front wing of the car. He fell to the ground, rolling clear of the car, and then started to scramble back towards his doorway. As he reached his doorstep, figures came tumbling from the other vehicles, running towards the injured man, whooping and yelling like primitive savages.

The forester managed to scramble painfully to his feet, but he was unable to reach the shelter of his doorway. He ran and limped past Harry's temporary hiding place and on into the deeper undergrowth. A man and two women were following. One of them was waving a torch about and Harry shrank to a crouch, attempting to remain still and silent while the pursuers passed him, intent on catching the injured forester. After they passed, Harry delved into his canvas bag and pulled out two of his previous 'come-in-handy' purchases – a crossbow and a bag containing a dozen quarrels – polished, hardwood arrows.

The three pursuers crashed on through the thinning undergrowth, fanning out and yelling to each other as they pushed through young trees and around thick rhododendron bushes. Harry waited until he was sure they were well past him and certain that the others were still on the grass patch, before following them. He had no difficulty in locating them. The injured forester was lying on the ground trying to avoid kicks and blows from his attackers. One of the assailants had found a rotting piece of wood which he was using to batter his victim, but pieces kept breaking off. The victim had just managed to crawl and roll to the base of a big tree and one of the women was leaning her back against the tree, blonde hair tumbling forward over her face and arms spread out to retain her balance as she aimed kicks at her victim's head.

The three assailants were consumed by their task, but Harry realised that others might be following, so anything he could do to help the injured forester would have to be done now. He focused his mind on his three previous tormentors and silently moved forward until he was within fifteen feet of them, but still hidden. Crouching lower, he hefted the crossbow in his hand, and braced it and himself against the side of a tree while he pulled a sharply pointed quarrel from his coat pocket. He could feel his heart pounding and his face sweating as he slotted the shiny hardwood bolt into the frame. He checked that the weapon was taut and ready to fire. Breathing out slowly, he lined the crosshair sight up onto the woman doing most of the kicking. The release mechanism was very light and sensitive and Harry fired before intending to. Nevertheless, the shaft flew true. He had meant to wound the attacking woman but the shaft took her through the throat, passing right through and pinning her to the tree immediately behind her. A look of shocked surprise appeared briefly on the beautiful face. The mouth opened wide as though to shout, but instead, blood spurted from the wound. Then a gurgle escaped from the dying woman's mouth, her arms fluttered aimlessly, and she slumped forward, hanging from the trunk of the tree, her head tilted forward, her face obscured by her long blonde hair which was now rapidly changing colour as the blood continued to flow.

The other two assailants stopped, standing rigid, frozen to the spot, until the other woman uttered a piercing scream and fled back through the bushes. The man dropped his wooden club and, in shock, walked slowly towards the dying woman, now pinioned to the tree. He stood for a moment, close in front of her, staring, apparently mesmerised. At this point, Harry released the second shaft. The power of the crossbow and the shorter range meant that the second quarrel would arrive with even more powerful energy than the first. It hit the man high in the centre of his back, squarely between the shoulder blades. The force of the missile pitched him forward and he slumped onto the body of the woman so that they both hung there, skewered to the treetrunk in a deathly embrace.

The injured forester was trying to crawl away into the bushes and Harry could hear the other woman still screaming as she ran to her friends. He stood still, registering the shock and horror of what he had done; then he decided that he had better get away into the protection of the forest as quickly as he could. He forced his way through the thicker bushes, then moved obliquely back towards the track leading behind the cottages, treading as carefully and quietly as his repaired legs would allow. He had to change direction because he could hear enraged and drunken voices coming towards him. The remaining men were thrashing their way through the trees towards the scene which Harry had just left. He passed the forester who was now staggering along, crouching and holding one arm around his ribs. He saw Harry and threw himself under a big rhododendron bush. Harry ignored him and kept moving, aiming to get around behind the cottages; but he missed his direction in the gloom and ran out in front of the nearest building. There was a shout from his right and he saw two men silhouetted against the headlights of several cars. They had seen him and were already running towards him, one of them brandishing something that appeared to be a sword or a very long knife.

Harry saw that the front door of the nearest cottage was still open and he made for it. His legs were tiring and slowing him, and the man with the sword was gaining on him. He turned for a brief glance over his shoulder, tripped, and fell headlong across the stone doorstep. His canvas bag cushioned his fall but he was winded. He looked around desperately for some means of escape, and saw what had previously looked like a stick when the forester appeared with it in the doorway. It wasn't a stick. It was a double-barrelled shotgun and it was lying under Harry's right hand.

Harry clutched at the gun, rolling over as he did so, at exactly the moment when the first pursuing man threw himself on top of him. Harry shoved the gun upright attempting to fend off the first blows. As the gun came up, the butt jarred against the doorstep, Harry's body rolled against the gun and his hand, now clutching the trigger guard, inadvertently closed around the double triggers. Both barrels fired. Harry's assailant had been very close and had taken a double shot of twelve-bore in the face and upper chest at point-blank range. As the lifeless body rolled away from him Harry stared, shocked at what had once been a man. Now it was just a torso culminating in a gory mess that had once been a head.

Harry heard a high-pitched yell from the direction of the cars. He scraped away the blood and tissue obstructing his vision and saw the other man running fast, back down the track away from the cars.

Harry turned away from the doorway, moving to his left past the front of the cottages. He was heading for the sanctuary of a thick and overgrown hedge beyond the further cottage, which marked the edge of the grass area. As he stumbled along he heard the cottage door slam behind him and felt some relief that the forester had probably reached refuge. He made it to the edge of the clearing and forced his way through a thinner part of the hedge, where he flopped down on the muddy turf, exhausted, gasping for breath and fearful of retribution.

Nothing happened for a few minutes but Harry could hear raised panicky voices coming from the forest on the other side of the cottages. He realised that he must leave the area as quickly as he was able to move. He tried to trot but couldn't, so he walked away from the cottages, breathing heavily and following the track as it wound further into the trees. In five minutes or so the cottages and the cars in front of them had disappeared from view. He paused, staying among the bushes and young trees that marked the edge of the track. He was beginning to worry about spending the rest of the night lost in the forest, so he thought he had better stay in contact with the main track until he could make his way back to where his van was hidden. He moved a few feet further into the bushes and began to work his way towards the cottages, keeping behind the first line of shrubs and bushes. He cursed to himself as he realised that he had lost his walking stick somewhere.

As the tree line opened out on either side of the track, Harry saw torches. They seemed to be waving about haphazardly and he deduced that they were searching for him. He dropped silently to the ground and wriggled into a gap between a clump of ferns and the straight trunk of a pine tree.

He heard the voices again. He couldn't hear exactly what they were shouting but they seemed to be yelling abuse and profanities at each other. Realising that he was close enough to be illuminated by a torch beam sweeping over him, he slithered backward, further into shrubs and ferns. He stopped again, having wormed his way into the space inside a big clump of rhododendrons. Although panicked and in shock, he was thinking clearly and he was certain that they were searching for him. He tried to work out the best way to go and, watching the movement of the torches, he decided to head back towards the main road while remaining well clear of the track

The torch beams now seemed more distant, suggesting that the surviving members of the group were passing along the track, following it further into the forest. They were using the torches to probe the vegetation on either side of the track but the torches didn't seem very powerful and one or two were already failing. At least one other torch was circling the cottages. Harry wondered if they had discovered his van. If they hadn't found it and he could reach it he'd have a better chance of getting away. Too many 'ifs', he thought. He needed a diversion and he had come prepared. In his haversack he had two wine bottles filled with petrol, their corks wedged in place with petrol soaked rags. They were primitive Molotov cocktails.

Harry crossed the track about fifty feet behind the vehicles parked on the track, just short of the cottages. He was closer to the main road now and could hear the occasional rumble of heavy vehicles from that direction. He was also more confident of his location and he believed he should be able to find his van.

He knew that as soon as he started the engine of his van his remaining enemies would hear him and by the time he extricated the van from its hiding place they would be on him. Although it was now very dark among the trees, Harry had better night vision than his pursuers because his eyes had not been affected by torchlight. His other advantage was that he was now calm, although breathless, and he was stone-cold sober, whereas the others were exhibiting various levels of excited inebriation.

Harry moved silently forward out of the bushes and slid into a ditch that ran alongside the track. There was muddy water in the bottom as well as short nettle shoots, but he didn't feel the discomfort. He waited and listened while trying to control his breathing. After a few minutes he reckoned that the shouting voices had moved still further away from him so he worked his way along the ditch, ignoring nettles and mud, moving closer to the nearest car, still intent on setting his diversion.

He stopped his progress along the ditch when he was within twenty feet of the car, then he searched about in his pockets until he found a book of matches. Carefully, he stood the two bottles upright in the sandy soil at the lip of the ditch, tore out a match and struck it. The first one he attempted to light snapped and dropped into the vegetation at his feet. Three more attempts resulted in matches flaring briefly then going out. Harry turned his body to provide more shelter for his matches, tore three more matches from the book and, holding them close together and close to the bottles, he struck them. The flare of the matches was bigger and lasted longer than the other attempts but the flame burnt the fingers holding them. Harry dropped the burning matches but not before managing to light the rag wrapped around the cork of one bottle. He used the bottle to light the wick on the second bottle, waited until it was well alight and then, stepping out on to the track, he threw it as far as he could, aiming towards a spot in the undergrowth on the other side, near the grass area.

For a few seconds nothing happened but then there was a bright flare of flame. He heard more shouting and could see some of the distant torch beams moving towards the flames, which were already dying down. Harry picked up the second bottle and threw it underarm, down the track towards the nearest vehicle, a Land Rover Discovery. The bottle hit the ground in front of the vehicle without exploding. It rolled underneath the Land Rover, between the front wheels. He thought it had failed and was turning away back towards the ditch when the home-made bomb blew up with a distinct 'whump'. Flames emerged from under each side of the car, while Harry set off through the undergrowth to where he hoped his van still waited.

Using the looming roofs of the cottages against the skyline as a guide Harry made his way towards his former hiding place. The van was so well hidden that he twice missed the spot, but he was relieved when he saw that it hadn't been discovered. He climbed into the driving seat, pulled the door closed until he heard the small click of the lock connecting, and then dragged the crossbow from his canvas bag. He wound the tensioning handle and fished two more hardwood bolts from his pocket, pushing them into the space where the left seat cushion met the seat back.

Then he sat perfectly still, listening and waiting.

The first set of flames had disappeared but the second set could be seen roaring through the upper part of the trees, nearly two hundred feet away. The car was obviously well alight and he could hear the crackle of the fire interspersed with sounds of screaming and shouting.

Then he heard the distinctive sound of engines roaring into life. They were making a run for it. He could now just make out the dim shape of the roofs away to his left and he could still see the bonfire he had created on the track. The noise of the fire was louder but he could no longer hear the other engines. Harry started his own engine and bulldozed the van back through the undergrowth. When he reached the edge of the grass patch he turned off the engine and looked around. There was nobody to be seen. Harry thought that the forester was still hiding behind his locked door. He ran around behind the van and disconnected a heavy balk of timber which had been tied by two ropes to the towing point on the back of the van. The timber had done a reasonable but imperfect job of wiping out his muddy tyre tracks.

Harry drove down the main track, then off to the side to circle the spot where flames from the gutted Land Rover were dying down. Within a few minutes he was on the main road and only two hours later he was bumping slowly along the riverside path towards the Motor Fishing Vessel.

He backed the van into its spot in the reeds, and picked up his bag and a few other bits and pieces before boarding the boat, unlocking the wheelhouse door and disappearing inside. He stripped off all his clothes, disgusted at the blood and flesh still stuck to them. Then he went down to the lower deck bathroom and stood under the shower for a full five minutes, soaping all over his body and thoroughly washing his thinning hair. He towelled himself dry as he walked into the main cabin, then dressed quickly, finally pulling on a set of white overalls which he buttoned on both wrists and up to his chin.

He went back up to the wheelhouse and located a cylindrical five-gallon steel drum which had been converted for use as a waste-bucket. He picked it up and took it out to the river bank. Then he fetched his discarded clothes and bundled them into the drum. Finally, wearing goggles and protective gloves, he carefully poured acid from a plastic keg onto the clothes. Smoke began to curl from the bin and the clothes started to disintegrate. Then Harry carried the bin with the remaining liquid into the reeds behind the van where he had dug a small hole for his rubbish. He disposed of the remnants of the still smoking liquid by pouring it into the hole.

It was nearly ten o'clock when Harry drove the van back down the path to Wareham. Once out of the town he pulled into an otherwise empty lay-by and changed the false number plates for the proper ones.

An hour later he parked the van among a number of other vehicles on a back street in Easton, before walking to his cottage.

Chapter 36

Bob led the way down the stairs to the superintendent's office. 'Let me do the talking,' he said.

Jim nodded and waited while Bob knocked on the partly open door, before following the senior detective into the room.

As usual, the station boss was making a show of being very busy, scribbling notes on the corners of a thick sheaf of documents with an expensive-looking fountain pen. The two men waited while the scribbling was completed with a final flourish. The superintendent put down his pen, moved the papers into an 'Out' tray and waved towards the chairs in front of his desk.

'Do you mind if I shut the door, sir? What I have to say is quite sensitive.' Bob was already extending an arm towards the door.

The superintendent appeared to be about to object, but then said, 'Right, shut it.'

Bob made sure the office door was firmly shut, then sat down, leaning forward with an earnest look on his face.

'Well, sir, we've moved a long way ahead. We have one suspect in custody and he has confessed. He seems to have suffered a major attack of conscience and he has responded positively to all the interview questions…'

'Who conducted the interview?'

'I did, sir, and the suspect's lawyer was present throughout, as was DS Creasy, and a representative from the CPS. The interview was duly recorded digitally and by a stenographer. The suspect was given plenty of time and proper breaks during the interview process as well as food and refreshments.' Bob trotted out all this in the hope of precluding a continuing trail of questions and interruptions. He paused, waiting for the superintendent to respond. For a few moments nobody spoke and the two senior officers stared at each other across the desk.

'Well, go on then.' The superintendent's voice betrayed some typical impatience.

'Yes, sir. To summarise, the man in custody has named nine accomplices and it looks as if that accounts for the whole gang. The story goes back several years to when these people were at university together. They found a mutual interest in free running...'

A puzzled frown appeared on the brow of the Superintendent. 'What's that?' he said.

Jim chipped in, thinking his boss would start to flounder at the concept of free running. 'It's a new kind of athletic sport, sir,' he said. 'Free runners run all over obstacles, up and down walls, rolling, leaping and tumbling as they go. You might have seen some of this on television a few years ago, but a lot of people would say that free runners are really just showing off to their friends. The idea is to get from A to B no matter what might be in the way.' He stopped speaking, having run out of words.

'Yes, I see.' Clearly the Super didn't 'see', judging from the hesitant way he spoke.

Bob charged on. 'These people formed a sort of social club. The FRUG they call it, apparently.' Cutting off the inevitable question, he ploughed on. 'It means Free Running Undergraduates,' he said. 'Anyway, one thing seems to have led to another and they started to combine socialising with their running, showing off to each other and looking for thrills. There is one other connection that I think drew them all together and that is that they all seem to be out of the top drawer...'

'What do you... oh, I see.'

Bob carried on as if there had been no interruption. 'The socialising led to excessive booze, then to performance-enhancing drugs, then to drugs just for kicks and after that, I think, they went out to find another way of getting their thrills, or kicks if you like.' He paused for effect and in order to draw in a deep breath. 'That, sir, is when they started to kill people.' He stopped.

'What on earth do you mean?' Shock was evident in the senior officer's voice.

'I mean, sir, that I now have reason to believe that this group of well-connected individuals, in seeking ever greater thrills and, I suppose, risks, have killed at least two people and maybe more. We also have an admission that they have attempted to murder at least one other man. And before you ask, sir, we have an admission and allegations to that effect from the prisoner we have in custody.'

Superintendent Holmes leaned back in his chair and asked pointedly, 'And who is that prisoner?'

'It is Sir Arthur Simmonds.'

The effect of this revelation was remarkable. The superintendent shot bolt upright in his chair. His eyes bulged, he started to lever himself to his feet, then flopped back down in the chair. 'My God!' he said, then again, 'My God.' Then, gathering his dignity round him like a cloak, 'But I know him. I've had dinner with him. He's a friend. He's a gentleman. Good God. You must be wrong.'

'He has freely admitted his active part in an attempt to beat and kick an elderly man to death, in killing the man's dog, in driving while unfit through drink or drugs, in conspiracy, and in attempting to pervert the course of justice.' Bob paused once more and the silence in the room was almost tangible. 'He has also made allegations that murders have been committed by his FRUG associates in the past and that more such crimes are being planned for the future.'

'But... but... Who the hell are these people?'

'When I tell you the names of the other nine alleged conspirators you will be even more shocked, I think.' Bob consulted his notebook and started to read from it.

'The Right Honourable Giles Wellton MP, former Minister of State for Rural Affairs; Sir Arthur Simmonds, Baronet, whom we have in custody; Jane Lockyer, who is an actress; Sandra Somerville, who, as you know, is a tennis player.' He looked up from his notebook, paused and peered across the desk at his boss who was leaning forward, resting his elbows on the desk and holding his head in his hands.

'Shall I continue, sir?' asked Bob. The superintendent nodded, still holding his head and staring down at his desk, so the DCI carried on. 'Then there is Henry Hayward, the TV presenter; Cornel Grovey, the Reverend Jeremy Wilberforce, Don Randell and Captain Roger FitzHarris, an army officer.'

'Is that all? It's like an extract from Who's Who.' There was considerable irony in the question, but the answer produced an even bigger reaction on the part of the superintendent. Bob flipped his notebook closed with a snap as he started to speak again.

'No, sir, it is not all. There's one other name which we need to consider in more detail. That is the barrister Ray Marsden, son of former Commander Sir Andrew Marsden of the Met, of Special Branch and before that of the Dorset Police.'

'That would be Ray Marsden, the man with the permanent "get-out-of-jail-free" card, the Villain's Friend?' The Boss seemed to have perked up a bit.

'Yes, it would, sir; but there's more to it than that.' Bob shifted uneasily in his chair, silently wishing he had a strong coffee in front of him. He took a deep breath and continued. 'The thing is that when we started to look into the beating up of Harry Chaplin we kept coming up against blanks. In short, somebody had made all the records, all the evidence, go away. We couldn't even find one single copper who remembered anything about it. It was just as if somebody had spirited the bashed-up body down from the sky and left it in a back street in Weymouth.'

'So, two questions: how did you get into the case in the first place, and what are you insinuating?'

Jim sat very still, wishing to intervene in the conversation and wondering simultaneously how long his Guvnor's patience would hold out.

Bob was wondering whether the station commander was deliberately being obtuse – or was he trying to play some bizarre form of 'devil's advocate'?

He puffed out his cheeks, fiddled with his notebook and started again. 'Can I take you back to our conversation at the beginning, sir? That was when I told you how I'd been to see Harry Chaplin shortly after he came out of his coma. I said that I found several short reports in the local papers, all seemingly describing a gang of youngish tearaways from out of town who were up to mischief. That is, not only a gang of young tearaways, but a gang of posh young tearaways. They had trashed a restaurant in Bournemouth, had caused a fight among the stalls at the Seafood Festival in Weymouth, and then this mashed-up body was dumped in Weymouth in the early hours of the morning. After that we found evidence of a car crash on Portland, on the road out of Easton. This turned out to be a very expensive car crash – an Aston Martin in fact.'

Bob paused again, waiting to see if the superintendent would interrupt. He didn't, so Bob continued. 'These people are all very well-connected and, perhaps due to their networking, they all seem to have done well in their different chosen careers. They've stayed in touch and they have a name for their little group. They call themselves Free Running Undergraduates and they use this as a kind of password, identifying themselves to each other – and they seem to shout it as a sort of war-cry when their blood is up. Are you with me so far, sir?' The superintendent nodded.

'Now here comes the difficult bit,' said Bob. 'It looks as though they are a crowd who go out seeking thrills, but being a few years older, the attraction of free running as a thrill provider has diminished. So they've replaced it with something else. It's a bit like bear-baiting, or dog-fighting, or bare-knuckle fighting, or cock-fighting, or any number of similar activities that involve illegality, blood, violence and risk, to the participants and to the watchers.

'What these people do...' Bob fiddled with his notebook, pausing to muster the right words: '...is get their blood and violence-based thrills from selecting a victim at random and beating him – or her – to death. We have reason to believe that as well as almost achieving this with Harry Chaplin, they have actually achieved their aim more than once in the recent past. They even probably film the event. It would be called a snuff movie.'

'Good God! You mean they have been going round casually murdering people for fun?'

'Yes, sir.'

'On my patch? Good God!'

'Possibly on our patch, sir, but not certainly.'

The meeting was interrupted by an abrupt rap on the office door. Without waiting for a response, the door was opened by DC Gerry Treloar. He looked towards the superintendent and received a cold glare for his trouble. The others turned to look towards him as he spoke.

'Very sorry to interrupt, sir, but something has come up and I need to speak to DS Creasy.'

'Is it important?' The Boss was still glaring.

'It is, sir, very important.'

'Oh, very well then; do it outside, but be quick.' Jim scraped his chair back, reached the doorway in two strides and disappeared through it with the detective constable.

'Carry on,' said the station commander as the door closed behind Jim.

Bob wondered whether he should, but then decided that he should carry on, in order to keep the focus of his boss's attention.

'Well,' he continued more slowly, choosing his words with care. 'You will remember what I told you about the problems we encountered when we started to look into the Chaplin case. There should have been a comprehensive, clearly documented set of records, including statements from the traffic officers who found the wrecked Aston Martin; investigation reports into the ownership of the car; an investigation into Chaplin; who found him, fingerprints, witness statements, house to house enquiries, reports about the fracas in Weymouth. But there was nothing. Abso-bloody-lutely nothing.' He stopped.

'Nothing at all?'

'Nothing – except some empty file covers with a title on the outside but nothing inside. My clerical assistant found them among a load of redundant stuff waiting for destruction –

luckily the idle bugger who should have destroyed them probably forgot.'

The superintendent spoke from behind steepled fingers: 'This station doesn't lose records.'

'No, sir, it does not. So I'm drawn to the conclusion that somebody cleared out everything that was anything to do with the Chaplin case once it was realised that he was still alive. And sir, I mean everything. The car remains were made to disappear, the files were stripped, notebooks and other papers, coppers' statements, like from the copper who found Chaplin's body, and even the coppers themselves. The traffic men who came across the crashed car were transferred, as was the desk sergeant, and probably others for all I know.' Bob stopped to draw breath, and to wonder what was keeping Jim outside all this time.

'Go on, Robert.'

So, we're becoming chums again, thought Bob. He continued speaking. 'We need to consider who would be able to do this and under what pretext. It would take a lot of clout – way above the pay grade of anybody here, but it would have been helpful if the man doing the shutting-down exercise had some knowledge of this nick and how it works.'

'Yes, I see.' The Boss was now 'on side.'

'Then there's motive, and of course there has to be money, a lot of money to fix and buy off all the people who might be involved. Of course there is one higher power that could help this...'

'Do you mean God...?'

'Not quite, but nearly, Boss.' The 'Boss' word had slipped out but Bob realised it had been unexpectedly helpful from the ghost of a smile that crossed the face of the man opposite.

He seized the opportunity and continued, 'So we need to find someone who has a great deal of power and influence, access to a fair amount of untraceable cash, authority within the police, and finally,' he paused to allow the effect of his words to register, 'and finally, motive. The motive in this case would be to protect one of his own – a son, perhaps?'

'Yes. Okay, spell it out.'

'This individual has to be very senior in the police. The ultimate power, which would at that time be really unchallengeable, would be national security, somebody with the authority of MI5, or perhaps even MI6. The motive, as I said, would be to protect one of your own, avoid a scandal, family disgrace, that sort of thing, and the money would come from the pockets of the criminals involved. Who comes to mind as a very senior police officer, with connections to the Security Services, connections to money, and, we now discover, a sharp-brained son with a lot of powerful connections of his own?'

'Marsden!' The superintendent uttered the single word with triumph.

'Exactly, Boss, those parameters seem to fit former Commander Sir Andrew Marsden of the Met, sometime member of the security services and former station commander in this nick – who also happens to have a clever son with an unfortunate connection to a gang of psychopaths.'

'Wow! Marsden! It certainly fits, and it fits the public perception of the man.'

Bob was about to respond when the door opened and Jim strode back into the room. He stood behind his chair and, addressing both men said, 'There's been a serious development.'

'Not with Simmonds?' said Bob.

'No, Guv, but I'm sure it's connected with our case.' He moved around and sat in his chair as he continued speaking. 'Earlier this morning Hampshire police had a call from a man in a distressed state. He was a forester working and living in the New Forest. Some time last night he was followed from a pub back to his cottage which is in the forest. He was attacked by a gang of what he called "Yuppies". He was badly beaten and he only survived, he thinks, due to the intervention of somebody else. He doesn't know who. Anyway, that person, man or woman – we don't know – shot dead two of the people as they were trying to kill the forester. He managed to get to his cottage and lock himself in. There was some more trouble and the gang eventually escaped in several high performance cars. One car was left behind, burnt out. Guv, it has – to start with at least – exactly the same MO as the Harry Chaplin case.' He stopped and sat, obviously excited, breathing heavily.

'Anything else?' asked Bob.

'Yes, there are three stiffs.' He rapidly corrected himself: 'Three dead, including one woman, and one man with his head blown off. Oh, and one fancy burnt-out four-wheel drive.'

'Have they moved or touched anything at the scene?' said Bob.

'No, Guv, I've asked the Hampshire boys to seal off the area and hold it till we get there.'

'Sir, I'd better go now,' said Bob. Then as an afterthought, he turned and said "Oh, one more thing, sir. We've got a witness to the attack on Harry Chaplin. We've shown him photographs and he's been able to pick out no less than three members of the gang!'

'Yes, right, I see. Okay, go now, but keep me informed when you can. We'll keep what we were talking about under wraps for now.'

'Right, Boss.' Both detectives were already stepping to the door.

'I've got a pursuit car waiting outside,' said Jim.

Chapter 37

Harry spent the next morning tidying up the cottage, clearing away the accumulation of free papers, pizza ads and a few letters which lay scattered on and around the doormat, before busying himself dusting, vacuuming and generally tidying up.

At about ten o'clock he finished tidying the cottage, made a cup of coffee, took it to the sitting room and settled down in front of the television. He sat staring at the screen, ignoring the cooling coffee while allowing his mind to wander over the dramatic events of the previous evening. He felt no remorse for what he had done because he firmly believed that he had been justified. He actually experienced a sense of satisfaction over the terrible revenge that he had exacted on a group of people who had originally set out to beat him to death for their own perverted amusement.

A random thought kept recurring to him, that the books were now balanced and it was time to end the battle – to distance himself from the life that had consumed him since emerging from his coma. He was tired of the solitary, secret life he had been building, and he believed he had done enough. After all, he thought, the gang was broken up; and while they had done him great damage, he had now killed four of them. He also believed that he had been lucky so far not to be caught, either by the gang or the police.

He started to drink his coffee, realised it was now cold and took it back into the kitchen where he made a fresh brew. Back in the sitting room, the television was still on but the screen was showing some particularly inane quiz show so he started pressing buttons on the remote control, looking for a news channel. Eventually he found the BBC News Channel, which was already in the middle of a bulletin.

'Police are investigating a multiple killing which took place yesterday evening in the New Forest. According to the only witness, Alfred Newman, a group of men and women who had been drinking heavily in a nearby pub, followed Mr Newman back to his home and attacked him. Then they fell into dispute with each other and fought among themselves. Police are searching for the owner of a Land Rover left burnt out in the forest near Mr Newman's home. Police are also searching for a number of other men and women and have called for witnesses to come forward. It is thought the motive might have been robbery.

'In other news, the search is continuing for the missing former government minister, Giles Wellton. It is believed that Mr Wellton may have suffered some sudden illness and a finger-tip search is being conducted around Wimbledon Common where Mr Wellton was last seen...'

Harry had heard enough. He sat in silence, sipping his coffee and continuing to meditate on recent events. Then he had an idea. He went back into the kitchen and returned with his laptop. He found the notebook where he had jotted down the names prized painfully from Giles Wellton and one at a time typed them into the Google search engine on the computer. He knew about Wellton and Sandra Somerville, so he typed in 'Jane Lockyer'. Immediately a list of websites was displayed.

The first site he opened was Wikipedia, which presented quite a lot of information about Jane Lockyer. He read that she was an actress who had worked mostly in repertory, interspersed with a few television roles and small parts in two films. He didn't recognise any of the productions listed but he read on. He learnt where she had been born, her age – twenty-seven – and was given an outline of her school and university career, which seemed unimpressive. He noted that her expensive education had generated not one single academic qualification.

He turned to another website and found that this one seemed to be advertising the acting skills of Jane Lockyer woven in with a whole lot of gossip column stuff about who she was dating, what shows she had appeared in and what she was about to appear in. He thought it could have been titled I'm Jane Lockyer: Buy Me!

Harry continued to scroll down the screen and came across a series of alluring photographs, mostly publicity shots but some others that could easily have graced the pages of Playboy magazine. He studied them reflectively. She was definitely one of the women in the photographs he had taken from Wellton's wallet but more than that, she was the woman he had killed only a few hours ago. As he stared at the voluptuous body barely clad in a few sensuous strips of clothing, he thought, without emotion, of the woman he had last seen pinned by his crossbow arrow to the broad trunk of an oak tree, wide-set blue eyes staring sightlessly, hands, feet and arms still twitching as blood poured unfettered from her throat and down across her ample breasts, soaking and staining the thin white silk blouse she had worn. Then the image had been covered as his second victim of the night fell across her, draped over her like a macabre tailor's dummy. He forced himself to think back to the dreams which had haunted him for so long. This was one of the women who had kicked him and stamped on him in a vain but violent and bloodthirsty attempt to kill him. She was dead and would not now be able to destroy any other life. He still felt no remorse, but a small, irritating speck of conscience kept emerging in his head, suggesting that perhaps he should now show some remorse.

He looked up Henry Hayward and Ray Marsden next. Henry Hayward was a smarmy TV chat show presenter given to wearing flashy suits and loud ties, but Ray Marsden was a different type altogether. There were several websites attached to his name; two of them included photographs of the man. Harry studied the photographs, one showing a well-built, youngish man dressed in the formal clothing of a barrister. The other one was a head and shoulders close-up of an unsmiling man with thick black gelled hair, wide-set, piercing eyes under bushy brows and a prominent nose above thin lips and a square clean-shaven chin. He was a barrister and, from what Harry read, a very successful one. Another entry said that he had recently been appointed Queen's Council. Harry noted that his father was a retired senior policeman with the Metropolitan Police, who had previously been active in Special Branch, and then later, it was thought, with MI5.

He moved on from the Wikipedia entry on Marsden and typed in Cornel Grovey. There wasn't very much about him but it suggested that he was an international playboy. His striking good looks and tall military posture shown in a few photographs seemed to have led him through the beds of a remarkable selection of 'Society' ladies and then, in a similar pattern, through a series of scandals and divorce courts.

The next name surprised him even more. Jeremy Wilberforce, it transpired, was actually the Reverend Jeremy Wilberforce. He was an ordained priest and Chaplain to the Bishop of Benchester. Harry sat there, in his chair, his remaining coffee growing cold, staring at the computer screen and wondering what kind of evil had possessed these people.

Harry couldn't find much information about the next two names he had. Don Randell was an international yachtsman and, surprisingly, thought Harry, openly gay. Roger de Launcey FitzHarris was an army officer in a swanky regiment and he came from a landed and well-to-do Scottish family. There were no photos of this man and very little supporting information on either of them.

The last name on his list was Arthur Simmonds. With yet another shock Harry discovered that the tall, distinguished young man shown in the inset picture was Sir Arthur Simmonds, a baronet who seemed to own a large chunk of Dorset, together with property in the West Indies, South Africa and elsewhere in Britain. He was described as a wealthy philanthropist and certainly looked exactly like a distinguished country gentleman. He was said to have paid for schooling and medical treatment as well as, sometimes, housing, for people who were injured, damaged or just down on their luck. The final entry practically floored Harry. Sir Arthur Simmonds was supposedly a major sponsor of the Chesil Clinic and Medical Research Centre near Weymouth.

This was the clinic that had so carefully and tirelessly taken in and nursed a broken man back to health. Harry simply couldn't understand any of it. He sat there, allowing his mind to wander and then trying to work out which of these men he had killed. He tried to suggest to himself that it didn't really matter. They had all been his enemies and now some of them were dead. But he couldn't leave it at that. He needed to know more, but since nobody else actually knew what Harry had found out, and hopefully what he had done, he also needed to keep a low profile. He couldn't go round asking about these people. He simply had to do nothing, but wait and see what, if anything, happened.

By the time Harry had cooked his frozen ready-meal lunch, he had also reached the conclusion that the time had come when he needed to fade quietly from the picture; move away and start to live a simple and easy life; to try to enjoy life once more, and perhaps even do something to compensate for the wrongs he had been drawn into committing. He began to feel a sense of calm and relaxation creeping over and through him as he realised that he had dealt with his demons.

When he switched on the television news later that evening he learnt the names of those he had dealt with and he was surprised to learn that the police were said to be seeking others and were close to making arrests.

Chapter 38

The unmarked pursuit car raced along the A31 dual carriageway at an illegal speed, discreet blue lights and headlights flashing, two-tone horn blaring. Both Bob and Jim had mobile phones clasped to their ears, trying to pick up as much information as possible before they arrived at the crime scene.

Just under forty-five minutes after leaving the police station at Weymouth they turned off the main road and down onto the roundabout under junction one, marking the beginning of the M27. They drove south towards Lyndhurst, then through the busy little forest town, still travelling south as they left it, but now more slowly, though still heralded by the two-tone horn signalling their progress.

Both men had placed their mobiles back in their pockets by the time the car bumped along the rough track towards the pair of rustic cottages in the forest. Bob peered through the window as their driver manoeuvred around the remains of the burnt-out Land Rover, now flanked by blue and white 'Police Aware' tape. The detectives were bounced back and forth as the car lurched through muddy ruts and holes, around the wreck and on down the forest track to the clearing. The whole area including the cottages, the track and the rough grass verges around the torched vehicle had also been cordoned off, and several figures dressed head to toe in hooded white overalls and blue plastic overshoes were moving around between the trees and undergrowth searching the crime scene.

A few minutes later the police car stopped at the edge of the churned-up lawn in front of the cottages. A detective from the Hampshire Constabulary opened the car door while Bob eased himself out. They shook hands with the Hampshire officer and then climbed awkwardly into white overall suits and overshoes. Then with Bob and the local man leading they walked off towards a white canvas screen in front of one of the cottage doors. Jim followed closely, a pace behind.

A policeman wearing a motorcycle traffic officer's uniform lifted a flap of the screen as they arrived. They stepped inside but both newcomers immediately turned away involuntarily. The others were already used to it but it took the Dorset men a minute or two to get used to the smell and the sight of the blood-spattered headless body.

'Any identification?' asked Bob.

'Yes, we think so, but we need DNA confirmation – you can see the state he's in. Anyway, I think we should look at the others first,' said the local man. He walked away without waiting for an answer and headed off to the left down beside the wall of the cottage before branching further to the left, moving off the track and weaving through patchy undergrowth, which gave way to a copse of tall trees surrounded by a grassy glade.

There were no screens here yet, and the scene which met them was like something conceived by Dante for his Inferno. The first thing to attract their attention was a constant buzzing coming from a cloud of flies. Beneath the flies was a big patch of blood on the ground, spreading out from the base of the tree and now congealing and turning brown. Above that stood a man in a dirty white shirt streaked with dried blood. He was slightly built, prematurely balding and clearly dead. His arms were thrown forward, hanging over the shoulders of the female corpse, which was wearing a flimsy blouse that had also once been white. The momentum of the man falling forward had pitched him against the white bloodless face of the woman, so that their lips were actually touching. It was a shocking tableau of an embrace of death. The cloud of black flies were buzzing audibly around and above the corpses, with hundreds of others crawling on the bodies and along the blood-soaked ground. The scene was completed by a small part of the hardwood shaft of a quarrel projecting from between the man's shoulder blades.

Jim craned his neck to peer around the dead man. He saw immediately that the quarrel had passed right through the body and into the lower chest of the woman. Looking again he could see another quarrel sticking out of the woman's throat, pinning her firmly to the tree.

Other police officers arrived and began to erect a tent around the grisly scene. Bob turned and spoke as he started to walk away. 'The first thing we need is a confirmed identification. Has anybody got any tea?' The three detectives walked purposefully, and in silence, back towards the edge of the grassy glade. By the time the trio reached the car several folding canvas chairs had appeared and Bob flopped into one of them. The others followed suit and they sat in silence.

Then Bob said, 'I doubt even the most experienced coppers have seen anything like that. It looks almost as though it has been set up as a tableau.'

The tea arrived. The Dorset men sat and waited. That was really all they could do because these crimes had taken place outside their jurisdiction. The local man disappeared towards the cottages.

Five minutes later, he was back. 'The woman is Jane Lockyer, the actress,' he said. 'Haven't got anything on the other two yet but it shouldn't be long.'

'Right,' said Bob, 'we've got enough to start with. We now know – or at least we have a good idea – of what these unsavoury buggers have been up to. We've got ten names, one of them in custody. I won't wait for the identification of these two. We'll get that radioed through as soon as they have something. Meantime, get on the blower – phone, mind, not the radio – and set up raids on every known address for this lot. I want them all pulled in. We'll also need warrants to search premises and vehicles, okay?'

Turning to the Hampshire detective he said, 'There's nothing else we can do here so I'm going back to Dorset straightaway. Thanks for your help; let me know as soon as you've identified the two male stiffs. Keep in touch with my skipper here. We've got to go and catch some very bad men.' He started to walk back to where the mud-spattered pursuit car was waiting.

Jim walked alongside his boss, but he looked aghast. 'That's a tall order, Guv; we have to find the addresses first, and there's at least nine of them, ten if you count the bloke we've got in custody. Some of these people are wheeler-dealers and they may have more than one place. Actually, some of them will have several addresses – the politician, for instance. There could be at least four or five other forces involved; that means multiple sets of judges or magistrates. It's gonna take some setting up, Guv.'

'Just get on with it, Jim.' The response was terse.

Back in the car, Bob stared straight ahead through the windscreen as they bounced back down the track and turned onto the Lyndhurst Road. The siren and blue lights came on again as the car picked up speed.

It was not until they were back in the outside lane of the A31 that Bob spoke again. 'Well,' he said, 'difficult or not, Jim, I want it done, and I want it done quick. You'll need help but I'll talk to the boss and you'll get it. It's just after four now and we should be back at the nick before five. I expect to have a preliminary identification of the two stiffs in the forest by then, and we already know the woman. I reckon most of the addresses will be outside the Dorset manor, so other people will have to tramp round the courts for the appropriate bits of paper.'

Bob stopped speaking as the car radio interrupted him. 'Whisky tango one two,' it said. 'Message for DCI Majury. Over.'

The driver answered immediately. 'Whisky tango twelve; roger. The DCI is listening. Pass your message. Over.'

'Whisky tango, we have two identifications for you. Over.'

'Whisky tango, roger: go ahead. Over.'

A different voice emerged from the radio. 'The idents are Cornel Grovey and Donald Randell. Addresses of all three involved have been located and sent by email to Weymouth. What is your Echo Tango Alpha? Over.'

The driver answered without waiting for his passengers, 'Doors open at 1645. Over.'

Bob reached forward, holding out his hand for the radio microphone. 'We'll set up a secure phone conference as soon as we arrive. Send your contact numbers by email. Over.'

'Roger that. Out!'

The blue lights took them easily through the early evening traffic and by a quarter to five Bob was climbing the front steps as quickly as he could, heading for the Super's office. Jim, with the help of Gerry Treloar and the duty sergeant, was organising a briefing for the half dozen or so police officers who had been gathered together ready for the proposed raids on the expanding list of addresses.

As he was winding up the briefing, the door opened and the station commander came into the room followed by Bob. Chairs scraped as the assembled team started to stand up. The superintendent waved them back down into their seats. 'Carry on,' he said.

Jim continued. 'We have at least five addresses to raid, one of which belongs to the man we have in custody, and another belongs to a man recently deceased. Regardless of that we will go in at 0600 tomorrow. The other five addresses will be covered by Hampshire and the Met, also possibly Surrey and Thames Valley. That is being coordinated by the Met. Remember, there is a total of six names on the list of those we want to arrest. When you go in I want you to search particularly for computers, mobile phones, cameras, tablets, iPods – that sort of thing. We also want to know if there are alternative addresses that we don't know about, so look for address books, notes, diaries and any other loose papers or files.

'Finally, if you make arrests, make sure you follow the process meticulously, make sure they're cautioned before you say anything else and do allow them to remain on the premises while you continue the search. Weymouth has been designated search headquarters and all team leaders will assemble here at 1200, when DCI Majury will hold a conference, which will determine what happens next. I will be going with the team to Poole and DCI Majury will be going to Bovington. Any questions?'

Several hands shot up. 'You haven't mentioned the Military Police or the Ministry of Defence Police, Skip. Have they been informed?'

'Good point...'Jim was interrupted by a familiar voice behind him.

'I'll do that,' said the superintendent.

Bob stood up, addressing the twenty or so police men and women. 'Thank you. Most of the people we will be looking for are well-connected. We think we've got the right names, but you can never be certain – so handle them with kid gloves – got it?'

Heads nodded. They had, indeed, got it. More hands were raised. 'What do we do about any other addresses we find, Guv? Do we go on to them?'

'No. Initially you report back here and any further action will be decided then.'

'Are we expecting any aggro? Any weapons likely?'

'No, aggression towards you from these people is most unlikely. And in the equally unlikely event that you find any kind of offensive weapon on the premises, you bag it up and take it with you. Don't enter into any discussion on the matter.'

'What do we do if their briefs turn up?'

'Like the subjects, treat them with kid gloves; be polite; be as nice as you can, tell them where you are taking any arrested suspects, namely here, to this Station, and tell them they are welcome to come to the Station in due course.'

There were several more questions, mostly answered by Bob but with some amplification from the detective sergeant. Then the room emptied, quite quickly, and the officers dispersed.

****

At a quarter to five the next morning, the teams assembled in the station. Half an hour later, ten vehicles set off in convoy, led by Bob Majury driving his own unmarked car. All the vehicles were showing flashing blue lights, and some with alternately flashing headlights.

As the convoy reached Dorchester, two vehicles broke away, heading north, and the rest drove steadily west.

At exactly 6 a.m., in Dorset, London, Hampshire and Surrey, teams of police men and women arrived at various front doors. Some rang bells, some burst through locked doors and one or two teams actually had doors opened for them.

In North Dorset, the detective sergeant leading the team actually telephoned the imposing ivy-clad house as their car entered the long tree-lined driveway leading to the building. The call was answered by a sleepy voice, wondering what was going on, but by the time the car and its accompanying van came to a stop in the courtyard, the door was already being opened. The warrant was flourished and the search began.

At the gates of the Royal Armoured Corps Headquarters at Bovington, things were not going quite so well. Despite the warning telephone call from Superintendent Holmes the previous evening, the two vehicles had been stopped at a lowered barrier by the main entrance to the camp. The guard had called the sergeant who had studied the warrant and grandly declared that it was not valid on Army land. Bob returned to his car, instructed the other vehicle to pull up alongside his, thus obstructing the gate, and then, seated in his car, he had started to make telephone calls, working from a list of numbers he had been given by Gerry Treloar. Forty minutes later, his temper frayed, he stood by the car under a light drizzle that had started, and watched as an officer, dressed in camouflage smock and trousers, and accompanied by a troubled-looking man in the uniform of the Ministry of Defence Police, approached the blocked gate barrier.

'Good morning,' said the officer as he arrived at the other side of the barrier. 'My name is Major Bennet. I don't know what you want, but this is Army land, you see, and you don't have jurisdiction. Sorry, old boy. Wasted journey, I'm afraid.'

Bob held his temper with difficulty. 'You haven't received a telephone call requesting your co-operation in a murder investigation?'

'Oh yes, received the call, old boy, but these things are for the Military Police, you see. Can't agree to co-operate without having our own cops look at it first, you know.'

Bob turned to the uniformed sergeant by his side, and spoke earnestly and quietly to him. He handed over a piece of paper and stood back as the sergeant climbed into his van and began to back it away from the gate.

The major, who now seemed to be finding the stand-off amusing, asked, 'Where's he going?'

Bob could see a young woman, dressed smartly in what, he presumed from the red cap she was wearing, was the uniform of a corporal in the Military Police. She was tripping along, quite quickly, down the roadway that led to the gate. Bob started to walk slowly back to his car. He climbed in, started the engine and in a series of moves, turned the car so that it was now sideways on to the gate, blocking any access or egress. He got out and walked back towards the barrier.

'I said, where's he going?' repeated the major, rather testily.

'Oh.' Bob glanced at his watch, smiled serenely, and put his arms on the barrier. 'Your colonel lives in Bovington village, I believe? I think we've got his address here.' He held out the paper in front of the major, where he could see it. The major looked uncertain for the first time, nodded, and said, 'Yes, that's it. Why do you want it?'

Bob smiled broadly. 'Well, about now, you see, my sergeant and his two constables will be breaking down the front door of that house, entering it at speed, shouting "Police!" and heading for the bedrooms. The house is in Bovington village and – as you will know – that is outside this camp and therefore clearly within my jurisdiction.

'They will arrest your colonel, to whom a recorded request for assistance has already been made from Weymouth, and, I understood, accepted; and they will charge him with obstructing the police in the course of a murder inquiry. They will drag him down the stairs, throw him in the back of the police van and return here. Then you will be allowed to cross this barrier to speak with your colonel if you wish. Of course, as soon as you step outside this barrier I will arrest you and both of you will be taken to Weymouth Police Station where you will be held in custody.'

'You bastard! He's got a wife and children. Oh, Christ, he'll slaughter me. Oh, shit!'

Bob walked away and sat on the front passenger seat of his car, letting the door hang open and watching the turmoil now taking place on the other side of the barrier. A second Ministry of Defence Police officer had arrived, as well as a tall, gleaming, imposing figure with a short leather-covered stick under his arm, who Bob thought might be the Base Sergeant Major. In this he was correct. Further back along the road behind the barrier other figures were making for the gate. Most of the Army people already around the gate were talking. None appeared to be listening, and the entrance gate was fast becoming a focal point for a farcical spectacle.

At this point, the headlights of the police van appeared further along the lane. The van was heading towards the gate. Bob waited patiently.

The van pulled up and as the police sergeant alighted from the driving seat, Bob opened the outer rear doors. Inside, a face red with fury peered out through the wire mesh wall of the retention 'tank' inside the van. The owner of the face seemed to be a small man, clad in a dark blue dressing gown. A pair of striped pyjama legs extended below the dressing gown and ended in naked feet. The mouth under a small bristling ginger moustache opened but Bob got his point in first.

'Colonel,' he said, 'I have ordered your arrest because I believe you are deliberately obstructing my inquiry into a serious crime. I am seeking to enter the premises occupied by one Captain Roger de Launcey FitzHarris, an officer under your command and resident within your establishment. This officer,' he pointed to the major, 'has deliberately barred my entry into your establishment, acting, I understand on your orders. I have also sent out a call to all police forces for Captain FitzHarris to be arrested on sight. Is there anything you would like to say before I slam this door and send you off to Weymouth?'

Within ten minutes the colonel had decided that he had made a grave mistake, which he blamed on guidance received from the major. The major looked distinctly crestfallen, his air of chippy superiority had disappeared and he just stood in silence. The colonel was then driven back to his home in Bovington village, and reunited with his wife and children. Prudently, during the previous visit, the police sergeant had actually knocked on the front door of the colonel's house despite his boss's instruction to break it down, albeit knocking very loudly; and he waited by the undamaged door while the colonel prepared himself to return to the camp.

At Bovington Camp, Bob and his team were just parking their vehicles outside the officers' mess, each vehicle now with an additional passenger in the form of a trim young female Military Police Corporal. One of these led Bob and his two search officers into an accommodation block while the other waited with the vehicles and the rest of the team.

Bob was led along a corridor, past men and women emerging in various stages of undress to start their working day. Eventually the Military Police Corporal stopped and rapped on a door. Nothing happened, so she rapped again, louder and longer this time. Again there was no answer, so Bob waited while the corporal went off back along the corridor in search of a key. She returned within a minute and opened the door. The door led into a small bedroom, furnished with a single bed, a desk incorporating cupboards, a fitted row of cupboards and drawers, a couple of easy chairs and a large wardrobe with internal shelves and drawers. An open door led off into a bathroom. The room was clean and everything seemed neat and tidy. It was unoccupied, and looked as though it had been for some time.

Bob wasted no time and told his officers to start searching, while the Military Police Corporal produced a mobile phone and started talking earnestly into it. After a conversation lasting several minutes she put the phone away and said, 'Apparently he's on leave.'

Elsewhere the raids and searches were proceeding more or less as planned. In Wimbledon, Sandra Somerville had made a fuss about the property belonging to a government minister who should have been contacted by the police. She had been arrested and held at the property while the search took place. Ray Marsden, the QC, had given surprisingly little resistance when encountered in his Westminster flat. He had even provided the keys to what he described as his cottage in Wareham. The flats of Jane Lockyer in Fulham, Cornel Grovey in Winchester and Don Randell in Poole, all of whom were known to have died, were easily opened and thoroughly searched, without encountering any problems. Henry Hayward was arrested in a recording studio and taken to his flat where he watched the search without protest, but the Reverend Jeremy Wilberforce could not be located. Nevertheless, his home in the grounds of the Bishop's Palace was opened and searched.

The original plan had been for the search team leaders to assemble back at Weymouth at noon, but, like many such plans, it proved too ambitious, so it was not until 5 p.m. that the last team leaders arrived at Weymouth.

A series of metal tables had been set up at the end of the briefing room and these were now filled with evidence – all tagged to show location, ownership – if known – and the date, time and circumstances of finding the item. The room was full, with about twenty police officers sitting or standing, most of them nursing mugs of coffee or tea. Bob Majury had been working the room, talking to officers from the other forces, picking up detail and flavour that may not have been included in the hastily prepared official reports.

Eventually, he made his way to the front of the room, called for attention, waited until everyone was seated and listening, and then started speaking.

'First, I want to thank you all for taking part in this operation…'

A voice from the middle of the room interrupted him: 'No problem, Bob, it was a nice day out!'

'Thanks, Jack, glad you enjoyed it. I know you all lead a boring life tucked away at the Yard!' A ripple of laughter died away as Bob continued. 'The thing is,' he said, 'that at first sight it looks as though your collective efforts have been successful. Thanks in part to these evil buggers' habit of recording what they do when they go out to get their kicks, we seem to have a lot of evidence, and most of our 'gang' seem to be fingered by it. What I must ask you for now, unless of course you've already done it, is statements from at least two officers who were present when any significant item of evidence was found. If there was a lot of it in one place, then you can put it in the form of a list; but to preserve the value of the evidence we've got, I want the circumstances, time and precise location of discovery stated, so there can be no question of some smart-arsed brief claiming it was planted or tampered with. Everybody with me on that?'

There were nods and mutters of assent from around the room. Bob waited a moment and then continued, 'We have, I believe, three suspects in custody…'

Jim broke in with the names: 'Sandra Somerville, Henry Hayward and Ray Marsden, as well as Sir Arthur Simmonds who we're already holding here. Jane Lockyer, Cornel Grovey and Don Randell are dead; which means we're still looking for the ex-government minister Giles Wellton, the Reverend Jeremy Wilberforce and Captain Roger FitzHarris…'

Bob started speaking again. 'Among all of those, and I know I don't need to tell you this, the one to watch most carefully is Ray Marsden, the Villain's Friend, the man with the golden "get-out-of-jail" card…'

There was a low rumble of voices from around the room. Few of those present were unaware of the reputation of the man who had been such a successful thorn in the side of the police.

Bob ignored the interruption and carried on. 'Knowing the man by his deeds, I am surprised that he came so easily, and has apparently co-operated. I sense that he's leading us down the hill to a trap, some sort of legal tripwire which he probably thinks won't even allow us to get him into the witness box. Who arrested him, please?'

A hand was raised from near the back of the room. 'I did.'

Bob turned to address the young Detective Inspector from the Metropolitan Police. 'Tell us about it, George.'

Detective Inspector George Curtis remained seated as he spoke. 'It was all very civilised, really. He was already up and dressing when we arrived. He didn't comment on the damage to the door, other than to say we would probably have to pay for it. He watched everything we were doing without comment, handed over the keys to his cottage, which is apparently more like a castle, and he just asked if he could make a couple of calls before we put the cuffs on. He didn't have anything to say, all the way down in the car. He just looked out of the window.'

'Who did he call?' Bob suddenly resembled a tiger about to pounce.

'He said he needed to call his chambers and speak to his clerk; and the other call was to his club to cancel a dinner engagement.'

'Did you verify this?'

The detective inspector looked uncertain. 'I… uh…'

'I mean, did you take the phone yourself, check the number and who was answering and then call them back?'

'Yes, I took the phone and spoke to the person on the other end, but it all seemed kosher so I didn't call them back.' The Met officer looked and sounded embarrassed as other eyes in the room turned to look at him.

'Pity that, George; he's a slippery bastard, and he might have been giving someone a heads-up.' He rubbed his chin with a hand and then said, 'Tell you what, George, we'll go back, without knocking. We're covered for the entire day by the warrant so we'll go back. I think that with Master Ray's contacts in the legal world it might just be possible that some little bird tipped him the wink when you applied for the warrant. That may be why he didn't register any shock or seem upset when he realised his drum was going to be turned over, in the smoke and in Wareham."

The detective inspector looked glum. 'Sorry, Bob,' he said.

'Don't worry about it, old lad. I think it might actually help us.' He turned to Jim who was seated on the left of the front row. 'Jim, I want you to go now. Make sure you've got the warrant and take your original team with you. Don't worry about the normal, obvious places; I want you to look for hiding places. Get a dog team to follow you, take up the floorboards, search the garden, the car and the non-obvious. If something has been put away in a hurry, it will be in a place that's already prepared, but easily accessible by anyone who knows. You may need to arrange some floodlighting.'

'I'd like to go with him,' said George.

'Do that.'

The two detectives left, heading for the car park, collecting two more members of Jim's team on the way.

Chapter 39

Harry sat slouched in his armchair watching the television screen, which was showing the ITV late evening news. But his mind was on other things and the various news reports had become merely a blur of coloured images accompanied by the drone of the newsreader. The news ended with a brief weather forecast and was then replaced by a noisy, intrusive advert for motor insurance, so he pointed the remote control at the set and switched it off. In the sudden silence he remained staring at the blank screen, as thoughts and worries continued to chase each other inside his head.

He felt tired and drained. The exertion of dumping Wellton's body at sea, together with the subsequent drama in the forest, had exhausted him physically and mentally. His adrenaline-inspired confidence of the previous evening had deserted him. He couldn't remember what he should do next. He tried to concentrate, but a nagging image of Wellton's corpse rising to the surface once more and somehow becoming linked to him, followed by the drama and danger that had suddenly surrounded him in the forest the previous evening, had left him feeling old and washed out. He realised that planning revenge was very different from actually taking revenge. The methods he had used to extract information from Wellton had sickened him. The anger that had consumed him as he resumed his life had now largely dissipated and he wanted nothing more to do with killing.

After ten minutes or so, he dozed off into a fitful sleep, lying back in the armchair until the central heating shut down and the warmth drained out of the room.

When Harry woke his head felt easier, and the nagging thoughts of what might have been had largely evaporated, leaving his mind clear once more. The room was quite cold and when he glanced at his watch he was shocked to see that it was two hours after midnight. His immediate inclination was to go to bed but he was awake and alert now, and he felt refreshed, so he fetched a jacket and put it on.

He spent the next hour reviewing his position and the options open to him. He realised that he had been lucky in the forest. He had been very lucky indeed; and he wanted to distance himself from the whole thing, while he still could. After a while he eased himself out of the chair, ambled off to check the front door lock and made his way towards his bedroom. Once he was in bed he found himself weighing the pros and cons of what life might now hold for him. He had accounted for a total of four of his tormentors but he thought the job wasn't really complete; nevertheless, he was now as far as he wanted to go, but there was one predominant train of thought that he couldn't get out of his head.

Enough was enough, he thought. He had stained his hands in his burning quest for revenge, and now, he felt the need to cleanse himself, to get far away from the evil with which he had become entwined.

He stayed awake in the darkened bedroom for quite a while, thinking of whether he really had a future at all, and if so, what it might be like. By the time he fell asleep he had reached a sort of decision. He knew what he must do, but not how he could do it.

Harry was awake by seven next morning. He felt more refreshed and less physically exhausted, but he decided to stay in bed and listen to the news on the radio. The first item on the morning news bulletin made him sit bolt upright and forget his maudlin thoughts.

'Concern has been expressed by several government ministers at the disappearance of the former Minister of State for Rural Affairs, The Right Honourable Giles Wellton. Mr Wellton has not been seen for several days and concerns have been expressed for his safety by his friends. Mr Wellton was last seen taking his usual morning jog around Wimbledon Common and police searches have been conducted throughout the area. In a separate development, Scotland Yard has reported that Mr Wellton is being sought by police, together with a number of other men and women, in connection with an ongoing investigation into a number of serious crimes. No other information has been forthcoming.'

Harry switched off the set and climbed out of bed. He shrugged into a dressing gown and headed for the kitchen. As he waited for the kettle to boil, he poured cereal into a bowl, still thinking, and mulling over what he had just heard. If the police were looking for Wellton in connection with others there was a good chance that the activities of the Frugs might have been brought to light. Of course, he thought, it might be that they were wrongly connecting Wellton with the massacre in the New Forest. Either way, it seemed to Harry, the police might just be about to relieve him of the burden of chasing his revenge. He decided that he should now quietly remove himself from the arena. He intended to disappear and try to wipe clean his own personal slate.

He spent the morning pottering about while considering his future. He hadn't been identified in the New Forest but it was obvious that someone else must have been present so the police would search for that person. He didn't know which of the men he had killed but he did know he had killed Jane Lockyer and he felt sorry for that, even though part of him justified the murder as having removed an evil killer, and perhaps saved another innocent man.

Harry decided that he would need to get rid of everything that connected him with the events in the New Forest. Most important was the crossbow, but the van and anything left in it would also have to go. He would change his banking arrangements and draw down a substantial sum of money to enable him to set up a new life. He decided to act as quickly as possible in order to avoid becoming embroiled in any police investigation, or a trial. He convinced himself that, in any case, there was nothing he could add as a witness at a trial other than to confirm the state of his injuries. But then he came to the conclusion that he couldn't even do that because he had been found unconscious and had remained in a coma for so many years. He was just like a parcel being passed for repair from expert to expert; things had happened to rebuild him, but he could add nothing to the question of how he had been beaten so badly in the first place. Dreams could not be used as evidence.

By the afternoon, the day, which had started bright and promising, began to turn windy with a heavy overcast, so Harry stayed indoors and used the time to develop his plan. He managed to set up an online bank account, then used his car to drive into Weymouth where he opened a building society account and transferred a large proportion of his remaining funds. When he returned he busied himself around the cottage, sorting out what he would take to his new life and what he would leave behind. He made a point of listening to both television and radio news bulletins, which, as the day wore on, confirmed his view that the police were onto the gang that had attacked him. Later in the afternoon a BBC newsreader stated that three people, a woman and two men, had been found dead in a remote part of the New Forest. Another man had been found with serious injuries and he was helping the police with their enquiries. The newsreader said this was believed to be a forest worker who appeared to have been the victim of an unprovoked assault. The names of the deceased were given as Jane Lockyer, an actress, Cornel Grovey, the international socialite and Don Randell, an ocean-racing yachtsman and a likely member of the forthcoming Americas Cup team. Enquiries were continuing and the police were stepping up the search for a number of other people believed to have been involved.

Harry sat still with his thoughts. So those were the people I have murdered, he thought. Guilt piled up in his head despite attempts to vindicate his actions by telling himself that they were bad people who had attempted to kill him, and therefore he had been justified in what he had done. With these thoughts he fell asleep on the sofa.

Chapter 40

It was dark by the time Jim Creasy and his team arrived at the wall enclosing the large ornate house which Ray Marsden described as his cottage, and there was only a little light from the thin crescent moon. Nevertheless, the team members were each equipped with powerful flashlights and in the back of the four-wheel drive response car was a battery of portable, self-contained floodlights. The twelve feet tall wrought iron gates had been left conveniently wide open so they were able to drive straight through and along the fresh-looking gravel drive to the parking space in front of the house. As they crunched to a stop by the imposing portico an unmarked white BMW Met pursuit car pulled up alongside. Then the whole area around the house and well into the surrounding grounds was suddenly illuminated by concealed floodlights.

'That's helpful,' said Jim, as he stood by the car allowing his eyes to adjust to the sudden glare. He tossed a bunch of keys across to one of the constables. 'You get started inside, and remember we're looking for discreet and unusual hiding places. I'm going to have a look around outside.' He set off, walking slowly and waving the beam of his torch from side to side as he worked his way around the grounds. There was a kitchen garden with a few vegetables but a lot of flowers, a stand of mature trees and, on the other side of a croquet lawn, a mixed orchard of twenty or so fruit trees.

He walked on, looking for sheds or other outbuildings. He threaded his way around the garden and through the trees twice and then walked around the inside of the tall wall. It was only on his third circuit of the garden that he decided to check a stout wooden door built into the wall. It was set into the perimeter wall and at first he had assumed that it was simply a side gate to the property. That was certainly what it looked like, but it seemed particularly robust, and it was secured with several impressive-looking deadlocks. He realised that if he couldn't locate any keys he was going to need some tools and more muscle to get through the door, so he started across the lawn towards the house.

He was approaching the house when he heard his name called. He quickened his pace and was met on the front steps by detective constable Frank Kelly, the younger of his two assistants.

'Skipper,' he said, 'come and have a look at this.' He led the way through what appeared to be a library and then into a room dominated by a giant television screen and separate sound system. They had to walk around the edge of the room because the fitted carpet had been rolled back and several floorboards pried loose. Nothing had been found under them. The young constable continued to the back of the room, and dragged a heavy sofa a few feet forward, revealing a glass-fronted cupboard which appeared to be filled with books. He watched as Frank lifted out the books occupying the top two shelves. Then working in the powerful beam of Jim's torch he fiddled around the edges of the back panel of the cupboard. Seconds later the panel was out and lying on the bare floor, revealing a second cupboard stacked with video tapes and discs. The two men hauled them out and passed them to the third member of the team, who dropped them all into a big plastic bag with a Currys logo on the side. When the tapes had been removed, three document boxes were revealed on the floor, previously hidden by the tapes. They went into another even bigger plastic bag.

Frank then produced a small digital camera and took a series of photographs of the hiding place, showing a sequence of pictures from the secret cupboard being fully open and empty, to closed and concealed. Jim made an appropriate note of what they had found and where and when it had been found, and got the other two to initial it. Then he resumed his search for keys. He looked in all the drawers and cupboards he could find on the ground floor and was about to climb the expensively carpeted stairs when he spotted a drawer in a small, ornately inlaid occasional table in the hall. He pulled open the drawer which contained two bunches of keys and several single keys which looked like car keys. As he gathered these up, he heard the voice of DC Kelly behind him.

'The obvious place, Skipper.'

The internal search now being complete, the four police officers pushed the floorboards back and tidied up the disturbed rooms as best they could before they all walked across to the gate in the wall.

Jim took the first bunch of keys and systematically tried each one in the lock. Nothing worked so he tried all the keys again, but without success. The gate remained stubbornly locked. A further ten minutes elapsed while he repeated the process with the 'house' keys and with all the other keys.

'Sod it! Frank, go and look around the outside of the wall, see where it leads to.' He stared at the stubborn gate in frustration. Examining it through the torchlight he noted that the timbers and the fittings were very solid, and apparently of more recent construction than the adjacent walls. Speaking mainly to himself, he said, 'It'll take a tank to shift that thing.' As he spoke, a thought flitted unbidden through his head. Why did a secondary exit gate in a perimeter wall need to be so solid? Then he heard Frank calling as he hurried back from the main entrance.

'Skipper! It's not a gate to the outside; there's a secondary wall. You can't see any gate on the outside.'

'Okay, that's a very good reason to keep going at this side. See if we've got any tools in the cars.'

Frank changed direction towards the cars parked in front of the building. He rummaged about in the back of the response car and emerged a few moments later holding a canvas tool bag in one hand and a big crowbar in the other.

As Frank returned he could see that Jim seemed to be examining the top and bottom of the gate. 'Look,' he said, 'there are vertical bolts top and bottom and those hinges could keep Fort Knox safe. We need to think of another way.'

'There is a way.' Frank pointed towards the hinges, then said, 'Two ways, in fact.'

The DS turned, waiting for more.

Frank continued, talking enthusiastically, 'There's a fairly heavy hammer in the tool kit. We use the crowbar like a chisel, and hammer out the mortar between the bricks till we can disconnect the hinges from the wall. If that doesn't work we can go round the other side and dismantle the wall in the same way. I can do it. I used to work as a bricky.'

'Right, go to it,' said Jim. 'There are plenty of garden chairs you can stand on to reach the top one, but start on the lower hinge.'

It took nearly forty-five minutes before they had both hinges detached from the wall, but the door still proved stubborn. After another ten minutes of combined heaving by the three men they managed to drag open the door to create a gap just big enough to pass through. Once through, they found themselves in a rectangular room surrounded by red-brick walls over a plain concrete floor. One end was dominated by a large projection screen, with an expensive-looking digital projector under a cover on a stand in the centre of the room. A dozen upright chairs were scattered around and the outer wall was lined with a row of four-drawer filing cabinets. The cabinets were locked but it only took a few seconds to jemmy open a couple of drawers using the crowbar. The first one contained several cans of sixteen millimetre film and the second seemed to be filled with an assortment of photograph albums, notebooks and box files. Frank opened one of the photograph albums and glanced inside. 'These need to go in the evidence bag, Skipper,' he said.

When they looked behind the projection screen, they found several top-opening padlocked wooden lockers and an array of different sized cardboard boxes. The crowbar made short work of the padlock hasps on the lockers, and the men began unloading more box files, DVDs, two lap-tops, portable printers and several expensive looking cameras, both video and still.

Jim eased himself out through the gap past the broken doorframe, pulled out his phone and keyed a single 'fast-dial' button. The call was answered almost immediately. 'Guv,' he said, 'we've been successful and found a lot of stuff that we can bring in, but there's much more. You need to seal this place off and get a recovery team out here as soon as you can to collect the rest of the stuff. You'll need a fairly big van and some heavy duty tools.' He waited while Bob responded briefly at the other end of the line, then said, as an afterthought, 'And for God's sake don't let that bastard Marsden out on bail. If he gets wind of what we've found he'll wipe this place cleaner than a shining pin.' He listened to the reply, said, 'Got it, Guv,' and put the phone away.

'Right, team,' said Jim as he squeezed back through the gap. 'We need to move everything we can back to the car, but we won't be able to carry all of this stuff away. Another team with better kit and a van is on its way. We wait here until they arrive and meanwhile we let nobody in. The place is going to be sealed off and taken apart, brick by brick.'

The team worked steadily for the next couple of hours, by which time they had removed the cameras and a number of files. The backs of both vehicles were full but there was a considerable bulk of equipment and documents still left in the secret chamber. The last items to go into the car were a Smith and Wesson automatic pistol and several magazines filled with ammunition. This had been found taped underneath a sliding metal drawer in a filing cabinet.

It was nearly midnight before the team arrived back at Weymouth Police Station. They offloaded all the evidence they had brought back and placed it under lock and key in the evidence room. Bob then told them all to go home and come back 'bright-eyed and bushy-tailed' at eight next morning.

Chapter 41

Harry reached his decision as he finished his breakfast. He felt calmer as he went through his usual routine of washing the dishes and tidying the kitchen. By the time he finished his task he noticed that the sky had turned dark grey and heavy spots of rain were already hitting the window. Intending to go out, he went to fetch his anorak, by which time the rain had increased, so he decided to wait and listen to the news on the radio, hoping the rainstorm would pass. The newsreader started his bulletin with the sensational announcement that police had arrested four men and one woman in connection with an ongoing multiple murder investigation and other serious crimes. The sensational nature of the announcement came in the names of those arrested. They were Sandra Somerville, the Wimbledon tennis star, Henry Hayward the television talk show host, Ray Marsden QC, the well-known criminal barrister; and Dorset landowner Sir Arthur Simmonds. The police were still looking for the Reverend Jeremy Wilberforce, Captain Roger FitzHarris, a serving army officer, and former government minister Giles Wellton.

He turned the radio off and sat counting on his fingers: four arrested, three dead, and three more missing. But of course one of those listed as missing was also dead – killed by his own hand. That would be the lot, he mused, with some satisfaction.

He left the cottage when the rain had reduced to an intermittent dribble and walked steadily up through Easton, using a stick to ease the ache in his right knee that now seemed to bother him on some mornings; he waited for the traffic, then crossed the road into the square. He joined the straggling line of people heading for the Tesco store, continued on past the store and then turned onto a rough patch of land used by local householders for free parking. The van was sitting in the middle of a row of nondescript vehicles and he glanced around discreetly before climbing in, still unnoticed, and drove away, bumping slowly over the uneven grass.

Harry turned onto the main road and drove north, down the hill through Fortuneswell, past a funfair setting up near the square, then on across the causeway and into Weymouth. In Weymouth he parked by the railway line in the B&Q car park, spent the next twenty minutes making a number of purchases, then a further ten minutes wrestling with the unfamiliar automatic payment and check-out machine, before returning to his van, throwing his shopping in the back and setting off, heading north once more.

An hour later, Harry pulled up in front of the barn he had rented in the remote countryside near King's Stag. He got out of the van, opened the doors to the barn, and found the bucket he had last used to torment Wellton, which he filled with water. He opened up the side and rear doors of the van and removed the loose items inside. Then he mixed a generous portion of Jeyes Fluid with the water and started to scrub the inside of the vehicle. He worked mostly on the roof, floor, doors and seat backs, not bothering too much with the front of the van.

As soon as he was content that he had removed all traces of what the van might have once contained he started a similar clean-up inside the barn. There were some stains on the concrete floor which he thought were probably bloodstains so he worked diligently on these. He found a short length of hose that he was able to fit over the water tap, so he could use it to soak the stains on the floor, interspersing this with more Jeyes Fluid and energetic scrubbing using a big yard-broom. When all this was finished he felt exhausted, so he eased himself into the front of the van to rest. Almost immediately he lapsed into sleep and dozed for nearly an hour. He woke feeling better but still tired. Heaving a sigh, he climbed out of the van and started work, rather more slowly, on his final task. Harry picked up the recently purchased broom and used it to sweep up all the loose detritus he could find in the barn. He carried and dragged the heap round to a clear area behind the barn, formed a small bonfire and lit it. He stood watching over the fire until it was reduced to a smouldering pile of grey ashes. Then he dispersed these with the broom, helped by the rising late morning breeze.

Harry set off once more in the van, avoiding the main roads and winding instead through a series of small villages, heading north into Somerset. Eventually he came across what he was looking for – a used car lot a mile outside one of the bigger villages. He pulled in and parked across a line of not-very-modern domestic, commercial and agricultural vehicles, climbed down from the van carrying his rucksack and strolled across towards a ramshackle office.

The office was occupied by a scruffy middle-aged and middle-weight man with a three-day growth of beard. He eased himself out of a torn and dirty imitation leather armchair, stopped chewing a sandwich, folded his newspaper and said, 'Can I help you, squire?'

Harry smiled and arranged his face in an expression which he hoped would make him appear friendly towards the scruffy lout. Maintaining the smile he said, 'I hope so. I've got a nice little Peugeot van for sale. Nice condition, low mileage, side doors as well. Are you looking to buy vehicles for stock?'

The greedy glint in the eye of the car trader belied his response. 'Not a lot of call for small vans like that,' he said. 'How much were you looking to get for her?'

'Well, I know what she's worth,' said Harry, slipping into the same terminology as the car buyer, 'but I don't want to hang about much and I don't need her now, so I might be able to go a bit lower. Cash sale, mind!'

These two factors seemed to help the car-trader to reach a conclusion and so an offer was made, and haggled over for nearly an hour. They walked around the van several times and took a short test drive. Eventually Harry produced the registration document and the van changed hands for half of what it was worth, paid in cash and accompanied by an agreement to drive Harry to Taunton station.

It took four more hours for Harry to travel in several trains to Weymouth, and then an expensive taxi to the square at Easton where he paid off the driver and walked back to his cottage. He was tired and hungry but satisfied with his day's work, which marked the successful completion of the first part of his plan.

The following day Harry started the second phase. He called two local estate agents and made appointments with them both. He was going to put his cottage up for sale and move on as soon as he could. Once this was settled he spent the next several hours sorting out the few essential items he would need to build his new life. The rest, he thought, could be sold with the cottage. After rearranging his bank accounts he was surprised to learn that with all the backdated pension, social security and insurance payments, and despite his purchases of a boat and two other vehicles, he was still worth just under half a million pounds. He was a man wealthy beyond anything he could ever have imagined before a gang of pampered thugs changed his life and his outlook on life.

But he didn't see the need for so much money and he didn't know what to do with it.

That evening, for the first time in years, Harry went to church. Without really thinking about it, he left the cottage and drove over the causeway and up through Wyke Regis, parking on the road outside the ancient village church of All Saints. He found the door open and went into the dimly lit interior, pausing before easing himself into a seat in the middle of a row halfway up the nave. There he stayed for nearly two hours. He prayed, which was something he had forgotten how to do; but sitting in the silent church he found the thoughts he could use to ask forgiveness, and arranged them into some sort of prayer. Faint, vague and fuzzy recollections of his childhood and youth passed through his mind as he begged forgiveness for the terrible things he had done. He felt a curious warmth in the otherwise chilly and empty church and he was comforted by it. When eventually he left the building, he saw a collection box placed on a table by the font. Without really thinking about what he was doing he put his hand in his pocket and pulled out a bundle of notes from the money he had been paid for his van. He casually stuffed several hundred pounds into the collection box. For the first time since being discharged from the clinic he felt clean, empty of worry and of anger, and even content as he walked slowly across the churchyard to his car.

The final thing he did that afternoon was to arrange long-term storage for his car with a small garage operating from one of the industrial estates in Dorchester. He paid in advance for a year's storage, arranged that he would telephone when he wanted the car to be collected from Wareham – for which he added a generous sum – and left the spare key.

For the first time since emerging from his coma, Harry slept easily and dreamlessly that night.

Chapter 42

The investigation now had a name. It was called 'Operation Kestrel'. This emerged later in the morning following Bob's latest briefing of the superintendent. It was the Super who had decided the investigation should have a name and what that name should be. He felt really pleased that at last he had made a real and important contribution.

Bob assembled his team in his big attic-like office at the top of the building. As well as Jim Creasy and Gerry Treloar, Detective Constable Frank Kelly and Mary Flint, Bob's admin clerk, were also present. The men from the other constabularies had left the previous night and were now compiling official reports on their activities to add to the growing piles of paper.

A selection of items from the large collection of evidence seized during yesterday's raids was now laid out on the big wooden table that occupied the centre of the room. Piles of papers, at least a dozen mobile phones, several laptops, cameras including digital, film and video, in addition to three cans of film, were spread out across the table. Everything was tagged with labels showing the time, date and location of the 'find', as well as the name and signature of the officer who had found the item. Jim and Gerry were seated at a different table, trying to gain access into some mobile phones and laptops, to see what they contained. A list was made of the images and messages found in each gadget and Mary was speed-reading through the piles of loose paper, attaching adhesive post-it notes to some of the documents, which she then placed inside separate files.

Bob was engrossed in reading the contents of the cardboard files that had been recovered from the house in Wareham. He finished reading the last of half a dozen files and threw it onto the table among the others. Stretching his arms above his head he interrupted the air of concentration around the table. 'That, lady and gentlemen,' he said, 'is the gold dust we have been looking for.'

The others stopped what they were doing and looked up, waiting for their boss to explain his remark. 'What we have here,' said Bob, waving his hand towards the scattered files on the table, 'is the collected and previously hidden reports on the Aston Martin crash. They also, for the very first time, show a direct link between former Superintendent, former Met Commander, former Met Deputy Assistant Commissioner and former M15 spook Sir Andrew Marsden, father of Mr Ray Marsden, in whose possession these incriminating files were discovered.'

Smiles appeared on the faces around the table and Bob leaned back in his chair looking smug. After allowing a few minutes for them to take it in he spoke, 'Well, there are several chunks of gold dust! But at the same time a great big piece of the evidence picture is now in place. We have moving and still photographs, some with dialogue, showing each of the people we have in custody, as well as others, in action – going about their vile and dirty work. But this lot is only the tip of the iceberg and from what I've seen brought in so far, we have a lot more incriminating evidence here.

'These vain and arrogant bastards really thought they were above the law. They thought they would never be caught, and if ever they were, why, their tame mouthpiece in the cells downstairs would call in heavyweight help, just as he did before, and enable them to walk free.

'We're going to have to look after this lot very carefully but there's a lot of other things to do. For a start, we need to pick up former Sergeant Gordon Crosskey, former Sergeant David Carpenter, former Police Constables Ken Martin and Paul Crimond. And invite them all back to the nick they once knew so well for a little chat.'

'Who are they?' asked Gerry.

'They, Gerry, are the desk sergeant, the traffic sergeant and the traffic officers who all decided to mislay their notes and retire at short notice, very likely, I would imagine, as much richer men than they used to be.'

'Wow,' said Jim. 'I'd like to be in on that one.'

'You will be, my boy, you most certainly will be, and you will not only learn from the experience, you might even enjoy it. Now, Mary, how's your shorthand? Good, I hope.'

In answer, Mary went across to her own desk and collected her shorthand notebook. She walked back across the room and settled herself in a chair opposite Bob, who was now seated on the other side of his table, elbows resting on the wooden surface and hands forming a steeple, ready to dictate his report. As Mary's pencil was poised over her notepad, Bob called across the room, 'Jim, break off from that; note the addresses and phone numbers in those files and start looking for those slightly bent coppers.'

It took half an hour to dictate the initial report. While Mary went off to her own desk to type up the dictation, Bob pulled on his jacket, straightened his tie and marched off towards the superintendent's office. He had nearly reached it when he was intercepted by one of the detective constables who had taken part in the raids the previous evening.

'Excuse me, sir,' said the young man. 'One of the "collars" from yesterday is demanding to speak to you. Getting quite agitated, he is. He says he has information that you need.'

'Which one is it?'

'Marsden, sir.'

A broad smile appeared on Bob's face. 'Well, well, well.' He said, 'How interesting, and how unsurprising. Go and see him and tell him I'm busy right now but I'll come along and see him as soon as I have time. Sometime later today that'll be. I'm sure he hasn't got anything else pressing to do so I expect he won't mind waiting. You can tell him that; but you mind out now, he'll steal the buttons off your tunic if you give him half a chance.'

'Right, sir.' The detective disappeared in the direction of the custody suite.

Bob continued to the station commander's door, knocked on it and waited the usual thirty seconds before the familiar voice called him in. He stepped inside, noting that for once – perhaps for the first time – the Boss was sitting in his shirtsleeves.

'I've come to bring you up to date, sir. We're very close to putting a case together for the CPS, but there have been developments, which means that in the last half-hour we have become much closer to being able to wrap up the whole case.'

'Including the probable corruption?' The Boss was choosing his words with care.

'Very much including the corruption,' said Bob.

'Tell me more,' said the Boss, rather unnecessarily.

'Well, to summarise once again, sir, we have four subjects in custody, one of whom has already confessed to his part in the assault on Harry Chaplin…'

'He can always retract that; he probably will when that lawyer gets to him again…'

'I don't think so, sir. I've spent a lot of time with the man and he knows there is no way out. He wants to co-operate and trade that co-operation for as much leniency as he can generate. He is also a credible witness, but of course he isn't going to incriminate himself in any of the other activities of this group and I'm not going to press him. However, as I told you, we also have an eye-witness to the attack on Harry Chaplin. He's picked the right photos out of a selection, but a good defence lawyer might challenge him over the time lapse between witnessing the incident and reporting it. We have three others deceased and we now know their names, but we also have plenty of evidence to incriminate them not only on this assault but on what, at present, appears to be a number of separate murders. Murders that have been filmed as 'snuff' movies. In short, sir, we've got these movies. We've also got still photographs and sound recordings. These idiots were actually filming their activities on mobile phones, tablets and cameras, and not only that, they were storing them in their homes – as sort of macabre keepsakes. There are also documents, letters, organising notes, directions; that sort of thing. We have bucketfuls of clear and undeniable evidence. Not forgetting the crashed Aston. They will all be going down, and I don't think the trial will take very long.'

'What, even Ray Marsden, the Villain's Friend? I'm sure he'll have something up his sleeve, don't you think?'

'Funny you should mention Marsden, sir; I've just been told he wants to talk to me.' Bob continued quickly, hoping to forestall an interruption he could see coming. 'We picked up a load of damning evidence last night from his house in Wareham. It was very craftily and expensively hidden, but my boys found it. Included in that evidence are the original reports of the traffic officers and others who dealt with the Aston crash and then took early retirement. I think it'll also finger his father. Incidentally, DS Creasy is trying to locate those officers as we speak…'

'Why do you think he wants to talk to you?'

'Well, sir, either he wants to slip me a bung, in which event I will have a witness with me whenever I speak to him – and of course any meeting will be recorded – or he might want to do a deal, drop the charges for turning Queen's Evidence, something like that I expect.'

'Well, I suppose you had better go and see him…'

'Oh, he'll keep, sir. It won't hurt to make him cool his heels for a bit longer, and anyway I have more to tell you.'

'Go on.'

'There are still three others missing. The soldier I'm sure we will pick up fairly soon and probably the vicar as well…'

'Vicar?'

'Yes, sir; well, not actually employed as a parish vicar. He's the Chaplain to the Bishop of Benchester so he's a Reverend. Anyway, he's done a runner, though he'll be picked up soon, I expect. But the other one, the ex-government minister bothers me. He went to ground several days before any police activity took place. He was in trouble from other directions: girlfriend, parliament, public scandal and so forth, so it's distinctly possible that he's done a runner, but if it is connected with our investigation, why did he take off so soon?'

'What do you think?'

'I don't think his disappearance is connected with Operation Kestrel. He went for a morning run and disappeared, leaving his expensive car in the park. What that says to me is either he was abducted or he wants to make us, and others, think he was abducted. But I have a funny feeling…'

'What kind of funny feeling?'

'I think he might be dead, sir, and we won't find him, or the body.'

'Why do you say that?'

'Well, we know that three of the gang are dead, but we don't know who killed them. If Wellton is not on the run, but dead, it suggests that somebody is hunting down the gang to exact a bit of revenge.'

'Who do you think that is?' The superintendent leaned forward conspiratorially and spoke in a whisper.

'I don't know,' said Bob, 'and anyway, my priority is catching the live ones. Also, we have photos of other, as yet unknown, victims; so there might be a lot of friends and relatives out there with a motive for revenge.' While he was speaking, he had already formed a view as to who might be hunting down these people, but he reckoned privately that if he was right then there was justification, and he had no intention of seeking that person out.

'I see.' The superintendent seemed to have run out of questions.

The two men sat in thought for a few minutes, then Bob shoved back his chair. 'I'll keep you in touch, sir,' he said as he moved to the door.

Having brought his boss up to date, Bob set off to see Marsden, but first he plodded back up to his office and picked up a few items from the collection of evidence. Before leaving the office he made sure that Gerry noted in the log they were maintaining that the items had been temporarily removed by the DCI. Bob strolled back down the stairs, thinking about the forthcoming interview. He had confidently expected that the 'Villain's Friend' would want to talk to him; but Marsden's demand had come rather sooner than expected. As he passed the front desk he collected a young probationer who was just signing in.

Addressing the desk sergeant, Bob said, 'Mind if I borrow young 236 here for a couple of minutes? All he'll have to do is listen to a chat. I'm going down to say good morning to Mr Marsden.'

'Good luck, sir!' replied the sergeant. 'It'll be good for his education.'

The probationer constable said nothing but turned meekly and followed Bob along the corridor leading to the custody suite. They arrived at an iron gate leading to the cells. It was guarded by a uniformed constable seated behind a desk on which sat a big, slightly dog-eared ledger.

'We're to see Marsden,' said Bob.

'Right, sir, he's in number six, and becoming a right pain in the arse!' The constable moved out from behind his desk, pulled a set of heavy keys from his pocket and led the way to cell number six. He selected a key, peered through the small observation hatch and then opened the door. He walked warily into the cell, eyes darting around, checking that all was as it should be. Then he stood in a corner, watching Marsden, who was seated on the spartan bunk, lolling back against the whitewashed brick wall. The only other furnishings in the cell were an upright wooden chair and a small wooden table set against one wall, on which stood a chipped enamel water jug and a plastic tumbler.

'You just stand over there in the other corner and listen, okay?' Bob waited while the probationer followed his instruction, then he pulled the chair into the middle of the room and sat on it. Addressing the prisoner he said, 'You wanted to see me, Mr Marsden?'

Marsden didn't immediately answer. He sat and swept his gaze slowly across the three men facing him, while Bob wondered what ploy the man might try. Then Marsden pulled himself upright, away from the wall, perched on the edge of the bunk and started to speak.

'Thank you for responding so quickly to my request to speak to the investigating officer,' he said, speaking the words carefully, but heavy with sarcasm. 'The thing is, I can help you to overcome all this nonsense, this silly misunderstanding. I am not a vindictive man but you will know my reputation as an accomplished lawyer, and I don't want the Dorset Constabulary to end up with even more egg all over their faces. All I need is for you, sir, to recognise the dreadful mistake that has been made, authorise my immediate release, sign an appropriate letter of apology and...' he paused, 'oh, and give me a written undertaking that the Force will compensate me fully for any loss or damage to my property. I can draft something for you if you like, then there would be no hard feelings, eh? After all, we're all on the same side. What do you say, eh?'

'I was told you had something helpful to say to me. Is that it? If so I've got other things to do rather than waste my time listening to your nonsense.' Bob started to rise from his chair, and the other two officers turned towards the door.

'No, wait, I do have something to tell you.' There was just a tinge of appeal in the voice.

Bob flopped back into the chair. 'Okay, tell me,' he snapped.

'The thing is, you have no evidence; well, certainly not against me.' Marsden spoke with more confidence.

'Explain!' The single word was barked out and seemed to echo from the walls.

Marsden took a deep breath and cast his eyes down, examining the concrete floor in front of his feet. He's making it up as he goes along – winging it, thought Bob, as he stared, stony-faced, at the top of Marsden's head. Slowly the head came up to face the detective.

'Well, I know that some rather wicked things have been done. I am a lawyer, a defence lawyer; and people have confided in me, and I have made a record of such confidences, but I must stress that I have had no other involvement. I have merely been asked to represent the interests of some friends, foolish friends, who have allowed themselves to be caught up in something rather sordid.' He stopped, waiting for a reaction.

'So you're telling me that you have no involvement in the matters we are investigating but you know what those investigations concern. You are prepared to provide evidence, hearsay evidence it seems, in relation to people you say were involved. Is that right?'

'Yes.' Marsden smiled as he responded.

'Then give me a name – now!'

'I'm not sure that would be ethical at this stage…' Bob waved a dismissive hand and started to move.

Seeing that the interview was about to be ended, Marsden spoke rapidly and earnestly, 'I'll give you two names,' he said. 'Cornel Grovey and Don Randell.'

The crafty bastard is giving me the names of the dead ones, Bob thought. Time to end this charade, he said to himself. Aloud, he said, 'But of course, Mr Marsden, those two men are dead.'

'No, surely not!' said Marsden . 'But I only spoke with them a few days ago. Dead, you say? How can they be dead? Oh dear, I really didn't know. But of course, I still have their depositions – that would help you to conclude the case, save you a lot of time and money, wouldn't it?'

'And you were not involved in any of this, other than as a legal advisor?'

'No, no, that's right.' Marsden was leaning forward, hands clasped together, in an appealing posture once more. Bob noticed a slight sheen of sweat on Marsden's forehead. He decided it was time to strike and he reached down to the large brown envelope he had placed on the floor beside his chair. Marsden watched, looking worried for the first time, as Bob withdrew a sheaf of photographs, ten inches by eight. These were some of the images that had been copied from two mobile phones, a Samsung tablet and a Canon digital camera, all found in the two hiding places in the Wareham property.

'You have depositions, you say?'

'Yes, yes.' Marsden was definitely showing eagerness as well as some worry now.

Bob smiled. 'Well, that's very kind of you, Mr Marsden,' he said. 'But you see I can go a little better than that. Incidentally, what an amazingly clever little facility you have, set into your garden wall. Oh, I suppose I should tell you that the door's broken now. But my boys found a most remarkable treasure trove in there, and of course in that charming little safe in your drawing room,' he chuckled before continuing '…behind your bookcase.' He stopped and peered at Marsden. The man sat rigidly on the side of the bunk, face now a shocked bloodless white, lips trembling, hands winding around each other.

Bob watched his victim like a hawk about to swoop, then he continued, 'I'm sure you know what we found, Mr Marsden. There is so much incriminating evidence – incriminating you, your friends and your daddy, that is – that it took several lorries to bring it all back here to a safe place. There is no way out for you. But before I leave you to have a good think about what life holds in store for you, have a look at these.'

He held the first photograph up in front of the prisoner, where he could see it clearly. It was a high definition colour photograph showing a man, unmistakably identifiable as Marsden, with his right foot raised in the act of kicking. The object he was kicking was the bloodied head of a man lying on sparse rough grass. Without waiting for a response, Bob produced the second photograph which again showed Marsden facing the camera and aiming a punch at a smaller figure who had his back to the camera. The location of this one seemed to be some kind of beach. The third photograph showed Marsden kneeling on another bleeding and broken figure, lying supine and surrounded by tall reed-like grass. This one was in black and white.

Bob continued producing photographs, all of which followed the same theme; some had been taken at night and some in daylight. One or two had been taken inside some sort of building. He watched Marsden's face as he silently held up each photograph. The man now sat stock still, his face ashen white, drained of blood, his hands and knees trembling.

Bob put the sheaf of photographs back into the envelope which he replaced on the floor; he then picked up an old brown cardboard file cover. He spoke quietly. 'I should also tell you, and you should tell your brief, that we actually have an eyewitness to the unprovoked attack you carried out in July 2010 at Portland Bill. Do you have anything else to say, Mr Marsden?'

Marsden stared ahead, eyes vacant, hands trembling slightly. He didn't answer.

'No, I didn't think you would.' Bob held up the cardboard file cover and said, 'Look at this, Mr Marsden. Do you know what it is?' Marsden didn't look at the file cover, but he shook his head.

Bob held the file cover closer to Marsden's face and shouted, 'Look at it!' Slowly the eyes shifted to focus on the brown cardboard. 'Read the title, Mr Marsden.' Bob gestured as though to throw the cardboard, but there was no reply.

Nevertheless Marsden was looking at the file cover and, almost imperceptibly, his lips were moving.

'Never mind,' said Bob. 'It says, "Traffic Accident Report, A354 18th July 2010. Sergeant M Crosskey." That is one of the documents that you got your daddy to deal with, to make disappear. But some silly person was daft enough to retain the original document and others like it. Habit, I suppose. Well, there you are; I just thought you'd like to know. Give you something else to think about other than the murder charges that are on their way. Oh, by the way, we've traced all of the former police officers who were involved, all of them who had a chat with your daddy and who are about to finger him with enough dirt to put him away for a long time. Who knows, they might even let you share the same cell. That'll be nice; you'll be able to look after the old boy, keep him safe from all those nasty fellows who might want a word with him in the nick. Just imagine how a very senior ex-copper, bent ex-copper, knighted for his work into the bargain, is going to get on inside one of Her Majesty's tougher penitentiaries. Do let me know if you want to talk about anything else. Good day, Mr Marsden !'

With that, Bob walked out, followed by the other two police officers.

Chapter 43

In Portland Harry had just said goodbye to the second estate agent. Each agent had suggested a figure which had seemed to Harry less than the property was worth, but he didn't really care. He just wanted to sell the cottage and its contents as quickly as possible, and with the least fuss. The cottage and much of its contents belonged to a different part of his life – a life he now wanted to leave behind, to forget, to abandon. It carried memories that he needed to erase for ever. He needed to achieve a kind of re-birth; and for that to happen, everything beforehand would have to go.

His plans were now well advanced. He had kept it all to himself, but then, he reflected, there was really nobody to tell. After a bread and cheese lunch he scoured the cottage, including the garden and the dustbins, to make certain there would be nothing left behind which might show anything of who he was or where he was going. Indeed, in relation to the latter, he wasn't yet really sure himself. He was just going to leave and let fate handle the rest.

After his lunch he collected the usual bundle of letters, flyers and leaflets waiting on the doormat. He skimmed through them, noted that there was nothing useful and threw the rest in his dustbin. Then he placed several packed travel bags and a rucksack just inside the front door. It took a couple of short journeys to transfer the luggage to the Astra, parked just a few yards further up the street; then he returned and locked his front door before returning to the car and starting the engine. Although the car had been standing idle for a couple of weeks, it started easily and Harry pulled away quickly, driving towards the causeway, and then on to Wareham.

In Wareham Harry found a parking place down near the riverside. He paid for a two-hour ticket; then, fixing the straps of his rucksack on his shoulders, hefting a bag in one hand and taking his rough-hewn walking stick in the other, he set off, following the narrow road out to the east side of the town. When he reached the end of the rows of terraced housing he climbed over a stile and followed a faint path across a couple of fields until he reached the riverbank. He strolled along the path, stopping occasionally to rest, until he saw his boat on her mooring. He passed the space among the reeds where he had last parked the van, and stopped to examine it in case he had overlooked anything previously. He hadn't, and the reeds were already starting to move back, encroaching on the one-time parking space.

Harry climbed aboard using his makeshift gangplank, unlocked the wheelhouse, dumped his luggage in the saloon, switched on the gas supply and brewed himself a cup of tea. Then he locked up the boat and set off back to where he had left the car. His return journey took less time than the outward one because he was no longer burdened with luggage and because he found a shorter route. He followed the riverbank until he reached the grounds of the Priory Hotel, then skirting round the hotel and the adjacent church, he emerged close to the car park and made much better time. Nevertheless, his two hours of parking were almost up. Harry checked that no-one was watching and bought another ticket from the machine, giving him another hour of parking. He carried the rest of his bags to the boat, returned well within the hour and drove back to Portland. He stayed only long enough to make a final check around his home, ensuring that everything was secure and that he had left no tell-tale trail.

The autumn weather was holding so Harry drove once more to Wareham, found the long-stay car park, locked the car, and, taking his stick, casually strolled the shorter route to the boat. Once aboard, he started both engines and waited a good half-hour for them to warm through before casting off the mooring lines. He felt a bit more confident this time, as *Spitfire* chugged down through Poole Harbour. After passing the car-ferry berths he guided the boat slowly towards Poole Quay Marina, spotted the fuelling berth on the opposite side of the fairway and steered the boat in, to bump rather inexpertly alongside the pontoon. The attendant was friendly and helpful and was happy to be paid in cash for the fuel. Harry filled up the diesel tanks as well as four twenty-litre cans that seemed to be part of the boat's equipment. He had no idea how long the fuel would last but he thought he could work that out as he went along.

The weather was still good, with only a light overcast beginning to cover the western sky, as Harry started the engines once more and signalled to the pump attendant, who let go the two mooring ropes and threw them onto the deck. The outgoing current helped the boat to drift away from the pontoon, so Harry was able to push the lever into forward gear, turn the wheel hard to starboard and head off across the harbour, following the main channel towards the entrance and the open sea. He had no difficulty in negotiating the Sandbanks Chain Ferry this time and he settled down to follow the line of buoys marking the outer approach channel.

After passing the outer fairway buoy, Harry kept going for another half-hour, then he set the auto-pilot to a southerly heading with the boat moving along at slow speed. He had a good look around but couldn't see any sign of anyone taking an interest in him, so he opened the after hatch and began to haul various things out. The wheelchair went over the side first, followed by the remaining ketamine and syringes; the contents of Wellton's wallet were followed by the wallet itself. Finally, with the boat now almost stationary and rocking gently from side to side, he searched once more through the interior of the vessel, gathering together various small items which he thought might connect him in some way to the demise of Wellton and his friends. The last things to go over the side – which, with a slight shock, he realised he had forgotten – were the crossbow and the remaining quarrels. He stared unhappily at the little wooden arrows bobbing beside the boat as he saw that the quarrels continued to float.

By the time Harry had turned his boat back towards Poole he noticed with some concern that the sky had darkened and the south-westerly wind had increased markedly. The waves were quite big now and they were hitting the boat on the port beam which made it roll alarmingly. However, the boat was well-found, sturdy and seaworthy, though not necessarily sea-kindly. By the time the green outer fairway buoy came alongside once more, Harry was feeling wretched. He had spent almost the entire return passage vomiting, retching and fearful. As he entered the calmer water of Poole harbour he felt worn out and mentally exhausted; but slowly, as he crossed the wide expanse of the outer harbour, he began to feel better. It was almost dark, and raining steadily by the time he tied up at his riverside berth; and he was feeling physically exhausted and in need of sleep. He decided to stay on the boat, and collect his car early next morning.

Chapter 44

Next morning, the former traffic sergeant Gordon Crosskey and the two retired traffic officers were arrested and brought to Weymouth for questioning. The former desk sergeant, David Carpenter, had died two years previously. However, his death did not prevent his banking records, along with those of the other retired police officers, from being examined.

It was very difficult for them to deny the connection between their concurrent decisions to retire from the police force at short notice in September 2010, and the sudden financial windfalls that arrived in each of their bank accounts. The two sergeants had received fifty thousand pounds each and the constables had been given thirty-five thousand pounds. Varying amounts of expenses had also been paid, in part apparently to cover the cost of moving permanently out of the county. The present state of each bank account showed no sign of any of this money remaining; it had all been long since spent.

When the evidence was put before them, together with the suggestion that they were not the principal target of the investigation, none of the three men denied their guilt. They were told that they would be charged with malfeasance in a public office but that in all likelihood – particularly if they co-operated – their previous records would be taken into account. Elizabeth Curry, who attended some of the interviews on behalf of the CPS, went so far as to suggest that sending them to prison would not be in the interests of the State. Each of the men agreed with some enthusiasm to give a full statement of how they had been approached, by whom, and for what reason. They were interviewed separately and they had been given practically no opportunity to collude before they were arrested, but their stories were remarkably familiar.

The former traffic officers agreed that Sergeant Gordon Crosskey and Constable Paul Crimond had been the first officers to attend the scene of the crash. They had checked the car but had found no one in it. They had found some bloodstains on the instrument panel in front of the driving position, and the windscreen was smashed; but otherwise, the interior of the car was remarkably undamaged. Externally, the car was a wreck. It must have left the road at high speed and smashed itself along and partially through a dry stone wall; and it was so badly damaged that they didn't immediately identify the car as an Aston Martin. They 'called in' the accident and set up traffic diversion barriers. Then they carried out a cursory search of the area, including the fields and buildings behind the wall. Since it was very quiet and they could find no sign of any other vehicle being involved, they continued with their patrol, and returned to the station just before two a.m. They weren't unusually interested in the follow-up because they both took the view that the crash was probably the work of some rich drunk who would be quickly identified from the car's registration number.

Next morning, Paul Crimond drove out on his own in a patrol car to check that the traffic diversion arrangements were working, and to take some photographs of the crash scene. He arrived at the scene shortly after 9 a.m. and was surprised to find that the car had already been removed. He looked around the area, took photographs of the damaged wall, measured the length of the skid marks on the road and looked through the gap in the wall, where he found body panels, a wing mirror and various other parts from the car. He photographed these, waited by the site to make sure the light morning traffic was flowing easily round the cones, and then returned to Weymouth Police Station, where he took his mid-shift break. He had a sandwich and a cup of tea before writing up his report, which didn't take very long. The report, along with those of his colleagues, was routinely put into the tray of the station commander before being taken for further action.

Apart from the usual chat about what might have happened to cause the crash, the incident was quickly overtaken by a lot of other events during the day after the crash. There had been a spate of minor road traffic accidents, the usual number of speeding tickets, a short chase after a 'boy racer' and the arrest of two uninsured drivers. All of these events had been recorded in the traffic officers' daily reports.

It was with some surprise, then, and not a little worry on the part of the traffic officers, when two mornings after the crashed Aston Martin had been discovered they were all summarily ordered to return immediately to the station.

When they arrived separately at the station they were each instructed to report to the station commander, who remained tight-lipped and not at all pleased to see his officers. Only Sergeant Crosskey could remember the boss's name at that time. He thought it was Chief Superintendent Croft. One of the others remarked that lowly constables were only favoured with a visit to the Chief Super's office if they were in the shit, and he and his colleagues, he said, 'had kept a clean sheet' – and the Chief Super was only very rarely seen outside of his office.

On arrival at the boss's office, each man was asked to confirm that the report in front of him had been compiled by himself and to confirm that he had no other documents related to the crash. Each man had responded by confirming that there was nothing other than a routine entry in their notebook. They were then required to hand over the notebook before being escorted by a silent detective constable to an interview room where they were instructed to sit and wait, watched over by another detective constable who would not allow them to communicate with each other. The two detective constables were not known to any of the traffic officers; indeed, they each confirmed that the plain clothes men were not from the Weymouth Station. Jim Creasy, who was doing most of the questioning of the former police officers, did ask each of them how he knew these men were, in fact, detectives. He got the same answer from each man: 'Because I was told they were.'

After a short wait, the first traffic officer, Sergeant Crosskey was called into an adjacent room, where he was curtly told to sit at a desk placed in the middle of the room. On the other side of the desk sat a balding middle-aged man dressed in an immaculate three piece suit complete with a gold watch chain and a scarlet silk handkerchief. He wore tinted glasses, had a small military-style moustache and was running to fat, which could not quite be disguised by the cut of the suit.

There was no hand-shaking and the interview was conducted in a hostile manner throughout. The man started by stating that he was a high-ranking officer who represented both Scotland Yard and the Security Services. 'You don't need to know my name, you just need to answer my questions,' he said.

He indicated two documents on the table and told the sergeant to read them and sign them. The first document was a copy of the key points of the Official Secrets Act and the second was an instruction and undertaking to regard the present investigation as Secret under the act. The paper threatened dire consequences if any part of the interview, subsequent discussion or the contents of the road traffic accident reports were later divulged to anybody. The sergeant, who was confused and worried about what he had become involved in, quickly signed the papers which were then snatched off the desk and shoved into a leather briefcase by the fat man opposite. He was then instructed to hand over his police notebook which was also deposited in the briefcase; a new police notebook was placed on the desk. 'Take that, it's now yours,' said the man.

The next part of the interview was bizarre. The interviewer leaned forward conspiratorially and explained, in a slightly gentler tone, that it would be best for the sergeant if he were to transfer out of the Dorset Constabulary, and even better if he were to resign from the police force. The man went on to suggest that the sergeant had stumbled inadvertently into a matter of national importance and that if he stayed in his present job he might be at risk. The type of risk was not specified but the sergeant was in no doubt that he was under threat from dark forces. The man then explained that if Sergeant Crosskey took the advice he had just been given, his interviewer would arrange for the sum of fifty thousand pounds to be paid into his bank account, together with a further sum of money to cover all his expenses in moving away. If he resigned from the Force, the interviewer would arrange for his retirement to be recorded as being for health reasons and he would be given an immediate full-career pension, index-linked. Sergeant Crosskey had already completed sufficient service to qualify for a basic pension and the offer just made to him was better than anything he could have imagined, so he readily agreed. Another document was then placed in front of him.

'All right, sign this,' said the interviewer.

Crosskey signed the document without hesitation and without studying it, then, as he put his pen away, he asked, 'What is this?'

'Your resignation from the Force! Now send the next one in and remember what you've signed. Breach the act and you'll go to prison. This interview is now ended.'

Feeling somewhat stunned, Crosskey left the room. He was met in the other room by the detective who had accompanied him from the boss's office. 'Follow me,' said the man.

Crosskey was taken to the locker room and instructed to clear his locker, watched by his escort. Then he was taken to the small Traffic Office, told to clear his desk and marched out of the building, for – as it turned out – the last time.

Each of the other two officers described the same uncomfortable experience, and each signed all the forms, including their resignations, effective that day. Jim asked them to confirm the financial offer made to them, which they did. He also asked whether the money actually turned up. 'Yes,' they said, 'it did.'

Jim finished questioning the last of the traffic officers and asked him to step outside and call the other two in. He started to tell them that although they would all remain under arrest he would arrange for them each to be granted police bail, and following this fairly simple process they would all be able to go home. But first, he said, transcripts of their interviews would be prepared and from these, statements would be drafted. He was in the act of explaining this and asking them to wait in the canteen, when there was a brief rap on the door, which was then thrown open.

DC Frank Kelly stood in the doorway, breathing fast from having run down the stairs. 'Sorry, Skipper,' he said. 'Something's turned up and the Boss wants to see you right away.'

Jim was confused at first. 'Which boss?' he said.

'The DCI.' With that, Frank turned and began to retrace his steps, quickly.

Jim repeated his instruction to the three former policemen to wait in the canteen, 'until someone comes to collect you and tell you to go,' he said, almost as an afterthought.

Bob spoke without looking up from the document he was reading as Jim entered the room. 'There's been a development,' he said. 'The Reverend Wilberforce has been found, or rather his body has been found. It looks very much as though he's topped himself. I want you to go over there now and check it out.'

'Over where?'

'Oh, it's a village near Benchester, near the Somerset border. The local bobby has taken charge. He seems a competent lad.'

'Guv, I can't go immediately. I haven't finished writing up the interview transcriptions yet, and then I've got to draft each of their statements. I've also told them we'll give them police bail.'

'Well, Mary can do the transcriptions. You know what they said so you can draft the statements now. Give them to me and I'll check them against the transcripts. Then they can sign them. By the way, how did it go?'

'Guv, it's red hot, what they've had to say. They were conned by this smart-alec spook or whatever…'

'Would that be smart-Andrew, smart-Sir Andrew, I mean?'

'From the descriptions they gave, it would, Guv. And what's more, I'm pretty sure each of these men would be able to pick out Sir Andrew in a line-up. What they have to say all pans out, identical. I believe they were honest coppers put under a threat they didn't understand and then offered an attractive way out provided they kept schtum – which they took. What we've got is an expanding case of conspiracy before and after the fact…'

'Why do you say "before the fact"?'

'Because somebody with a lot of push made that car disappear from the scene of the accident before one of our coppers went to see it early the next morning. Sir Andrew is tied into this right up to his eyebrows and the connection is, before you ask, from Sir Arthur Simmonds through Ray Marsden then to his dad, who puts the fear of God into four straight coppers, and who finally hands over all the evidence to his dodgy son.'

'…who is daft enough to hang on to it all as a keepsake.' Bob allowed himself a little chuckle as he finished speaking.

Jim turned once more as he reached the door. 'What about the other one? The army one, I mean?'

'He's still missing and the military police are after him now as well as us. I've put out alerts at the ports, railway stations, airports and so on. He'll be caught before long, you'll see.'

Chapter 45

Harry was ready to leave. He had, to all intents, moved out of his cottage. A set of keys was held by each of the estate agents who were competing to sell the building. The keys to the barn had been posted back to its owner and the van had been sold for cash, with the correct number plates now re-installed so its recent use would be unlikely to be linked to its former owner.

Harry was pretty sure he had everything he needed on board the boat and he had sufficient fuel to take him a long way away, as well as plenty of cash to buy more if he needed it. He was vague as to where he was going. All he was sure of was that he wanted to distance himself from the place where his former life had been so roughly wrenched away from him.

Now he was waiting for a weather 'window'. Every day he listened to all the BBC and Shipping Forecasts. He had been waiting for a couple of weeks now, mostly aboard the boat but occasionally returning to the cottage. He had even once made a start to his journey, first taking a couple of seasickness tablets before heading down river and across Poole Harbour. However, by the time he passed the Chain Ferry at Sandbanks he could see lines of breaking waves building up from the south-west, so he turned the boat round and made his way back into the harbour and up the river to his solitary berth. Then the kwells took full effect and he fell asleep for the rest of the day.

Still waiting for a suitable break in the weather, Harry turned the radio on to catch the latest long-range weather forecast and found himself listening to the news.

The newsreader moved smoothly into the next item and Harry's attention was instantly alerted. Moving quickly, he reached across to turn up the volume on his small portable receiver.

'…and in a further development in the multiple murder inquiry being conducted by the Dorset police, a spokesman has announced that the body of the Reverend Jeremy Wilberforce, formerly Chaplain to the Bishop of Benchester, has been discovered in thickly forested land in West Dorset. It is understood that the Reverend Wilberforce took his own life, although no formal announcement has been made. The Bishop of Benchester has said that the discovery is very sad indeed and that Jeremy Wilberforce must have been a troubled man, but he had hidden his difficulties, and this added to the tragedy that a man who had provided so much help and comfort to others had felt unable to ask for help for himself. A memorial service will be held in Benchester Cathedral on…'

Harry turned off the set. He waited a few minutes before switching it on again and just caught the end of the weather forecast.

That evening he tuned in to another forecast where the forecaster talked for some time about a strong anti-cyclone establishing itself over the south of England. There was some light reference to an Indian summer, and calm winds were predicted but with rapidly cooling temperatures and a significant risk of fog in the Channel.

Harry decided he would wait no longer. The time had come for him to leave and finally sever his ties. He would slip his mooring lines early the following morning. Unfortunately, Harry had not yet learnt much about tides.

The journey started well and the sea remained calm. He had to stop the boat and hold his position against the strong flood tide coming in through the narrows but after ten minutes of cavorting about, sliding on to the edge of a mud bank but then

– mercifully – straight off again, he managed to follow a few fishing boats out through the narrows.

His passage down past Studland Bay and the white columns of Old Harry Rocks was uneventful and he took the idea of 'Old Harry passing Old Harry Rocks' to be a good omen. The sturdy little Motor Fishing Vessel chugged easily down the Purbeck Peninsula, rounded Peverill Point and turned west towards the towering cliffs of St Albans Head. Here he ran into the full force of the flood tide. The light westerly wind had now backed to become a light south-easterly and as he came closer to the massive headland he experienced, for the first time, the phenomenon known to sailors as 'wind over tide', and Harry began to learn just how turbulent the sea could become when the 'wind over tide' phenomenon was superimposed on an already existing tidal race, such as the one off the St Alban's headland. Although still under clear skies the *Spitfire* started to be thrown around among solid and breaking waves. Twice, the small boat broached; but Harry didn't know what was happening. All he knew was that his vessel seemed to be heading for disaster as the boat slid sideways down the steep back of a towering wave, and arrived in the trough of the wave heeled so far over that she was almost lying on her beam. But the Motor Fishing Vessel was tough and sturdy and she had been built from a design intended to survive heavy seas as a working fishing boat.

Harry cowered, terrified, clinging on to any fixture he could reach inside the wheelhouse, as the boat gradually righted herself, slowly responded to the demands of the autopilot and started to climb the front wall of the next wave. As the boat reared and plunged, sometimes slamming down deep into the bottom of a wave trough with walls of water high on either side, Harry's world was coming apart. The noise of the sea outside was competing with a constant crashing and banging from inside the boat. Harry was too frightened to feel seasick; he didn't know what to do so he didn't do anything. But after fifteen minutes, the conditions began to ease and after a further five, the *Spitfire* was once more cruising westward through benign seas; and the only remaining noise came from loose objects still rolling about in the saloon and cabins.

Harry couldn't understand why his boat, and apparently only his boat, had been thrown around in a sea that had suddenly become wild and distinctly unfriendly. As the boat emerged from the turbulent race his heart rate eased but he began to feel sick and bruised from sudden contact with various parts of the wheelhouse. Then he looked at the big and confused seas now behind him, and he realised that he wasn't going to drown; and so his demeanour improved. However, the experience left him with a healthy respect, bordering on fear, for the power of the sea.

He might have been comforted had he known that far up on the headland, a volunteer watchkeeper from the National Coastwatch Institute was monitoring the progress of the small vessel through powerful binoculars.

'He's ploughing straight through the Race,' said the man with the binoculars. 'He's either very bold or he hasn't a clue about what he's running through.'

'I think he just doesn't know what he's doing,' remarked his colleague, with greater perception than he realised.

'He's through the Race now but we'll keep an eye on him as long as we can, then call Portland Bill if he's still heading their way. The Portland Race might actually do for him if he tries to take that one on as well.'

Half an hour later, the big seas and overfalls had completely disappeared and Harry's little boat was making good progress through fairly calm waters, heading for the distinctive shape of Portland Bill. In the Coastwatch Lookout Station set on the higher ground a few hundred yards to the north of the big red and white lighthouse, one of three VHF radios suddenly crackled into life.

'Portland Lookout, Portland Lookout: this is St Albans Lookout, St Albans Lookout, on channel sixty-five. Over.'

The lead watchkeeper, Barry Grant, reached across to the microphone. 'St Albans, this is Portland. I read you loud and clear, good morning and how can we help? Over.'

'Portland, this is St Albans, good morning. About seven miles due east of you, there is a small vessel. Looks a bit like an old Admiralty Motor Fishing Vessel. Can you see him? Over.'

'Stand by.'

The radio became silent for a few moments, before Barry spoke again. 'Yes, St Albans, we can see him. He's heading west, probably doing about nine or ten knots. Is there a problem? Over.'

'Portland, this is St Albans. We have monitored him passing through St Albans Race heading into a full flood spring tide. Not to put too fine a point on it, he doesn't seem to know what he's doing. He's broached twice and it's only the boat that got him out of trouble. We just thought you might keep an eye on him in case he wants to try his luck with the Portland Race. Over.'

'St Albans, this is Portland. Thank you for that. We'll watch him and if he looks like getting into trouble we'll tell the coastguard. Have a good morning! Out.'

Roly Weston, the second watchkeeper in the team of three, now had the massively powerful gantry-mounted telescope trained and focused on the small brown vessel doggedly closing the distance to Portland Bill. The third watchkeeper, Jack Farnham, was carefully scanning the big coloured display of the state-of-the-art radar. 'I think I have him,' he said. Then a few minutes later, 'Yes, that's him. I'm auto-tracking him and he's heading due west, showing ten decimal five knots.' They settled down to monitor the progress of Harry and *Spitfire* as they motored steadily westward.

Roly, still peering through the big telescope, added more information. 'That's a fairly old boat by the look of it – looks quite solid though, and I can only see one person. One head keeps bobbing out of the wheelhouse door, then ducking back in.'

Right in front of the lookout, about half a mile due south of the lighthouse marking the southernmost point of land, the sea had turned white, almost as though the water was boiling, giving a remarkable contrast with the calm sea all around. As usual, there was a collection of about fifteen smallish boats moving around the edges of the rough water of the Portland Race. These were mostly local inshore fishing boats, with a few dive charter boats and a couple of local yachts.

Jack spoke again from the radar position. 'If he maintains this heading he's going to steer right into the centre of the Race. He might have scraped through St Albans, but in these conditions he probably won't survive if he carries on.'

As it happened, these three men keeping watch at Portland Bill that day were all retired from full-time employment but they were all experienced seamen, two of whom ran their own sailing yachts, and they were each blessed with that special sense known as 'a seaman's eye'. They could tell from the behaviour of the small vessel that it was not being handled well. It was failing to interpret and anticipate the small waves that were already beginning to knock it about, contributing to the slightly erratic course being steered.

The three watchkeepers discussed the options open to them as the small boat crept inexorably forward across the sea towards probable disaster.

Roly said, 'We need to get him to turn south until he has the white water on his starboard quarter.'

'We could call the coastguard and tell them that he's heading into danger,' said Barry, who was also now watching the small boat through binoculars, 'but by the time they think about it, even if they call out the lifeboat, that bloke will already be in the Race and the lifeboat might be looking for a wreck.'

Roly was still peering through the big telescope. 'Well, whatever we do,' he said, 'we'd better do it quickly, or he's going to be in really big trouble.'

Jack crouched forward, straining to see the small intermittent contact on the radar. 'I still have a fairly good contact,' he said; then, 'We've got at least twelve local boats out there. I wonder if any of them are monitoring channel sixty-five. Most of them know it's the dedicated Coastwatch channel.'

Before he finished speaking, Barry had already grabbed the radio microphone. 'All stations, this is Portland Bill Coastwatch transmitting on channel six five. Any vessel reading this transmission, in the vicinity of Portland Bill, come in please. Over.' He stood by the radio, waiting, the microphone in his hand.

A minute ticked by and then a broad Dorset accent emerged from the speaker.

'Hello, Portland, this is *Barracuda Two* here. I'm fishing bass, just off the Shambles Bank. Over.'

'I have him on the radar.' Jack was working the controls to set a marker on the contact that appeared to be *Barracuda Two*. 'The target boat is exactly one point seven miles bearing one zero zero from *Barracuda Two*.'

Barry keyed the radio microphone immediately: '*Barracuda Two*, you have a small Motor Fishing Vessel approximately one and a half miles east of you, heading west at about ten knots, description brown wooden hull with a light-coloured wheelhouse. His progress seems erratic and he's heading right for the centre of the Race. He's already had a problem with the St Albans Race and we think he will be in real trouble if he gets caught in the Portland Race. Can you intercept him and tell him that the Race is dangerous? And can you suggest to him that he should turn south for five miles and go around the Race to the south? Over.'

After a slight delay the voice emerged once more from the radio. 'We're always pleased to help you boys. Arter all, you looks arter us. I'm on me way. *Barracuda* out.'

The watchkeepers saw *Barracuda Two* turn east and accelerate to close the Motor Fishing Vessel. Within six minutes the two vessels were alongside each other. For another couple of minutes they both continued towards the turbulent white water of the Race. Then the watchkeepers saw the two vessels turn to a southerly heading. They stayed together for perhaps a mile, then *Barracuda Two* peeled off and turned back towards his previous fishing spot.

'Well, that seemed to work,' said Jack.

'Let's see what he does,' said Roly, 'and let's hope he follows the advice he's been given.' He turned away from the big telescope. 'Time for a brew, I think.'

****

On board *Spitfire*, Harry was giving silent thanks for the nautical guardian angel who had suddenly materialised alongside his boat and suggested that it would be better to head south and avoid the Portland Race. The skipper of the other boat had been succinct in his choice of words: 'Only a bleedin' idiot would continue goin' that way. You a bleedin' idiot, are ye? If ye are, and ye go on into the Race in that tub, ye'll likely be a dead bleedin' idiot!'

'Right, what do I do?' shouted Harry across the fifteen foot gap between the two boats.

'Turn ninety degrees to port – that's to the left, see? Go south for at least five miles. Where are ye headed?'

'Er, south, okay?' Harry shouted back rather uncertainly.

'Yeah, south. Ye've got a compass, have ye?'

'Yes.'

'Well, point the boat towards the big 'S' on the compass card. At least five miles; that'll take you about forty minutes. Got it?'

'Yes. Thank you.'

Harry's thanks were lost in the roar from the twin outboards on the other boat as it performed a tight turn to starboard, back to the fishing grounds.

Harry watched the miles ticking off the distance indicator, while frequently glancing to his right towards the huge white-topped waves all apparently fighting each other for their small part of the sea. He was very glad of the advice he had received.

It took nearly two hours before the Portland Race was left behind, and Harry felt dog-tired by the time he set a course due west, out into the wide expanse of Lyme Bay. He had been on his feet almost continuously since leaving the riverside berth. His knees ached and his legs felt like jelly. He had already experimented with the fairly simple task of setting the autopilot, so working carefully and methodically he engaged it now on a westerly heading. He decided to sit on the comfortable wheelhouse bench and watch the autopilot for a few minutes to check that it was working properly. Within less than a minute he was leaning back against the cushioned backrest, fast asleep.

Up in the lookout the watchkeepers were still monitoring the progress of the small wooden boat as it motored across Lyme Bay. *Barracuda Two* had already reported his meeting with the Motor Fishing Vessel. He related the instructions he had passed to the other vessel, announced that its name was *Spitfire*, declared that it was not equipped for fishing and concluded by saying that the skipper of the vessel 'didn't have a clue, and shouldn't be allowed out without his mother!'

Barry acknowledged this and asked how many people had been seen on board the *Spitfire*.

'One half-wit! *Barracuda Two*, out.'

Barry keyed the microphone and thanked *Barracuda Two* for his help and wished him a successful day's fishing. There was no answer. *Barracuda Two* was back on his fishing ground.

'I've still got the MFV on radar but the contact is becoming very intermittent. He's ten miles west of us now and he seems to be making good a west sou' westerly course. Can you still see him, Roly?' Jack was adjusting the 'clutter' and 'gain' controls on the radar as he spoke.

Roly was still peering through the big telescope, looking out to the west. 'Yeah, I can still see him, but only just. It's getting hazy in that direction.' His voice was slightly muffled by the viewing end of the big telescope. Then, 'Hold on,' he said, 'I've lost him.' Then a moment later, 'We've got fog forming out to the west, and to the south. Visibility is now down to about four miles but the fog is moving and expanding, so it'll get a lot less.'

Half an hour later, the bank of thick sea fog rolled in over the cliffs to engulf the lookout. First the tall lighthouse, a quarter of a mile south of the lookout, turned hazy, then it disappeared altogether. Other nearby buildings were swallowed up as the fog became thicker, until nothing could be seen except the cliff edge and the grass in front of the lookout. Then the watchkeepers heard the mournful sound of the automatic foghorn coming from the lighthouse. 'We better ring the coastguard and tell them that visibility is down to two hundred metres,' said Jack.

A further three hours passed before Harry was woken rudely and suddenly. The noise of a ship's foghorn was so loud and penetrating that it made Harry's ears hurt. Momentarily, his whole world seemed to consist of nothing but the blast of the foghorn. He was completely disorientated as he stared into white nothingness. His little wooden world seemed to be floating in space but he had no time to contemplate this. As he stared into the thick fog, he watched with horror as a huge blue-painted steel wall emerged out of the white nothingness surrounding him. He stood between the bench and the wheel, rooted to the spot as the towering blue side of an enormous ship bore down upon him. He didn't know what to do, but there wasn't anything he could do. The ship hit the small vessel a glancing blow, but the effect was to bounce the *Spitfire* back off the side of the bulk carrier. The relative speed of the two ships caused the incident to be over within moments. In fact, the MFV bounced along the bulk carrier's side for less than one minute before the big ship disappeared back into the fog. Harry had been knocked to the wheelhouse deck and for a long while he just lay there, stunned, while the fog seemed to become even thicker, swirling in and around the *Spitfire*.

Harry realised his engines were still running, and, dazed from his dramatic awakening and sudden shock, he crawled across the wheelhouse deck and pulled himself to his feet before looking out of the cracked port window. At first he didn't know what to make of what he saw. The whole port side of his little ship seemed to be wrecked. He stared, mesmerised, at this for a while, wondering what he could, or should, do. Then it slowly began to dawn on him that he was still afloat and still chugging through sea which was now glassily calm. He turned and looked down into the saloon, expecting to see water swilling about, but there was nothing.

As he recovered his wits and the shock began to wear off he felt bolder, so he slid open the port side wheelhouse door and stepped gingerly onto the deck. The timber bulkhead surrounding the deck was completely smashed, with much of it having already fallen over the side. But apart from this, the only damage seemed to be scuffs and scrapes along the hull, interspersed by patches of blue paint. He almost wept when he realised how narrowly he had escaped. Then he decided to look at the instruments in front of the wheel. The autopilot had disengaged and *Spitfire* was now apparently wandering on a generally southerly course.

Harry tentatively turned the wheel and watched the compass card slowly revolve until the boat was pointing roughly west. But the bows kept turning. He turned the wheel back the other way, overshot again, and then again until he eventually managed to find and hold an approximately westerly heading. He pressed the button re-engaging the autopilot and to his considerable surprise, it worked. Once under automatic guidance he was able to inch the controls around a degree at a time until he was again heading due west. He was now wide awake and determined to stay awake. As he stood behind the wheel, images formed in his mind of a time working as a deck hand in a big ship. Was that me? he thought. If it was, he wished, belatedly, that he had taken more interest in the navigation of small boats.

As the day wore on, the light easterly wind sprang up again and the fog started to disperse. Harry turned to the chart-plotter and fiddled with it until he believed it was showing an accurate position. As the remaining mist continued to thin he found, with some surprise, that he was able to relate the little coloured screen to the rocks and headlands he could now see appearing a couple of miles to the north. After zooming in and out on the chart-plotter his confidence started to return and he reckoned he was passing somewhere to the south of the estuary of the River Dart. He altered the heading of the autopilot so that he would be able to pass clear of the next headland – Start Point.

The last recorded sighting of Harry's boat was made that evening by the Coastwatch crew at the Bass Point lookout, near the Lizard Peninsula. They made an entry in their log that they had seen a small wooden Motor Fishing Vessel heading west at about ten knots in a fairly calm sea. They also reported that the vessel appeared to have sustained major damage all along its port side, consistent, they thought, with a collision. They were concerned at this and decided to telephone Falmouth Coastguard and report what they had seen. Falmouth responded by diverting a Royal Naval Search and Rescue helicopter from the big Naval Air Station at Culdrose. The Sea King was already airborne carrying out winching practice off the mouth of the Helford River, and was soon heading for the last reported position of *Spitfire*.

When the helicopter arrived at the estimated last position of the damaged boat it started an expanding square search, but by this time the sun had set and visibility was deteriorating rapidly. The big powerful Sea King was equipped with radar but the wooden structure of the boat presented a very poor return so no contact was picked up. The crew carried on searching for over two hours but the intermittent mist and fog together with the drift of twilight into night meant that they were unsuccessful.

Indeed, as the evening grew darker, the only thing they expected to be able to see were the boat's navigation lights. They didn't see any navigation lights for the simple reason that Harry had not thought to switch them on.

About the same time that the helicopter search was taking place, the sixty-thousand ton bulk carrier *Grace II* reported to Falmouth Coastguard that she might have been in collision with a small fishing vessel. Once this information was digested, a broadcast was put out on the Coastguard frequency, channel sixteen, asking all stations to look out for a small unnamed fishing vessel which might have been damaged in a collision with a larger ship.

Both Bass Point and Portland Bill stations heard the broadcast and responded. Portland reported that they had guided a small wooden Motor Fishing Vessel around the Portland Race and that the name of the vessel was *Spitfire*. They followed this with a full description and gave the position, course and speed of the vessel when last seen. Bass Point reported having seen the boat passing the Lizard and added the ominous information that the boat they saw appeared to have suffered major damage, probably from a collision. As a result of this, a search of the area bounded by the Lizard, Land's End and the Scilly Isles was started at first light next morning. The all-weather lifeboats from Falmouth and Newlyn, assisted by another helicopter from Culdrose, were directed to search for wreckage as well as the *Spitfire*.

No boat, and no wreckage was found – and the *Spitfire* was never seen again.

Chapter 46

It took a lot longer than expected to complete the process of checking the statements of the three former traffic officers against their interview transcripts. Jim had worked quickly to draft the proposed statements but it was after three before he even left the station to drive up to Benchester. When he arrived, he had to park outside the gated entrance to the Bishop's Palace and then crunch down the long gravel drive to the massive front doors of the building. Here he was met by a detective constable from the local county force.

Once inside, he was first introduced to a remarkably young-looking but very solemn-faced bishop. Jim said a few words which he hoped were appropriate before he and his companion were handed over to an equally glum young woman who was introduced as the bishop's secretary. After the brief introduction she led the way through the Palace, emerging eventually into a small, dimly lit room, where lay the body of the Reverend Jeremy Wilberforce. The body was laid out on a trestle table and the room was lit by groups of candles set on cloth-covered tables surrounding the trestle.

Without speaking, the secretary handed a small notebook to the other detective, who passed it to Jim. When he opened the book he saw that the first few pages were blank but then he found a page across which was scrawled, 'I'm so sorry. Forgive me.' The same words were repeated on other pages, becoming progressively more difficult to read. Many of the pages seemed to be water-stained.

Jim looked at the body, which was dressed in the black garb of a priest. The eyes were dilated, the hands were curled as though gripping something, and there were traces of vomit over the chest and arms.

The secretary answered Jim's unspoken question: 'He was found in woodland near here, lying among clumps of belladonna plants, and it looks as though he had been eating the berries. We'll know more after the autopsy.'

'Anything else found on him?' asked Jim.

'A few coins, a watch, pens, nothing significant.'

'Right, I'll need to go back now. Can I take the notebook?'

'If you sign a note to say you've got it.' The other detective held out a pen as he was speaking.

Jim scribbled out a receipt on a piece of paper provided by the secretary, and placed the notebook into an evidence bag, carefully avoiding touching it with his hands; then, turning to the DC, he shook hands and made his way back through the Palace to where his car was parked at the front gates.

Two hours later he walked back into the DCI's office at Weymouth.

Bob looked up. 'You didn't take long, but while you were out there's been another development.' Jim dropped into the chair facing his boss across the table and waited.

'We've got the soldier. Well, actually we haven't got him. He's been picked up by the Military Police and they seem reluctant to let us have him. The Super is rounding up some high profile help to put pressure on the military to release him into our custody.'

'Where did they catch him?'

'Rheindahlen.'

'Where's that?'

'In Germany. It's a big British military base.' Bob doodled for a moment on a pad of paper lying on the table, 'Apparently they want to court-martial him for being absent without leave. They seem to think that outranks multiple murder.'

'So what happens now?' Jim walked over to the electric kettle as he posed the question, then he held up a mug. 'Tea?'

Bob angled his head briefly, in assent. 'Well, we've nearly got it wrapped up. Assuming there were ten in the original gang, we've got four in custody, one who's coughed everything, four dead, one by his own hand, one in military custody and one missing.'

'Unfortunately, it's the big one who's missing,' Jim said, between sips of coffee.

'I don't know. I think Sir Arthur Simmonds is the prize catch. He's swamped in remorse and will make a very good witness. Hayward is also looking decidedly unpleased with himself and I don't think it will take much to get a confession out of him. We've also got this.' Bob swept his arm expansively over the pile of cardboard files sharing the end of his table with a big cardboard box containing an assortment of digital phones, compact cameras, video discs, tablets and film canisters. 'This lot' – he waved his arm again – 'is absolute dynamite, absolute bloody dynamite, and it's going to blow any defence nonsense right to kingdom come and back again.'

'How were the traffic cops' statements?' asked Jim.

'More dynamite, but rather special dynamite, which I think we should go and discuss with Mr Ray Marsden.' He placed heavy emphasis on the 'Mister'. While speaking, Bob climbed slowly to his feet, rummaged in the cardboard box, and pulled out a small camera, two mobile phones and a tablet. 'Here, you take these,' he said, handing the bundle of gadgets to the detective sergeant. 'I'll take the traffic files and statements.'

Ten minutes later the two detectives stood outside Marsden's cell while the custody sergeant's assistant unlocked the door. Marsden was lounging back on the Spartan bunk, reading a dog-eared paperback and still looking remarkably out of place in his smart blue pinstripe business suit and highly polished shoes. Except now, the expensive Savile Row jacket had been folded carefully and placed on the end of the bunk; and the once crisp white shirt was now adorned with dark sweat stains and broad red braces.

Although his previous air of superiority had not entirely deserted him, Marsden was not nearly so cocky as he had been at first during Bob's earlier visit.

'Oh, good afternoon. I imagine you have at last come to let me out.' He swung his legs off the bunk as he spoke. 'Well, no hard feelings, chaps, we all make mistakes. But this is a big one, easily cleared up with about a quarter of a million in compensation.' As he finished speaking he stood beside the bunk, casually brushing dust from his trousers.

Bob ignored the taunt. 'I've brought something else you might like to see,' he said. 'You remember the photographs I showed you? Well, have a look at this.' He stood squarely about three feet in front of Marsden and held up the tablet so Marsden could see it. He pressed the start button and a remarkably clear video image filled the screen.

The video showed a wide expanse of grass, with what appeared to be a cliff edge in the background. The lighting suggested it was filmed in late twilight. The camera panned around slowly to the right, taking in first one, then another sand-filled golf bunker. Then the picture panned back to the left and zoomed in on the blood-covered body of a man lying on the ground. The body lay completely still and as the video continued, another man ran a few paces from out of the frame to the right and aimed a savage kick at the head of the unmoving body. The head jerked unnaturally to the side. The neck was broken. The same man stepped forward again and kicked the body. On the other side a woman had also started to kick the corpse, but it was the kicking man who was closest to the camera. The assailant then paused and stared straight into the camera. He wiped sweat from his forehead and as he did so, a gold Rolex wristwatch became visible on his wrist. It was the same watch that now adorned the wrist of the prisoner. Marsden stared at the remarkably clear picture being held in front of him, which showed his own face, his loose tie, his crisp white shirt, his waistcoat and his watch in stark detail.

Neither detective spoke as the blood drained once more from Marsden's face and the book slipped from his hand to fall in a flutter of pages to the cell floor. Marsden fell backward, flopping onto the bunk, his head leaning forward, clutched in both hands.

'Look up, please, Mr Marsden,' said Bob. 'There's much more than that to show you, or perhaps you would like to have Mr Grayson-Cummings in to watch the show. But we can wait for that, because we have a great deal more where that came from. You remember, I'm sure, how I told you we'd found your hiding place. We also found a lot of the toys and gadgets used by your bloody-fool friends; actually, they had hiding places as well. It's amazing, I think, how a bunch of toffs, with thousands wasted on trying to educate them, can be so incredibly stupid, not only to run around killing innocent people just because they're there, but also to be even more stupid and tuck away all the evidence we could possibly need. It leaves me gobsmacked, it really does. I think you're just a bunch of cretins who never grew up. I think you've committed at least seven murders, and you've filmed and photographed them. But we've got the films and photographs – and we've got an eyewitness; that's somebody who actually watched you lot performing your perverted games. You know, you're so stupid I almost feel sorry for you. Do you have any comment to make, by any chance?' With that, Bob shook his head from side to side and laughed.

They watched in silence for several minutes while Marsden sat on the bunk, holding his head in his hands. Bob was a great believer in the power of silence. He moved a little closer to Marsden and started to speak again. 'We've got the files, Mr Marsden; we've found the coppers who were bought, and they've all made statements. They will pick out your daddy in a line-up and what they have to say will finish your old man – oh, but I already told you that, didn't I? We know all about the crashed Aston Martin and we have a very co-operative chum of yours – Arthur Simmonds – singing his heart out.'

Bob stood in front of Marsden, continuing deliberately to taunt and needle him. 'As I said, how clever of you to ensure you kept a full and comprehensive record of all your little games; all your fun; all your arrangements and all your pathetic "get-out-of-jail" efforts. I wonder why you did that? Could it be that by keeping all those murderous records you'd be able to keep your psychopathic chums in line? I also know now that you kept a complete record of what your daddy did to get you off the hook and make all that difficult evidence go away. Why did you do that? Was it because you couldn't even trust your own father? Your daddy was a pretty important man at that time and he used his position to scam a few simple coppers into selling their souls for a few quid. I wonder how he's going to cope with slopping out. Any comment, Mr Learned Counsel?'

Marsden remained still for a moment, then he shot up from the bed, throwing himself, arms outstretched, fingers clawing, towards Bob. He had finally lost it. The suave tormentor of the law was no more. The realisation of what he was, what he was about to become and what the future held in store for him was too much, and his last throw was to attempt violence once more. He hurled himself across the cell, fingers outstretched, clawing towards Bob's face.

But the DS was too quick for him. As the tall man shot forward, Jim swung and kicked him sharply on the side of his left knee. The knee buckled and Marsden went down, clutching at the corners of Bob's jacket. Bob brought his arm swiftly down and used the edge of the tablet to knock Marsden's wrists away. The barrister fell hard to the floor, landing on his right side. He lay there, massaging his wrists and breathing hard. 'You bastards,' he snarled. Jim reached down and pulled one of his arms back behind him. The DCI pressed the alarm bell, while keeping his eyes on the now writhing form on the floor.

The cell door was flung open and the constable appeared in the doorway, 'asp' in his hand.

Bob held up his arm towards the constable, palm outward and said, 'It's okay. He just got a bit excited; but there is something else I want to tell him before we go.' He turned towards the figure on the floor, who was now sitting, his back propped against the edge of the bunk, still massaging his wrists, staring at Bob, his face a mask of hate.

Bob didn't move; he just leaned down towards Marsden and said, 'I thought you would like to know that you are not the only one in custody. We also have your friends Sandra Somerville, Sir Arthur Simmonds and Henry Hayward in here as well.'

Marsden looked up, apparently mentally calculating. But then Bob continued, 'Oh, yes; you are probably wondering where your other friends are. Well, Captain FitzHarris has been arrested by the army and will be coming here soon and…' he paused for effect: 'as you know, Jane Lockyer, Cornel Grovey,

Jeremy Wilberforce and Don Randell are all dead.' He tucked the files under his arm, handed the tablet to Jim, turned to face Marsden and said, rather formally, 'Good afternoon, Mr Marsden.' Then he left the cell. Jim followed him and, together, they walked back towards the DCI's office.

When they reached the office, there was a red light winking urgently on the desk-mounted telephone. Bob picked up the phone while still standing and listened. He turned towards the door, calling, as he left, 'The Super is anxious to see us, both of us – now!'

A few minutes later Bob tapped on the partially open door of the station commander's office and was surprised at the immediate invitation to come in. The two men walked into the office and were waved towards chairs. The big boss was, for once, smiling. 'Well done!' he said. 'It looks like you have the case largely wrapped up. I can add a bit that you won't yet know. Former Deputy Assistant Commissioner Sir Andrew Marsden has been interviewed under caution in the presence of the National Police Complaints Commission and a senior officer from the Security Service. He has been arrested on multiple charges of perverting the course of justice and malfeasance in a Public Office. Also, following the statements made by Sir Arthur Simmonds and the traffic officers you interviewed, former Chief Superintendent Alex Croft – also some time of the Metropolitan Police – has been arrested. He has also admitted offences likely to prejudice the course of justice but has claimed to have been acting under duress from Sir Andrew Marsden.' He sat back, triumphant and satisfied. Then he added, 'So bring me up to date regarding the others.'

Bob cleared his throat noisily, shifted on the uncomfortable chair and started to speak. 'I think we have accounted for almost the whole gang of active psychopaths, sir. We have four in custody here. One is held by the army in Germany, but we'll get him here when the protocol is sorted out; and we have four dead, one by his own hand.' He stopped for a moment before adding, quietly, 'One still missing, I'm afraid.'

'Well, from what I've seen, we have more than enough evidence to proceed. Wellton is a very well-known face so he won't be able to stay on the run for very long.' Superintendent Holmes looked pleased with himself. 'Although he was a very successful politician, he has trodden on a lot of toes and like others of his ilk, he doesn't actually have many real friends. He'll be picked up in due course, you mark my words.' The superintendent finished speaking and sat, smiling across his desk; a rare event, Jim was heard to remark – some time later.

The interview was obviously over so the detectives trooped out of the bright, smart office, returned to their own, and began the task of collating, categorising and cataloguing the evidence. This task was enormously demanding at the start, and as more searches and further background investigations continued, the mass of evidence became huge, so several other officers were drafted in to help.

Chapter 47

It was nearly eight months before the murderers were brought to trial. By this time they had become notorious, and were described in the press as 'The Snuff Gang'. When the army eventually handed over Roger FitzHarris he had already been tried by court-martial in camera on the suitably vague charge of bringing the army into disrepute. He had been sentenced to be Dismissed the Service with Disgrace – so he arrived in the custody cells in Weymouth as plain Mr FitzHarris.

After being formally charged and interviewed by Robert Majury and then again by Jim Creasy, he was packed into a secure prison van and taken under police escort to join the others on remand at Winchester. 'Joining the others' was not strictly correct, because the surviving gang members were all kept separate from each other and from the other inmates. They were kept in close confinement and watched, day and night, largely to prevent attempts at suicide.

With FitzHarris's arrest there were five defendants behind bars, with a sixth member of the gang still missing. Despite this it was decided to proceed with the trial of all six, trying the missing man in his absence.

The trial lasted six weeks, much of the time being devoted to the production and description of the wealth of evidence that had been turned up. One of the problems that had to be overcome was the absence of bodies, and indeed the identity of most of their victims. The only person known to have survived an attack by the gang had disappeared. He had been last seen sailing westward in a small damaged boat in indifferent weather patterns, but the boat had disappeared without trace and so had Harry. Nevertheless, during the third week of the trial the body of an unnamed elderly man, thought to be a tramp, had been discovered in a shallow grave in woodland near Blandford. Shortly after this, a partially decomposed body was discovered in a cave under the cliffs near Golden Cap. Fragments of clothing and other items found on the body as well as DNA traces linking the corpse to shoes taken from the gang helped to establish that these were the remains of the man depicted in the video that Bob had shown to Ray Marsden.

Marsden himself tried early in the trial to slither out from under the hammer of justice by claiming to be insane. It didn't work and the judge, who had seen Marsden perform previously in court, was not hoodwinked. The former barrister was duly sentenced along with the rest of the gang. As soon as sentence was passed he was stripped of his appointment as Queen's Counsel and then barred for life from practising as a barrister or in any other legal or quasi-legal appointment.

All five members of the gang were given life sentences and four of them, including Sandra Somerville, were sentenced to serve a minimum of forty years before becoming eligible for parole. The pronouncement of the 'guilty' verdict was made against a background of loud wailing and sobbing from the former Wimbledon star.

Sir Arthur Simmonds was told he would serve a minimum of fifteen years before becoming eligible for parole but the final ten of those years would be suspended providing his behaviour during the first five years was acceptable. Having already pleaded guilty, he accepted the sentence with dignity, standing upright in the dock, head bowed. As sentence was passed he was heard to say, 'My Lord, I am so sorry.' The judge ignored the remark and moved on to the next sentence.

The three traffic officers were all given suspended sentences of three years in the case of the sergeant and two years for the two constables. They were each ordered to forfeit the money they had been bribed with, failing which they would be required to serve their sentences in prison.

Sir Andrew Marsden had already been tried and found guilty on a number of counts, including conspiracy, perverting the course of justice, bribery and malfeasance in a public office. His sentencing had been delayed on the order of the judge who presided at both trials. In the meantime, his knighthood was removed. When the main trial ended, former Commander Andrew Marsden was brought into the dock for sentencing and when he was told to rise to hear his sentence he was standing beside his son. The judge solemnly addressed each of the five charges and pronounced a sentence of four years for each conviction. Marsden was observed to relax visibly as he calculated that with these sentences running concurrently he would only serve two years, less when his time on remand was taken into account. Then the judge dropped his bombshell. The sentences, he announced solemnly, amounted to the most he was allowed to impose; but, he said, he was directing that these sentences would be served consecutively. Marsden's face fell and he staggered, clutching at his son as the realisation struck that he was going to spend at least ten years in jail. He was a broken man. The arrogance and pride washed away from him to leave him standing, shaking slightly, a sad, broken and lonely old man.

His deputy, Chief Superintendent Alex Croft, later Commander Alex Croft, was given a suspended sentence; but all of his Metropolitan Police and Dorset Constabulary pension rights were removed.

Superintendent Holmes was transferred from Dorset to head up a newly formed Wessex Anti-Terrorist Force. He was pleased.

Bob Majury retired six months after the end of the trial and Jim Creasy was awarded accelerated promotion to the rank of detective chief inspector. Gerry Treloar was promoted to sergeant in the uniformed branch and Mary Flint left the Force to get married.

After having served the first two years of his sentence, Sir Arthur Simmonds' health began to deteriorate. An order was granted that his sentence should be terminated on compassionate grounds, but he died in a prison hospital.

Exactly three months after the conclusion of the trial, a Brixham-based trawler dredged a black plastic-wrapped bundle from about four miles offshore in Lyme Bay. It was landed at Portland Port and taken away by the police. When the bundle was opened up, the remarkably well-preserved remains of Giles de Courtney Wellton MP, former Minister of State for Rural Affairs, were discovered. A post-mortem examination was conducted which showed serious injuries to the feet and lower legs of the corpse. Further to this, significant traces of the drug ketamine were found and it was decided that the probable cause of death had been an overdose of ketamine. DNA tests confirmed the identity of the remains, and the body was buried in an unmarked grave, without ceremony.

Chapter 48

When Bob Majury retired, he fretted around his home for the first few months, feeling grumpy and dissatisfied. He missed the mental fencing and occasional excitement he had experienced as a senior detective. His wife Aileen suggested a hobby and he decided to take up golf. He applied to join a local club, paid for the requisite twenty lessons from the club pro but found the game tiring, cold, frustrating and irritating. He sold his almost new clubs through the Dorset Echo for just under half of their value and morosely went in search of something else to fill his time. Again at the suggestion of his wife, he joined a gym and worked diligently at removing the excess weight he had piled on over recent years. That helped, and as he trimmed down he felt fitter and brighter, but he still needed something to occupy his time, other than walking his newly acquired retriever and pottering about in his garden.

Then Aileen came up with a brainwave. She hit upon the idea of encouraging Bob to take up genealogical research. She hit the target! Bob found he was almost back in his old world, chasing down ancient identities, visiting parish churches in search of their records, and poring over microfiche in various county historical branches. He joined several research societies, visited the National Archive at Kew and started to build an impressive family tree.

Bob came of Anglo Irish parentage and while he found it relatively straightforward to research his English mother's side of the family, he kept running into irritating dead-ends when following up his Irish father's side. After a while he came up with an idea. He and Aileen would take an extended holiday to Ireland. Aileen received the idea with enthusiasm and in the early summer they set off, driving in Bob's new Volkswagen Passat Estate, bound for the ferry port at Holyhead.

They drove in a leisurely fashion across south-west England and up through Wales, stopping overnight at a couple of country pubs, one in Somerset and one on the edge of Snowdonia. Eventually, they splashed through steady rain and boarded the high-speed ferry at Holyhead in the early afternoon. By evening they were comfortably lodged in a big new multistorey hotel just off Dublin's O'Connell Street, happily wallowing in typical Irish hospitality, good wine and fine fare.

They stayed in and around Dublin for a week enjoying the sights and the atmosphere. Bob was often heard extolling the virtues of Guinness, which he declared to be far superior to the version sold on the other side of the Irish Sea.

At the end of the week they left Dublin heading south for the County of Wexford where Bob intended to start his serious research. They stopped at a couple of villages, again enjoying the hospitality and what Bob had learned to call 'the craik' which loosely translates as 'the fun'. He was occasionally picking up snippets of the information he was looking for, but most of this came from parish records or extensive searches through usually wild and overgrown cemeteries. The parish records were almost invariably incomplete and churchyard searches took a long time. Engaging local people in conversation and asking if they knew of families with the surname Majury turned out to be a useless and disappointing pastime. Bob found that so long as the Guinness flowed, legions of ancient Majurys would be recalled. But then he would subsequently discover that none of them ever existed and he was just being fed the stories 'to be kind and helpful to the Englishman'!

However, despite the repetitive false leads he was invited to follow, Bob was able to establish a broken but consistent trail of his otherwise unknown Irish ancestry. As he and Aileen wandered slowly south, through gently rolling hills and rich green pastures, the name Majury started to crop up more often.

They were staying in a tiny village on the banks of the upper Slaney River at an inn which also did duty as village shop, hairdressers and post office during the day, when they fell into conversation with a farmer who couldn't identify any local Majurys but he recommended that they should go further south following the course of the river towards the town of Enniscorthy, where they might be more successful.

Aileen and Bob rose late next morning, and by the time they had ploughed through 'a full Irish breakfast', packed their cases and completed the obligatory chat with their landlord, it was nearly lunchtime before they were ready to leave. Finally, having refused a 'jar' to slake their thirst before they left, they set off heading generally south, using a network of tiny lanes, passing back and forth across the river on old stone bridges, and meandering through small villages. The countryside was green and fresh from overnight rainfall, and verdant fields dotted with black and white cattle alternated with stands of ancient deciduous woodland. Bob was enjoying life, happy in the relaxation that seemed to be invested in the deep south of Ireland, when he spotted a signpost announcing the existence of the Monastery of St John and St Joseph.

A mile or so further on they entered the village of New Ross, where they came across a second signpost. This one described a Franciscan monastery with an entrance one mile further, on the right. It also said that fruit, vegetables and flowers could be purchased from the monastery, in addition to afternoon tea. There was no bar or pub in the village so Bob and Aileen decided to journey on and stop at the monastery.

After the village, the tiny lane crossed the river once more and then joined a modern, wide, well-made road, 'courtesy of the European Union,' Aileen said. The sun was shining and the afternoon became warm. There was very little wind, and practically no traffic – unless a Jersey cow blissfully grazing on the grass verge could be counted as such. Shortly after passing the cow, and wondering whether he should try to find someone to whom he could report the lost animal, Bob came across a big signboard announcing the location of the Monastery of Saint John and Saint Joseph of Wexford. A small private road lined by tall poplar trees led off to the right, behind the noticeboard. They turned onto the road and followed it for another mile where they rumbled over a cattle grid. Just beyond this was yet another sign welcoming visitors to the monastery, adding the information that the monastery had beautiful and extensive gardens, pick-your-own fruit and a 'homely' tea room. They decided to break their journey here, have some tea and maybe pick some fruit.

They drove through imposing, ornate, wrought iron gates and on down a long gravel-covered driveway bordered by ornamental trees, flowers and shrubs. To either side, rich green grassland rolled away into the distance. The setting was idyllic.

After nearly three quarters of a mile they approached another, smaller gateway, this one tended by a smiling monk wearing a dark brown hooded habit. He leaned forward and said in a lilting tone, 'Welcome to the monastery, my children. What would you be looking for? What can I help you with?'

Aileen, who was driving, said they would like to see the gardens and then perhaps pick some fruit, and maybe stay for tea.

'Well now, that's a good choice, so it is. You just follow this little road until you see the parking sign, then you can walk around the gardens. You will see one of our novices in charge and he will show you where you might pick some fruit, and flowers if you've a mind. We don't charge for the flowers, they are after all belonging to God, but a donation for the poor would be welcome.'

Aileen nodded her thanks but before she could respond, the monk spoke once more. 'You will see, I am thinking, Brother Harold near the fruit gardens and he will help you to pick whatever you want. Mind now, he will not speak to you, for he is still a novice and forbidden to speak before Vespers – but you can tell him what you want and he will help you.'

Aileen did manage to thank the monk this time, but before she could drive off, the monk leaned forward once more, pointing with his right arm in the direction of the fruit gardens. 'Why, there is Brother Harold now. Go and find him and he will help you.' Aileen followed the direction of the pointing arm and saw another figure, similarly clad in a dark brown cowled habit. This one had the cowl pulled up to cover his head. She drove on for perhaps two hundred yards, stopped in the indicated parking space and they both climbed stiffly out of the car. Bob walked across towards the monk who turned to face him, hands clasped together in front of his chest as if praying.

Bob stopped in his tracks and stood stock-still. Brother Harold remained standing on the grass at the edge of the track, unmoving, smiling at Bob. He nodded his head slightly. Bob opened his mouth but couldn't speak. The monk's head appeared to be tonsured, and his chin sported a small grey beard, but the features riveting Bob to the spot were the bright, clear blue eyes and wide, tanned, open face with faint scars on the left temple. Bob could hardly believe what he was seeing, but he was staring at the face of the man he knew as Harry Chaplin. Eventually he spluttered 'You… You're Harry, Harry Chaplin.'

The monk bowed assent and, still clasping his hands together and smiling, he turned and led the couple silently in the direction of the gardens.

The End

#0074 - 160418 - C0 - 210/148/20 - PB - DID2172493